The Brink of Ecstasy

"If I do not kiss you now, I will go mad."

Her heart pounded in anticipation as Shane lowered his head and his mouth moved ever so slowly to claim hers. It was as if he were giving her time to back away if she did not want this.

But she did want it.

She ached for it.

For him.

With a sudden wanton impatience that startled her, she turned toward him and raised her lips to meet his.

There was nothing tentative about this kiss. It was fierce and wild, hungry and passionate. On and on it went, a man and woman exploring their feelings for each other and discovering unexpected depths and heights.

With a flash of insight, Kathleen realized it was the clinging of a man and woman who believed the light of love had been forever extinguished in their lives and were now discovering that perhaps they were wrong.

Other **AVON ROMANCES**

Kiss Me Goodnight

Marlene Suson

AVON BOOKS  NEW YORK

AVON BOOKS
A division of
The Hearst Corporation
1350 Avenue of the Americas
New York, New York 10019

First Avon Books Printing: May 1998

For my three very special Kathleens:
Kathleen M. O'Reilly
Kathleen Ann Heron
Kathleen Michelle Heron
with love

KISS ME GOODNIGHT

Chapter 1

Beneath a dark, threatening sky, Shane urged his sorrel gelding toward the top of a rock-crusted Irish hillside as bleak and barren as his own heart.

When he reached the crest, his breath caught. Despite the black storm clouds blowing rapidly toward him, he abruptly reined his mount to a halt and stared in startled pleasure at the vale, lush and green, spread below him.

As Shane gazed at the emerald land, he was seized by the strange feeling that he had come home at last.

But that was absurd. Aloysius Shane Howard Howell, sixth Marquess of Sherbourne, had never before been to this spot. Until he landed at Dublin two days earlier, he had never even been to Ireland.

Furthermore, Shane, whose title was English not Irish, had never felt truly at home anywhere, not even at Sherwood, his country seat in Lincolnshire. There he had been born and raised, and there his dead wife and now his son were buried.

A strange serenity settled over Shane like a soft Irish mist. He could not remember when he had last felt so at peace, certainly not since the onset of his son's fatal illness. A lump rose in his throat at the memory of little Jeremy. Something in Shane had died with his five-year-old son.

He feared it was his heart.

Below him, a stream tumbled merrily down a small cascade, then foamed and rushed across the valley floor. Even before he raised his gaze and saw the impressive Palladian mansion on the hilltop opposite him, Shane knew where he was.

Canamara.

At last. An unexpected burst of pride surged through him. This beautiful vale and the mansion beyond were part of his Irish estate, which he had never seen.

As Shane rode down the hill, wind from the fast-approaching storm ruffled his mount's mane and pushed black clouds across the valley's sky, blotting out the sun and casting a chill over the land. The smell of rain about to fall permeated the air.

As he reached the bottom of the hill, the first drops of what promised to be a downpour spit from the clouds. Shane pushed the sorrel to a gallop toward the mansion, hoping to escape a thorough drenching.

In his haste to reach shelter, he did not slow when the lane snaked into the trees and shrubs along the stream. Galloping around a curve, he found himself almost upon a stone bridge, hardly wider than a footpath.

As his mount thundered onto the span, he caught a flash of black on it. To his horror, he realized a woman in a hooded cloak was hurrying across the bridge ahead of him.

And the span was too narrow for his horse to pass her.

Although Shane tried, it was too late for him to stop the racing sorrel.

Apparently hearing the horse behind her, the woman dropped down onto the bridge's low stone side wall and swiveled, lifting her feet upward to the top of the wall.

Shane held his breath, hoping her admirable presence of mind and quick action would save her. But as the sorrel flashed past her, he heard the rip of cloth and a groan that struck terror into his heart. Had she not been quick enough?

Before his gelding was fully stopped, Shane was out of the saddle and swinging to the ground.

Shane ran back toward the woman. She still sat on the stone side wall of the bridge, the flounce of her full black skirt trailing on the ground. As he closed the gap between them, he called anxiously, "Are you hurt?"

"*Nil*, no thanks to you." She swung her feet down from the wall, planted them firmly on the bridge, and stood up. Relief coursed through Shane.

"Kill me, were you trying to do?" The lilt in her low contralto voice delighted Shane's ear.

He started to deny her charge. But as he reached her, his words died in his throat. Her hood had fallen away from her head, and tumultuous waves of hair, the color of the finest burgundy, tumbled about her shoulders. Eyes as green as the isle on which she lived were set in a face that, although flushed with anger, would haunt a man's dreams.

She was several inches shorter than his own six-foot-two. Her shapeless black cloak hid her body, but he was certain it would be slender and delightfully rounded in all the right places.

A wave of desire surged through Shane, startling

him, for he'd not felt anything like it since before his son died five months ago.

Her skin was pale perfection, as soft and smooth as Devonshire cream, and Shane longed to lick it, every last lovely bit. Erotic images of undressing her to do so tormented him, and his fingers itched to make his fantasy become a reality.

"I am vastly sorry." His voice came out deeper than usual. "I did not see you until I was upon you."

His apology only seemed to make her angrier. Her eyes flashed like summer lightning.

"So it's English you be?" Her tone left no doubt she considered this an unpardonable sin. "And even more of a fool than most of your kind."

Perhaps because of the musical lilt to her lovely voice, her charge more bemused than irritated him. "What makes you say that?"

She gave him a withering look. "Only a damn fool rides around a blind curve at a gallop!"

No one had ever dared call the Marquess of Sherbourne a damn fool—at least not to his face— and he could not help smiling at this novel experience.

"Smiling are you, when a miracle it is your beast did not trample me?"

Her feisty spirit, a refreshing change from the simpering women he knew, delighted him. He smiled placatingly at her. "And I thank God for the miracle."

"Why, now, are you trespassing on the Marquess of Sherbourne's land?"

Shane bit back the answer that sprang to his lips: *I cannot trespass on my own land.* That would betray his identity.

He wanted to remain incognito during his stay

at Canamara. That's why he'd decided to adopt his two middle names and declare himself to be simply Shane Howard, not Aloysius, Marquess of Sherbourne.

Among his family and friends, he had always been called Shane rather than Aloysius, which had been his late father's name too. He felt his jaw clench involuntarily at the thought of his father. What irony that they shared the same name, when no two men could be more different.

Now Shane had come to Ireland, where he was unknown, in search of quiet and seclusion in which to try to come to terms with the death of his adored son and, in the wake of that tragedy, with the empty loneliness of his own life, which no longer seemed to have any meaning.

Jeremy's death was not the first tragedy to strike Shane. When the wife he'd loved so much had died giving birth to their son, his grief for her had been intense. Then, however, he'd had Jeremy to raise and to love. Now Shane had no one.

To reveal his true identity would preclude finding the tranquil escape in Ireland that he so badly needed. Should it become known he was the marquess, he would be required to meet and entertain his neighbors and tenants and to submit to endless, meaningless ceremony.

Shane wanted none of that. He was heartily sick to death of boring, empty ritual.

To assure his anonymity, he'd deliberately dressed in an old riding coat and worn buckskin breeches that made him look more like an itinerant peddler than an English lord. He'd even taken the precaution of removing his signet ring from his finger and carrying it in his pocket.

The woman asked, "Don't you know, Sher-

bourne has ordered all trespassers on Canamara be
dealt with harshly."

That was nonsense, and Shane inquired, "Then
why are *you* trespassing on Canamara land?"

"I am not. I live here."

"At the great house?" he asked, startled, for she
had neither the look nor the manner of a servant
and, in his absence, only servants lived there.

"Nay. I rent a cottage over there." She gestured
toward a path that branched off from the one he
was following. "I warn you it will go hard with
you if you are found trespassing."

"I am not trespassing," he answered sharply.

She raised a brow inquiringly.

"I . . . I am here by Lord Sherbourne's invitation." Would that impress her?

Clearly it did not, for her expression turned as
cold as winter snow. "So it's a friend of Sherbourne
you are." The hatred in her voice as she uttered his
name confounded him. "That'll win you no welcome among folks here, none at all."

Her statement both startled and puzzled Shane.
"Why is that?"

Her lip curled in a sneer. "Notorious Sherbourne
is for being the cruelest and most uncaring of all
Ireland's absentee English landlords."

"Oh, come now," he protested. As Oliver Radnor, Canamara's agent, had pointed out repeatedly
in his reports, Shane was the most generous landlord in the county—perhaps in all Ireland—and it
cost him dearly.

Canamara's pitiful income would be far greater
if Shane were to do as other English landowners
had and subdivide the estate into tiny plots that
could be leased to Irish tenants, desperate for land,

for exorbitant rents that were more than the ground was worth.

But Shane had absolutely refused to subject his tenants to this abhorrent system of rack rents.

He had been told repeatedly that the Irish were an ungrateful lot, and this woman's statement proved it. "That is not true, and you know it," he protested.

With an angry swipe, she brushed an errant lock of hair away from her face, drawing his attention back to that glorious burgundy mane. His hands involuntarily tightened into fists to stifle his impulse to bury them in her hair.

"You think not?" she scoffed. "Ask anyone here, and they'll tell you the same."

Before he could defend himself, she looked down at her skirt trailing on the ground.

"Ruined my skirt, you and your beast did."

"I will buy you another."

She gazed skeptically at his plain coat frayed at the cuffs, unruffled shirt, worn breeches splattered with mud, and scuffed boots. "You look as though you can ill afford to buy anything—even a razor for yourself."

Goaded, Shane shot back, "And you have a tongue like one."

"Nicked you with it, did I?" Her emerald eyes gleamed mischievously. She smiled for the first time, and it was so luminous it took his breath away. "Had you a looking glass, you would see my comment was justified."

Shane raised his hand to his chin and winced as he rubbed the rough stubble there. Although he had shaved before resuming his journey early that morning, it did not take his beard long to grow. Dark as it was, it stood out against his fair skin.

"My apologies. My hand tells me you are right."

Her beautifully arched eyebrows rose above her laughing eyes. "Another miracle, an Englishman who actually admits a woman—and an Irish one at that—is right. But then, I have known no *poor* Englishmen. Your countrymen in Ireland have all grown rich at our expense."

Considering his clothes, chosen because he did not wish to call attention to himself, and his unshaven, travel-worn appearance, Shane was not surprised she would mistake him for a poor man, rather than the rich lord of the realm he was. "Have your dressmaker send the bill for a new skirt to me."

Her smile widened, sorely tempting him to kiss those full, red lips.

"Sure, and will she be paid?"

Shane managed to say with a straight face, "I will scrape together the money somehow. Why do you look so doubtful? I not only admit when I am wrong, even to an Irish woman, but I am also a man of my word."

Her brilliant green eyes narrowed scornfully. "No Englishman is a man of his word."

Her determination to find fault with everyone English rankled him. "I promise I will prove you wrong."

Her doubting expression ruffled him more than her sharp tongue. Certainly she was a provocative change from his countrywomen who agreed with everything he said and hung on his every word.

Not that Shane entertained any illusions that they did so because they found him brilliant and irresistible. What they found irresistible was his title and his fortune.

And the fact he was a widower.

He liked the way this Irish woman's gaze met his steadily and directly. None of those sly, coquettish glances from beneath her lashes that too many women of his acquaintance employed on him.

She asked crisply, "The bill for my skirt, to whom and where am I to have it sent?"

"To Shane Howard at Canamara." He waved his hand toward the mansion on the hilltop. "I will be there for a few weeks."

"And why would the high-and-mighty Sherbourne be inviting the likes of you to stay in his great palace that he never deigns to visit?"

As Shane considered how to answer her, the rain that until then had been light suddenly intensified, beating down hard on them. Without thinking, Shane reached out and pulled the hood of her cloak over her lovely hair to protect it. As he did so, his hand lightly brushed her cheek, and he felt her start.

But apparently not from pleasure, for she glared at him. "And now it's a soaking I must endure. Were it not for you, home I'd be by now."

"Have you far to go?"

"A quarter-mile." The temperature had dropped sharply, and she shivered.

Shane, loath to part from her, said, "I will take you there."

"Sure, and how will you be doing that when you have no cart or carriage?"

The husky timbre of her voice sent a shiver of pleasure through Shane. "My mount will carry us both."

She looked as scandalized as if he'd just invited her to share his bed. Considering her singular effect on him, that sounded like a wonderful idea.

And one he intended to pursue while he was at Canamara.

"Ride like that with a stranger and an Englishman at that?" she responded indignantly. "Indeed I won't."

"Do not be a fool. I will deliver you to your door in a fraction of the time it will take you to walk there."

Anger sparked in her marvelous eyes, turning them to emerald fire. "An even greater fool would I be to trust you to do so."

With that, she turned and struck out on the diagonal path that angled away from the stream. A running footman might have envied her speed.

Shane had never before had his honor questioned so bluntly, and his temper snapped. Cursing under his breath, he retrieved his horse, mounted, and rode after her. What the hell did she think he was going to do to her—ravish her on the back of his horse in the pouring rain?

Her black cloak was thoroughly wet by now and plastered against her body, revealing the unconscious sway of her slender hips as she walked.

His manhood stiffened at the thought of what it would be like to have those hips undulating beneath him in his bed. For the first time in months, his body, numbed by grief, felt truly alive.

When he caught up with her, she faced straight ahead, refusing even to glance at him.

"You are wet and cold. Be sensible and let me take you up on my horse. I swear that you will come to no harm at my hands."

She did not look at him. "How can I believe that? They are English hands."

"Damn it, but you are the most stubborn woman I have ever met."

Exasperated, he guided the sorrel a few steps ahead of her, then stopped. As she hurried past him, he reached down, grabbed her beneath her armpits, and easily hauled her up, depositing her sideways in front of him. He was startled by how light she was.

His unexpected maneuver apparently so surprised her that for a moment she remained frozen. He had her firmly lodged in front of him, urging the sorrel forward, before she began to fight him.

He wrapped his arms around her, locking her arms to her sides and her body against his. The soft, tantalizing weight on his left arm told him he'd encircled her just below her breasts.

She struggled frantically to squirm free from him. Her hip rubbed against him in a way that sent desire rushing through him. He tightened his grip around her.

"Stop fighting me," he whispered in her ear. "You will succeed only in frightening my horse into trying to throw both of us." *And in driving me mad with lust*.

A long shudder shook her. Shane could not tell whether it was from being cold and wet or from fear of being thrown. Apparently the latter, because she suddenly stopped squirming. He was not such a fool, however, as to release his grip on her.

As the gelding lengthened its stride, her breasts bounced gently against Shane's arm. They were surprisingly full for a woman as slender as she was. He fought the urge to take them in his hands, to hold them, to caress them, to . . .

Shane ruthlessly cut off that train of thought and tried to concentrate on the path ahead.

He failed miserably.

Her fresh floral scent, quite unlike any perfume

he had ever breathed, filled his nostrils. Her wet hair curled about the edge of her hood and tickled his chin. Her hip rubbed rhythmically, seductively against his loins.

So hot was the lust that boiled through him, he wondered wryly whether her earlier fears of riding with him might have been justified.

He was the one, however, who was suffering. What had he let himself in for?

The longest ride this side of eternity.

Shane suppressed a groan and urged the sorrel to a still faster pace. How long had it been since he'd wanted a woman as much as he now wanted this one? Certainly not since he'd married his late wife.

Could it be his heart was not as dead as he had thought?

Or had this Irish spitfire's scent and hip merely intoxicated him with their erotic promise?

He clenched his jaw and forced himself to study the countryside instead of dwelling on the tempting morsel in his arms.

As the path traversed the hillside, it followed roughly the course of the stream flowing below. The water was so clear that he could see fish gliding about beneath its surface.

Since boyhood, fishing had been one of Shane's favorite pastimes, and his mother had claimed Canamara offered the best fishing in the world. He was so eager to try it that he carried in his saddlebags a small container of worms stored in moss.

"That stream looks to offer excellent fishing," he remarked aloud.

"It's said to be the best in County Kerry for trout and salmon."

Then this had to be the stream where his grandfather had taught his mother to fish. "I can scarcely wait to try it."

The woman twisted her face toward him. "You must have Sherbourne's permission first." Again she spit his name out as though it left a bad taste in her mouth. "But seeing as you're his friend, no worry have you."

The bitterness of her tone prompted Shane to ask, "Do you like to fish?"

She nodded. "As though I'd have any opportunity here."

The only other woman Shane had known who enjoyed fishing had been his mother. She had taught her son, much to the displeasure of his father, who felt that such rustic delights were beneath the future Marquess of Sherbourne. "I should be very pleased to have you join me here in the sport."

"Sherbourne and Radnor would never allow one of the Irish to contaminate this stream by fishing it."

Her mention of his agent reminded Shane it was growing late. By the time he left the woman at her home and rode on to the mansion, Radnor most likely would have left the estate office for the home that was provided for him on Canamara's grounds. Perhaps Shane would save time if he stopped at Radnor's cottage before going to the great house. "Can you direct me to where Mr. Radnor lives?"

"At the top of the hill." The woman gestured toward the mansion.

"No, I don't mean the estate office. I am looking for the cottage where he lives."

"No cottage for little Ollie," the woman scoffed. "Lives in the great house, he does, as though he were His Lordship himself."

"You sound as though you do not much like Mr. Radnor."

"I'd like him better if, instead of apologizing for having to carry out Sherbourne's orders, he'd refuse to do so or resign in protest."

That made no sense, but before Shane could question her further, they emerged from the trees into a lovely green meadow. Ahead, a low wall of native stone surrounded a substantial two-story cottage of the same material.

Pink, white, and yellow roses grew along the wall, and colorful boxes of flowers hung beneath the windows of the dwelling. Tall maples shaded it.

"It's in that cottage I live."

Shane should have been relieved that his ordeal of transporting this tempting baggage was about to end. Instead he did not want to part from her.

Since he had come upon her, he had felt not only desire for her, but a strange euphoria and lightness of spirit. The bleak, suffocating fog through which he had been stumbling for so long faded into a lighter mist where he might find his bearings again.

By the time Shane stopped the sorrel beside a gate that led into a neat, well-tended garden beside the cottage, the heavy rain had spent itself, the sky had brightened considerably, and only an occasional drop fell.

He noticed a small plaque in the wall next to the gate that read Rose Cottage and observed aloud, "You have a fine home, perfectly named."

"And dearly I pay for it," she retorted.

That puzzled Shane. Although he had never visited Canamara before, he went over the ledgers that Radnor sent every quarter and could not remember a Rose Cottage on the rent roll. Yet the name sounded familiar to him, though he could not place why.

He lowered the Irish woman to the ground, irrationally missing the pressure of her hip that until then he'd regarded as a diabolical instrument of torture.

Shane hoped she would ask him into the cottage for a cup of tea as a reward for bringing her home. "Here you are, safe and unharmed, Miss—?" He waited expectantly for her to supply her surname.

"Mrs. it is, not miss."

Although the sky had brightened, the day suddenly seemed grayer and colder than it had earlier when the rain beat down on them. Shane's happiness evaporated.

Unfortunately, his lust for her did not vanish with it, even though his honor would never permit him to make love to another man's wife. Not even to this woman who so intrigued him.

"As to my name, no need have you for it," she continued. "Our brief acquaintance is ended."

Shane was unaccustomed to feminine rejection, and it took him by surprise. "How can you say that when we will both be living on the same estate? Can we not be friends?"

Even as the words left his mouth, he cursed himself for asking. Mere friendship with this glorious creature was not what he wanted. In fact, it would be pure hell.

"No Englishman is a friend to the Irish." Her expression turned as dark as the sky. "Especially not one that's a guest of Sherbourne's."

Again she spit out his name as though it left an evil taste in her mouth. Shane thought of the many warnings he had been given about the hostility of the Irish toward the English. In some cases, it might be justified but, damn it, not in his. "Is that my only thanks for bringing you home safely?"

"For that, I do thank you. And now it's dinner I must be seeing to." She turned away. Moving with a fluid, sensual grace that made Shane again ache with desire, she walked up the path to the cottage without a backward glance at him.

Clearly he had not impressed her as she had him.

Nor had he aroused in her the powerful attraction that she had in him. Which was just as well, since she was married.

Still, he wanted to know her reason for loathing a man she had never met before. He called after her, "Why do you abhor Lord Sherbourne so much?"

She stopped at the cottage door and turned, her eyes glittering with anger and hatred. "The heartless bastard murdered my husband."

Chapter 2

Kathleen McNamara would long cherish the expression of shock and horror on Shane Howard's handsome face when she revealed to him what a fiend his friend Sherbourne was. Past time it was for the marquess's English friends to learn the truth about his cruel, evil character.

Her own reaction to this stranger, though, unnerved her. Not even her beloved Patrick on first meeting had made her pulse race as this Howard did.

And he a damn Englishman at that.

How could she be such a fool? She knew the callous contempt with which Englishmen treated Irish women.

Yet he had been polite and concerned for her well-being. Most Englishmen would have trampled her on the bridge and not even bothered to stop. Most certainly they would not have ridden out of their way in the rain to take her home.

His behavior was not all that puzzled her. He looked more Irish than English with his black curling hair, fair complexion, strong-boned face, and smiling mouth.

Nor had Kathleen ever seen an Englishman who

had his color of eyes—that distinctive bright blue of the Irish. A haunting sadness lurked in their depths, as though a great sorrow had befallen him.

Before he could recover his voice, Kathleen hurried inside Rose Cottage, shut the door behind her, and barred it to ensure she would have no further conversation with him this day.

Shaken by his effect on her, she hoped he would take the hint and leave quietly. If he pounded on her door, she would turn him away.

She prayed she would have the strength of will to do so.

Before she faced him again, she needed time to quiet her racing pulse and turbulent emotions and to recover the good sense with which she had been born.

Nor did she want to answer the questions Mr. Howard would surely put to her about how Sherbourne had murdered her husband. Not when her four-year-old daughter was home and might overhear them talking. Brigid knew only that her father had died fourteen months earlier. The grim details of how he'd met his end had been kept from her.

Kathleen waited behind the door, her heart thudding, for the stranger's next move.

A seemingly endless minute, then a second one ticked by before she heard the sound of his horse riding away. She peeked out the small window shaped like a porthole in the door to watch him gallop toward Canamara's mansion.

She'd wanted him to leave, so why did she feel so unaccountably disappointed to see him ride away?

Much agitated, Kathleen shed her sodden black cloak, reeking of wet wool. She went to the row of wooden pegs on the wall of the hall that led from the front door to the kitchen. Garments hung from most of the pegs, but she located an empty one next to her daughter's forest-green coat.

Once she deposited her cloak, Kathleen found herself drawn back to the round window. She could still see Shane Howard in the distance. His retreating figure held her gaze like a magnet. Although his garments were worn and his appearance unkempt, he had an unconscious air of authority about him.

She shivered—not that she was cold. Despite her wet hair and damp clothes, Kathleen felt overheated from her encounter with this stranger.

What manner of man is this Shane Howard that he affects me so?

His strength had surprised her. He'd swung her up before him as though she weighed no more than a stone.

As he pulled her against him, she felt the ripple of his powerful muscles. The warmth of his body seemed to permeate to the very marrow of her bones.

Yet there was a gentleness about the way he held her protectively against him. And for a few moments in the shelter of his arms, she had forgotten all the responsibilities that weighed so heavily on her shoulders.

When his arm settled beneath her breasts, a shudder of desire and excitement vibrated through her.

Her unsettling response to him had intensified as the sorrel reached a gallop. Her breasts bouncing lightly against his arm had generated another kind of heat, long absent, that curled deep within her. That she should feel it at all was shocking enough, but its strength was even more stunning to her.

When they reached Rose Cottage, she had found herself regretting that the ride was about to end and Mr. Howard must put her down.

Have I gone daft?

Kathleen had loved, still loved, her dead husband, her own Patrick. Although too impetuous and impatient, a kind and generous man he had been, and he'd paid for those virtues with his life.

After such a husband as Patrick, how could another man, a stranger, unleash such disturbing sensations in her?

Especially when he was one of the hated English.

And not only was he an Englishman, but most unforgivable of all, one well enough acquainted with her husband's murderer, Lord Sherbourne, to be invited to use Canamara's mansion.

"Mama, what are you watching?"

Turning away from the round window, Kathleen held out her arms to her four-year-old daughter. Brigid hurled herself into them, hugging her mother fiercely. The faint scent of lavender soap clung to the little girl.

Kathleen kissed her child, her heart brimming with love for her, and returned her hug, then affectionately stroked her fine dark hair, so like her father's.

Since Patrick's murder, Brigid had been the center of Kathleen's life. The little girl had become even more attached to her mother, as though she feared she might lose her too. Unfortunately, that was a possibility, given Kathleen's clandestine activities.

She released her daughter. "And what is it you've been doing while I was at school?"

"I played with Theresa. She and her da walked

me home. And she wants me to stay with her one night soon. Please, Mama, say I can."

Kathleen was not certain she could bear being separated from Brigid even for a night, and she said noncommittally, "We'll see, darling. What did you do after you got home?"

"I helped Maggie make shortbread biscuits." Brigid smiled proudly.

Kathleen suspected her daughter's "help" had consisted mostly of sampling the dough and the finished product.

Brigid confided, "Maggie says a fine cook I'll make."

Kathleen smiled. "That's high praise indeed."

Maggie, their girl of all work, was actually a woman several years older than her mistress's twenty-six years.

Kathleen studied her daughter lovingly. She was small for her age and slender. She had inherited not only her father's hair, but his laughing, cornflower-blue eyes and impish smile.

"Mama, I wish I had a da like Theresa does."

Brigid's voice and expression were so wistful, a lump that felt the size of a boulder rose in Kathleen's throat. She dropped to one knee so that she would be at her daughter's eye level.

"You had a father who was even better than Theresa's, sweetheart."

A single tear trickled down Brigid's face. "But I don't have one anymore."

Kathleen hugged her daughter to her. "No, you don't." Brigid had been so young when her father was killed that her memories of him were fading quickly now. "Your da was such a good man that God called him to heaven to be with Him."

"Then God should give me another da in his

place. Mary Margaret says she got a new da after God took hers to heaven. It's not fair for God not to give me another da too, after He took mine."

"It is not for us to question God, Brigid," Kathleen said firmly as she released her daughter and stood up. "And well you know that."

"Mama, you tore your skirt."

Looking down, Kathleen saw the gap where the side of her black skirt was ripped from the waistband.

Although she had managed to pull herself up on the stone side wall of the bridge before Mr. Howard's sorrel nearly trampled her, she had not been quite so quick with her full skirt. Before she could yank it up after her, one of the horse's hooves had caught it, tearing the cloth.

"It's nothing. I must have snagged it on a branch." Kathleen decided against telling her daughter about the horse, fearing the incident would alarm the child. "Is Maggie in the kitchen?"

Nodding, Brigid accompanied her mother to the big room that was the center of life at Rose Cottage. As Kathleen opened the door, she was met by delicious odors of bread warming and of meat and vegetables simmering.

Maggie, short and broad with hair the color of carrots and a face full of freckles that had never faded, looked up from the pot she was stirring over the turf in the fireplace.

"Late ye are, lass, and wet too." Maggie lifted the spoon from the pot, then replaced the lid, and reached for the ever-present kettle of hot water. "A cuppa tay ye'll be wantin'. Sit yerself down and, in a minute, ye'll be havin' it."

Kathleen sank gratefully onto one of the cushioned settles that flanked two sides of the large oak trestle table. A vase of pink roses, which she had picked that morning from the bushes that grew next to the wall, brightened the table's center.

"And soakin' wet your hair is," Maggie noted as she poured boiling water into the chipped china teapot. "A towel yer mama is needin', Brigid. Go upstairs to the linen closet and bring one down."

The little girl obediently hurried off to fetch one.

Towels could be found closer than that. Nor was Kathleen's hair all that wet thanks to Shane having pulled up her hood. Maggie's final sentence alerted Kathleen that the woman had something to tell her that was not for Brigid's ears.

As soon as the child was out of earshot, Maggie said quietly, "Seamus Malone stopped by wantin' to talk to ye." Her eyes narrowed. "What be goin' to happen tonight?"

"Don't ask," Kathleen answered sharply, silently damning Seamus for raising Maggie's suspicions.

He was the second of Conn Malone's four sons. Conn had devoted his life to turning the land he leased from Sherbourne into a thriving farm complete with a large, comfortable house for his family and a handsome barn.

Last month, Devil Sherbourne had repaid Malone for being such an excellent tenant by raising his rent beyond what he could possibly afford.

The Malones had been driven from their land with only the clothes on their backs, as though they had been illegal squatters instead of exemplary tenants.

Tonight the secret society that Kathleen helped lead, the Knights of Rosaleen, would exact retribution for Sherbourne's unconscionable actions.

Maggie frowned. "Wastin' me breath I am sayin'

this, but I'm wishin' ye'd not go. Too dangerous, it is."

"What we do tonight has to be done, Maggie." Kathleen spoke in a whisper to make certain her daughter did not overhear her. "I will not allow my husband's murderer to benefit from the Malones' years of hard labor."

"And what'll ye be tellin' yer little one about where you'll be?"

"What I've told her before. I'll be helping the midwife with a difficult birth."

"It's yer daughter ye should be thinkin' about."

"I am thinking of her." And Kathleen would gladly give up her position with the Knights if only there was someone else to lead them. "I do this in the hope that by the time Brigid is an adult she will have the rights our and our parents' generations have been denied."

Maggie planted both her hands on her broad hips. "Sure, and what if ye be caught with the Knights? It's hangin' by the neck ye'll be."

"I have to go." *Who else is there?* Ironically, Kathleen's silent question was the same one Patrick had asked her when she had vigorously protested his becoming involved with the Knights.

Unfortunately, though, what had been true then was still true now. The men in the neighborhood were brave and goodhearted. But other than Conn Malone, not a one of them was a leader. Conn's age and crippling rheumatism prohibited him from leading the Knights on raids. Without a captain to do that, they quickly disintegrated into a drunken mob that posed its greatest danger to itself.

Maggie snorted. "No need have the Knights with a woman tagging along."

Thank God Maggie had no idea Kathleen was

not merely doing that but, disguised as a man, was the Knights' leader, their Captain Starlight. Only Conn Malone, his son Seamus, and one other man in the area were privy to this carefully guarded secret. The other Knights all thought her a male stranger from County Cork sent to lead them. How shocked they would be to learn their Captain Starlight was a woman.

Brigid ran back into the room and handed her mother the towel she had found. Kathleen's thoughts drifted back to Shane Howard. She rubbed her hair vigorously, as though by doing so she could also rub him from her mind.

She was more successful, however, with drying her hair than with excising the Englishman from her thoughts.

Kathleen told herself she would not see him again, but she knew that he would be difficult to avoid while he lived at Canamara.

Worse, she *wanted* to see him again.

That was what most disturbed her. To soothe her conscience, Kathleen attributed this eagerness to her hope she could persuade him to spread the truth in England about the true character of her husband's murderer, that devil incarnate, Aloysius, Marquess of Sherbourne.

Chapter 3

S hane galloped toward Canamara's mansion, his thoughts in turmoil. The Irish beauty had struck him with her verbal lightning bolt accusing him of murder, then she'd gone inside the cottage and slammed the door behind her.

What in hell could she be talking about? Shane had never in his life killed anyone.

Her charge, as ridiculous as it was false, so shocked Shane that he'd gaped at the closed door in stunned silence.

He should have dismounted, marched up to the cottage, and demanded an explanation from her then and there, refusing to leave until he got it.

But evening was upon him. Shane had been in the saddle since early morn. He was cold and wet, hungry and exhausted. The ever-changing Irish sky was growing darker again, promising another bout of heavy rain before he could reach the mansion.

Shane would confront the woman, as provoking as she was exciting, on the morrow. He knew where to find her.

He was so shaken by her accusation that he was almost to the mansion before it occurred to him that if her husband was dead, she was no longer another man's wife and therefore untouchable. Rather she was a widow free to do as she chose. Once he'd convinced her that "his friend" Sherbourne could not possibly have had anything to do with her husband's death, perhaps . . .

His spirits rose. The day inexplicably seemed to brighten again, even though the rain had resumed and was growing heavier by the minute.

While Shane had been with her, the black cloud of grief and loss and futility that had engulfed him since his son's death had lifted a little. Like a bright shaft of sunlight, she had penetrated the gloomy darkness, promising a brighter day ahead. He hoped to see a great deal more of her while he was at Canamara.

His thoughts turned to this estate his maternal grandfather had left him. It was the least profitable of all Shane's holdings, and his man of business in London constantly urged him to sell it.

But Canamara had been his mother's home, the place where she had grown up. When he was a small boy, she'd told him about the estate, its house, and its people with such love in her voice that he could not bear to dispose of it.

And as Canamara's agent, Oliver Radnor, often pointed out, Shane had only himself to blame for its poor return. Not that Radnor advocated resorting to rack rents. Rather, in his reports on Canamara, he repeatedly lauded Shane for continuing his grandfather's policy of refusing to employ this device to extort every penny possible from the land.

The agent had also expressed his gratitude effusively for Shane's not forcing him into what he termed the "untenable position" of having to collect these exorbitant rents.

On Shane's ride from Dublin today, he had been appalled to see the shameful effect this cruel practice had on the land and its people. Too many of the estates he'd passed were divided up into crazy quilts of tiny parcels that could not possibly support even a small family. Invariably their inhabitants, adults and children alike, were hollow-eyed, pitifully thin, and dressed in rags.

When Shane dismounted in front of Canamara's mansion, the rain was falling in torrents again. Cold and wet, he hurried beneath the great portico's sheltering roof. Water dripped from his cloak as he crossed to the entrance and loudly banged the knocker.

Minutes passed without an answer. Shane frowned and banged again. Clearly the small staff he employed to care for the house was not accustomed to having visitors.

Finally the door opened, and Shane stared in astonishment at a footman wearing rich blue and gold livery and a condescending expression. Shane had not thought any footmen presently worked at Canamara, and certainly none who would be dressed in such lavish livery.

The servant examined Shane, making no effort to conceal his disgust at the visitor's wet, bedraggled appearance. He would most certainly have looked down his supercilious nose at the caller, except the footman was nine inches shorter than Shane, making this impossible.

"The likes of you should not be seeking admittance here," he said with an audible sniff of disdain. "This is the carriage entrance for the quality. The servants' entrance is where you belong."

Shane had never before been mistaken for a servant. Startled, he said sharply, "That is not where I belong."

The footman looked pointedly beyond Shane to his mount beside the portico. "Then where is your carriage?" His accent was English, not Irish.

"I came on horseback, bearing a letter from England for Oliver Radnor." Shane doubted what the Irish woman had told him could be right, but he said, "I understand that he lives here in the great house."

Instead of confirming whether this was true, the footman sniffed again. "I shall see whether the master will speak to you. I doubt he shall have time, however, for he has a most important engagement tonight."

"Master?" Shane asked in surprise. "Lord Sherbourne is not in residence." *Not yet.*

"I refer to Mr. Radnor."

"His Lordship's agent? Why do you call him master?"

Clearly startled, the servant demanded rudely, "Who do you think you are to question me?"

Holding on to his temper in the face of this incivility, Shane said sharply, "I know very well who I am, a friend of Lord Sherbourne. He has graciously given me the use of Canamara during my stay in Ireland."

The haughty footman's eyes narrowed. "More likely you are one of those evil, unshaven Irish scoundrels that prey upon upright citizens."

First Shane was mistaken for a servant and now for an outlaw. Well, he'd not wanted to be recognized as Lord Sherbourne. Perhaps, he thought wryly, he'd accomplished his goal a little too successfully.

"I have a letter for Radnor from His Lordship."
Shane pulled from his coat pocket the note he had
written before he left England, instructing that "his
good friend Shane Howard" was to be treated exactly as if it were His Lordship himself who was
visiting Canamara, and he was to be housed in the
marquess's own bedchamber.

The odious footman looked at the letter in disdain. "How am I to know you are not an Irish brig-
and who set upon Lord Sherbourne's unlucky
friend and robbed him of his money, this letter, and
even his life?"

For the second time that day Shane had been accused of murder. Outrage as strong as a rogue
wave swept over him.

"And do I speak like an Irish brigand too?" he
demanded in his most frigid, most correct British
accent. "Or do I speak like an English friend of
Lord Sherbourne's?"

Shane noted with satisfaction that the footman's
contemptuous expression dissolved into confusion.

The servant picked up a small silver tray from a
table by the door. "Place the letter on this." His
tone implied he would not touch a missive that had
been contaminated by the caller's handling.

Shane dropped the letter, sealed with the signet
ring that he carried in his pocket, on the salver.

As though he were the lord of the manor and
Shane a lowly peasant, the footman ordered, "Wait
there, you, while I give this to Mr. Radnor."

By "there" the footman meant outside on the
portico where Shane still stood. The odious servant
had not even extended the rudimentary courtesy
of inviting him inside while he waited, or of reliev-
ing him of his dripping cloak.

So insolent was the servant that Shane was

tempted to reveal that he was Canamara's owner and to dismiss him on the spot. But to make his real identity known now would defeat Shane's purpose in coming to his Irish estate.

The servant disappeared through one of four interior doors symmetrically placed about the hall, closing it behind him.

Shane promptly stepped across the threshold into the two-story high great hall and looked around curiously. Stripping off his wet cloak, he marveled at how the hall managed to combine both grandeur and eye-pleasing simplicity.

No murals decorated its off-white walls. Intricately carved plasterwork divided the ceiling into a large diamond in the center surrounded by six triangles. Shane dropped his gaze to the floor. Alternating tiles of white and black marble had been inlaid in a geometrical pattern that mirrored precisely the square and triangular plasterwork pattern on the ceiling.

The hall was exactly as his late mother had described it to him. How much as a child he had wanted to come with her on her visits here, but his father had forbidden it. He would not allow his son and heir to leave England.

One of the doors off the hall stood ajar. Certain it must lead to the dining room, he went to it, pushed it open farther, and found that he was right.

The long mahogany table had been set for two with fine porcelain, crystal, and silver. It looked as though a visitor of great prominence was to be entertained at dinner.

Who could the guest be? Since Shane had not been expected, the table obviously was not set for him. He recalled the footman mentioning Radnor's "most important engagement."

Although Shane did not know Radnor, he had met the agent's predecessor and father, Thomas. The elder Radnor had been the estate's agent during the final two decades that Shane's grandfather had owned it and had served with such loyalty and distinction that Shane had not hesitated to appoint his son to succeed him.

Shane was satisfied that he'd made a good choice. In Oliver's monthly reports to his employer, he wrote in great detail of the many improvements he made on the estate, especially in the housing for its dependents.

Occasionally when Shane went over Canamara's accounts, which Oliver sent quarterly to him in England, the charges for whitewash of tenants' cottages and thatch for new roofs seemed excessive. But since Shane wanted his Irish estate to be a pride to him—and to the memory of his mother—he did not object.

Shane had only one complaint against Oliver Radnor. Unlike Thomas's terse, straightforward reports, his son's were effusive to the point of fawning. While such sentiments might have gratified some of Shane's peers—certainly they would have pleased his father—they merely made him impatient and uncomfortable.

Shane turned away and moved back into the hall. The door through which the footman had vanished was flung open. A short, stocky man hurried into the hall, carrying the opened letter to Radnor in his left hand.

Shane stared in surprise at the man's costly dress. His silver brocade coat with matching waistcoat worn over black silk breeches would have been appropriate for the most elegant of London dinner parties.

Had Shane not known Canamara belonged to him, he would have thought he was looking at its owner.

Indeed, Shane was not entirely certain of the man's identity. Agents did not dress in such splendor, and the man before him bore no resemblance to Thomas Radnor, who had been thin and at least five inches taller.

This man stood no more than five-foot-four, but his body was well proportioned. He was handsome enough, with regular, if somewhat bland, features, which at the moment were puckered in worry.

Unlike the rude footman, the newcomer managed a smile, and said heartily, "What a pleasant surprise, Mr. Howard. I welcome you to Canamara."

"I am glad someone does," Shane muttered.

The man's face grew anxious. "I am deeply sorry, sir, if our reception of you was not all it should have been, but you find us at a disadvantage. I fear Lord Sherbourne neglected to inform us you were coming."

He must be Radnor, Shane decided. He sounded just like the letters the agent wrote. And Shane reacted now as he did to Radnor's letters—with a touch of impatience.

"It is most unlike His Lordship to send us a guest without warning," the man continued, "and we are caught by surprise."

It was unlike His Lordship to send any guest at all. In the six years since Shane had inherited Canamara, he had sent only one, Robert Sutton, and that had been nearly a year ago. A lump rose in Shane's throat at the thought of poor Robert, whose

journey here had ended tragically in his death.
"Are you Oliver Radnor?"

"Yes, I am Lord Sherbourne's agent."

*No cottage for little Ollie. Lives in the great house, he
does, as though he were His Lordship himself.* Shane
had not believed the Irish woman, but now . . .

The pompous footman appeared in the doorway.
"Bring in my saddlebags from my horse," Shane
ordered.

The servant could not have looked more outraged had Shane demanded that he swim across
the cold Irish Sea to England. Quivering with indignation, he said, "I am a liveried English footman, not a common Irish porter."

"Do as you are told, Dobbins," Radnor snapped.

The footman obeyed the agent, but not without
casting a fulminating glance at both him and
Shane.

Shane said to Radnor, "That wretched man is
more insolent than a duke's London footman. I am
amazed you tolerate him."

"You must forgive Dobbins. He was convinced
you must be an Irish robber posing as His Lordship's friend to gain entrance here. I must confess,
Mr. Howard, it was a surprise to myself as well as
Dobbins that a friend of His Lordship's would arrive on horseback without carriage, luggage, or
valet."

Although Radnor maintained his respectful, dif-
ferential manner, the way he accentuated the word
valet told Shane he considered this servant indis-
pensable to any man with the slightest pretension
to being a gentlemen.

Shane's valet shared Radnor's opinion. He had
been much distressed to learn he was to stay behind in England. He would be far more distressed,

indeed shocked, were he to see the clothes Shane had brought with him to Ireland.

Determined to pass as a man of no consequence in order to assure the anonymity he sought during his visit, Shane had acquired a wardrobe of worn, inconspicuous garments from a Wrexham rag-picker while on his way to Ireland.

"I need no valet, and I preferred to travel from Dublin by horseback," Shane told Radnor. Not only did doing so cut hours off the journey, but he had not wanted his first view of the Irish country-side restricted by the confines of a traveling car-riage. "My baggage should arrive by wagon tomorrow. I have all that I need for tonight in my saddlebags."

"You are very lucky to have arrived here at all," the agent said. "Englishmen do not travel alone through the Irish countryside, for it is crawling with Irish scum who delight in waylaying, robbing, and killing them.

"I had no idea such crimes were so common here," Shane said.

"Oh, yes. Indeed, a guest His Lordship sent us last year, a Mr. Robert Sutton, was killed as he trav-eled back to Dublin on his way home to England. I warned him of the danger, but he would not lis-ten." Radnor sighed mournfully. "Such a tragedy."

Yes, it had been. Robert Sutton had been one of Shane's closest friends, and he still missed him.

He had learned of his friend's death only two days after Jeremy's physician had told him his son would not live another six months. Shane had been devastated by the double blows.

Even now, being reminded of them sent his spir-its plummeting, and he realized how wet, hungry, and very exhausted he was.

Radnor said, "I must write Lord Sherbourne immediately and warn him again about the dangers of letting his friends travel as you did."

A weary Shane hardly heard him. "Please have someone show me to my apartment."

Radnor looked deeply pained. "His Lordship very kindly instructed me to give you his own bedchamber, but I fear it is not ready. It is shut up, and all the furniture is beneath dust covers. It must be cleaned and aired and the bed made up before it will be habitable. It will be some hours before it will be ready."

Bone-tired, Shane could not entirely stifle a groan.

"Since I know you must be exhausted from your journey, may I suggest that I show you to a guest bedchamber for tonight only," Radnor continued. "We will move you into His Lordship's rooms tomorrow before your baggage arrives."

Eager for a bath and shave, Shane said, "Yes, the guest chamber will do for tonight. I also require a hot bath before I go down to dinner."

Radnor was clearly dismayed when Shane said he would be down to dinner, and the agent's expression provoked Shane's curiosity about the mysterious guest who merited such an elaborate table.

"Please tell the cook I will be in the dining room in one hour." Given the way the table was set, Shane was certain serving his dinner then would be no challenge to the cook.

Alarm flitted across Radnor's face before he managed to hide it behind his deferential manner. "Surely, Mr. Howard, after a tiring day in the saddle, you would prefer a tray be brought to your room rather than being required to dress again for dinner."

Appealing as a tray in his room sounded to the weary Shane, he intended to discover why the agent was so anxious that Canamara's visitor not use the dining room tonight. "A tray is unnecessary. I will come down to dinner in an hour."

Although Radnor could not entirely conceal his displeasure, he said politely, "As you wish, sir. Now let me show you to your temporary quarters."

The agent led Shane toward the end of the hall, where a straight staircase connected to an arched opening on the floor above.

"After you have shown me up, Mr. Radnor, please make certain a groom takes care of my horse. Tell him to leave the tack beside him in the stable. I like to take early morning rides."

Radnor, who had reached the foot of the stairs, stopped abruptly and spun around to face Shane, clearly agitated. "Mr. Howard, you cannot ride by yourself."

"Why not?"

"You do not know the estate. It is very large, and you are certain to get lost. I will assign a groom to guide you." Radnor started to ascend the stairs rapidly, as though bent on cutting off any protest from Shane.

If that was the agent's intent, he failed. Shane said, "I have no need of a guide. I have an infallible sense of direction, and I prefer solitary rides."

Particularly when Shane hoped to see the widow McNamara again. He could not help smiling at the prospect.

Radnor's pace up the stairs did not lag, but his profile hardened. "I am sorry, sir, but I cannot allow you to ride alone. It is far too dangerous!"

"Dangerous," Shane echoed incredulously. "How so?"

"Secret societies of Irish troublemakers are very active in this area. These ungrateful wretches despise all Englishmen, even one as good to them as Lord Sherbourne. They want to drive all us Englishmen from the island. They would not hesitate to beat, torture, or even kill you, should they come upon you alone."

Not once in any of his long, effusive letters to Shane had Radnor mentioned such bands operating in the vicinity of Canamara. Instead he had assured his employer that all was peace and calm. Shane's eyes narrowed. "Lord Sherbourne said nothing to me about such problems."

"Did he not?"

Radnor sounded puzzled, which in turn puzzled Shane. "I cannot believe I am in any danger. The Irish ruffians will have no idea who I am." *And neither do you, little Ollie.*

"Your name will not matter, only that you are an Englishman. I cannot permit you to ride alone," the agent said sharply.

"Can you not?" Shane challenged.

They had reached an arched opening at the top of the staircase, and the agent stopped and faced Shane.

"Pray, forgive me for speaking as I just did," Radnor said humbly. "But I assure you it was prompted only by my deep concern. You must understand that I feel personally responsible for the safety of the marquess's guests, and I consider it my duty to ensure it. I failed once to save a friend of His Lordship. I cannot bear to fail again."

Shane could not quarrel with this. "I do understand."

They passed beneath the arched opening into a long hall. Instead of turning left, which Shane knew from his mother's detailed description of the house led to the best apartments, Radnor turned right.

"I was surprised to learn that you lived here in the great house." Shane wondered what explanation the agent could offer for this usurpation. "Lord Sherbourne said you occupied a cottage on the grounds—Rose Cottage, I believe he called it."

Shane had belatedly remembered why the name of the house in which the Irish woman lived had sounded familiar to him. "But when I went there, I discovered another family living in it."

The ruddy color bled from Radnor's face, and he looked rather green. "I . . . I . . . have let Mrs. McNamara, a poor widow whose husband was killed in an unfortunate accident on the estate, use the cottage." As he talked, his voice grew more certain and animated. "Had I not done so, the poor woman would have been homeless, for she is destitute and has nowhere to go. And being a bachelor, I did not need an entire cottage."

"How did her husband die? I was shocked to hear her claim Lord Sherbourne murdered him."

"Such nonsense." A nervous smile twisted Radnor's lips. "Merely another example of what a hysterical, irrational race the Irish are. They persist in exaggerating and distorting everything. Lord Sherbourne never in his life saw her husband, but since McNamara met his fatal accident in Canamara's park, she accuses its owner of murdering him."

"Was McNamara one of my"—Shane caught himself before he gave away his identity and hastily inserted—"my lord Sherbourne's workers?"

"Nothing so honorable as that. McNamara was a poacher. The gamekeeper mistook him for a deer and accidentally shot him."

Before a horrified Shane could ask how the gamekeeper could have made such a ghastly mistake, the agent hurried on, "Mrs. McNamara is an honorable woman who begged her husband to give up his lawlessness, but he refused to listen to her."

Having met the fiery Mrs. McNamara, Shane could not imagine her begging for anything.

They reached another hall at the end of the one that led from the staircase, and Radnor turned left into it.

"She could not help what her husband was. The lout left her a penniless widow with a small child. I could not turn them out, leaving them to starve without a roof over their head."

Shane recalled the woman had indicated she paid high rent. "You charge her nothing?"

"How could I, given her circumstances? Lord Sherbourne is such a kind and generous man that I knew he would want me to act as I did."

"Then why did you not inform him of your action?" *Or of McNamara's death?* But Shane could not ask the latter question without risking betrayal of his identity.

"But I did," Radnor assured him.

"Then why does Lord Sherbourne think you still live in Rose Cottage?" Radnor was beginning to trouble Shane.

The agent looked perplexed. "I cannot imagine, unless it slipped his mind."

"I have always thought His Lordship had an excellent memory," Shane said dryly.

"Or perhaps my letter to him on the matter went

astray. I shall write His Lordship immediately and inquire whether he received it. Speaking of letters, if you have any for posting, give them to me. I handle all the mail myself after discovering the servants were not entirely reliable in this matter."

Radnor stopped at a door at the far end of the second hall. "This is one of Canamara's finest guest chambers."

Shane knew he was lying. But he had no idea why Radnor would do so and bring Shane to this chamber instead. It made no sense, and set him to wondering whether this was the only lie Radnor had told him. Had the agent's "missing" letter about McNamara's death ever been written?

The room was small and sparsely furnished, hardly the best Canamara had to offer, but it would do for one night. All Shane cared about now was shedding his wet clothes, shaving, bathing, and filling his empty, growling stomach.

As Radnor turned to leave, a scowling Dobbins appeared with Shane's saddlebags, dropped them inside the door of the room, and vanished. Radnor followed the footman out the door and shut it behind him.

Shane strode to the single window in the small chamber, drawn by a melange of discordant sounds outside. The window offered him an excellent view of the stables and a large chicken coop, filled with clucking, crowing fowl.

He turned away in disappointment. His mother had told him that the windows from his grandfather's bedchamber offered an unparalleled view of Canamara's lovely park, and Shane had looked forward to seeing it.

That view was one of the reasons Shane had instructed in his letter that he be given his grandfather's apartment. The second was his mother's stories of a secret staircase her father had built. It connected his bedchamber to his private gun room, which had a hidden exit into the rose garden.

Shane's grandfather had used the hidden stairs when he secretly entertained fugitive Irish Catholics, with whom he sympathized.

His mother had first told Shane of the passage when he was a small boy. Since then, he had eagerly looked forward to the day he could explore it himself.

Now, though, he was more concerned with puzzling out why Radnor had given him this decidedly inferior room for tonight. Did the agent have some reason for wanting to keep him away from the other wing of the house where the better chambers were located?

What the hell was going on?

And what was the truth behind Mrs. McNamara's allegations?

Shane suspected traveling incognito to Canamara would prove to be far more illuminating for him than if he had come as himself.

And his usually unerring instincts warned him he would not like what he discovered.

Chapter 4

Shane removed the miniature of Jeremy from his saddlebag and placed it on the table beside the bed he would use tonight. He never went anywhere without this portrait of his dead son. The excellent likeness of the boy had been done a year before his death. As Shane looked at the image of his son's fair, delicate face with enormous blue eyes, he felt as though his heart were bleeding.

A knock at the door announced the arrival of two pretty young maids delivering a copper tub for Shane's bath. They answered his greeting with inarticulate sounds, their gazes carefully averted.

After depositing the tub, they scurried hastily out again as though they feared for their lives in his presence.

They returned a few minutes later followed by three other young maids. Each girl staggered under the weight of the two large, heavy pitchers she carried.

Shane was disgusted that maids, not manservants, should have to bring such a heavy burden up the stairs. But after meeting that odious Dobbins, he was not surprised that the maids were pressed into such service.

The first maid marched across the floor to the tub, looking to neither the left nor the right, and dumped the contents of her containers into the copper tub. The others deposited their pitchers just inside the door of Shane's room and fled as though the black death contaminated the chamber.

The first maid hurried back to the pitchers by the door, straining visibly as she picked up two of them.

Always the gentleman, Shane went over to her. "Here, let me take one of those."

As he tried to take the container in her left hand, she started so violently that water splashed from it over his jacket and shirt. Her pretty freckled face blanched in terror. "Sorry I wet ye, Yer Honor."

"A little water can do no damage. I was trying to relieve you of one of the pitchers. They are too heavy for you to carry both of them."

Although she looked incredulous, she silently relinquished a container to Shane, and he picked up a second one. After she emptied the one she still carried, he dumped the contents of both of his into the tub.

They repeated this process a second time. Disconcerted by the girl's obvious discomfort, Shane pointed to the two remaining pitchers. "I'll empty those."

"Anyt'ing else ye want?" The maid's gaze remained fixed on Shane's wet shirtfront while her fingers nervously pleated the cloth of her apron.

Trying to put her at ease, Shane stepped toward her with a smile. She jumped away from him as though his nearness would have burned her flesh, and she made a hasty sign of the cross.

Nonplussed, Shane asked, "Why are you so frightened of me? You have no reason to be."

"Sure, but I do, for a friend of Lord Sherbourne's ye be."

"Why the devil should that frighten you?"

"It's a divil His Lordship be." Her expression told Shane she firmly believed this. "A cruel, murdering monster!"

Her eyes suddenly widened in fright, and she clamped her hand over her mouth as she apparently realized what she'd said to a friend of the devil himself.

"He is nothing of the sort." All the unjust charges leveled that day against Shane had tried his patience to the limit. Irritation crept into his voice. "Why would you think that?"

Instead of answering him, she tried to sidle toward the door.

"Stay," he ordered, wanting some answers.

"Please, sir." Her voice trembled with fear. "A good girl I be."

"What are you talking about?" Shane asked, baffled.

Her face turned as fiery red as her hair. Again edging toward the door, she said bitterly, "Ye think I don't know what services Englishmen expect of Irish maids?"

Belatedly grasping her meaning, Shane exclaimed, much affronted, "Not this Englishman!"

The apprehension on her freckled face betrayed her certainty that he lied, and she would pay the price.

Never before had his character and integrity been challenged as they had been since he had reached Canamara. "I will do you no harm. Nor will His Lordship. What is your name?"

"Siobhan."

"Thank you for bringing my bath, Siobhan. I require *nothing* else of you. You may go now."

The girl turned and ran from the room as though the devil were hard on her heels, and shut the door behind her.

Disturbed that he should be unjustly considered such an ogre by one of his servants, Shane stripped off his traveling clothes, depositing them in a heap on the floor. He climbed into the tub and lay back in the relaxing water, letting its warmth soothe his weary muscles.

With all but his head submerged, he soaked lazily, contemplating how unlike Thomas Radnor his son had turned out to be.

Shane had met the father shortly before his own grandfather, Lyon Fitzgerald, died. He'd sent Thomas Radnor to England to deliver a letter to Shane in which he praised its bearer as the most honest and capable of men, who had served Canamara and its people long and well.

Knowing Shane would soon inherit the estate, his grandfather urged him to retain Thomas as his agent and steward, for none knew better than he how to manage Canamara.

The sensible, plain-talking senior Radnor had impressed Shane, who assured him that he would keep his position after Grandfather died.

Radnor then added a request of his own. His only son, Oliver, had returned to Canamara after being educated in England. The elder Radnor was training the young man to become the agent of a large estate. It was the father's fondest wish that upon his death, which was surely years away since he was still a vigorous man of seven and forty, his son should succeed him as agent at Canamara.

Thomas Radnor, however, died in a fall from a horse only four months after the demise of Shane's

grandfather. Good honest agents for Irish estates
were hard to come by. Believing the senior Radnor
would have trained his son well, Shane had ap-
pointed him to succeed his father.

Shane pushed himself to a sitting position in the
tub. He wished he could soak until the water was
cold, but he intended to be in the dining room before the end of the hour he'd allotted himself. He
wanted to discover who the mysterious dinner
guest was.

After he finished bathing, shaving, and dressing,
he'd used only forty-one minutes of his hour. He
was impatient to see the view from his grandfather's windows, and he would have time to do so
before dinner. He might also discover whether
Radnor had a reason for not wanting him in the
family wing of the house.

The hall outside his room was quiet. He opened
the door a crack to confirm no one was about, then
hurried down the hall and turned right into the
long corridor that led to the other wing, where the
master's suite was located.

He expected to find maids bustling about his
grandfather's apartment, making it ready for his
surprise visit. But when he reached his destination,
the door was closed, and he heard nothing inside.
He knocked lightly on the door. When he got no
response, he tried the door, and it swung inward.

Shane stepped inside a spacious bedchamber furnished with heavy masculine pieces, including an
enormous tester bed with a carved oak canopy and
comfortable, commodious wing chairs.

Despite what Radnor had told him, not a single
dust cover was in evidence.

And the apartment was clearly already occupied.
A man's jacket of blue superfine had been tossed

over the back of one of the chairs. On the round table beside this chair rested a cut crystal wineglass with a half-inch of wine still in the bottom. An open book lay on the table beside the bed.

Shane sniffed the air. Not only did it not have the stale, stuffy odor of a room long shut up, it was fresh and scented with a familiar blend of orange, cinnamon, and cloves.

His mother used to make the same potpourri at Sherwood. He still missed her, that lovely, vibrant Irish lass who had been both the delight and the anchor of his childhood and his youth.

As Shane passed the door to the dressing room, he saw a man's shaving equipment lying on a washstand below a large mirror in a gilt frame.

He stepped into the dressing room. Brushes were scattered across the top of a chest of drawers. The door to the wardrobe was open, and he saw costly raiment hanging in it.

Shane returned to the bedchamber and went over to the windows that lined the two outside walls of the corner room. His mother had not exaggerated. His breath caught at the views from the two angles the windows offered of Canamara's gardens and park and the hills beyond.

In the corner where the windows came together was a small writing table that provided whomever used it with a breathtaking sight.

Shane glanced down at an opened letter that had been dropped on the table. The missive was addressed to Oliver Radnor.

So not only was the agent living in the great house without permission, but apparently he was occupying its prime apartment.

Frowning, Shane moved to the table that held the crystal wineglass. He picked it up and sniffed the wine, an excellent claret, that had been left in the bottom.

No wonder the footman had called Radnor master. The agent was enjoying the life reserved for Canamara's owner.

Was that why Radnor wanted to keep the surprise visitor away from this end of the house? Had he hoped to conceal that he'd appropriated his employer's privileges for himself?

Even if that had been Radnor's aim, Shane thought he'd have wanted to move his belongings out of the suite he'd purloined as quickly as possible. But clearly, he'd done nothing.

Lives in the great house, he does, as though he were His Lordship himself. Shane felt a new respect for the widow McNamara and a stronger faith in her veracity. So why did she think he'd murdered her husband?

He pulled out his pocket watch. Although he still had eleven minutes left of his hour, he would go down now to the dining room.

As Shane headed for the door, he passed a solid front mahogany cabinet standing against the wall. He wondered if it contained mementoes of his grandfather's, but he did not want to take the time now to look.

Shane stepped into the empty hall. As he neared the arch at the top of the central staircase, he heard a querulous female voice coming from the steps. "Ollie, lovey, why'm I dressin' like this fer dinner if it's in yer rooms we'll be eatin'?"

Shane stopped before he could be seen by whoever was on the stairs and listened.

"A waste of me beautiful gown, it is."

"Shut up," Radnor ordered brusquely. "You have no cause to complain. I paid for that damn gown, and we will eat wherever I say."

"But ye promised we'd be eatin' in the fancy dinin' room tonight. Sure, and ye know how much I'm wantin' that."

So the mysterious dinner guest was a she, and Shane was about to meet her.

"If the widow McNamara comes to dinner"—the unseen woman's voice took on a jealous edge—"I'll wager it's in the dinin' room she eats with all them fancy plates and goblets and such."

Shane stiffened at this tidbit that the woman he had met on the road dined with Radnor at Canamara. So that was how she knew the style in which he lived. He wondered whether Mrs. McNamara came frequently.

"It is none of your concern where she dines, Fee," Radnor snapped.

"Such a rush ye be in to get me to yer bedchamber tonight, lovey."

The couple reached the top of the stairs, and Shane saw a flash of a red satin skirt, then the profile of a voluptuous woman. As she stepped through the arch that led from the stairwell, she almost bumped into him. Her eyes widened.

"Well, well, and now who's I seein'?" She looked and sounded like a cat who'd just discovered a tender, tasty mouse.

Even if the neckline of her gown had not been cut so low it left almost nothing to the imagination, the bold, thorough appraisal she gave Shane would have told him what kind of woman she was.

So this was Radnor's "most important engagement."

Shane's presence in the hall clearly nonplussed Radnor. "Mr. Howard, what are you doing here?" he asked in consternation.

"Mr. Howard, is it?" the woman echoed, all but licking her lips. "Fiona's me name."

Shane nodded an acknowledgment to her and told Radnor, "I am going down to dinner."

"But you are early." Radnor sounded as though Shane had committed a grievous offense.

He shrugged carelessly. "No more than a few minutes."

Fiona eyed Shane as though she wished *he* were the main course on tonight's menu.

The strumpet's boldness made him thoroughly uncomfortable. And his certainty that she and Radnor were about to cavort in his grandfather's bed, in the very bed where his mother had been conceived and born, angered and offended him.

But he gave no indication of this as he said smoothly, "Mr. Radnor, I find the guest room I have been given inadequate. Have my belongings moved to Lord Sherbourne's apartment while I am at dinner."

That would, at the very least, force Ollie and Fiona to move the site of their "activities," if not thwart them altogether.

The agent stiffened as though he'd been prodded with a sword point, but when he spoke it was with great politeness. "Surely you can wait until morning. The servants cannot—"

"No, I insist it be done while I am at dinner." Shane began descending the steps. "Be so kind as to see to it immediately."

He was certain he heard Radnor cursing under his breath, but he did not glance back toward the agent. He wondered with amusement what Fiona would say about being shuttled to yet another location for dinner.

When Shane entered the dining room, he was not

surprised to see that one of the two covers had been removed from the table.

Although the food was excellent, the loneliness that had been his constant, unwanted companion since the death of his son gnawed at him as he sat in solitary splendor at the long table.

For a little while this afternoon with the widow McNamara the gnawing had stopped, but now it was back stronger than ever. Shane wished that she were dining here tonight with him.

And just what was her relationship with Ollie Radnor that he had given her his home to live in?

Remembering what Fiona had said, Shane wondered whether "little Ollie" collected the "rent" from the widow in her bedroom at Rose Cottage.

That would explain why he denied receiving monetary rent, while she claimed to be paying dearly for the roof over her head.

Standing on the stump of a felled tree, Kathleen McNamara concluded her instructions to the three dozen men before her in the secluded meadow. She had taken care to deepen and roughen her already husky contralto voice so that she sounded like a man. "Remember the safety of all rests upon carrying out your instructions exactly."

Here and there a torch illuminated the pitch-blackened faces of the men, who looked rather like escapees from an African slave ship. Their dark faces contrasted sharply with the large, loose-fitting white shirts they wore over their clothes.

Unlike the men Kathleen led, she did not wear a white shirt, but a green military uniform, decorated with gold braid, that identified her as their Captain Starlight, one of the names Irish secret societies gave to their leaders to protect their real identities.

They often wore masks for the same reason, so no one thought it odd that a hood of green silk covered her head, both hair and face. Holes had been cut in the cloth for her eyes, nose, and mouth.

She'd also bound her breasts and padded her shoulders and waist to make herself look more like a man. Apparently she had succeeded, because none of the men had questioned her sex.

The Knights were gathered tonight in response to Devil Sherbourne having driven the Malones—father, mother, and four grown sons, two with families of their own—from their farm and rented it to a friend of his, an Englishman named Tilton.

All the improvements the Malones had made on the land, including the home and other structures they had built, now belonged to Sherbourne. His Devilship had even seized the fine herd of cattle that they had bred and raised.

The Malones had been allowed to leave with only the clothes on their backs. The marquess claimed that all else, down to the cooking utensils in the kitchen, the linen on the beds, and the clothes in the closets, belonged to him.

And so it did now, for no authority in Ireland would dare question an English marquess.

Although Kathleen's group had adopted the garb of the infamous Whiteboys, they were not members of that secret society but of another, called the Knights of Rosaleen, which shunned the Whiteboys' brutal practices.

And she reminded the men of that now. "Remember, no person is to be harmed. We seek justice, not vengeance."

One of the black-faced men grumbled loudly, "No justice can us Irish find in Ireland. Only the damn English who stole our land from us have justice."

"That is why we are here tonight—to obtain a small measure of the true justice the English and their law deny us," Kathleen retorted.

"Woe be the day the ould Lion died and left Canamara to his divil grandson," a voice deepened by age said.

"A far greater woe for us were the day the Lion's daughter married an English lord," another man said. "That's the birth of our troubles."

Kathleen nodded in silent agreement. *How could any Irish woman have betrayed her people with the evil English as Maureen Fitzgerald had? And spawned as her son that devil Sherbourne?*

Aloud Kathleen cried, "And now we shall inflict a bit of justice on Sherbourne for having robbed the Malones of all they have built with their years of hard labor."

"It's not enough to hurt His Divilship's purse alone," a disgruntled voice called. "It's a good thrashing them English Tiltons deserve for comin' here and takin' the land away."

"Better yet, hang them from a high oak tree," another man shouted. "Think twice then, the English will before they'll be stealin' the rewards of our blood and sweat."

Kathleen held up her hand to silence the dissenters. "Listen to me. We do not obtain justice for ourselves or sympathy for our cause by wounding or killing the English. Remember that. The Tiltons are not to be harmed, only the property."

"Sure, and that's more kindness than we was showed," a bitter voice that Kathleen recognized as Seamus Malone's cried. "Dragged me poor ma out o' her own kitchen while she were cookin' dinner and knocked me da down when he tried to help her."

An angry murmur ran through the men.

"Rather be seein' the house and barns in ashes and rubble, than havin' the likes of Sherbourne and them Tiltons benefitin' from our toil," Seamus said.

"And deny Sherbourne any benefit we shall," Kathleen assured him. "What more fitting retribution for the greedy devil than to make his property worth far less?"

Someone said, "I hear a friend of his be visitin' his great mansion on the hill."

Word of a newcomer traveled fast across hills and fields and bogs of west Ireland.

Recalling her meeting with Shane Howard, a little shiver of excitement rippled through Kathleen. Her jaw clenched, and she tried to kindle for him the same revulsion she felt for Devil Sherbourne, but she could not muster it. Silently she cursed her own weakness.

"A story to take back to his evil friend, we'll be givin' him tonight," another man cried.

Trying to push Shane Howard from her mind, Kathleen called, "Sure, and enough talking we've done. Time now to act."

A cheer went up from the assembled men.

Kathleen marched at the head of the Knights in her captain's uniform, leading them toward the Malone farm.

What irony that she, who had so adamantly opposed her husband's heading this secret society while he was alive, should now captain them in work she had once deplored.

"We came here as teachers to preserve, not to destroy," Kathleen had argued passionately with Patrick. "We came here to save and pass on to future generations the culture, language, history, and legends of our land. We came here to help make certain that the damn English fail in their efforts to obliterate our past. We did not come here to fight them with knives and cudgels and pitchforks."

Once Patrick would have agreed with her, but he had changed in the months they had lived in County Kerry, teaching at illegal hedge schools, which sought to educate Irish children in their culture that the English were so anxious to obliterate.

"Unless the rapacious English are stopped, not merely the Irish culture but the Irish themselves will be obliterated," he had argued back. "No future we'll have, as well as no past."

"No future *you'll* have if the English kill you," she'd cried.

"I have to lead them, Kathleen. The men do not lack courage but they lack leadership ability. Without me to guide them, they'll disintegrate into a drunken mob and be killed."

So far, though, only Patrick had died. Sherbourne had ordered his cold-blooded execution, leaving the knights without a Captain Starlight to lead them.

In her grief, Kathleen had sworn that her husband did not die in vain. She quickly realized that if she were to ensure that he had not, she must assume his leadership of the Knights.

More women would be widowed as she had been and children orphaned unless a firm leader took over the reins of the organization. Kathleen had too much affection for the Irish parents of her students to let this happen.

Her most compelling reason for following in Patrick's footsteps, however, sprang from her frustration and fury at the gross injustice of his slaying having gone not merely unpunished but entirely ignored by the authorities. Delighted she was to inflict whatever small damage she could on her husband's murderer.

Still Kathleen's spirit quailed before the responsibilities to her daughter, students, and Knights that weighed on her. Both the latter activities were dangerous and could land her in a gaol or worse. She did not want Brigid to be robbed of her one remaining parent.

Most happily would Kathleen give up both teaching and the Knights if only there were someone to replace her.

They neared the substantial Malone farm. It was well past one in the morning, and all the windows in the main house were dark.

Kathleen gave the signal, and the Knights glided in different directions like silent shadows through the night.

The horses were freed from the barn and the poultry and pigs from their pens.

Apparently the Tiltons were heavy sleepers, for no heads appeared at the house's windows to seek the reason for the animals' noise.

Once the animals were safe, Seamus Malone hurled a blazing torch into a pile of hay inside the barn he had spent so many hours helping to build.

The flames flashed through the dry hay, quickly engulfing the wooden interior of the barn. The Knights torched the other outbuildings too.

This was the signal for the men who had invaded the house to roust its occupants from their beds.

As Kathleen and the other Knights waited for the Tiltons to be led from the house, the flames leaped into the night sky, brightening it with an eerie light.

This must be what a day in hell looked like,

Kathleen thought. The acrid smell of burning wood and hay filled her nostrils and burned her eyes and throat.

Her stomach roiled as she watched the destruction the Knights wrought. Such a waste. Such a damn waste!

Minutes passed. Ash and cinders drifted down on them. Kathleen tapped her toe impatiently. They had to hurry now before someone saw the fire and spread an alarm.

Finally, two men and two women in their nightclothes were led from the house at pistol point, their arms loaded with bundles. Kathleen had ordered that they be allowed to take with them as much as they could carry in their arms, which was more than the Malones had been permitted.

The first man in this procession was burly, with an awkward gait, large protruding ears, and bushy hair. A jagged scar ran down his cheek from the corner of his left eye to his chin.

Although Kathleen had not seen Ben Tilton before, she recognized him instantly. She had thought the sinister description she'd heard of him must be exaggerated, but if anything it had been understated. Seeing him in the flesh, she could not suppress a shudder. He looked to be the perfect companion for a devil.

Tilton roundly cursed the Knights and swore vengeance on them in language that would have shocked a jack-tar.

While Kathleen was perfectly willing to believe that Devil Sherbourne would have such repulsive friends, Tilton was the antithesis of Shane Howard. She could scarcely believe one man could have two such disparate friends. If she ever saw Mr. Howard again, she must ask him what he thought of Tilton.

A tingling excitement gripped her at the thought of Shane. Shocked, she tried to push him from her mind by focusing on the man and two women who sullenly followed Tilton from the house.

Kathleen had been told the other man was Tilton's brother, but in the light cast by the leaping flames she could see no resemblance between them. The women looked nearly as rough as Tilton did, but they let him do the talking—or rather the cursing.

They were led to a copse a safe distance from the burning buildings and tied there.

As the Knights dispersed, Tilton shouted after them, "Lord Sherbourne will 'ang all you Irish bastards for this night's work. And you"—he turned small eyes glittering with rage on Kathleen in her captain's uniform—"'e'll 'ave you drawn and quartered."

Kathleen could barely suppress a shudder. Yes, she thought as she slipped into the night, Devil Sherbourne surely would if she were caught.

And then what would happen to Brigid?

Chapter 5

As the first gray light of the dawning day crept into the room, Shane awakened with a start from an unnerving dream in which the widow McNamara demanded he be hanged for murdering her husband.

He stared up at the big oak canopy of the bed that had been his grandfather's. When he'd gone upstairs after dinner the previous night, his meager baggage had replaced Radnor's belongings in the suite. Even the miniature of his son had been moved to the table beside the canopied bed.

Shane tossed back the covers and climbed out of bed. He liked to rise early, and he was eager to sample the fishing in the enticing stream that flowed near Rose Cottage.

He loved the sport, and he'd long ago discovered he often did some of his best thinking while waiting for a fish to bite. So when he was troubled or in a quandary, he often sought relief with his fishing pole, but not since his son's fatal illness. Too many memories of fishing with Jeremy in the stream at Sherwood had kept him from picking up a pole again at his English estate.

As Shane dressed, he told himself he merely

wanted to try the fine sport this Irish stream offered. The possibility that while doing so, he might
see the widow McNamara again had absolutely
nothing to do with his eagerness.

Still, he would pass her home on his way to the
stream. If his luck were in, he might see her and
invite her to fish with him.

Shane removed the worms he'd brought from
their moss-filled container and placed them in a
small wooden box, which his mother had given him
years ago. He would use his grandfather's fishing
tackle stored in the gun room on the floor below.

He did not doubt the gear would still be there.
His grandfather had kept the windowless room
locked, and he'd had the one key to its only visible
door. A few days before his death, he'd sent the
key to Shane with a cryptic reminder of the gun
room's two secret entrances.

Shane had known from his mother that one
opened directly to the outside. The second revealed
a secret staircase that led up to this bedchamber.

He strode over to a Celtic cross attached to the
wall and pushed the top of it. The paneling next to
the cross swung open, revealing the narrow staircase. He marveled at how carefully the panels had
been fitted so that the opening was undetectable.
Had he not known the secret, he would never have
found the passage.

The staircase, thick with spiderwebs and dust,
had clearly not been used since before his grandfather's death seven years ago. Its dank air, stale
and moldy, made him cough.

Before entering the passage, Shane grabbed a
candlestick with a lighted, half-burned taper, and
an old shirt he'd bought from the Wrexham rag-
picker.

Using the shirt to brush away the worst of the cobwebs, he sneezed so hard from the dust he nearly blew out the candle flame that penetrated the blackness for only a foot or so ahead of him. Slowly he picked and groped his way down the narrow, steep stone stairs. At the bottom, he pressed a button in the wall, and again a panel swung open.

The windowless gun room was as dark as the stairway, and Shane held up the candlestick to inspect it. Glass-fronted cases, holding a variety of the weapons that had given the room its name, lined three of the small room's walls. The fishing tackle rested against the fourth. He swallowed hard as he saw the small bamboo rod that must have been his mother's when she was a child.

Shane shut the opening that concealed the staircase, marveling again at how undetectable the panel was in this room too, once it was closed. Nor could he see the secret door that opened outside. The only visible entrance to the gun room was a door that led into a back hall, and a heavy bolt had been thrown across it to prevent access.

After choosing the gear he wanted, Shane pressed another spring, this one disguised as a bell pull, to open the hidden door to the outside. He stepped into a lovely little rose garden next to the house and breathed deeply of its perfumed air.

The other three sides of this arbor were enclosed by a circular boxwood hedge, taller than Shane, with only a narrow opening in it. No one beyond the hedge could see if someone were to use the secret door. Here too, he marveled at how carefully the exterior stones of the rustic had been cut and fitted to hide the opening.

Slipping out of the rose garden, Shane headed

down the hill toward the meandering stream at an angle that would take him by Rose Cottage.

A profusion of trees and shrubs with leaves ranging through a dozen shades of green, silver, and copper were arrayed along both banks of the stream. They had been far too carefully placed with an eye to contrasting and complementary hues and shapes to be the random work of nature.

The grass beneath his feet was wet, and water drops from a recent shower fell from the leaves of the oaks and beeches and plane trees in the park. Again Shane breathed deeply of the fresh, grass-scented air of early morning after a cleansing rain.

As he passed the gate to Rose Cottage, his rapid gait slowed drastically. Disappointment gripped him when he saw all the shutters were still closed, except for one slightly ajar on the upper floor. He detected no sign of life other than a thin wisp of smoke drifting toward the east from the cottage's chimney.

His step slowed and some of the spring went out of it as he continued down the hill to the stream. He had not admitted to himself how much he'd hoped to see Mrs. McNamara again. Surely by the time he finished fishing, she would be up and about.

Shane reached the bank of the stream and walked along it for several yards to where the frolicking waters plunged over a salmon weir.

He pulled the wooden box from his pocket, extracted a worm from it, and baited the hook on the bamboo rod he'd selected. As Shane cast his line skillfully into the bubbling stream, he thought of the man to whom this pole had belonged.

As a boy, Shane had listened with envy as his mother talked of her father, so unlike his own. His grandfather had taken her everywhere with him and had taught her to ride and fish.

Shane's mother, not his father, had taught her son to fish. His father, to whom appearance was all, considered it beneath the dignity of an English marquess to indulge in such a pastime.

From all his mother had told him of her wise and witty father and from the many treasured letters he'd written his grandson, Shane had loved him without ever seeing him.

Shane's own father had been determined to keep his son from knowing Ireland and that part of his heritage. Unfortunately, that had been back in the days when Shane had still foolishly tried so hard to please his aloof, disapproving father.

By the time Shane concluded this was impossible and he had no reason to continue trying, his grandfather was dead.

Now standing where the old man might have fished, Shane bitterly regretted not having come to Canamara while his grandfather still lived. Perhaps they could have fished and taken long walks together. Melancholy gripped Shane.

A tug on the fishing line told him he had hooked a fish. When he pulled it from the water, he saw it was a disappointingly small trout. He detached it from his line and threw it back into the stream.

A prickly sensation crawled up the back of Shane's neck, as though someone unseen were watching him. He turned and scanned the foliage behind him but saw no sign of anyone.

His imagination must be working overtime.

Shane baited his hook with another worm from the small box and cast his line as far into the middle of the stream as he could manage.

Several more minutes passed before his rod suddenly bent with the weight of a fish, clearly much larger than the previous one had been.

It was feistier too, putting up a fight that demanded all of his attention. It yanked and twisted, feinted and fought while Shane struggled to bring it in.

When his aquatic adversary finally leaped above the surface, revealing itself to be a salmon, he was thrilled by its size.

The salmon proved to be one of the most exciting challenges he'd faced with a rod and hook.

After he finally landed the trophy and dropped it at his feet, the feeling that he was being watched pricked him again.

This time, a slight movement behind a bushy yew tree told Shane he was not merely imagining other eyes upon him. Someone was skulking about there.

Recalling Radnor's warnings about marauding Irish, Shane wondered if he should have brought his pistol with him.

The night before his arrival at Canamara he had stayed at an inn on the road from Dublin. There, in the tap room, he had listened to a local English property owner's hair-raising tales about Irish ingrates.

But having seen the starving faces on the land around the inn, he'd had little sympathy for the complainer.

Since Shane treated his tenants very differently, he expected no trouble at Canamara. Perhaps, though, he was overly confident of their gratitude for his refusal to exploit them.

He was about to find out. He moved toward the yew, ordering in his most commanding tone, "Come out from behind there at once."

"Me, do you mean?" inquired a surprised voice that clearly belonged to a little—a very little—girl. "I's the only one here."

Shane stepped around the yew and faced his "stalker," a beautiful, diminutive child with an oval face so perfect it nearly took his breath away. Her large, solemn eyes, as blue as the sky on a perfect day, were strikingly framed by curling black lashes. She studied him with undisguised curiosity.

So much for the dangers of marauding Irish, he thought wryly.

The girl's skin, as creamy as fresh milk, contrasted sharply with her long dark hair, which badly needed a comb and brush. She looked as though she had just tumbled out of bed and had immediately escaped outside.

The buttons on her green coat had been fastened, as though she'd been in a great hurry, in the wrong holes. A flannel ruffle, which no doubt belonged to her nightdress, peeked from beneath the coat's hem.

Shane suspected her parents would be much surprised to discover she was not safely in her bed. He guessed her age to be about four—a little younger than Jeremy when he died.

A wave of pain poured through Shane at the thought of his dead son. He could not see a child near Jeremy's age without again mourning his loss. "Why are you hiding here, watching me?"

"I don't wanta scare the fishes away."

He wondered why she thought she would, but before he could ask, she said, "I wants more t'an anyt'ing to fish."

She spoke with such wistful longing that she rekindled in Shane memories of his dead son.

Jeremy had loved fishing as much as his father did. How excited the little boy had been whenever a fish, no matter how small, took the bait and he could haul it in. Closing his eyes, Shane could see his son yet, dancing about on the bank with glee and proudly swinging his latest catch.

Shane's melancholy deepened as he recalled the happy hours he and the boy had spent together at Sherwood's stream. Jeremy had still been a toddler when Shane had first taken him fishing.

For his son's second birthday, Shane had given him a small rod. A suffocating lump rose in Shane's throat as he remembered how proud his son had been of that rod and of the first fish, a trout not much bigger than a tadpole, that he'd caught with it.

Even before his son had been born, Shane had vowed to be the kind of father he himself had wanted. He would give his child, whether boy or girl, the patience, love, and attention that he'd never had from his own father.

Then his wife had died giving birth to their son. Stricken as Shane had been by her death, he had forced himself to overcome his grief so he could concentrate on raising their newborn child.

Shane's own mother had been so important in his life, he could not imagine growing up without one. He'd been determined to be both mother and father to his son and had devoted himself to Jeremy, spending hours with the child. Shane no longer went to London for the season but remained instead at Sherwood with his son because he did not wish to expose Jeremy's tender young lungs to the city's dirty, smoky air.

What irony that the boy should have died of consumption anyhow.

"Why's you looking so sad?" the child beside him inquired.

Before Shane could answer, the salmon at their feet gave a dying flop, drawing her attention to it.

"Ne'er I've seen a fish that big before." Awe colored her voice.

"A prime catch," Shane agreed.

"T'at other fish, why'd you t'row it back?"

So she had been watching him then too. "It was only a baby, and I wanted it to be able to grow up and become a big one like this is." Shane gestured toward the salmon at his feet.

"T'at's nice of you." She nodded her head vigorously in approval. "I likes you."

"The feeling is mutual, I assure you."

She looked puzzled. "Mutual, what's t'at mean?"

"It means we share the same feeling. I like you too."

She smiled at him and turned her attention back to the fish at his feet. "What kind is it?"

"A salmon." Shane picked it up and dropped it into his creel.

"Oh, t'at's Mama's favorite fish," she confided.

She was such a lovely little thing that she all but took Shane's breath away. She reminded him of the stories his mother used to tell him about the *daoine sidh*, the good fairy folk of Ireland. He wondered whimsically whether she could be one of them.

"And where do you live, *sidhe*, in a magic fairy rath in the woods?"

That clearly startled her, and she assured him earnestly, "Oh, no! I'm no *sidhe*, truly I'm not."

"You look like one," Shane teased.

"Mama says fairies don't really exist, but I t'ink she's wrong."

Shane agreed with her mother, but he smiled and

asked, "Why do you think she's wrong?"

"Me friend and I found one of the little people's caves," she confided. "It's near here. Would you like to see it?"

He nodded. "Perhaps when I am done fishing."

"Have you seen a *sidhe*?"

"No, but I'm certain they look like you."

She knit her brows, clearly perplexed. "But how can you know if you haven't seen one?"

He chuckled. "Because you look just like the ones who visit my dreams."

Her eyes were as big as guinea pieces now. "I do?"

Shane nodded.

She considered this in silence for a few seconds, the tip of her little pink tongue poking at her upper lip. Then her eyes narrowed suspiciously. "You're funning me."

"No," he fibbed. "Tell me, then, who are you if you are not a *sidhe*?"

"Brigid," she replied, as though no further identification was required.

"My name is Shane. I am very pleased to meet you, Brigid."

He was about to ask her where she lived when she said, "Don't you know, you can't be fishin' here."

"Why not?"

"Cuz the fishes here belong to the bad man that owns this land."

Shane stiffened at this slander. "Why is he a bad man?"

Brigid did not seem to notice the sudden edge to his voice. "Keeps all the fishes for himself, he does, and won't let anyone else have t'em, though he ne'er comes here."

Shane's face hardened. He did not deserve the hatred some of his Irish tenants clearly had for him. Nor had he rescinded his grandfather's order that each leasee might take two fish a week from Canamara's streams. Shane would happily have permitted more had he not feared overfishing would deplete the supply.

"Well, *sidhe*, I am a friend of the man to whom the fish belong, and I assure you he is not bad. He has given permission for me and anyone else I wish to accompany me to fish here."

"I ne'er fished. I wants to more t'an anyt'ing."

She sounded so wistful that Shane picked up his spare rod and held it out to her. He wished now that he had brought his mother's childhood rod with him. But how was he to know he would be joined by this little Irish elf?

"Would you like to fish with me?" he asked her. "You are welcome to use this rod, although I fear it is too big for you."

Brigid eagerly reached for the long bamboo pole, but as she touched it, she jerked her hand back as though it had burned her. "Oh, but only growed-ups can fish."

She looked hopefully at Shane. "Do you t'ink maybe I'm growed up enough now?" The tip of her tongue poked worriedly at her upper lip as she awaited his answer.

Shane laughed. The charming little cherub was clearly as excited about fishing as Jeremy had been. "I think you may be. Try it, and we will see."

Her face glowed with excitement as Shane handed her the pole and dropped down on the ground beside her. He pulled the small wooden box from his pocket. "Let me show you how to bait your hook."

He extracted a worm from the box and deftly attached the wiggling creature to the hook.

"But you be hurtin' the worm," she said anxiously, her face puckering in a distressed frown.

Shane looked down at her. The morning breeze ruffled her tangled hair, and he could not stop himself from gently pushing a dark wisp of it back from her lovely little face. What a dear, sweet child she was. "No," he assured her.

She regarded him dubiously, her eyes as blue and guileless as a cloudless sky.

Shane put the box of worms back into his pocket.

"Why d'you have worms in t'at box?"

The little elf was as inquisitive as Jeremy had been, Shane thought pensively. Unlike many fathers, he'd always enjoyed answering his son's endless questions.

"Why're you sad?" A concerned frown creased Brigid's face, and she touched his hand with her own small one as though to offer him comfort.

Much moved, Shane forced a smile to his lips. "Was I? I did not mean to be. I was thinking about the box. I have rubbed its wood with a few drops of oil of ivy berries. In an hour or so, the worm smells like the oil, and fish find that irresistible."

Brigid's tongue pushed at her lip again. "Ir'sis'ible? What's t'at mean?"

"That you must have whatever it is."

"So the fish, it has to have the worm?"

He nodded again. "Precisely. Now let me show you how to cast your line."

When he had finished demonstrating and the hook with the wiggling worm had disappeared below the bubbling surface, he handed the pole back to her.

"I wants to throw the hook in the water."

"You need a shorter pole to do that, Brigid. Perhaps another day we can fish, and I will bring a smaller rod for you."

Instantly her little oval face brightened with excitement. "Sure, and you're sayin' we can fish again?"

"If you want to." Shane was surprised at how much he hoped she would.

"O' course I wants to!"

But delighted as Shane was at her eagerness, he realized he was usurping her own father's position, and he had no right to do that.

Before he could say anything, however, Brigid observed, "You talk funny. Where's you from?"

"From across the sea."

"I's ne'er been on the sea, but Mama has," she confided.

He wondered if her mother was English, but before he could ask her, her rod dipped.

"A fish!" Brigid shrieked in excitement. "A fish, I've caught."

Shane tossed his own rod aside, and knelt behind her, placing his hands over hers, his left on the rod and his right on the reel, guiding her enthusiastic effort to land her first fish.

She was so small, so fragile. Memories of another child he had helped like this lashed at him. He pushed them away to concentrate on this fish, *this* child.

The fish put up a poor fight. When they pulled it in, the trout was only a little bigger than the one he had thrown back.

When Brigid saw its size, her tongue poked anxiously at her upper lip again. "T'row it back, must I?"

"Not when it is the first fish you have ever

caught. You are always allowed to keep your first one. Now let's see if you can land another, bigger one."

Shane pulled the wooden box from his pocket and opened it. "This time you must bait your hook yourself." He half-expected the little girl to shudder and refuse to touch one of the wiggling creatures.

Instead she picked one out without hesitation, but then she looked up at Shane with anxious eyes. "And sure are you I won't be hurtin' it?"

"You won't hurt it." Shane hoped he was not lying to her.

Satisfied, her tongue pushed again at her upper lip as she concentrated on attaching the fat earthworm to the hook.

Shane again cast her line into the water and handed her the pole. Feeling more contented than he had in months, he sat down beside her.

She utterly charmed him, but the past had taught him to distrust such contentment. Too often for him, it had preceded unforeseen tragedy.

Chapter 6

When Kathleen awoke in the big feather bed she shared with her daughter, her eyes felt as though they had weights on them.

She had not gotten home until nearly three that morning. She'd changed out of her uniform in the shed behind the house, but she'd still stank of smoke. Using water from the kettle Maggie always kept warm over the embers of the turf fire in the kitchen, Kathleen had washed her hair and scrubbed herself with lavender soap to rid herself of the odor.

But she could not scrub away the memories of the flames and the destruction, and her heart ached.

When she'd finally crept up the stairs to her bedroom and slid beneath the covers beside Brigid, dawn had been no more than an hour away. Her daughter, always a sound sleeper, had not so much as twitched.

After Kathleen fell asleep, she dreamed of the English stranger she had met on the bridge the previous afternoon. Her intense physical reaction to Shane Howard, which she had tried so hard to suppress from her conscious mind, had surfaced in her dream, and its erotic content shocked her.

Since Patrick's death, Kathleen had been faithful to her husband's memory. That had been easy, she realized now, because she had not been attracted to another man until she met Shane Howard.

When her husband was alive, Kathleen had always enjoyed the marital bed. Her ride home with Mr. Howard's arms around her and her body pressed against his had aroused in her all the restless, gnawing need that she'd firmly subdued after Patrick's death. Even now she felt her nipples pebble at the memory of her breasts brushing against the stranger's arm.

She cursed herself for her unseemly reaction. How could she have any feelings at all for one of the hated English, especially when he was a friend of her husband's murderer? Her weakness shamed her, and she felt like a traitor to both Patrick and her proud Irish blood.

Kathleen rolled onto her side and forced her eyes open, expecting to see her daughter's face on the pillow beside her own. She blinked in surprise. Brigid's half of the bed was empty.

What a rare morn it was for her sleepyhead daughter to be up before Kathleen. The child must have gone down to the kitchen to join Maggie. Still, it was unprecedented for Brigid not to wait for her mother to awaken.

Concerned, Kathleen dressed hurriedly and brushed her tumultuous hair into some semblance of tidiness but did not take time to pin it up. She hurried downstairs to make certain her daughter was there.

Maggie was alone in the kitchen.

"Where's Brigid?"

Maggie looked up from stirring a pot of breakfast oatmeal. "In bed, I thought. She's not been here."

Frowning, Kathleen went into the hall and called her daughter. Only silence answered her.

Kathleen went outside but found no sign of her daughter anywhere within the wall of native stone that marked the grounds of Rose Cottage.

Her heart pounding with foreboding and fear born of a mother's love and concern for her child, Kathleen looked wildly around the empty yard. Her breath came in frightened pants.

The wind blowing up the hill whipped her hair about her face. Impatiently pushing it away, she noticed the gate was ajar. Running to it, she bent down. In the dewy grass, she made out the faint outline of small footprints pointing toward the stream.

Brigid must have gone down to watch the fish frolicking in the water, even though she had strict orders not to go outside the wall surrounding Rose Cottage without permission. An obedient child, she had not broken this rule before.

What on earth could have possessed her to do so this morn?

Not long before Patrick was murdered, Brigid had discovered him fishing in the stream. She had begged him to let her fish too.

Knowing what he was doing was both illegal and dangerous, Patrick, who had no great patience with his daughter under the best of circumstances, angrily shooed her away, saying her watching had frightened the fish off and she must leave. His real reason for not wanting her there was the stiff punishment meted out to an Irish tenant who dared to fish in the streams of his native land without the owner's permission.

Patrick had not been fishing for sport or to feed himself. He had taken the risk because the potato harvest had been poor the previous year, and many of Canamara's Irish tenants were half-starved. The fish he caught went to them.

When Brigid—who could be as stubborn as her father—persisted, he told her only grown-ups were allowed to fish, and she had to wait until then.

After that, Patrick took care not to fish again where his daughter might see him, but the damage had been done. After his death, she asked her mother every other day whether she was "growed up" enough to fish yet.

Finally, Kathleen told her the truth. Even if she were old enough, the bad man who owned Canamara permitted no one to fish there anymore.

Kathleen pushed open the gate and hurried down the hill into the wind. It whipped her hair and her skirts out behind her.

"Brigid, where are you?" she called, the wind blowing her voice back at her.

No answer. Kathleen's heart leaped into her throat, pounding harder with escalating fear. Could her daughter have fallen into the water?

Kathleen reminded herself that Brigid was a good swimmer. But what if she had hit her head when she fell into the stream? Kathleen broke into a run.

If something were to happen to Brigid, if she lost the child to death as she had Patrick, she could not bear it. Her daughter was the most precious thing in Kathleen's life.

And all she had left of Patrick.

She ran as fast as she could. As she neared the artfully planted foliage that screened the stream, the wind carried Brigid's excited cry to her. "Gettin' away, it is," she cried in Gaelic. "Help me."

A deep male voice responded, also in Gaelic, assuring her "it"—whatever that was—would not escape.

Who the devil could he be? Kathleen wondered. And, more chillingly, what was he doing with her daughter?

Kathleen honed in on Brigid's squeals coming from the bank a little downstream. She stopped abruptly when she saw a man kneeling behind her daughter, his arms around her and his hands over hers on the fishing pole she held.

"Now, pull your catch in," he instructed her daughter.

His voice sounded familiar to Kathleen, but she was too distraught over her daughter to identify it. Brigid, however, appeared to be in no danger from him. He was merely teaching her how to fish.

He turned his head a little, and Kathleen belatedly recognized him.

Shane Howard!

Kathleen's fear for her daughter receded. Slowly the racing beat of her heart and pulse returned to normal. Watching the man who had seriously disturbed her night's sleep, kneeling with his arms around Brigid, teaching her to fish, Kathleen realized that she instinctively trusted him with her daughter.

But why should that be so when he was a hated Englishman?

Frowning, Kathleen studied his handsome, chiseled profile, feeling the same potent attraction to him that she had the previous afternoon. Why did this Englishman affect her so?

She had told herself fiercely that she hoped she would never see him again, but now she could not smother a surge of joy at the sight of him.

Remembering how it had felt to be encircled by those strong arms of his, Kathleen was shocked to discover she envied her daughter standing within their muscular protection.

She moved silently to a bushy yew only a few feet from the pair on the bank and, undetected, watched Brigid and Mr. Howard.

Kathleen felt tears burning at the back of her eyes. It should have been Patrick kneeling there with Brigid.

But even if he were alive, Kathleen doubted that he would be doing so. A good husband had been Patrick, but if she were honest with herself, he rarely paid much attention to his small daughter. Nor had he displayed the patience with her that this stranger did now.

Kathleen had blamed it on Patrick's growing up with seven brothers and no sisters. She'd told herself he was simply unused to little girls and awkward with them. But she'd feared it was more than that. Patrick had desperately wanted a son. During her pregnancy, he had planned all the things he would do with the boy. When their baby turned out to be a girl, he seemed to lose interest in her.

Now Kathleen marveled at how the Englishman gently corrected her daughter's inexpert handling of the rod and explained to her what she must do.

He was clearly used to dealing with small children. Was that because he had some of his own? Kathleen could not fathom why she should feel the painful stab she did at the possibility that he had a wife and children.

She quickly forgot everything but her delight at her daughter's gleeful shrieks and beaming countenance.

Brigid hauled a medium-sized trout from the water. "Oh, how big it is! See how big!" She danced exuberantly on the stream bank, her face shining with pride and triumph. "Oh, I loves to fish!"

Kathleen looked from her daughter to Mr. Howard's face. She was baffled by the sad, haunted look in his eyes as he looked down at the little girl.

Brigid looked eagerly up at him. "Take me fishing tomorrow, please."

A shadow fell over Mr. Howard's face, and he said with a sorrow that tugged at Kathleen's heart, "Your papa should be the one to take you fishing."

The happiness evaporated from Brigid's expression. "No da has I." Her shoulders slumped, and she stared at the ground. "I wants a da so much."

Her daughter's melancholy tone and dejected posture nearly brought tears to Kathleen's eyes. She had been so busy with all the demands upon her since Patrick's death, she had not fully appreciated until this moment how deeply Brigid longed for a father.

"Where is your mama?" Mr. Howard asked.

"Sleeping. Most of the night, she was gone helping a babe be born."

Kathleen's breath caught. Thank God Brigid did not know the truth.

The little girl looked up at the man beside her, and her despondent expression gave way to a brilliant smile. "Would you be my da?"

Kathleen clapped her hand over her mouth to smother her gasp.

A small, choking sound escaped Mr. Howard.

"Oh, please." The little girl grabbed his hand and clung to it. "Please, be my da. I like you lots, and it's you I want to be my da."

He dropped down on one knee beside her and

smiled. "I like you lots too, Brigid, but I am afraid it is not as simple as that." His tone was kind and sympathetic. "We are not allowed to choose our parents. God does that for us."

The Englishman's gentle, thoughtful response to her daughter softened Kathleen's heart toward him.

"I pray to God every night to give me a new da," Brigid confided sorrowfully, "and He hasn't." Her face suddenly brightened. "But now He's sent me you." Her expression darkened again. "Don't you want me for your daughter?"

"I would love to have you as my daughter," he assured her, sounding as though he meant it, "but you are not. And only your mama can choose a new da for you."

Kathleen stifled a groan. He had no notion of how stubborn and determined Brigid could be. Now her daughter would hound her to death, begging her to make Mr. Howard her father.

But would that be so bad? a perfidious little voice within her asked.

Had she lost her mind? She didn't even know this man.

Nor would Kathleen ever marry a damn Englishman, especially not a friend and guest of Patrick's murderer.

Chapter 7

Both the sun's upward climb and Shane's stomach told him it was long past time he went back to the house for breakfast. But he hated to part from this enchanting elf. Astonishingly, Brigid even made him forget Jeremy and his agonizing loss for a little while.

Shane's time with her had been the most pleasant he'd spent in months. He would happily pass the rest of the morning with her. The time for good fishing, however, was over. Furthermore, her mama would surely discover soon that she was missing and raise a hue and cry.

Shane put the two trout Brigid had caught in his creel with his salmon.

"What's you doin'?" she asked in alarm.

"We must go," he said as he stood up. "It is time for breakfast. I will carry your fish for you."

"Don't wan'a leave," the child protested, her lower lip jutting out stubbornly as he began gathering up the fishing gear. "I's not hungry. Can't we keep fishing?"

"No, *sidhe*, the fish take a nap when the sun is as high in the sky as it is now."

Reluctantly, she surrendered the rod she'd been using and stood up.

Behind them, an unforgettable contralto voice, husky and so sensual it sent a shiver up Shane's spine, asked, "Brigid, what are you doing here?"

Shane, who had heard no one approach, whirled around. His heartbeat quickened at the sight of the widow McNamara.

Her thick, beautiful hair, crackling with electricity, tumbled loosely about her shoulders like a cascade of burgundy wine. She looked as though she'd just gotten out of bed. The thought of her there sent desire bolting through him with the intensity of lightning.

His gaze settled on her lips. To his hungry eyes, they looked even more kissable this morning than they had yesterday.

"Mama!" Brigid cried.

Shane started. Good God, Mrs. McNamara was the little elf's mother.

"You know you are forbidden to leave the yard without permission," the widow scolded her daughter. "Nor are you to go off with strangers like this." She glared at Shane.

He smothered a groan. She must think he had enticed her daughter to accompany him. Another black mark against him in the widow's mind.

"But, Mama, I had to."

The widow's eyes flashed green fire at Shane. Brigid was innocently miring him deeper in her mother's bad graces and perhaps even a scandalous mess.

"Sure, and why is it you *had* to?"

"To fish with S'ane."

"I swear I did not lure your daughter here," he interjected quickly. "I was already fishing when she came upon me. If I had not had the feeling I was being watched, I would not have discovered her hiding behind that yew."

The widow turned to her daughter. "And did you do that, Brigid?"

The little girl nodded, and Shane inhaled a long, deep breath of relief.

"I didn't wanta scare the fishes away."

An odd light shone in the widow's emerald eyes and her beguiling lips twitched at her daughter's explanation. "I see. And why did you leave our yard without permission, Brigid?"

"But, Mama, you said when I was growed up, I wouldn't have to ask permission anymore, and I'm all growed up now," Brigid said proudly.

"And what makes you think that?" her mother asked, her wrist hooked challengingly on her hip.

Brigid smiled beatifically, her expressive eyes glowing, her little cheeks puffed with pride. "Because I fished and I caught two fishes and only growed-ups can fish—remember Da said so."

Shane could not suppress a grin at the little girl's peculiar logic. Her mother rolled her eyes.

"How did you come to be watching Mr. Howard fishing?"

"His name's S'ane," Brigid corrected. "When I wakes this morn, I looks out the window and sees him carrying his fishing poles."

Her mother looked pointedly at the buttons of Brigid's green coat fastened in the wrong holes and the flannel ruffle poking beneath it. "You know you do not go outside in your nightdress."

"But me coat, I put it on."

"That's not enough." The widow held out her hand to Brigid. "Come, we're going home so you can get properly dressed."

The little girl's face fell. In what Shane suspected was a ploy to distract her mother, she asked, "Is the babe you helped be born a boy or girl?"

Shane was startled at how much this simple question seemed to fluster the widow. It was a moment before she managed to answer, "A dear baby girl. Now—"

"Are you a midwife, Mrs. McNamara?" Shane interjected, wanting to know everything about this fascinating creature who had reawakened his numbed emotions.

"No. No, I'm not," she said quickly.

Too quickly. Shane wondered why she should be so nervous. Could it be she had been with a lover? Had she told her daughter the story of helping with a birth to conceal the real reason for her absence? He was disconcerted by how much the possibility that she already had a lover disturbed him.

"I sometimes assist at difficult births." The widow took her daughter's hand firmly in her own. "Now come, Brigid. We must get home."

Shane wished the widow had taken his hand instead of Brigid's. He ached to feel the softness of her skin against his palm—and to enjoy the gentle caress of her fingers on other parts of his anatomy.

Using her free hand in what was an obvious delaying tactic, Brigid pointed to the creel Shane held. "Mama, two fishes, I caught. Show her, S'ane."

"He doesn't need to show me." Mrs. McNamara pulled on her daughter's arm. "I am impressed, but the fish belong to Mr. Howard, not to you."

The little girl's bright face puckered. "T'ey does so belong to me. I caught t'em. S'ane didn't."

"But he has Lord Sherbourne's permission to catch them. You do not." The widow's expression told Shane that the mere mention of his name left a nasty taste in her mouth.

Irritated by her unwarranted disdain, Shane retorted, "Yes, Brigid does."

The widow looked at him in astonishment. "What?"

"His Lordship told me I might invite a guest to join me anytime," Shane improvised hastily, "and I asked your daughter, so you see she does have permission. The trout she caught are hers."

"Sherbourne would be furious with you were he to learn you not only let one of his Irish tenants fish in his sacred stream but then allowed her to keep her catch."

"Nonsense," Shane replied testily, "he would not mind in the least."

"You do not know His Lordship very well, do you?"

"I know him far better than you do. You have never even met him. Furthermore, you wrongly hold him guilty of a crime he did not commit. How could he when he was not even in Ireland?"

Mrs. McNamara gave him a warning look, nodding her head slightly toward her daughter as she did. "I'm not wishing to discuss that subject now."

Shane comprehended her silent message that they not talk of her husband's death in front of her daughter. Undoubtedly, she wanted to protect Brigid from learning of the ugly circumstances surrounding her da's death.

"No, of course not." He glanced down at Brigid, then looked up at Mrs. McNamara, silently berating himself for having broached the subject. "I should not have said anything."

With her daughter's hand clasped firmly in her own, she headed up the path toward Rose Cottage.

Although Shane had not been invited to accompany them, he fell into step beside them.

He detected a faint whiff of Mrs. McNamara's fresh floral scent. He longed to bury his nose in her soft, flowing hair so that he could drink more deeply of her unique perfume. This thought prompted another part of his anatomy to ache to bury itself in her too.

"Mama, S'ane says I looks like a *sidhe* he sees in his dreams."

Brigid's mother swiveled her head to regard him. "Sure, and surprised I am he knows what a *sidhe* is."

"Why're you surprised, Mama?"

"Because he is an Englishman. They are ignorant about such things."

The scorn in her voice irritated him into saying sharply, "I may be English, but I am not ignorant, especially not of the *daoine sidh*."

Brigid looked up at him as though he'd suddenly grown horns and a tail. "You be an Englishman?" She sounded dismayed and incredulous.

He nodded, both taken aback and hurt by the child's reaction.

Her face scrunched up in a puzzled frown, and her tongue pushed at her upper lip as she studied him thoughtfully. Finally, she said, "But he don't act like one, Mama. And he speaks Irish."

Her mother's beautiful green eyes narrowed and hardened with suspicion. "Sure, and how is it, Mr. Howard, that a man of corrupt English blood speaks Gaelic as though he's one of Ireland's native sons?"

He tried to ease the sudden tension with a smile and a teasing answer. "No doubt you will be horrified to learn that fine Irish blood mingles with the corrupt English in my veins.''

She looked more bemused than horrified. ''Ah, so that is where the Irish blue of your eyes comes from.''

Shane felt inordinately pleased that she had noted the color of his eyes. It reassured him an attraction as strong as his for her could not be entirely unreciprocated.

As they turned onto the path that led up the hill to Rose Cottage, the widow asked, ''Where is your horse?''

''I walked.''

''What, an Englishman who walks rather than rides!'' she exclaimed derisively.

Her daughter's eyes widened. ''You ride, S'ane?''

When he nodded, she cried, ''Oh, teach me, please!'' In her excitement she tugged at his sleeve. ''I wants to ride so much.''

''I will be happy to teach you.''

The little girl beamed, but her mother groaned. ''You have no horse, Brigid.'' The widow turned to Shane, looking at him through narrowed eyes. ''And where's it I'm to find a horse worth her riding that costs five pounds or less?''

Thinking her anger stemmed from being forced to admit the most she could afford was five pounds, he said quietly, ''I did not mean to embarrass you. I will find her a horse worthy to ride and stand the cost.''

''It's not embarrassment I'm feeling! A horse for Brigid, I can afford. But you damn Englishmen will not permit us to own one worth more than five pounds!''

''You cannot be serious!'' Shane exclaimed in shock.

"More serious I can't be. Your English law prohibits it."

It was not *his* law. Indeed, he had known nothing of it, and now that he did, he was appalled.

The widow's face tightened. "And if a horse we have be worth more, an Englishman has only to hand us five pounds and the horse is his."

"That is shameful!" Now Shane understood why, in a country noted for its fine horseflesh, the few Irishmen he'd seen on horseback rode such sorry nags.

She looked at him as though she could not believe his response, and he told her with quiet sincerity, "I had no idea that was the law. I am as disgusted as you are by such injustice."

At the gate to Rose Cottage, the widow passed through it with her daughter and started up the walk without a backward glance at Shane. He had hoped she would invite him to join them for breakfast, but she clearly had no intention of doing so.

Well, he was not about to let her escape him so easily this time.

"Wait!" He held up his grandfather's creel. "You have forgotten Brigid's fish."

The widow turned and walked back toward him. The graceful, unconscious sway of her hips sent a surge of desire through Shane. He stepped through the gate and handed her the creel. As she took it from him, she nearly dropped it. "Why's it so heavy?"

"S'ane's salmon's in it." Brigid hopped from one foot to another. "You forgot to take it, S'ane."

"No, it is no longer my salmon." He grinned at the little girl. "I am giving it to you and your mama." He looked up at her mother. "She told me salmon is your favorite."

As she flipped open the top of the wicker basket, the widow's eyes widened. "So big it is!"

Shane wryly wished that her expression was half so impressed when she looked at *him*.

The widow stared hungrily at the salmon for a moment before trying to hand the creel back to Shane. "We can't accept—"

He cut her off in mid-sentence. "But you must." He clasped his hands behind his back, refusing to take the basket from her. "I will not take the creel until you have accepted the salmon."

Shane thought she would be pleased. Instead her expression turned wary and suspicious. "Sure, and what price are you asking in return?"

"Breakfast this morning is all." He ignored the fire in his loins, which tried to dictate a very different answer.

"Oh," Brigid cried, "please do eat with us, S'ane."

The widow looked as though she wanted to clap her hand over her daughter's mouth, but before she could object, he said hastily, "I am delighted to accept your invitation, Brigid."

Her mother looked aghast. "Very plain's our fare, Mr. Howard. You'd be much preferring the food served at the great house."

"But I much prefer the *company* at Rose Cottage," he assured her with a grin. "Surely breakfast is a fair trade for the salmon."

From the look Mrs. McNamara gave him, she must consider any time in his presence an exorbitant price to pay. That stung him, but he continued placatingly, "I will even clean it for you in the bargain. Why do you look so astonished?"

"Amazed I am a friend of Sherbourne would know how to clean a fish."

"I am a man of many surprises." Shane followed the widow around to the back of the house.

As he gutted and cleaned the fish with quick, expert strokes, he said, "I understand, Mrs. McNamara, that you are all alone in the world except for your daughter."

Brigid, who had followed them, piped up, "Her da and sister live in Dublin."

"I am surprised you have not gone to live with them." Was it a lover who kept the widow here? Jealousy chewed at Shane. "Why do you remain in County Kerry?"

"Mama teaches," her daughter answered for her.

"Brigid, you know you are not to speak of that!"

The widow's tone was far sharper and more reproving than Shane had yet heard her use toward her daughter, and he wondered why.

"But a nice man, S'ane is, Mama. He—"

"He is English, Brigid! You know no Englishman can be trusted."

God Almighty, the widow made Shane feel as though he were the worst sort of scoundrel simply because he was English. "This one can!"

"Can you now?" Mrs. McNamara looked both hopeful and incredulous. "And you a friend of Sherbourne?" She turned to her daughter. "Time it is for you to get dressed."

"But Mama—"

"You'll not be sitting down to breakfast till you're dressed."

Apparently the firmness in her mother's voice convinced Brigid further argument would be futile. She headed for the cottage.

After she was gone, Shane said, "So you teach at the local charter school." He knew from Canamara's accounts that he contributed a considerable sum each year toward the school's upkeep.

The widow looked appalled. "As though I'd have anything to do with that hellhole!"

For a moment his hands stilled on the fish, and he gaped at her. "What are you talking about? I don't understand."

"Clearly, there's a great deal you do not understand about Ireland and your countrymen's violation of it and its people."

He opened his mouth to rebut her charge. Then he remembered the sorry hovels on tiny plots of ground that he'd seen on his ride from Dublin.

"Please," he said quietly, "I have no wish to debate you on an empty stomach. Will you grant me a truce at least until we have finished eating?"

The widow reddened. "Yes, of course." She sounded a little sheepish.

She led him through a half-door into a kitchen, a large yet cozy room, where two places were set at a trestle table. Mouthwatering odors of cinnamon, brewing coffee, and baking bread perfumed the air and sharpened Shane's hunger.

A sturdy woman with hair the color of carrots stood before the hearth, stirring something in a copper pot suspended on a hook hanging from an iron crossbar.

"Are you not eating this morning, Maggie?" the widow asked.

"Too hungry to be waitin' for dawdlers like you, I was," the woman replied.

Maggie turned her square, peasant face toward the widow. When she saw Shane, astonishment registered in her expression. He hoped that meant the woman was not accustomed to seeing a male visitor at Rose Cottage.

Especially not for breakfast.

"And who is it we have here, Kathleen?" Maggie inquired.

So the widow's name was Kathleen. Kathleen McNamara. A lovely name for a lovely woman.

"Mr. Howard is a guest from England staying at Canamara's great house. Brigid invited him to breakfast with us."

"And he accepted?" Maggie blurted incredulously.

"Yes." Kathleen turned to Shane. "This is Maggie O'Brosnan."

As Shane acknowledged the introduction, he held out the salmon he'd caught and cleaned.

"Holy Mother!" Maggie exclaimed. "Sure, and that monster can't be for us."

"Oh, but it is." He thrust it into her hands.

Maggie looked down at it hungrily. "It's a feast we'll be havin' for dinner."

Kathleen had not defined Maggie's role in the household, and Shane wondered whether she was a servant or a relative.

From what Radnor had said of the widow's financial situation, she could not afford a servant. Yet she had said she could buy a horse for her daughter. Nor did the cottage look as though she could barely make ends meet.

Copper pots and kettles hung from hooks by the fireplace. Handsome china was displayed on an oak dresser along the wall opposite the fireplace. A cloth of fine Irish linen covered the large trestle table, set with pretty stoneware, and a crystal vase filled with a handsome arrangement of pink roses brightened the center.

The hard benches that usually flanked trestle tables had been replaced at this one by more comfortable settles with cushioned seats and backs.

A profusion of herbs and flowering plants grew in pots resting on the ledges of the room's diamond-paned windows. A patchwork quilt decorated the wall.

Such a pleasant, inviting room. Shane could not remember ever having been in a kitchen before, and its homey comfort surprised and pleased him. He could see why the cottage's residents preferred to eat here.

Maggie left the pot she had been stirring at the stone fireplace to set another place for him at the table.

Kathleen invited him to sit at the newly laid place while she and her daughter took the two across the table from him.

Shane wished he could think of some reason to exchange seats with Brigid so he could sit beside her mother, perhaps close enough for their thighs to touch. He recalled the way her hip had rubbed against him as they rode the previous day, and a fresh wave of desire arced through him.

After Maggie brought the food to the table, Kathleen urged her to sit down with them for at least a cup of tea, but she declined. "Chores I'll be doing now."

She left the kitchen, presumably to do them.

As the widow had warned Shane, the breakfast fare was plain. But it was also excellent. The oatmeal had been seasoned with cinnamon, the toast spread with fresh butter, and the aromatic tea brewed to just the strength he liked it.

Nor did the company disappoint him.

As they ate, Brigid plied Shane with questions about England, which he answered patiently and honestly until she asked, "And the King, do you know him?"

To answer truthfully would risk betraying himself. But neither did he want to lie to her. Instead he decided to give her an answer that would distract her from her original question.

"Well, Brigid, I am afraid I have a problem. You see I am very bad at walking backward. Can you do it?"

Her tongue poked at her upper lip. "I t'ink so."

"Why would she want to?" her mother asked.

"Because if she is ushered into the King's presence, she cannot turn her back on him, and she must leave by walking backward a long way across a great hall in a very full skirt."

"How silly," Brigid said.

Shane grinned and said to her mother, "Out of the mouths of babes . . ."

"No baby am I!" Brigid cried. "Growed up, I is. I caught two fishes."

Shane and her mother exchanged smiles of mutual amusement at Brigid's indignation. His breath caught at the beauty of Kathleen's smile.

Lord, but he ached to bury his fingers in her veil of burgundy hair that fell loosely about her shoulders and kiss her smiling mouth.

"Mama, did Maggie tell you Seamus stopped yesterday to see you?"

That startled Shane from his sensual reverie.

Her daughter's question clearly discomforted Kathleen. Who the hell was Seamus? Her suitor? Her lover? Was that whom she had been with last night? Shane felt jealousy prick at him again. "Who is Seamus?"

"A neighbor." Kathleen stood up abruptly. "Excuse us, Mr. Howard. I must be getting ready to leave."

Shane, who had intended to linger over breakfast

as long as possible, was chagrined at this curt dismissal. He stood up too, saying irritably, "Shane. My name is Shane."

"I told you S'ane was his name, Mama," Brigid said.

He smiled at the child, then turned to her mother. "Breakfast was excellent, Mrs. McNamara. Thank you."

"Welcome, you are." Kathleen took her daughter's small hand firmly in her own. "Time to go upstairs, Brigid. Say good-bye to Mr. Howard."

"Good-bye, S'ane." Brigid let her mother lead her toward the door, but after a few steps the little girl stopped and looked back at him. "Will you dine with us tonight, S'ane?"

"Brigid—"

He interrupted her mother's protest. "There is nothing I should like to do more, *sidhe*," he replied truthfully.

"Sure I am you'd be preferring to dine at the great house," Kathleen said.

He grinned. "Having enjoyed one meal at Rose Cottage, I would not dream of passing up another."

Brigid said with great seriousness, "Besides, Mama, we'll be eating the salmon he gave us, and you always tell me when someone gives us somet'ing, we must offer to share it with him."

Kathleen looked down at her daughter, her frown dissolving into a smile, and her eyes filled with pride and love. "Yes, darling, you are right. We must."

"So you will come, S'ane?" The little pixie hopped from one foot to the other in her excitement. "Do you like salmon?"

"It is my very favorite fish, just as it is your mother's."

"Very kind of you it is, t'en, to give it to us," the little girl replied in what he guessed was a perfect imitation of what she had heard her mother say on other occasions.

"And very kind it is of you to invite me, *sidhe*. I can hardly wait for tonight."

"Go upstairs, Brigid, and ask Maggie to brush your hair while I see Mr. Howard to the door," her mother said in a voice that brooked no opposition.

Shane wondered if Kathleen meant to retract her daughter's invitation once she was out of earshot. *Over my dead body!*

But instead, as Kathleen showed Shane out, she said in a low voice, "Please, I beg of you not to say anything to anyone about my teaching."

Shane did not understand why she would care. He might have teased her had the graveness of both her expression and her voice not warned him this was no laughing matter. "No, I will not. You have my word on that."

She looked at him with such doubt and concern in her eyes that he wanted to take her in his arms and kiss the anxiety from her face.

He conquered that impulse and sought instead to reassure her with speech. "I fear you think the word of an Englishman is worthless, but I assure you that once I have given mine, I have never broken it."

He stepped outside and turned back to face her. "I will see you tonight."

And I intend to learn what worries you so.

Chapter 8

"**M**ama, can S'ane be my da?"

Kathleen, surreptitiously watching Shane stride up the hill from Rose Cottage, smothered a sigh. As she'd feared, her daughter wasted no time in launching her campaign.

She silently cursed Shane for having put the onus on her. True, only she could choose another da for her daughter, but that would require marriage. How could Kathleen explain to her innocent four-year-old daughter that what this—or any Englishman—wanted from an Irish woman had nothing to do with matrimony? They thought it beneath them to marry one of "that inferior race."

Kathleen did not want her daughter to pin her hopes on Mr. Howard during his brief visit here. Her little heart would be broken when he returned to England, as he soon would, never to be heard from again.

"As Mr. Howard told you, it's not as simple as that, darling. And I'm thinking he's not a man to be wanting a daughter."

If only he did want Brigid—and her mother too. That errant thought shocked Kathleen. From where had it come? The effect the man had on her was unnerving.

"S'ane does so want me! He says he'd love to have me as his daughter."

"He was being polite, darling," Kathleen said gently.

"No, he wasn't." Brigid stamped her small foot for emphasis.

"And you shouldn't have invited him to dinner tonight."

"Why not? Your favorite fish he gave us, and we must ask him to share it with us."

Brigid was right. The Irish prided themselves on their hospitality, and Kathleen should have invited him. She would have except for the powerful, disconcerting attraction that she felt for him. It was unlike anything she'd experienced before, even for Patrick, and this frightened her.

"Besides, I wants him to come," Brigid said.

So, deep in her heart of hearts, did Kathleen, but she would not admit that aloud. "He ate here this morning, Brigid. That is enough."

And Kathleen had enjoyed breakfast with Shane far too much. She'd been shocked to find herself imagining what it would be like to do so after a night of sharing her bed with him. Even now, she felt her nipples grow taut at the thought, followed by a quickening in her belly.

Why was it that Shane Howard affected her as no man had, not even her own Patrick?

And Howard, a hated Englishman and a friend of Patrick's killer, she reminded herself for the umpteenth time.

Much agitated, she hurried into the hall, grabbed her black hooded cloak from its peg, and wrapped it around her. As she set out for the hedge school she taught, she detected a faint residue of Shane's distinctive spicy scent on the cloth from their ride together yesterday, and she shivered a little.

The damn man haunted her!

The less she saw of him, the better.

As Shane returned to the house through the hidden entrance to the gun room, he realized this had been the happiest morning he'd spent since his son's death. He left the fishing gear where he had found it, then used the secret staircase to reach his bedchamber.

There, as he passed the impressive mahogany cabinet, taller than he was, he stopped to see whether it did indeed contain his grandfather's mementoes. To his surprise, the cabinet doors were locked, and the key was missing.

Radnor must have it. Shane went downstairs the normal way. As he crossed the white and black marble floor of the hall, a loud, rough voice sounded through the withdrawing room door, which stood slightly ajar. "Ain't staying in no bloody inn. Me's staying 'ere."

"You will stay where I tell you, Tilton. Your choice is an inn or go back to England, preferably the latter."

Oliver Radnor's voice was so harsh and angry that Shane did not instantly recognize it.

"You were brought here to prevent what happened during the night, you worthless bastard, and you failed completely."

Shane frowned. What had happened during the night?

Radnor snapped, "Now get the hell out of here."

The door to the withdrawing room banged open, and a large man stalked into the hall. The evil-looking brute had ugly, protruding ears and a scar that ran down the side of his face.

When he saw Shane, he snarled, "You lazy Irish bastard, get to work 'stead of spying." He stormed out the front entrance and slammed the door hard behind him.

Radnor appeared in the doorway, his usually bland face furious. "Yes, damn you, before I—" When he saw Shane, he broke off with a choking sound and his ruddy color bleached away. The agent had obviously thought Tilton had been talking to a servant in the hall.

With clear difficulty, Radnor forced his lips into a smile. "Good morning, Mr. Howard." His tone was suddenly so much more pleasant that he hardly sounded like the same man. "I see you are a late riser. Would you like breakfast now?"

"No, I'm not particularly hungry this morning." Not after his breakfast at Rose Cottage. "Who the devil was that man?"

Radnor hesitated, then parried, "Why do you ask?"

He's trying to determine how much I might have overheard of their conversation. "I ask because I am not accustomed to being accosted as I come down the stairs and then accused of spying."

"He's merely an employee on the estate."

"What was he hired to do—frighten small children?" Shane asked in exasperation.

"He was hired to provide security, but he has proven to be unsatisfactory."

"I gathered that," Shane replied. "I overheard the end of the conversation. What happened during the night that he failed to prevent?"

The color that had been returning to Radnor's face faded again. "Uh, a wretched gang of Irish hooligans calling itself the Knights of Rosaleen attacked and burned the Malone farm."

"Conn Malone's farm?" Shane blurted in shock.

Radnor's gray eyes narrowed to mere slits. "How is it you know him?"

"I do not," Shane replied hastily, "but before I left England, Lord Sherbourne praised him to me as the best tenant he has on Canamara. He asked me to look him up while I was here."

Alarm flashed in Radnor's eyes so briefly that had Shane blinked he would have missed it.

The agent sighed sadly. "Yes, Malone was our best tenant. Poor man, now he and his family have nothing left."

"Was any of his family hurt?"

Radnor nodded. "Yes, I am sorry to say. He and his sons were beaten and their wives were raped by the hooligans' leader, who calls himself Captain Starlight."

"Why would Irishmen beat and rape their fellow Irish, then drive them from their home, and destroy all they have worked for? It makes no sense."

"No," Radnor agreed. "The Irish rarely make sense. Envy undoubtedly prompted their actions against the Malones. The Irish do not like to see anyone, even one of their own, have more than they do. Frankly, Mr. Howard, I find it very strange that His Lordship would have asked you to call on an Irish tenant. Why did he?"

"He thought from what his grandfather wrote him about Malone I would enjoy meeting him." Actually, it was what both Shane's grandfather and his mother had told him. She had been an only child, and as she grew up, she'd regarded Conn Malone as the older brother she did not have.

Shane said, "Perhaps I will call on the Malones

and see if I can do anything for them."

"I fear that is impossible," Radnor said quickly. "They were so frightened by what happened last night, they could not remain here. They have already left for County Clare to stay with a married daughter."

At that, Shane belatedly remembered his original mission to obtain a key to the locked cabinet in his bedchamber. When he asked Radnor for the key, the agent said, "I do not have one. The old master kept it locked. Before he died, he sent the key to Lord Sherbourne."

The only key Shane's grandfather had sent him was to the private gun room. So why was the cabinet locked? "How strange. Why would the old master have done that?"

"Apparently it contains private papers that he wanted no one outside the family to see. I once offered to ship it, still locked, to His Lordship in England, but he said he had no interest in whatever it might contain."

Another lie. Shane wished he could accuse the agent, but that would betray his own identity.

As Kathleen reached the gate to Rose Cottage that evening, Oliver Radnor was turning away from the front door. She checked her step. Little Ollie had been kind and helpful to her after Patrick's death, but she did not particularly like the agent, thinking him a weakling who lacked the courage to stand up to his evil employer.

When Radnor saw her, he hurried down the walk to her. As usual, he was dressed in an expensively tailored coat and breeches of costly fabric. She sometimes wondered if Devil Sherbourne himself dressed any more richly than his agent.

"Ah, Mrs. McNamara, there you are. I must talk to you."

She stopped at the gate, her hands tightening on it as he hurried toward her. "Now?" she asked, trying to hide her dismay.

Her nocturnal activities last night had allowed her less than two hours' sleep, and she had hoped to come home early for a nap before Shane arrived for dinner. Instead she had been detained at school and was much later getting home than she should have been.

Shane would be coming any moment for dinner. And she wanted at least a little time to ready herself. Although she would never have admitted it to anyone else, she had been looking forward all day to their dinner together.

"Yes, now," Radnor said. "It is very important."

His somber expression alarmed Kathleen. "What is it?"

"Most unpleasant business, I fear. A lawless mob of Irish hooligans attacked the Tiltons last night."

Kathleen's heart began beating triple time. Could there have been a traitor among the Knights last night who had recognized and betrayed her?

She managed to feign a perplexed expression. "Tiltons? Who are they? I do not recognize the name."

"The new tenants, the friends of Sherbourne, who took over the Malones' farm."

Kathleen suppressed a shudder as she recalled the burly Tilton and the jagged scar from the corner of his eye to his chin. What peculiar friends His Devilship had—straight out of hell itself.

Radnor continued, "The poor Tiltons. Their house and all the other buildings including their barn were burned to the ground."

She had to bite her tongue to keep from telling him none of the buildings belonged to the Tiltons. "Was anyone hurt?" Kathleen asked, although she knew that no one had been.

"Aye, they were. The bloody Irish cowards—at least a hundred of them—beat the Tilton men and violated their wives."

Kathleen gasped.

Radnor looked gratified. "I knew you would be shocked by such brutality."

Indeed she was shocked, but by the false charges of assault and rape against the Knights. The Tiltons must have lied about what had been done to them in an attempt to inflame the English landowners against the Irish.

"These evil outlaws call themselves the Knights of Rosaleen and their leader, Captain Starlight. That ugly scoundrel was the most brutal of the lot. He was the one who brutalized both of the Tilton women."

This accusation left Kathleen as bemused as she was angry. Radnor had no idea how impossible that would have been for the captain.

"Filthy cur!" Radnor said. "Have you any idea who he might be?"

"Sure, and what kind of people do you think I associate with, Mr. Radnor? I'll not be having you think I'm acquainted with any man who would go about the countryside abusing innocent women."

"What of his followers? Surely you must have heard some gossip."

"A busy woman I am, Mr. Radnor." To cover her unease, she reached down and made a show of selecting a yellow rose from the bush beside the gate. "No time have I for idle gossip." Kathleen hated to lie, and her statement was true as far as it went.

"If you should hear anything, I hope you will come to me. The evil scoundrels robbed the poor Tiltons of all their belongings."

This accusation was too much for Kathleen to let pass. She looked up from her study of the rose bush. "But is that not the same thing Sherbourne did to the Malones?"

Radnor's sudden scowl did not dissuade her from continuing. "As I recall, *they* were allowed nothing but the clothes on their backs. You said then that everything else on the farm belonged to Lord Sherbourne, including the Malones' clothes, made from cloth they had spun and woven themselves, which they were forced to leave behind."

"*I* did not say that!" the agent protested. "You must understand. I merely repeated what Lord Sherbourne ordered me to say. If you only knew how hard I argued against his evicting the Malones." Radnor's expression turned sorrowful. "Believe me, I begged, I pleaded on their behalf, but His Lordship would not listen to me."

"Sure, and a fool he is not to do so."

"And greedy," Radnor admitted. "He insisted everything on the Malone farm and in their house was his. You cannot know how heartsick I was when I was forced to carry out his order to oust them."

"Forced?" Kathleen demanded scornfully. "He would not have forced me."

Still, little Ollie sympathized with the woes of the Irish and did what he could to mitigate them. He often lamented to her the unpleasant duties Lord Sherbourne ordered him to perform, but he was clearly too weak to refuse to carry them out.

"Sherbourne told me if I did not do as he commanded, I would no longer be his agent."

"Then find another position on an estate where the landlord is not so greedy as Sherbourne is," Kathleen suggested.

"If only you knew how much I would give to be able to do so, but the marquess warned if I leave his service, he will make certain I never work again. And he will."

"I can't believe any man would be so petty and cruel," Kathleen exclaimed in disgust.

"Believe it of His Lordship. He has forced me to do so many things that are abhorrent to me." Radnor brushed his hand across his eyes as though he were wiping away a tear. "My only consolation is I have been able to talk him out of doing some of the worst things he has proposed."

"Have you now?"

Radnor nodded gravely. "If you think it has been bad here, I tell you it would have been far worse were it not for me. This knowledge is the only thing that enables me to continue."

"I do not see how things could be much worse," she said candidly.

"Believe me, they could," Radnor said fervently. "His Lordship truly is a devil."

From the moment he'd left Rose Cottage after breakfast, Shane had looked forward to enjoying the company of Kathleen and Brigid again at dinner. As the hour grew closer, he found himself increasingly impatient, and he set out for the cottage a few minutes early.

He moved at a leisurely pace down the hill until he saw Oliver Radnor talking to a woman at the cottage gate. Her back was to Shane, but her burgundy hair and handsome figure assured him it was Kathleen, and his pulse quickened.

She bent her head to study the yellow roses on

the bush beside the gate, giving him an unimpeded view of the agent's expression as he watched her. Shane could not remember when he had seen a look of such undisguised lust on a man's face. With her attention on the roses, Kathleen was clearly unaware of Radnor's prurient expression.

Shane had been growing increasingly troubled about the agent. Now disgust merged with suspicion in his mind.

When Kathleen looked up at Radnor, his face was instantly bland again, but a few seconds later his expression turned to a scowl. She had clearly said something he did not like.

Shane decided it would be better if the agent did not see him arriving for dinner. He slipped back into the trees that surrounded the meadow and waited for the man to leave.

Radnor soon started up the hill, and Kathleen went into Rose Cottage. Shane waited until the agent was out of sight before stepping from his own concealment and continuing on to the cottage.

As he opened the gate, a little pink whirlwind burst through the door of the cottage and raced toward him, crying gleefully, "S'ane, S'ane."

A band tightened around his chest as he was reminded of the welcomes he used to receive from his son whenever he'd returned home. He swallowed hard.

Then the whirlwind was upon him, scattering all other thoughts. She grabbed one of his hands in both of her tiny ones and led him into the cottage. "Mama's upstairs," Brigid confided.

Shane stopped by the staircase that led to the upper floor. "While we wait for her, tell me what you did today."

Brigid complied with such enthusiasm that he

could not help but smile. Since breakfast, his own day had been dull. The two armed grooms Radnor had assigned him guided him on an oddly circumscribed ride of the park. Although their route perplexed him, the park's beauty had filled him with pride.

Shane heard footsteps on the stairs and looked up to see Kathleen descending. His breath caught at the sight of her beautiful face scrubbed clean. Unlike the ladies of the *ton*, she used no artificial enhancements. And she needed none.

As she reached the bottom of the stairs, though, he noticed that her emerald eyes were dulled by weariness. Dark circles beneath her eyes marred the creamy perfection of her complexion. Clearly, she had not gotten much sleep last night.

Kathleen greeted Shane in her husky voice that made him feel as though warm, mellow whiskey was being poured over him.

She led him and Brigid into the kitchen, where Maggie was at the hearth.

She gave Shane a welcoming smile and said, "Sit down. Dinner ye'll be havin' in a minute."

Kathleen looked at the table and protested, "But Maggie, there are only three covers."

"A man that's a guest at the great house won't be wantin' to eat with a servant."

"You are also my dear friend, and none of us will eat until you join us," Kathleen said firmly as she went to the dresser for another place setting.

Although Shane had never in his life eaten at a table with a servant, he was not at all high in the instep. Besides, he sensed Maggie was his ally, and he welcomed that. "I too insist on your joining us." He smiled at the servant. "I would be much insulted if you were too inhospitable to eat with me."

Maggie smiled back. To Shane's delight, she picked the seat next to Brigid, leaving him to share the other cushioned settle with Kathleen. He waited until she sat down before sliding in beside her. Although he did not touch her, he moved so close, her floral scent tantalized his nose.

After tasting the salmon, Shane told Maggie with total honesty, "This is delicious. You are an excellent cook."

She blushed like a schoolgirl. "Thankee, thankee." She turned to Kathleen. "Forgot to tell ye, I did, Mrs. Finnegan returned yer *Vicar of Wakefield* book."

"The Trials of Dr. Primrose, Latter-day Job, I call it," Kathleen said with a smile.

Shane chuckled. "An apt title, but all's well that ends well."

"I do like the book's happy ending," Kathleen confessed. "Life has too many of the other kind."

"Isn't that the truth!" Shane exclaimed, thinking of his dead wife and son.

A sudden gleam in Kathleen's emerald eyes warned Shane a verbal shaft was coming his way. "Especially in Ireland, thanks to Englishmen like His Devilship who reduce us to serfs in our own land."

"Ireland has its own parliament," Shane pointed out, surreptitiously edging closer to her on the settle.

"And more corrupt and beholden to the English crown than your own, it is." Kathleen gave an angry toss of her head, and tendrils of hair drifted about her face.

Shane stifled his longing to brush them back as an excuse to touch her soft cheek.

"Nor does Parliament represent the people," she

continued. "How can it when four-fifths of Ireland's people are Catholic, and most of the remainder Protestant dissenters—and all of them are prohibited from holding office or sitting in Parliament."

"I agree that is shocking," Shane said sincerely.

"And shocked I am you agree," Kathleen shot back. "Now I know why you've come to Ireland. Run out of England you were for your views."

Shane laughed. "Not at all. Englishmen are more liberal than you think."

"Perhaps poor ones like you are, but I wager you never discussed politics with your friend Devil Sherbourne."

Shane did not want to defend his "friend" Sherbourne. Nor did he want to argue politics with her or, for that matter, any other subject.

What he wanted was to kiss her lovely mouth and other equally exciting spots on her tantalizing body, so close now to his on the settle that he could feel her heat.

Since he could not do that, he turned the conversation back to books, a safer topic than politics. "As a teacher, you will be interested in a new kind of book published in Scotland. It is called *The Encyclopaedia Britannica,* and its third and final volume will be out soon."

"I have seen the first volume." Kathleen's face mirrored her disdain.

"Clearly you were not impressed," Shane observed in surprise.

"Oh, I think it an excellent concept, but its accuracy leaves something to be desired. For example, it identifies California as a large country in the West Indies."

Shane, whose own perusal of the volume had

been desultory, was impressed that a woman would have caught this mistake. Most females of his acquaintance would not know *what* California was, let alone *where*.

He wanted to ask her about her teaching. However, after giving her his word that morning he would say nothing to anyone about it, he hesitated to ask questions in front of Brigid and Maggie, fearing Kathleen might construe that as breaking his promise.

He looked around the pleasant, comfortable kitchen with its plants and softly glowing turf fire. How much more at home he felt here than he ever had in the grand state dining room at Sherwood with all its gilt plasterwork and silver serving dishes.

When he finished eating, he leaned against the back of the settle, much contented. Once again, both food and conversation had been excellent.

Shane lingered after dinner to enjoy more conversation, but Kathleen's fatigue pricked him with guilt. He should not be keeping her up, and he took his leave much earlier than he wanted.

As she escorted him to the door, he told her bluntly, "I would love to stay, but you are plainly exhausted, and I cannot in good conscience remain any longer."

She looked up at him as though she could not quite believe her ears.

"What is it?"

She smiled. "Your acuteness astonishes me. And goodnight to you, Mr. Howard."

"Shane," he corrected.

"Shane," she repeated softly in that beautiful, husky voice of hers that oozed with unconscious sensuality.

His desire to kiss the lovely mouth from which this spoken music came overwhelmed him, but she shut the door before he could act upon it.

Much disappointed, he turned away.

He intended to return to Rose Cottage tomorrow night, and she would not be so easily rid of him then. He promised himself he would not leave without claiming his first kiss from her.

For the next twenty-four hours, however, he would have to settle for imagining what kissing her would be like.

Chapter 9

B rigid slipped from the bed the following Wednesday morning, awakening Kathleen. Pretending to still be asleep, she listened to the quiet rustling of her daughter's hurried dressing. Silently Kathleen cursed Shane Howard.

Since Brigid had met him, she talked of little else but "S'ane." However, neither Kathleen nor her daughter had laid eyes on the man for five days, not since he'd dined with them the previous Friday night.

This morning was the fourth out of five and the third in a row that Brigid had arisen so early, hoping Shane would go fishing and she could join him. Kathleen was certain he would disappoint her daughter yet again by not coming, just as he had the other three mornings.

Damn the man! Breaking Brigid's heart, he is! Kathleen should have known better than to let an Englishman, especially a friend of Devil Sherbourne's, get near her daughter—or her.

Not all of Kathleen's anger at Shane was on behalf of Brigid. Despite her own hostility toward Englishmen, she had liked him, thinking him very different from his other countrymen she had met.

And a long time it'd been since she'd enjoyed herself so much as she had with him Friday night. He had seemed so perceptive and truly concerned about her that she'd thought he cared. When he left, she'd expected to see him soon again.

Exhausted, she had slept late Saturday morning. She and Brigid were to accompany Maggie that morning to visit her sister. Knowing how tired Kathleen was, Maggie let Kathleen sleep and took Brigid with her.

Kathleen followed them, arriving about one P.M. Maggie told her that Brigid had been up early that morning, waiting at the gate for Shane to appear.

When he did not, Brigid returned to the house with a doleful face, and Maggie could scarcely coax any breakfast down her.

The Rose Cottage trio stayed with Maggie's sister until noon Sunday, when Kathleen and Brigid set out for dinner at the Sullivans.

Most parents of Kathleen's students were too poor to contribute money for their children's schooling. But the Irish, being a proud and generous people, insisted upon having her and Brigid to Sunday dinner with them as a small payment toward their children's education. This week had been the Sullivans' turn.

Back home, Brigid was up early the next morning, looking in vain for Shane to come. He did not appear the following day either. Nor was he likely to do so this morning.

Kathleen suspected he might already have returned to England without so much as a good-bye to either of them.

She got up and went to the window. Her daughter was hanging impatiently on the gate. When Brigid finally realized Shane wasn't coming, she would drag herself slowly back to the house, her body slumped in dejection, as she had the previous mornings.

Kathleen clenched her fists angrily. *Damn you to hell, Shane Howard!*

As Shane walked down the hill toward Rose Cottage, he wondered whether Brigid would appear. In the hope she would, he'd brought with him the small pole that had been his mother's when she was a child.

He had missed the little sprite the past five days, but his enthusiasm for seeing her mother again had dampened considerably.

When Rose Cottage had been deserted both Saturday and Sunday, Shane's disappointment had been so acute it surprised him. He could scarcely believe how much he'd come to want Kathleen and her daughter's company.

They were like a bright Irish sun breaking through the choking black cloud of grief and loneliness that had enveloped him since his son's death.

When he'd been with them, the time had flown by far too rapidly. Without them, the weekend seemed interminable. Furthermore, he found it strange they'd said nothing Friday night about going away the next day.

Shortly after noon Sunday he paid his second visit of that day to the cottage to see if they'd returned. On the path between the gate and the house, he'd met a thin, wiry man with unkempt graying hair and a hammer in his hand.

"Who are you?" Shane demanded suspiciously.

"Do men's work fer the widow. Been fixin' some loose boards on her root cellar."

"Do you know where she and her daughter are?"

"Brigid be with Maggie, who's visitin' her sister." He examined Shane with suddenly hostile eyes. "Ye be an Englishman?"

"Yes." Shane was taken aback by the hatred that flared in the man's eyes at this admission. "How long will Brigid be at Maggie's sister's?"

"Dunno." The man shrugged. "Several days maybe."

"And Mrs. McNamara went with them?"

"Nil."

Shane frowned. "Do you know where Mrs. McNamara is?"

The man gave him a sly, calculating look. "It's Seamus ye should be askin' that of."

Shane's face must have betrayed his shock, for the man cackled, "Sure, and Seamus'll know." He stepped past Shane and hurried out the gate.

No wonder Kathleen had not mentioned going away for the weekend. Jealousy seared him, quickly followed by disillusionment. He took parenthood very seriously and he had thought Kathleen did too. She'd struck him as a good and loving mother, much like his own had been. It was one of the things he most liked about her.

But a good mother would not send her daughter away with a servant in order to go off with her lover for several days. Did Kathleen not appreciate what a treasure she had in Brigid?

He was so upset that he had to find a way to work off his anger and restlessness. He planned to see the Lakes of Killarney during his stay in Ireland, and he decided he would ride to them that very afternoon.

Finding them even more beautiful than he had

been told, Shane lingered among them for the next two days, not returning to Canamara until late Tuesday night.

Now, as he neared Rose Cottage, he spotted Brigid hanging on the gate. She ran to meet him, and he felt like dancing an Irish jig in his joy at seeing her again.

"Hoping I was you'd be fishing this morn," she cried. "May I go with you?"

"Certainly, *sidhe*."

"Looking for you I was yesterday and the morning 'fore t'at, but you didn't come," she complained.

He looked at her sharply. Did that mean that her mother had cut short her assignation with her lover, Seamus? Had they had a fight?

"Why didn't you come?" Brigid pressed.

"I was away at the Lakes of Killarney." He showed her the small rod. "I brought this for you to use."

"Oh," she cried, jumping up and down in excitement, "a pole just my size, it is. May I carry it?"

Delighted by her enthusiasm, Shane handed it to her.

Watching from behind the curtain of her bedroom window, Kathleen felt dampness rise in her eyes as Shane gave the small fishing pole he carried to her delighted daughter. The rod was the perfect size for Brigid, and Kathleen wondered where he had found it.

From the vantage of her second floor bedroom window, she'd seen Shane coming before her daughter did. Despite her anger at him, Kathleen's heart had given a happy leap that, if she were honest with herself, had as much to do with her own emotions as with her daughter's.

He had not left for England after all.

The smile that had glowed on Shane's face when he'd seen Brigid warmed Kathleen's heart—and other parts of her body too.

Whatever the reason for his absence the past few days, lack of affection for her daughter clearly was not it.

As they walked toward the water, Brigid carried the small pole proudly with one hand and reached for Shane's with the other.

Kathleen watched as they disappeared hand in hand into the greenery that screened the stream from her. She admired the grace with which Shane moved. He would, she suspected, be a wonderful dancer, and she loved to dance. Not that she'd had a chance to do much in recent years. Patrick had hated dancing, perhaps because he was so poor at it, and he could rarely be coaxed into doing it.

She threw on her own clothes quickly, brushed her hair, leaving it loose, and hurried after them. When she neared the stream, she stopped about twenty feet from the bank to watch Shane show Brigid how to cast her line with the small pole. He was clearly a man who both enjoyed children and had considerable patience with them.

When he finished his instruction, he handed Brigid a small wooden box. She sat down and, with her tongue teasing her upper lip, concentrated on baiting her hook with a worm from the box.

Kathleen started forward, and her foot crunched a twig.

Shane looked around at the sound. Seeing her, his eyes narrowed and his face hardened in cold displeasure.

Her heart plummeted. That was not at all the reception she'd expected from him. He'd seemed so caring Friday night, and now he acted as though he loathed the sight of her. *He's just like every other damn Englishman.*

He strode quickly to Kathleen. Brigid was so intent on her hook that she didn't notice. Shane's expression had not softened one whit by the time he reached Kathleen, and her frayed temper exploded.

"You broke my daughter's heart, Shane Howard!" she hissed at him.

"Would you care?" He kept his voice low, apparently so Brigid would not hear him, but his face twisted in contempt, and his tone would have frozen boiling water. "You are the more likely one to have broken her heart."

What the devil was he talking about? "Poor Brigid has waited at the gate for hours every morning since you dined with us, hoping you'd take her fishing."

His eyes were as hard and cold as blue ice. "She was not there Sunday morning."

"But she was Saturday, and you did not come."

"No, because I was afraid she would disturb you. I knew how tired you were, and I wanted you to sleep late."

Kathleen felt a little sheepish at learning that his concern for her had been responsible for his absence.

"Imagine my surprise when I showed up that afternoon and the cottage was deserted." His voice dripped with sarcasm.

"Why are you so angry at me?" Kathleen demanded.

"I will be bluntly honest with you, Mrs. McNamara. I have only contempt for a mother who sends her child away so she can be with her lover."

Kathleen was so dumbfounded that she forgot to keep her voice down. She all but shrieked, "I would never do such a thing! What are you talking about?"

"The man fixing your root cellar said you'd sent Brigid away with Maggie for several days so you could be with your lover. How could you desert your child like that?"

Rage as fast and hot as a wildfire consumed Kathleen. She sputtered incoherently, too angry to talk.

"Don't be mad at Mama, S'ane. She didn't send me away." Brigid had laid down her new fishing pole and come up to them.

Shane looked as startled to see her beside them as Kathleen was. "Did you not go with Maggie Saturday to her sister's, *sidhe*?"

She nodded. "Cuz Mama was still sleepin', but she came after us, and we stayed all night, and the next day me and Mama went to eat at the Sullivans."

Shane's expression was such a comical mixture of surprise, relief, embarrassment, and chagrin that it lowered Kathleen's temper to slightly below the boiling point.

Before she ask him how he could think she would ever desert her daughter, Brigid gazed up at him with adoring eyes. "What's a lover, S'ane?"

Clearly discomforted, he stammered, "It . . . it . . . is . . . ah . . . ah . . . a man who loves a woman."

"Everybody loves my mama," Brigid assured him. "So she has lots o' lovers."

Kathleen choked.

Brigid smiled at Shane. "And you is my lover."

It was his turn to choke, and color flooded his

face. "No, sweetheart, ah—" He broke off, for once clearly at a loss for words.

"Why not?" Brigid demanded indignantly. "Doesn't you love me, S'ane?"

"Yes, but—"

"Then why isn't you my lover?"

Clearly flustered, Shane gave Kathleen a beseeching look, which she ignored. After what he'd said about her, he deserved to flounder about.

"*Sidhe*, you have to be grown up to—"

"I is growed up! I catch fishes."

Kathleen giggled.

"I mean," he amended hastily, "you have to be even more grown up—like your mama is."

"Oh," Brigid piped, "is you saying I has to be a mama 'fore you can be my lover?"

Finally taking pity on Shane, Kathleen interjected, "Something like that, darling. Now you had better go fish before they take a nap."

Brigid ran back to the stream, and Kathleen would have followed had Shane not placed a restraining hand lightly on her arm, sending a flash of warmth through her. Why did this man's touch affect her so?

Kathleen looked at him questioningly, noting with amusement his color was still considerably heightened from his conversation with Brigid.

"Thank you, Kathleen, for rescuing me from the quagmire my tongue buried me in."

She arched an eyebrow. "So now I am Kathleen again, not Mrs. McNamara, shameless, negligent mother?" She could not keep the edge of anger from her voice.

He winced. "Please accept my deepest, most heartfelt apologies for that. But you see, I thought you an exemplary mother, and I was never so shocked in my life as when that man said what he did."

The obvious sincerity of Shane's apology and the plea in his Irish blue eyes cooled what was left of Kathleen's anger at him.

He asked, clearly puzzled, "Why would he say that?"

"Cathal probably realized you were English. He despises the English and believes it every Irishman's duty to lie to them."

That was true enough, but Cathal was also a friend of Seamus Malone, who was infatuated with her. Kathleen suspected Cathal had been trying to discourage any competition with his friend, but she kept this conjecture to herself.

From the stream bank, Brigid waved her little rod. "Mama, see my pole S'ane brought me."

Kathleen looked at it, then at Shane. "Where did you get it?"

He smiled. "It was m—" He broke off abruptly, as though he'd almost said something he shouldn't, then finished lamely, "I found it among the fishing gear at the house."

Kathleen's curiosity was aroused. "What were you about to say?"

"Nothing," he mumbled, turning quickly to Brigid.

His evasive answer intensified Kathleen's curiosity. Perhaps she was not the only one who had secrets to hide.

When they left the stream that morning, Shane carried in his creel another large salmon he had caught and two trout that Brigid and her mother had pulled in.

As they approached the gate to Rose Cottage, Brigid again invited him to breakfast.

He looked up quickly to see Kathleen's reaction. Although she gave her daughter a quick look, she did not object as she had the first morning. He dared to hope he was making progress with her, despite his blunders at the stream.

She looked particularly lovely this morning with her hair drifting about her face in the breeze, and he longed to brush his fingers through it, longed to kiss her enticing lips.

When Maggie saw Shane entering in the kitchen, she turned to the dresser and took out another plate and mug for him.

She joined them at the table as she had Friday night. After all the trouble Shane's tongue had gotten him into earlier, he was quieter than usual.

Initially the conversation revolved around the weekend visit to Maggie's sister. Had Shane not already been convinced Kathleen had been there too, he would have been now.

He was still deeply embarrassed about his false accusation. He had to admit he was as much to blame as Cathal. The man had not actually called Seamus Kathleen's lover. In his shock and jealousy, Shane had inferred that.

Erroneously, he hoped.

Maggie hurried through her breakfast and left the table "to be gettin' at me work upstairs."

As Shane sat with Kathleen and her daughter in the warm, inviting kitchen, redolent with delicious cooking odors, the strange feeling he'd had when he first saw this valley returned even more strongly: He had come home at last.

He would gladly trade the fine dining room at Canamara, or for that matter, the Sèvres porcelain, sterling silver serving dishes, and Beauvais tapestry wall hangings in the state dining room at Sherwood for this cheerful kitchen with its pots of herbs and flowering plants, and its sweet-smelling turf fire in the stone hearth.

He would trade too the company of the lords and ladies who vied for invitations to dine at Sherwood with him for that of this fiery Irish lass and her enchanting daughter.

From upstairs, Maggie called down to Brigid that she needed her help. Clearly reluctant to leave the kitchen, the little girl obeyed the summons with dragging steps.

Much as Shane enjoyed Brigid, he was pleased at this opportunity to be alone with her mother. He suspected Maggie had deliberately given it to him.

The child was scarcely out of the room, however, when Kathleen stood up. "I must get to work too."

He could hardly ignore so pointed a hint as that. Trying to hide his disappointment, he rose slowly from the table. "May I walk you to school this morning?"

"Where I might be going is none of your concern."

The sharpness of her answer surprised Shane. "Why do you refuse to talk about what you do? You act as though teaching were a crime."

"In Ireland it is."

He would have thought she was joking but her tone made clear she was not. "I do not understand."

"And I've no time to be explaining."

"Breakfast was delicious, if too short." He smiled at Kathleen. "Will you let me return your hospitality by dining with me at Canamara?"

Shane thought the invitation would please her.

Instead she looked as though he'd insulted her. "What is it?"

"Sure, and I thank you for asking. But under that roof I'd never set foot!"

Shane frowned. "But I understand you have dined there in the past."

"Never have I done so! Not once!"

Her scandalized answer reminded him of the contradictory tales she and his agent told about her occupying Rose Cottage. "Radnor says he lets you live rent free in this cottage."

"*What?*" She planted both hands indignantly on her hips. "Sure, and I can't believe he told you that, for I pay a pretty sum for it. I had not thought little Ollie a liar. A weakling to be sure for not standing up to his devil master, but not a liar. But if that's what he told you, then a liar he is!"

Until Shane had discovered Radnor living in Canamara's best bedchamber, he would have rejected that possibility too. He quirked a questioning eyebrow. "Is he? What rent do you pay?"

Shane choked at the amount she named. "You jest. How can you possibly afford such a sum?" The amount would tax the resources of even a well-to-do widow.

Her face set in lines of implacable determination. "I will not allow Sherbourne to drive me from here until—" She broke off abruptly and stared down at her cup.

"Until what?" Shane prodded.

"Until—ah, until I am ready," she finished lamely.

He wanted to press her further, but from the stubborn set of her jaw, he knew that would be a waste of time and, worse, might damage the fragile rapport between them.

Instead he asked, "Do any of Canamara's other tenants share your hatred of Sherbourne?"

"Any?" she asked scornfully. "Sure, and they all do."

He was certain she exaggerated, but if that were true, the Irish were indeed as ungrateful a lot as their detractors claimed.

Kathleen tossed her long hair in a defiant gesture, and it rippled about her in a way that made him ache to comb his fingers through those fiery strands. "If you do not believe me, visit Killoma. See what the people there think of Sherbourne."

Killoma was the principal village on the Canamara estate. Its residents could not possibly have any complaint against him. Why, during the past two years, he had paid out so much for lime and new thatch in the village, he must have whitewashed and reroofed every structure there.

Yes, he would visit Killoma. He'd do so this very day. As Shane left the kitchen, he looked through the diamond panes of the windows toward the parklike landscaping along the stream. "What a beautiful place Canamara is."

"Beautiful it was before Sherbourne inherited it," Kathleen said scornfully. "A fine man was the old Lion. Writhing in his grave he surely is at what his grandson's done to the estate."

"What are you talking about?" Shane was sick of all her disparagements of him. "You have only to look at this beautiful vale to see His Lordship has been an excellent steward of the land."

"Granted, whatever can be seen from the great house is pristine. God forbid the view from there be compromised should His Almighty Lordship ever deign to visit. But ride beyond that, and see what you find."

"I will, and then I will challenge your unjust exaggerations."

"No," she retorted hotly. "Then, unless you are blind and stupid in the bargain, you will have a very different opinion of your friend Sherbourne."

Chapter 10

❦

After Shane left, Kathleen kissed Brigid good-bye and set out for her hedge school.

As she walked, she regretted her challenge to Shane to visit Killoma. She fervently hoped he would not go there. Since His Devilship had leased the Malones' farm to the Tiltons, tempers had been running high against Englishmen in general and Sherbourne in particular.

Even before the injustice to the Malones, the villagers had intensely hated their landlord—and with good reason. Kathleen feared for Shane's safety in Killoma, should it be learned he was a guest at Canamara and a friend of His Devilship.

He might be severely beaten or even killed.

I could not bear to have that happen to him. The strength of this emotion startled Kathleen. How could she feel so strongly about a man she had known only a week—and an Englishman at that. She tried to tell herself it must be because she'd be the one responsible for his going to Killoma.

If he goes. She prayed he would not.

Shane's rapid stride along the rutted, muddy dirt road began to flag, and he wondered how much farther it was to Killoma. His long, brisk walk toward the town had left him sweaty and thirsty.

He had opted to visit the village on foot because he wanted to mingle among the residents without betraying that he was a hated Englishman staying at Canamara. He spoke Gaelic fluently enough to pass for an Irishman.

Were he to ride into town on any horse in the estate's stable, however, his mount's obvious value would instantly alert the natives that he was English. For the same reason, he ignored Oliver Radnor's instruction to take two armed grooms when he went anywhere.

Besides, Shane thought with amusement, he did not look, at the moment, to be worth robbing. He wore a frayed and mended shirt, pants, and an ill-fitting coat, to blend in better among the villagers. Although clean, his clothes were faded from long usage.

Were he dressed in the elegant raiment of a marquess, he would stand out like a peacock in a yard full of chickens. None of Killoma's residents would open up and talk to him as he wanted.

His mother had told him about the popularity of the Boar's Head Public House, the center of social life in Killoma, and Shane would make that his first stop.

Above him, the ever-changing Irish sky, which had been sunny and blue when he left Rose Cottage, grew darker and more threatening. He hoped he could reach the Boar's Head before the heavens dumped their gray weight on him.

Rounding the side of a hill, Shane stopped at the sight of a sorry collection of buildings in the hollow ahead of him. The filthy cottages were splattered with mud. Large sections of their roofs were bare of thatch. *Surely this cannot be Killoma.* Then he saw a sign on the road that confirmed it was.

Where the hell was the prosperous village that Radnor had glowingly described in his letters? Where had all the money Shane had expended for whitewash and thatch gone?

On the edge of town, he passed an ugly, sprawling building with all its windows broken out. Several emaciated children, none of them older than Brigid, played on the bare dirt around the structure. He wondered what it could be.

Shane strode along the main street until he came to a plot of land where a half-dozen gaunt men sat on makeshift benches within the stone ruins of what had once been a building's foundation and walls. A stone fireplace rose starkly from the rubble.

Compared to the tattered garments these men wore, Shane looked positively prosperous in his ragpicker's clothes. He was the only one even wearing shoes.

The men eyed Shane with hostile suspicion.

"What ye be wantin' here, stranger?" a red-haired man of perhaps thirty demanded in Gaelic. He held a big earthenware jug in his hands that seemed too large for his thin frame.

"An ale house to wet me whistle," Shane replied in the same tongue. His colloquial answer in Gaelic dissipated a little of the antagonism he sensed from the men.

"Lookin' ye are at the only place passin' fer that in Killoma," an old man with thin limbs gnarled by age and rheumatism said.

"What happened to the Boar's Head?" Shane asked in surprise.

"Devil Sherbourne," one of the men said succinctly.

So Kathleen truly was not the only person in the neighborhood who regarded him as a diabolic reincarnation.

"Lookin' ye are at all he's allowed us to keep of the Boar's Head," the old man said. "Ordered it destroyed more'n two years ago, His Devilship did."

"What?" Shane could scarcely believe his ears. He had inquired only three months ago in a letter to Radnor whether the Boar's Head was still as popular as ever, and the agent had assured him it was.

Frowning, Shane asked, "But why would Sherbourne order it torn down?"

"Bastard afeared we might waste a minute or two enjoyin' ourselves 'stead of slavin' fer him all our wakin' hours," the ruddy man said. He turned to the gnarled old man. "Ain't that right, Finn?"

Finn nodded his agreement.

"Who told you His Lordship ordered it demolished?" Shane asked sharply.

"His agent, young Radnor," Finn replied.

The lying bastard! Shane could scarcely believe the magnitude of his agent's devious double-dealing that he was discovering. Was anything Radnor had written him the truth?

"Little Ollie does weep and cry o'er how no choice has he but to carry out His Devilship's orders, but carry 'em out he always does," the red-haired man said scornfully.

"Ain't that the truth though, Eamon," one of the other men agreed.

They passed the big jug around. When it reached Shane, he lifted it to his lips and took a sip of whiskey so raw and harsh he nearly choked on it. He quickly passed the container on to Finn. "Why do you call Sherbourne His Devilship?"

Every pair of eyes turned to stare at Shane as though he were a half-wit.

Finn lifted the jug to his lips with his gnarled and twisted hands to drink from it. "That's what the bastard be—the devil incarnate."

"What has he done to you?" Shane pressed, determined to learn everything that had fired these men's palpable hatred for him.

"What ain't the devil done?" Eamon's words were a little slurred from too much whiskey. "Robbed us of our land, our homes, everything we worked so hard to earn."

"A-turnin' in his grave, the ould Lion must be at what his high-and-mighty English grandson be doin' to us." Finn took another drink from the jug before passing it on to Eamon. "Sure, and a fairer, kinder landlord we could not have asked for than the ould Lion."

"But the Lion has a stoat for a grandson," Eamon sneered as he lifted the jug to his mouth.

Shane stiffened at being called a stoat, that savage little carnivore that killed animals much larger than itself. Even people told of being attacked by the creature.

After taking a large gulp from the jug, Eamon passed it on. "Murdered poor Patrick McNamara, His Devilship did."

Shane started at the mention of Kathleen's late husband. Why the hell did everyone believe he had murdered the man? "I heard McNamara's death was an accident."

He should have kept his mouth shut. Shane could feel the men's hostility descend again like a heavy curtain. They looked at him as though he were Judas Iscariot.

"Accident, was it?" Eamon scoffed. "Forced down on his knees with his hands tied behind his back and shot through the head with a pistol, he was."

Horror twisted Shane's gut. Each succeeding revelation was more devastating than the one before. Nothing was as he had thought at Canamara.

"His Devilship's orders, it were," Finn said. "Carry them out, poor Alban, the gamekeeper, was told, or His Devilship would turn him and his family out to starve."

As Finn was talking, a handsome young man, tall and robust, with arms heavily muscled from hard labor, strode up to the group. The newcomer's clothes were in better condition than those worn by the others in the group. He even had on boots, scuffed and worn to be sure, but still he was the only man besides Shane who was not barefoot.

Finn shrugged. "What's a man like Alban to do when he has a wife and nine wee ones to feed?"

"Nothin' excuses murder, especially not that one," the newcomer said, eyeing Shane suspiciously. "A good man was Patrick McNamara."

"And a fine lass his widow be too," Finn chimed in. "Lucky for us the day they came to County Kerry."

Keeping his gaze fixed on Shane, the newcomer said, "Not lucky for the McNamaras, though, thanks to His Divilship."

"But maybe lucky for ye, Seamus," Finn said slyly.

Shane started when he heard the man's name. Was this the Seamus who called on Kathleen?

"Sweet on his widow, ye be," Finn continued, confirming Shane's suspicion.

He stared at Seamus through narrowed eyes. He wished to hell the man wasn't such a handsome, muscular specimen. Seamus's face with its chiseled planes, broad jaw, and bright blue eyes beneath sandy-colored, curling hair would turn any woman's head. Jealousy clawed at Shane.

"Maybe His Divilship did you a favor, Seamus," Eamon chimed in.

Seamus glared at Eamon so fiercely, the smaller man backed up a step and said hastily, "Only funning."

"Sure, and didn't Cap'n Starlight gave the divil his due last week," Finn interjected hastily, clearly hoping to change the subject and defuse the tension between Seamus and Eamon.

"Who is Captain Starlight?" Shane asked.

"And why'd you be wantin' to know?" Seamus demanded.

"A name such as that would stir any man's curiosity."

"A friend of Divil Sherbourne's is visitin' Canamara, I hear, and from the description I think you're him." Seamus glared at Shane. "Am I right?"

All eyes turned to Shane, and an ominous silence descended as they awaited his answer. If he was to have any hope of winning their trust, he could not lie to them now. "Yes," he admitted.

An ugly murmur ran through the men.

"Sent you to spy on us, did His Divilship?" Seamus demanded.

"No, he did nothing of the sort!"

"Then why is an English friend of His Divilship dressed as you are?" Shane's self-appointed interrogator asked. "Decked out in satins and lace, you'd be—unless it's a spy you are."

"I am no spy!"

"Maybe we ought to kill this friend of the divil the way he had poor Patrick McNamara killed." Seamus's face twisted with hatred. "Send the divil his friend here with a ball through his brains and our compliments."

A cheer went up at that.

Shane perceived he was in real danger from the men around him. Thank God, they did not know his true identity. If they did, he strongly suspected he would have no hope of escaping alive.

As it was, it might be a near thing.

"Tell us the truth," Seamus ordered. "His Divilship sent you to spy on us."

"He did not!"

"How is it, then, you speak Gaelic as though you was one of us? His Divilship wouldn't be hobnobbing with the likes of you. Hates everything Irish, he does."

"That is not true." And it wasn't. Shane was proud of his Celtic blood.

"Sure, then, and what is true?" one of the men demanded belligerently.

"I taught Gaelic to his son."

"Never would Sherbourne have allowed that," Seamus scoffed. "His Divilship considers himself as English as his damn father was."

"Aye!" a man cried in a slurred voice. "Bastards, both of them."

If these men only knew the truth about the miserably unhappy relationship Shane had had with his father. He said quietly, "It was the present Lord Sherbourne's express wish his son learn Irish."

"His son's tutor were you, then?" Finn asked.

Indeed, Shane had been Jeremy's tutor. The boy had no other. Shane had loved teaching his son. "I was." His answer was not technically a lie.

"And you taught the divil's spawn Gaelic?"

Shane bridled at hearing sweet, innocent Jeremy called the devil's spawn, but his own safety depended on his hiding his anger. "I did," he answered, "and the boy spoke it fluently."

Seamus stood threateningly in front of Shane. "And now you can be our messenger to His Divilship. Go back to England and tell him we will be treated with the dignity that is every man's right or Canamara will be ashes.

"And tell His Divilship too, if e'er he shows his face in County Kerry, as dead as Patrick McNamara he'll be."

Chapter 11

After dismissing her pupils from their make-shift classroom beside a remote hedgerow of hawthorn, elder, and dog rose, Kathleen walked home along the same route she always took.

As she neared the bridge where she had first seen Shane Howard last week at this same time of day, her heart quickened.

Thinking of him put a spring in her step that had been missing for a long time. Or maybe the spring was in her heart.

Kathleen had almost convinced herself Shane would not have heeded her challenge to ride into Killoma and talk to the people there about Sherbourne. Still, she would like to see with her own eyes that he was safe.

She rounded the curve to the bridge and stopped abruptly. Shane stood there with two horses, one a bay gelding, the other a brown mare outfitted with a sidesaddle.

Kathleen's breath caught and her heart pounded like a *bodhran* drum during a battlefield charge. "Sure, and what are you doing here?"

"Waiting for you. I hoped you would come this way." He sounded hoarse and his eyes looked haunted, as though he had suffered a severe shock. Gone was his easy smile. "Ride with me."

Kathleen wondered what had happened to make him look as he did. "And stepping above myself I'd be to sit atop one of His Devilship's mounts."

Shane's beautiful blue eyes turned so bleak that her heart went out to him. "Ride with me, please." His voice betrayed his great agitation. "Show me what you were talking about this morning. Show me what I cannot see of Canamara from the great house."

"Why?" she asked bluntly.

"I could scarcely credit what you told me, but I did as you suggested and went to Killoma. You were right. I was shocked by what I saw and heard."

His anguished expression confirmed his words. *Why, he truly cares, even though he's English!* Kathleen's already dimmed hostility toward him faded as quickly as the light on a winter day.

"I want to see with my own eyes how bad things are on Canamara. Please, show me."

Although Kathleen no longer doubted his sincerity, she was puzzled. "But why bother? You have obviously discovered what I said about your friend Sherbourne is true. Or do you require further proof?"

Anger as hot and fierce as summer lightning flashed in his eyes. "I do not—" He broke off and fell silent for a moment, as though he were trying to regain control of his temper.

When he spoke again, it was in a more subdued tone. "I want to see with my own eyes the full extent of what is going on here."

Kathleen looked longingly at the spirited mare Shane held by the reins. It had been so long since she had been on a horse worth riding.

And deep in her heart, Kathleen wanted to be with Shane Howard, whether afoot or on horseback, although she would never admit that aloud. Instead she said, "At least you no longer try to defend Sherbourne. For that reason, I will go with you."

Shane helped Kathleen mount the mare, then swung himself up in the saddle of the bay. Once again, Kathleen found herself marveling at his grace.

His frayed and mended clothes were sadly inferior to Oliver Radnor's expensive, tailored garments. Despite that, he cut a far handsomer figure than little Ollie did in his fine ruffled shirt and silk breeches.

Odd, though, that a marquess, especially one as rich as Sherbourne, would take notice of Howard, let alone consider him such a good friend he would invite him to stay at Canamara.

As they set off in the direction Kathleen chose, she pointed to the high hill rising ahead of them. "That is Kincaid Mountain. It conceals from the great house some of the worst damage that Sherbourne has inflicted on Canamara."

"And what is that?"

She preferred that he view it for himself. "You'll not be needing me to tell you. Soon enough you'll be seeing with your own eyes."

"And you intend for me to make my own judgment." He smiled at her, although his eyes did not lose their grim set. "You are a wise woman."

This innocuous compliment filled Kathleen with warmth. Why did she feel so absurdly pleased by it? She told herself it must be because an Irish woman rarely enjoyed respect from an Englishman.

Shane continued, "I do not think I would have believed the situation in Killoma if I had not seen it myself."

"It's a fair regret I suffered this morn after goading you to talk to the people there. I hope they were not, er, unpleasant to you."

That wry smile she loved curved his mouth. "It was most enlightening until they learned I am a guest at Canamara. After that, it was a near thing whether I would escape with my skin."

His words stabbed at Kathleen's heart. If he had been hurt or killed, she would not have been able to live with herself. *You should not care so much!*

But she did. Very much.

How much shocked her.

"Sorry I am for suggesting you go to Killoma," she said with sincere contrition.

"Your concern for my continued good health delights me." His smile was strained and vanished quickly. "Tell me why Captain Starlight and his followers destroyed the Malone farm."

His request so surprised her that it was a moment before she managed to say faintly, "Ask Oliver Radnor. He knows."

Shane's face hardened. "Whether he would tell me, however, is another matter."

"Why wouldn't he?"

Shane answered her with a silent shrug.

Kathleen frowned. "I don't understand."

"Neither did I at first."

Her frown deepened at his cryptic reply. "But you do now?"

"Yes." This brusque answer and the hard, angry set of his face warned her against probing further.

They rode on in silence. Kathleen deliberately chose a path that took them high up on Kincaid Mountain, past the base of a tall granite outcropping. From there Shane's first view of the valley beyond would be panoramic.

When they reached the base of the outcropping, Kathleen reined in her horse. "We'll stop here for a minute."

After Shane followed her lead, she gestured toward the valley below them. "Behold the Vale of Kincaid."

The land in the long, wide valley was rich and green, but it was scarred by a maze of low stone walls that divided it into a patchwork of small plots.

From the corner of her eye, Kathleen surreptitiously watched Shane to gauge his reaction.

He stared down incredulously for a long moment. "*That* is the Vale of Kincaid?" He sounded bewildered. "Why the devil are all those walls there? It looks like a rabbit warren."

"So it does," Kathleen agreed, pleased by his dismayed reaction. Shane might be English, but he clearly had a good heart. "You see before you the fruit of Sherbourne's rack rents."

Shane stared at her incredulously. "But Sherbourne abhors rack renting. He does not allow it."

"Hah! Perhaps that is what he tells his friends in England, but you see before you the truth of the matter."

He looked as though he had been stunned by a sneak blow beneath the belt. Why, he was far and away the nicest Englishman Kathleen had ever met.

And the most exciting.

Ashamed of herself for such a thought, she

forced her attention back to the land below them. "The only difference between Devil Sherbourne and most of the other absentee landlords of the English ascendancy is that he eliminates the middlemen. He has done his own subdividing of the land until a poor tenant must starve in order to pay the rent on his miserable bit of ground."

Shane shook his head back and forth like a man in shock. "I cannot believe it," he muttered. "I cannot believe it."

"Believe it! The truth lies below you." Still, Kathleen's heart went out to him in his disillusionment. He clearly liked Sherbourne, and now he saw the marquess for what he really was.

His face turned as hard as the rock outcropping beside them, and rage glinted in his eyes. "Let us ride down to the valley. I want to see this close up."

Chapter 12

When Shane and Kathleen neared the bottom of the hill, she stopped her mare by a gorse bush, covered with painful thorns and yellow flowers. "Wiser we'd be to leave our horses and walk from here if you're of a mind to be talking to people."

Shane understood instantly. His mount would brand him as a privileged Englishman, and he would be as unwelcome as he had become at Killoma. He dismounted, helped Kathleen down, and tied their horses to the gorse bush, carefully avoiding its thorns.

They were perhaps ten yards from the first of the stone walls. This one had been built on the lower slope of the hill. As they walked toward it, he noticed a mound of stones in the upper corner of the tiny plot. "What is that?"

"A tenant's home."

Shane could scarcely believe Kathleen's answer, but when they reached the plot, he saw the mound covered the entrance to what was little more than a cave dug into the side of the hill.

A woman, thin, worn, and dressed in rags, emerged. She smiled when she saw Kathleen.

"And a good evenin' to ye, Mrs. McNamara." Her voice indicated both her respect for the widow and her pleasure at seeing her.

Kathleen returned the woman's smile. "Good evening, Mrs. O'Malley."

The woman gave Shane a speculative perusal. "And who's this ye've with ye?"

"A friend of mine, Shane Howard."

Kathleen's referring to him as her friend pleased Shane inordinately and gave him hope that in time he might convince her to become more than merely his friend.

"And will we be seein' ye two together, then, at the Lughnasadh dance?" Mrs. O'Malley inquired.

Kathleen and Shane answered simultaneously:

"No," she said.

"Perhaps," he said. Although this was the first he had heard of the dance, he was instantly determined to persuade Kathleen to go with him. *Lughnasadh* Day, which marked the beginning of the final quarter of the Celtic year, was August 1. Since today was July 29, he had not much time to convince her.

Mrs. O'Malley smiled. "Have you time for a cuppa?"

"We thank you for your kind offer," Kathleen answered, "but we can't stop."

Shane waited until he and Kathleen were well away from the O'Malley hovel before observing, "I would not have thought she could afford to serve us tea."

"And you've the right of it. That's why I refused. We'd be using the little bit she's hoarded for when illness strikes."

"Then why would she offer to share it with us?"

Shane asked, touched and puzzled by such generosity.

Kathleen smiled at him, that lovely smile that lit her eyes and seemed to glow from her very soul. "The Irish are a hospitable people, and we share whatever we have with our guests. We've a saying, 'Blessed with a potato to eat and a potato to share with a stranger, a poor Hibernian is happy.' "

As they walked the narrow paths that wound through the valley, they passed one tiny plot after another where the tenants lived in sorry hovels that Shane did not consider fit even for animals.

He could scarcely believe the poverty and squalor that surrounded him. It was worse than what he had passed on his ride from Dublin, which had so horrified him.

Nausea churned his stomach. Kathleen clearly sensed his distress, for she touched his arm comfortingly, and her lovely eyes were filled with understanding and empathy. He grasped her hand gratefully, and she let him continue to hold it as they walked on.

What he saw before him was as different from the Kincaid Valley that Oliver Radnor had described in his letters to Shane as hell was from heaven.

The rent roll that Radnor sent to London each quarter was brief, no more than a score of names with the modest amounts they paid for their land. Yet twice that number inhabited this valley alone.

Shane knew the names on the rent roll Radnor sent because his grandfather, who had taken a personal interest in all his tenants and their families, had talked about them in his letters. At each hut, Shane asked Kathleen who lived there. Not one of the names did he recognize.

Yes, he thought bitterly, a devil did control Canamara but, contrary to what everyone believed, it was not Sherbourne. He was as much a victim as his tenants. Radnor must be collecting many times the amount of rent he forwarded to his master.

Yet Shane had no one but himself to blame. He should have come to Ireland years ago, but he would not leave his son. And the voyage across the stormy Irish Sea would have been too much for the delicate Jeremy.

Everyone Shane and Kathleen met as they walked—male and female, adult and child—greeted her with as much warmth as Mrs. O'Malley had. They all seemed to know her, and she was clearly liked and respected by the vale's residents.

Shane felt very proud of her—and very proud to be walking at her side. He knew the friendly greetings he received were due to his being with her.

Only one person did not appear happy to see her, and that was a ragged urchin of about eight. When he saw her approaching, he turned around and started back in the direction from which he'd come, but she called out to him. "Come here, Jimmy Farrell."

He stopped, reversed direction again, and reluctantly approached her, his gaze fixed anxiously on her face.

"And where were you today?" Kathleen asked.

"Sick I was," he replied sullenly.

"Sick of studying your lessons. And sick you've claimed to be four times the past fortnight. If you're absent another day, it's a talk with your parents I'll be having."

He hung his head. "Yes, ma'am."

Shane studied Kathleen curiously. He'd noticed that when she talked to the Irish she adopted their speech patterns, but when she talked to him she sometimes spoke more formally.

As Jimmy hurried off, Shane asked Kathleen, "Where is your school?"

"Over there." She gestured vaguely toward the west. "How is it you are a friend of Devil Sherbourne?"

Certain that she was deliberately trying to change the subject, Shane asked softly, "Why are you so anxious to avoid talking about the school where you teach?"

She gave him a searching look. "When I know why you're a friend of the devil's, I'll talk to you about it."

"Sherbourne is a better man than you think." But was he? Shane burned with humiliation at how Radnor had hoodwinked and robbed him and caused untold misery to his tenants.

"Why do you insist on defending him?" Hatred flashed in Kathleen's eyes.

"I think you would be very surprised to meet Sherbourne." Undoubtedly that was the understatement of the decade.

They had taken a winding, roughly circular route through the valley. Now they neared the slope where they had left the horses.

They passed one of the worst hovels Shane had yet seen. A toddler played in front of it, his wobbly, unsteady gait making Shane smile despite his grim thoughts. Clearly, the child had taken his first steps quite recently.

The toddler suddenly tripped and tumbled flat on his face into a muddy puddle that was deeper than it looked.

Reacting instinctively, Shane broke into a run. He vaulted the low stone wall and hauled the boy, choking, sputtering, and covered with mud, from the puddle. Pulling out his handkerchief, Shane cleaned the muck from the child's nostrils and mouth.

The frightened toddler responded by screaming at the top of his lungs, which told a relieved Shane the child was in no danger.

The boy grabbed Shane's coat in his little fists, clinging to him. Shane hugged the toddler to him, ignoring the mud that coated his front. As Shane gently soothed and reassured the child, his screams slowly diminished into frightened sobs.

Kathleen ran up to Shane, undisguised admiration for him shining in her dazzling emerald eyes. "Never have I seen a man move so quickly."

Shane felt as though the queen had just awarded him a medal of valor. He winked at her. "You see I have one or two redeeming qualities after all."

Their gazes locked, and a blush crept up Kathleen's cheeks.

A woman so thin she looked skeletal ran from the wretched hut carrying a baby in her arms.

"Oh, me poor Timmy," she cried. "All right is he?"

"Yes, he is merely frightened." Shane still cuddled the scared boy, who continued to cling to him.

Kathleen said, "Mrs. McNulty, this is a friend of mine, Shane Howard."

Again he felt a tingle of happiness that Kathleen referred to him as her friend.

"And a fine friend too," Timmy's mother said cordially. "It's most pleased I am to meet ye."

"How is little Maurea?" Kathleen asked.

"Worse. Me poor sweet child." Mrs. McNulty brushed a tear from her eye, then looked hopefully at Kathleen. "And would ye be havin' a minute to spare to visit her? She'd love seein' ye."

"Certainly." Kathleen looked at Shane. "Will you be wanting to wait out here?" Her expression implied that no Englishman would set foot in such a sorry hovel.

"No, I will carry Timmy inside for his mother." Not that Shane had any other choice, the way the child was clinging to him.

Mrs. McNulty led the way. The women had to duck their heads to pass beneath the rotted board that served as a makeshift header for the crude entrance. Shane was forced to bend his knees as well as his head, and even then he felt the back of his neck brush against the opening.

Although he had tried to steel himself for the worst, what Shane found inside this cave dug into the side of the slope was even more abysmal than he could possibly have imagined. The side and back walls as well as the floor were damp dirt. Drafts blew through the front wall of rough, ill-fitting stones.

But what shocked him most was the sight of a pathetically thin little girl. She lay listlessly on a sparse layer of straw.

Other than a rough wooden cradle for the baby, the straw was the only thing resembling a bed in the hut. He wondered where the rest of the family slept. Shane was sickened that human beings were forced to live this way.

He looked up and saw Kathleen studying him. Their gazes met, and she smiled at him with obvious approval and—did he dare hope?—affection.

As if embarrassed by what she had revealed, she turned quickly and hurried to the little girl's side. "Maurea, I have missed you so."

"Mrs. Mc—" The rest of Kathleen's last name

was lost in a cruel fit of coughing that shook the little girl like a willow caught in a fierce winter wind.

Shane shuddered at the terrible sound, feeling as though he had been thrust into a waking nightmare as memories swamped him of his helpless vigil at his son's bedside. Jeremy had coughed this way before he died, struggling and gasping for each precious breath, just as Maurea did now.

Anger twisted in his gut. No child as sick as Maurea should be in this damp, drafty cave.

Kathleen knelt beside the cot and gathered the little girl to her, stroking and holding her until the coughing subsided.

Maurea opened her mouth again, but Kathleen placed her finger over the child's lips. "No, don't talk. It makes you cough. Let me tell you a story about the *daoine sidh*."

The little girl smiled, and Kathleen launched into a tale.

"Those are me Maurea's favorite stories," her mother told Shane. "She always seems a little better after Mrs. McNamara's been here."

Kathleen told her tale in a low voice to keep from waking the baby in the mother's arms, holding her little listener's rapt attention.

Shane had never known another woman like Kathleen, fiery yet caring, passionate yet intelligent, a loving mother and teacher. The more he saw of her, the more he was intrigued and attracted.

Mrs. McNulty laid her baby in the cradle and held out her arms to her son who was still clinging to Shane. "I'll take Timmy."

At first the boy continued to clutch Shane's coat

with his dirty little fists, but eventually his mother coaxed him to come to her.

Her eyes widened. "Oh dear, Mr. Howard, ruined yer coat Timmy's done. All muddy it is, and such a fine coat."

Shane looked down at the frayed and mended coat that he had gotten from the Wrexham rag-picker. Even without the mud, it was anything but fine. Yet compared to the rags the McNultys wore, the shabby garment must seem quite grand.

"Please, do not worry. It is an old coat."

But Mrs. McNulty's concerned face told Shane she would fret about it. Determined to put her mind at rest, he resorted to fiction. "Timmy did no damage to it, for it was already in very sorry condition before I grabbed him. I always wear this coat when I am doing the dirtiest of my chores. You cannot blame all of the mud on him."

The woman looked so relieved that Kathleen paused in her storytelling and rewarded Shane with a smile of gratitude.

"So it's a farmer you be," Mrs. McNulty said.

Having told the men in Killoma he was a tutor, Shane decided he'd better stick to that. "No, a tutor."

Kathleen gaped at him in obvious astonishment.

Mrs. McNulty looked impressed. "Then it's a teacher you are, like Mrs. McNamara. The best ever we've had, she is."

Shane did not doubt this praise was deserved.

Mrs. McNulty's face clouded suddenly as though she realized she'd said something wrong, and she hastily told Kathleen, "Not that your late husband weren't a fine teacher too."

So Patrick McNamara had been a teacher. Shane

frowned. Why would a man of his learning and position become a poacher?

"Thank you," Kathleen said gently. "My husband cared deeply about his students."

Mrs. McNulty turned back to Shane. "Would ye be wantin' somet'ing to eat?"

He looked at the pathetically small pile of potatoes in the corner and politely declined. They had not enough to feed themselves. No wonder the woman was so thin.

"Where's your husband, Mrs. McNulty?" Kathleen asked. "I didn't see him."

"Working off his duty to Sherbourne, he is."

At a loss to understand what she was talking about, Shane asked, "What do you mean, 'his duty'?"

Kathleen answered for her. "In addition to the exorbitant rent His Devilship charges, he requires each of his tenants to work without renumeration a considerable number of days each year on the land he retains for himself. How many must your husband contribute, Mrs. McNulty?"

"Twenty-four this year 'tween start of plantin' and end of harvest."

"That's outrageous!" Shane blurted.

"Aye, and how me Tom begrudges the time. But what can we do?" Mrs. McNulty shrugged her thin shoulders hopelessly.

"One more example of the kind of landlord His Devilship is," Kathleen said to Shane.

"But a taste of his own, Cap'n Starlight gave Divil Sherbourne last week," Mrs. McNulty observed.

Kathleen looked quellingly at her. "What can you be talking about?"

"Oh!" The woman clasped her hands to her

mouth, staring at Shane in dismay. "One of the Knights, I thought himself."

"*Nil!*" Kathleen retorted.

Mrs. McNulty looked horror-stricken. "Holy Mother, what've I done?"

The poor woman looked at Shane with such fear and distress that he took one of her rough, work-worn hands in his own and said softly, "You have done nothing that need worry you. I swear to you, as God is my witness, that I will never repeat to anyone what you said here today."

She looked so relieved that Shane gave her hand another reassuring squeeze before he released it.

Kathleen looked down at the little girl on the straw. "I must go now, Maurea. I miss you very much, and I hope you'll be back with me soon. If you aren't by next week, I'll come again to visit you."

As Kathleen turned toward Shane, her eyes betrayed she knew as well as he did that she would be visiting the girl here the following week.

As Shane followed Kathleen outside, Mrs. McNulty asked, "Will ye and himself here be goin' to the Lughnasadh dance?"

"No," Kathleen replied.

"Himself hopes to change her mind," Shane said with a grin.

Once he and Kathleen were out of Mrs. McNulty's hearing, she said in a voice fraught with suspicion. "So it's a tutor you are. How is it a tutor's a friend of a marquess?"

"I tutored his son." Shane told himself again he was not truly lying.

She looked at him incredulously. "Why would His Devilship invite a tutor to stay at Canamara as though he were a grand lord?"

"I was ill, and he thought Canamara might be a good place to recover." Again, Shane picked his words with care, not wanting to tell her an outright lie. Indeed he had been sick—sick at heart over his son's death—and he had thought he might find solace on his Irish estate. "I had never been to Ireland before, and I always had a great yearning to visit."

"And why is it you never mentioned before you are a tutor, especially when you knew I'm a teacher?"

"Ah, but you refused to talk about your work, so I decided tit for tat," Shane improvised hastily.

Anxious to turn the conversation away from himself, he pointed toward a roofless cottage of native stone about twenty feet up the flank of Kincaid Mountain. "What happened there? It looks as though it was abandoned before it was completed."

Kathleen looked in the direction he pointed. "It was. The McNultys began building it before the old Lion died. After His Devilship inherited, he raised their rent so high they couldn't afford to thatch the roof, and they were forced into that miserable cave where they live now."

Shane's thoughts returned to the sick child on the pathetic straw bed. "If poor little Maurea is to have any hope of surviving, she must have a better place to live."

"I know." Tears shimmered in Kathleen's eyes. "When she was first stricken, I took her to Rose Cottage, but Radnor said if I didn't move her out immediately, he'd have to evict me. I was heartsick, but all I'd accomplish by trying to keep Maurea was to rob my own daughter of a roof over her head."

"Why did Radnor say he would evict you? No doubt, he blamed Sherbourne."

She nodded. "Little Ollie said if His Devilship were to learn what I had done, not only would I be evicted, but he'd be discharged as agent. He dared not take that chance."

"Bastard," Shane muttered.

Kathleen smiled, obviously pleased. "So at last you admit what kind of man your friend Sherbourne really is."

He decided it would be wiser not to try to correct her mistaken impression now. Instead he asked, "Has a doctor seen Maurea?"

"Even if the McNultys had the money, which they don't, the only doctor in the neighborhood is English and doesn't lower himself to treat the common Irish, whom he regards as subhuman. He confines his practice to members of the gentry."

"That is a damn crime!"

Kathleen nodded as she sidestepped a puddle in the path. "I heartily agree with you."

"Even if I am an Englishman?" he inquired wryly. The more he learned about Canamara, the better he understood and appreciated her bitterness.

"The strangest Englishman ever I've met."

"Why do you say that?"

"You've a heart," she said succinctly.

One I am in danger of losing to you.

Kathleen continued, "I thought no Englishman had a heart."

"Ouch, I might have known you would sting me with that viper tongue of yours."

She grinned saucily at him. "But my viperous tongue speaks only the truth."

He raised his eyebrows. "Does it now? Then tell

me why Captain Starlight and his followers burned the Malones' farm.''

She hesitated for a moment, as though she was trying to decide whether to trust him. ''And why'd you be wanting to know?''

''I cannot understand what this Captain Starlight hoped to accomplish by such a terrible deed.''

''As Mrs. McNulty said, he gave Devil Sherbourne a bit of his own. And why is that so terrible?''

''I fail to see the logic. It is the Malones, not His Lordship, who suffer the most from having their farm burned. Are they not as Irish as this Captain Starlight?''

Kathleen tossed her head. ''So they are, but it's Sherbourne, not Captain Starlight, who made the Malones suffer.''

Shane's anger rose at her eagerness to attribute everything wrong at Canamara to him. ''What do you mean? It was a mob of Irishmen who torched their farm. And for no reason except they were jealous of the Malones, who had prospered through their hard work and deserved the fruits of their labors! So now the Malones are homeless, and their fine farm lies in ruins.''

Kathleen looked at him as though he were talking gibberish. ''Homeless they were before their farm was torched. The Knights destroyed it to repay Devil Sherbourne for driving the Malones from the home they'd built with their own hands and robbing them of the fruits of their labor.''

Now it was Shane who was baffled. ''What are you talking about? That mob drove the Malones from their home last week.''

''*Nil*, His Devilship did that three weeks ago, allowing the Malones to take nothing with them but the clothes they wore. Sherbourne leased everything else on the Malone farm, down to the contents of their cupboards, to that ugly friend of his, Ben Tilton."

Shane could scarcely comprehend what Kathleen was telling him. The Malones evicted? Tilton, a friend of his? He had never seen the man until their unpleasant encounter in Canamara's hall last Friday. He asked in bewilderment, "What are you talking about?"

"I am telling you those Irish *patriots* burned the Malone farm and drove the Tiltons from it so that they would not reap the profits of the Malones' years of labor."

You were brought here to prevent what happened during the night, you worthless bastard, and you failed completely. At last, Shane understood what Radnor had been telling Tilton that day.

Horrified, Shane ran his fingers distractedly through his hair, thinking of all Radnor's lies. "My God, I cannot believe this."

"Now you see why everyone despises Devil Sherbourne."

Yes, he did. Kathleen's expression radiated implacable loathing that ate like lye at Shane's heart and soul.

If she learned his true identity, could he ever hope to redeem himself in her eyes?

Chapter 13

"I have seen enough," Shane said. "We can return to the horses."

His face was grimmer than Kathleen had yet seen it, and his voice more strained. Devil Sherbourne's handiwork, the hodgepodge of tiny plots and dirt hovels into which the Vale of Kincaid had been divided, clearly shocked and disgusted Shane.

His reaction pleased Kathleen enormously. He was the first Englishman she had met who showed any sympathy for the plight of the Irish. She'd never thought to find an Englishman she could like, but she did like Shane.

Perhaps she already more than liked him.

This traitorous thought startled her. She turned abruptly down another path as though by doing so she could also leave her wayward thoughts about Shane behind. "We'll go this way, for it'll take us directly to the horses."

As they walked in silence, she tried resolutely to fix her attention on the path ahead of her, but she could not put the scene at the McNultys' from her thoughts.

When little Timmy had fallen into the muddy hole, Kathleen had been amazed at how Shane had instantly vaulted the fence and rescued him. Most Englishmen would have had their noses so high in the air they would not have noticed the child, let alone saved him.

She had been even more astonished at the caring and skill with which he had soothed the child. Recalling, though, how quickly he had established a rapport with Brigid, Kathleen should not have been surprised.

As she'd watched him with Timmy, she'd been beset by the nagging—and surprisingly painful—suspicion that Shane must have children of his own to be so good with them. In truth, she'd been secretly relieved to learn he was a tutor, which would explain his easy rapport with children.

He must be an excellent tutor. Shane had a way with children that many men did not. Her own Patrick, teacher though he'd been, had not possessed that skill—even with his own daughter.

Although Shane was still silent, Kathleen noticed that as they walked, his gaze roved about, taking in everything. His bleak expression told her he was as sickened as she was at what had been done to this beautiful vale.

When they reached the gorse bush where they had left their horses, he untied them, gave her a leg up, then sprang gracefully into his own saddle.

As they rode back up Kincaid Mountain, Shane appeared lost in somber thoughts.

"A ha-penny for your thoughts," she offered.

"Only a half-penny?" A small smile tugged at his lips. "You do not think them even worth a whole penny?"

She smiled too. "We Irish are a frugal lot."

His smile faded. "From what I have seen today, you have good reason to be."

They reached the base of the rock outcropping on Kincaid Mountain, where they had stopped earlier to look down on the valley.

"Can we stop here?" Shane asked. "I would like to go up on top of the rocks. Would you mind?"

"Not at all." Kathleen was in no hurry to lose his company.

Shane dismounted and reached for her. When he placed his hands on her waist, heat and excitement flooded through her at his touch. She marveled at his strength as he lifted her easily off the sidesaddle. He set her gently on the ground, as though she were some fragile, cherished treasure.

He led the horses away from the path. Leaving the reins to drag on the ground, he took her hand in his. His strong grasp sent another wave of warmth—and wanting—through her.

He guided her carefully up the steep trail, narrow and rocky, that led to the top of the outcropping, about twenty feet above where they had left the horses.

Once she stumbled and would have fallen had he not instantly pulled her against his hard body to steady her. He held her tightly to him for longer than was really necessary.

His breath was hot and sensual against her ear. His cheek brushed hers before he let her go. Had it been an accident?

Kathleen hoped not. She found herself wishing he had kissed her too.

He seemed reluctant to free his hold on her hand, and so hers remained locked in his grasp. Not until they reached the top did he release it, and she instantly felt bereft.

From this vantage point, they could see both the Vale of Kincaid and a second valley to the left of it. Shane's face darkened as he saw the land there had also been divided into a patchwork of tiny plots.

"What about the remainder of Canamara that cannot be seen from the house?" he inquired. "Has it been chopped up as cruelly as these two valleys?"

Kathleen nodded.

As though her answer had knocked him from his feet, he sank down on the rock outcropping, covered here and there with patches of wild grass. "I cannot believe what I have seen today."

Kathleen dropped down beside him. His eyes were tormented as he gazed over the land spread beneath them. She reached out instinctively to take his hand in hers, offering him silent comfort.

His long, tapering fingers closed tightly around hers as though she were his lifeline, and she felt her heart turn over.

His head was bowed, his black hair thick and curling every which way. She admired his strong profile with its straight, well-formed nose, and the hard line of his jaw that contrasted with the sweep of long black eyelashes.

He turned to look at her, and the agony in his eyes tore at her heart. He looked as though he blamed himself for what lay below them, yet none of it was his fault.

Did he think because he'd admired his employer and was now disillusioned that somehow it was his fault? Sherbourne had been kind to Shane, allowing him to use Canamara. Indeed Kathleen was incredulous that the marquess had done so. She did not want to believe His Devilship capable of the smallest generosity to anyone. "Now you know what your friend Sherbourne's character really is."

"Sherbourne knew nothing of this," Shane burst out with such vehemence that Kathleen started and jerked her hand away from his.

"Of course he did," she answered scornfully. "It was all done on his orders."

"You are wrong."

"Just because His Devilship was good to you, doesn't mean he's also good to his Irish tenants. Believe me, I am sick to death of listening to Ollie Radnor wail about how much he hates to carry out Sherbourne's cruel orders even as he does so."

Shane's jaw clenched, but he said nothing.

"A very different place was Canamara when Sherbourne's grandfather owned it. If only the old Lion had not died. Or more to the point, if only his foolish daughter had married one of her own instead of His Devilship's father, so much better it'd been for all of us."

"And far better for her too," Shane said absently.

Kathleen looked at him in surprise. "Why do you say that?"

"Theirs was a very unhappy marriage—or so I have been told."

His voice throbbed with raw emotion as though the unhappiness had somehow affected him. Kathleen waited for him to continue, but he did not. Instead he rubbed his eyes with his hands as though he were suffering from a sharp headache.

"What is it?" she asked.

"Please, tell me what happened after the old Lion died." His grasp tightened on her hand. "Please?"

He already looked so distressed that she hated to add to his pain by describing those black days when life had changed so drastically for Canamara's tenants. "Why dredge up that unhappy time. What good can it do?"

His eyes hardened with determination. "I intend to do everything I can to right the wrongs here, but I must know what happened."

Although she was touched by his clearly heart-felt desire, she pointed out, "Not that you have any power to right them."

"Perhaps I have more than you think."

"Because Sherbourne has been kind to you?" Kathleen tried to temper her words to take the sting of accusation from them. "If you think you can persuade him to treat his Irish tenants better, you are a dreamer."

"Am I?" The look he gave her was so fierce that a little shiver ran through her. For all his gentleness and rapport with children, this was not a man to cross. He was a man of strength and determination.

Not that it would get him anywhere against the powerful Marquess of Sherbourne.

"I want to know everything that happened here after the old Lion's death," Shane said.

"I was not here then, although I had visited as a child. My aunt married a man who was one of Fitzgerald's tenants back then. A more beautiful place than Canamara I'd never seen." She shook her head sadly. "My husband and I came here two years or so after the old Lion died. When he was alive, no need was there for us here. I can only tell you what I've heard about the time before that."

"Tell me what you heard." The firm strength of his hand clasping hers, the determined set of his face, and the sincerity in his eyes told Kathleen this was a man she could trust. She felt it all the way to the depths of her soul.

"Life was good on Canamara before the Lion

died." The stony ground on which she sat was hard, uneven, and uncomfortable, but in Shane's company she did not care. "He was much loved and respected, and I am told a better landlord could not be found in all Ireland."

With his free hand, Shane picked up a stray twig from the ground in his long, slender fingers and absently rubbed its bark with his thumb. Kathleen thought of what it would be like to have those fingers on her body, and another burst of heat enveloped her.

"Did the trouble begin as soon as the old man died?"

Such an odd question, she thought. Gathering her scattered wits, she tried to remember what she had heard about that period immediately after the Lion's death.

"No, not at once," she said slowly. "Radnor's father was the Lion's agent, and he managed to keep things much the same as they had been when the old man was alive, but he was killed only four months after the Lion died."

"So, as I suspected, that's when the changes began."

The bitter twist to Shane's mouth puzzled Kathleen. "Why did you suspect that?"

Shane stared down at the Vale of Kincaid, his face as hard as the granite outcropping on which they sat. He seemed lost in thought, and he did not answer her. She was not at all certain he had even heard her question.

A thick Irish mist swirled in about them, enveloping them in its cool dampness, and softening the view of the valleys beneath them.

After a moment, Kathleen continued, "Apparently, it would not have mattered whether Ollie's father was killed or not. It turned out that the elder Radnor had been lying to Sherbourne, telling him he was carrying out his orders to increase the rents, when he was not."

Shane's head whipped around, anger darkening his eyes. "How is it you know so much about the business of Canamara?"

"Little Ollie told me."

"Did he now? What else did he tell you?"

"Even if his father had lived, he could not have kept up the deception much longer, for he had not the money to forward to Sherbourne for the rents he'd claimed he'd collected. After he died, little Ollie was hard pressed to make up the difference so his father's reputation would not be posthumously besmirched, but somehow he managed it."

"I am certain he did." Shane's voice dripped with sarcasm. "Let me guess the rest. Little Ollie said Sherbourne ordered the land be divided and redivided and the rents raised."

"Yes." Kathleen stared moodily into the mist. "With each passing year, His Devilship grew greedier, ordering the land divided into smaller and smaller plots and increasing the rents until they are higher now than the land is worth."

"Why do the tenants pay them? Why do they stay?"

"Sure, and what else are they to do?" Kathleen demanded hotly. "They're Catholics. They were stripped of their own land. All the professions are closed to them." Her voice rose in indignation at the wrongs that had been done them. "They are permitted no way other than farming to feed their families. What are they to do?"

"They could go elsewhere."

"Where? Land is a precious commodity in Ireland. Rack rents such as His Devilship collects here prevail everywhere in Ireland."

A light breeze pushed the gray mist about them like drifting smoke, blotting out the scene beneath them and enclosing them in their own private world. Silence reigned between them for a few moments.

Shane broke it. "Why did you say you were not needed here when the old Lion was alive?"

"He'd set up a secret school on the estate for the Irish children of the neighborhood. After Fitzgerald died, his grandson ordered it closed, and the teacher had to flee to escape arrest."

"Why a *secret* school?"

"Only there can Irish children learn their native language, history, legends, and traditions."

"But surely they can learn that in the charter school as well. Why do you look at me as though I am mad?"

"Not only do its students learn nothing about their country's past, they learn nothing—or very little except how to labor in a woolen mill. The unfortunate children consigned there are nothing but slaves. An Irish parent will do almost anything to keep his child from that hellhole."

He gaped at her. "Are you serious?"

"I do not lie! You must have seen it when you walked into Killoma today. It's an ugly old building on the edge of town with all the windows broken out and not a blade of grass around it."

Shane's expression of utter horror told Kathleen more clearly than words that he had noticed the school.

Another minute passed before he asked, "But where do you teach?"

Kathleen gave him a searching look. Did she dare trust him with her secret? If he betrayed her . . . She had no desire to end up in a gaol. Yet her instinct—or was it her heart?—told her Shane would not betray her.

He apparently guessed the reason for her hesitation, for his grasp tightened reassuringly on her hand. "Your secret is safe with me, Kathleen."

She decided to take the chance and believe him. "I run a hedge school."

"What the devil is that?"

"A secret school that teaches the children what they cannot learn elsewhere. Since the English have outlawed such schools in Ireland, people are afraid to house them. So classes are often taught on the sunny side of a hedge. My own are. My husband was invited to come here to teach the children in such a school. After Sherbourne murdered him, I took over his position."

Shane visibly flinched. "You teach both boys and girls?"

"I welcome whomever can come. Why do you look surprised?"

"We have dame schools in England, but only girls attend them."

She could feel the heat of anger flaring in her cheeks. "And women are capable only of teaching their own sex? I teach both boys and girls every subject my husband did, including Latin and mathematics. I am not as ignorant as you think."

"I think nothing of the sort! You are the most intelligent and well-informed woman I have ever met." The admiration in his brilliant blue eyes was unmistakable.

Kathleen felt a new wave of heat—this time a

pleased blush—rising in her cheeks at his compliment.

"I am surprised, though, given what you have told me, that Radnor permits your school to continue."

"He thinks it vanished with my husband's murder. Little Ollie does not know that I took it over. We move its location every few weeks to keep from being discovered."

Shane looked at her in alarm. "What would happen if you were caught?"

"Nothing good."

The admiration for her in Shane's eyes made Kathleen feel ten feet tall.

"You are the bravest woman I know, *aon alainn*."

Beautiful one. Kathleen's heart somersaulted.

Their gazes met and held. Invisible lightning seemed to arc between them.

Slowly their mouths came together. At first hesitantly, a man and a woman, curious yet uncertain, exploring the powerful, mysterious attraction that drew them to each other.

Their kiss was gentle, tentative, lips lightly brushing lips, two persons in search of a kindred soul, each reaching out to the other, yet unsure, perhaps even a little frightened of what they might find.

Then the smoldering embers of passion sparked and flared, and they kissed each other with a growing hunger that sent tremors of longing through Kathleen.

Shane's arms went around her, muscular arms rippling with power, crushing her to him as though he feared she might try to escape him. He groaned and whispered, "You feel so good."

So did he. Kathleen drew comfort and strength

from the strong arms around her. She should have been shocked at the wanton way she kissed him back, yet all she felt was the rightness of it.

Kathleen returned his embrace, and he groaned again with pleasure.

His hands moved upward, and he loosened the pins that held her hair atop her head. With his fingers, he combed it down about her shoulders. "Such glorious hair," he murmured, "untamed like you, and the color of finest burgundy, *alainn*."

Beautiful. And he made Kathleen feel that way.

Shane held her face between his hands, and his lips sought hers again. Their kiss was wild and hungry, the melding of mouths and long dormant passions blossoming like exotic flowers in a barren desert.

He tasted like his scent, spicy, exciting. Desire burned within Kathleen like a flaming brand.

He lifted his mouth from hers, and his lips traced the sensitive cord of her neck.

"Oh," she gasped and then, "Oh" again as a delicious pleasure curled through her. The terrible loneliness that had wrapped around her like a shroud since Patrick's death seemed to dissolve.

She had the strange feeling that she had come home at last, here on this rock outcropping hidden in the mist beneath a gray Irish sky in the arms of this man she had known only a week.

Yet she felt as though she had been waiting for him all her life.

His hand smoothed her hair, then slipped beneath her cloak to cup her breast gently, as though he held a precious treasure in his hand. His thumb massaged her nipple through her cotton gown. It hardened and she arched with pure pleasure.

God help her, she should not be doing this, but she never wanted Shane to stop.

Chapter 14

Shane never wanted to stop.

Kathleen's passionate response, as honest as the woman herself, thrilled him.

As his thumb teased the taut, pebbled crest of her breast, his rigid manhood throbbed, making him long to bury himself in her sweet depths.

She was life, renewal, resurrection calling him back from the frozen sepulcher of grief in which he had been entombed since Jeremy's death.

A joy Shane had not felt in months, had thought he would never feel again, surged through him.

He tunneled his hands into her glorious hair, and its burgundy silk lightly caressed his fingers like a soft breeze.

Shane recaptured her mouth in a kiss that was ravenous with his hunger for her, and she returned it with equal passion, wrenching a moan of surprise and pleasure from him.

He had never met her like. She was unique, this Irish beauty with her sharp tongue and caring heart.

Shane brought his hand down, his knuckles lightly resting on her left breast so that he could feel the racing tempo of her heartbeat, which matched his own.

Then he cupped her breast gently. As he held its sweet weight, new ripples of desire coursed through him.

He buried his face against her creamy neck, loving the soft warmth of her skin.

The mist embraced them, like a soft gray cocoon spun specially for them by a *daoine sidhe* to shelter them from the world.

Lord, how Shane ached to lay Kathleen down, strip her clothes from her beautiful body, and make love to her until they soared together to the heavens.

Yet he knew it would be a mistake to take her now. It was too soon, and she would bitterly regret having succumbed to temptation so quickly. He did not want that to happen.

He had known this woman only briefly, yet he knew that he wanted more than merely a tumble in the hay. But how much did he want? He was not yet certain himself.

That question too, he must answer before he took her.

Furthermore, Kathleen deserved so much better than a rough, uneven bed of rock and grass with only the cool Irish mist to cover her.

Sighing in frustration, he withdrew his hand from beneath her cloak, gave her a final kiss, and stood up. "I had better take you back to Rose Cottage before I forget I am a gentleman. You are far too much temptation for me."

Shane held out his hand to her. She took it, and he helped her to her feet.

Her eyes were as soft as green velvet and dreamy. Shane was delighted that their brief interlude had affected her as much as it had him.

He led the way down the narrow path beside the rock outcropping so that if she stumbled or slipped he would be there to catch her.

When they reached the horses, Shane looked down at the Vale of Kincaid, but the mist had thickened still more and hid the valley in its gauzy grayness.

Now he knew why Kathleen and his other tenants despised him. In light of the outrages that had been committed in his name without his knowledge, their animosity was richly deserved. Had Shane been one of them, he would have felt as they did.

Wearily, he helped Kathleen onto the mare, mounted his own bay, and rode in brooding silence toward Rose Cottage, cursing himself for not having come to Ireland years earlier.

Ending the evil that had festered and corrupted Canamara for so long would be no easy feat and could, in fact, be filled with dangers and pitfalls. He thought of the final communication he had received from his friend Robert Sutton, who had been killed as he returned to Dublin from Canamara.

Three days after Shane learned of Robert's death, he had received a cryptic note from him, posted from Killarney. In it, Robert wrote he was returning early from Ireland to discuss the shocking information contained in his earlier letters to Shane.

Shane, however, had received no earlier letters from Robert.

Speaking of letters, if you have any for posting, give them to me. I handle all the mail myself.

Now Shane feared he understood why none of

Robert's previous correspondence had reached England.

As they neared Kathleen's cottage, she observed, "You are very quiet."

"Yes, you have given me much to think about. I am shocked and sickened by what I have seen today."

She gave him a searching look. "And I am shocked that an Englishman would care in the least."

"You know too few Englishmen."

"One is too many!"

"Until me?" he asked gently. "Or were your kisses back there a lie?"

She blushed scarlet. "Until you," she admitted softly.

Such a surge of happiness swept over him that it caught him by surprise. He reached across the distance that separated their horses and grasped her hand, soft and small, in his larger one. "Let me take you to the Lughnasadh dance, *alainn*, please."

Her hand trembled a little in his. "It will not be stately English dancing, but Irish jigs and reels."

"All the better." He loved the Irish dances that his mother had taught him as a child. "Please, say yes."

She smiled. "Very well."

Happiness flared in him at her answer, then died into embers as he wondered whether he would ever be able to convince her that he'd been ignorant of the atrocities carried out in his name.

Before Shane could repair the damage, he needed all the facts. And that meant he must ask Kathleen a question he dreaded. He postponed doing so for as long as he could.

When they reached the edge of the meadow surrounding Rose Cottage, however, he could delay no longer. "Please, let us stop here a moment."

Kathleen glanced at him, clearly surprised, but she complied. Something in his face must have warned her, for she asked, "What's wrong?"

He shifted his reins and reached for her hand, grasping it firmly. "I hate to cause you pain, Kathleen, but you must tell me about your husband's death. Why do you allege Sherbourne murdered him?"

He saw in her magnificent eyes the anguish she felt at the loss of her husband. "Because he did!"

"How?" Shane asked hoarsely.

She stared bleakly ahead. "The potato crop failed, and some of the tenants were half-starved. Yet Canamara's park teems with game—deer, ducks, geese, pheasants—and its streams with fish."

Her voice choked with emotion. "Only a mere sampling of this game and fish could have saved the tenants and their children from hunger. But no, His Devilship would not permit so much as one bird or trout to be used for such a humanitarian purpose. Little Ollie begged him in vain."

Shane's hands doubled into clenched fists that he longed to use on that lying snake.

"My Patrick, he was not a man to stand by and let children starve in the midst of plenty."

"So he began poaching?" In Patrick's position, Shane would have done the same. He found himself torn between admiration for the man's courage and jealousy over his wife's love for him.

"Yes," she admitted, "not for himself but to feed the hungry. His Devilship ordered that anyone caught poaching would be punished to the fullest extent of the law."

"But that punishment is transportation, is it not?"

"Yes, transportation to the colonies aboard a convict ship that is no more than a floating coffin."

"Is that what happened to him?" If so, it contradicted what Shane had been told in the village. "Your husband died at sea?"

Kathleen's mouth twisted in a grimace. "No, His Devilship ordered that if his gamekeeper discovered Patrick poaching, he was to kill him—to execute him—and then to say he had been killed while resisting arrest." Tears welled up in her eyes.

Shane's heart went out to her. Such injustice as she described enraged him. And the reason behind it baffled him. "Why would Sherbourne have singled out Patrick and ordered him killed like that?"

"Apparently he'd discovered somehow that my husband was a leader of the local dissidents—"

"But, Kathleen, it makes absolutely no sense for Sherbourne to order your husband killed."

"His Devilship wanted to be rid of Patrick permanently."

"He would have accomplished that if your husband was transported."

"Little Ollie said Sherbourne wanted to make an example of my husband to dissuade others from following in his footsteps."

"Sherbourne is not that stupid," Shane said in disgust. *Radnor might be, but I am not. Or am I, to have let the bastard get away with what he has all these years?*

She frowned. "What do you mean?"

"From the blood of martyrs springs rebels. Sherbourne knows that as well as I do. Why do you think it was His Lordship who ordered your husband killed?"

"Certainly it was not the gamekeeper's wish to kill him," she retorted indignantly. "So guilt-ridden is poor Alban over it that he hasn't been entirely right since then."

"Then why did he fire the gun?"

"He had no choice. Sherbourne ordered that if Alban failed to do so, he and his family would be turned out and His Lordship would make certain the poor man never found employment elsewhere. What is a man with nine children under the age of twelve to do? Let them starve?"

"How could Sherbourne have ordered Alban to kill your husband? His Lordship had never set foot in Ireland."

"The same way he orders everything else— through the written instructions he sends to Ireland." She shook her head. "If only he would listen to Ollie."

"Perhaps he has listened to him too much!" Shane thought of all the glowing letters from Radnor about how wonderful life at Canamara was, of all the charges for whitewash, thatch, and repairs that had never been made to its buildings, and of the huge sum in rents that Radnor must have collected and kept for himself.

"If only that were true," Kathleen said. "Ollie does what he can to help."

To help enrich himself. "Such as?"

"He lets Alban and his family remain in the gamekeeper's cottage, even though he can no longer perform the duties, and Ollie sees that the family has food. He takes it from the larder at the big house."

"How kind of him," Shane said with heavy

irony. He intended to talk to Alban as soon as possible.

"I must be getting home," Kathleen said.

They urged their mounts forward across the meadow to Rose Cottage. Shane caught a bright flash of movement on the path between the gate and the cottage. "Brigid is coming to greet us."

By the time they reached the little girl, she had opened the gate and was headed up the path toward them. "Oh, S'ane, will you dine with us tonight?"

Given his present mood, he probably should refuse, but the thought of a solitary meal spent contemplating the sins he was falsely accused of committing did not appeal to him.

"If your mama will allow me to come to the table in all my dirt, *sidhe*." He dismounted and helped Kathleen down, saying to her, "I promise I will wash the worst of it off me and remove my muddy coat before I sit down."

She smiled her agreement.

He finished tying the horses to the gate. As they started up the walk, Brigid grabbed his hand. Shane remembered another little hand that he had once held like this as they walked together, and he had to struggle to retain his composure.

"Why did you and mama go ridin' without me?" The little girl looked up at him with a pout.

"I had business today, *sidhe*, but I will take you another day."

The pout disappeared. "You promise?"

"I promise."

"And it's a promise you'll be keeping," Kathleen said with a laugh. "Brigid will see to that."

When they entered the kitchen, Maggie grinned

and winked at Shane. "Stayin' fer dinner are ye? I've set a place."

Much as he enjoyed the company at dinner, he discovered he had little appetite for food after what he had discovered that day.

He caught Kathleen watching him sympathetically as he pushed bits of potato and the salmon he had caught that morning around his plate, trying to conceal his inability to eat it.

Maggie eyed his plate. "So yer not likin' me cookin' tonight?"

"It is delicious," he assured her, "but I was so shocked by what I saw this afternoon in the Vale of Kincaid that it robbed me of my appetite."

"To yer credit that is," Maggie said.

The glow in Kathleen's eyes told him she seconded this opinion.

Much as he would have liked to linger in the cheerful, homey kitchen for hours after they finished eating, he left fairly quickly. He needed and wanted to start immediately righting the wrongs done in his name.

At the door, he lifted his mud-stained coat from the peg where he had left it and said to Kathleen, "Thank you, *alainn*, for showing me the truth about Canamara. I would not have believed it otherwise."

Her emerald eyes were filled with understanding and sympathy. "No favor I did you, I fear."

A strand of her burgundy hair drifted across her cheek, and Shane gently brushed it away from skin as soft as the finest velvet. Her lips parted a little, and he felt her slight tremor beneath his fingertips.

He succumbed to the temptation of her mouth, kissing her lightly. Her lips silently welcomed his, and he wrapped his arms around her and deepened the kiss.

When at last she pulled away from him, they were both breathless, and he wanted more. Much more.

But first he had much to do.

When Shane reached Canamara, Dobbins opened the door to admit him. The supercilious footman stared, clearly scandalized, at Shane's muddy coat.

"Have a hot bath brought up to my rooms as quickly as possible," Shane ordered. "And you and the other footmen, not the maids, are to carry the water up."

The footman looked even more scandalized. Clearly outraged, he exclaimed, "We footmen are English."

"So am I. What has that to do with anything?" After the shocking revelations the day had held for Shane, he had reached the end of his patience with this overbearing jackass. "If you wish to continue as a servant in this house, you will bring the water. Do I make myself clear?"

For a moment, the footman stared at him in shock before nodding sullenly.

Glancing behind Dobbins, Shane caught sight of Siobhan in a doorway, grinning widely. Clearly she had overheard his conversation with the footman. He moved toward her, stepping into the shadow cast by the wall.

She curtsied to Shane. "And would ye be wantin' dinner, too?"

"No, I have already eaten."

She curtsied again and turned away.

Oliver Radnor walked into the hall. Since the day

after Shane's arrival, Radnor had dressed in considerably less grand coats and breeches, but tonight he again wore a green satin coat, white silk breeches, and stockings.

This was the first time Shane had seen the agent since learning the horrifying truth about Radnor's stewardship of Canamara. Shane was so enraged that he was hard-pressed not to strangle the bastard.

But Radnor was a clever one. Shane would be a fool to betray quite yet that he had caught on to the agent's swindles.

Shane's own life might well be in danger. After his discoveries today and the note he'd received posthumously from Robert Sutton, Shane no longer believed an unlucky stroke of fate had put his friend in the wrong place at the wrong time. Shane strongly suspected Radnor had ordered Robert murdered.

After all, the bastard had ordered Kathleen's husband killed on his own authority, then laid the blame on his employer.

Shane would have to be very careful.

"Good evening, Mr. Howard," Radnor said politely.

"Good evening. You appear to be going out tonight," Shane said blandly, wondering if Radnor would be calling on Fiona.

"Yes, I am."

Shane moved out of the shadow toward the staircase, and the light of the chandelier fell directly on his muddy coat.

The agent's nose wrinkled in disgust, and he blurted, "Good God, man, where have you been? You look as though you tumbled into a pig sty."

Even pigs would not live as badly as the McNultys

do, thanks to you. "I slipped and fell into a mud puddle."

Radnor frowned. "Where was this? One of the grooms said you went riding alone. Where did you go?"

You would love to know, would you not, little Ollie? Shane knew the agent's question was not nearly as innocuous as he made it sound. "I rode about the park. Such a lovely, peaceful place."

"Yes, it is, but after what happened to the poor Malones, you must take at least one armed groom with you. I would hate to have to notify Lord Sherbourne that some evil has befallen you. Remember that poor friend of His Lordship's, Mr. Sutton, was murdered as he rode alone."

Shane stiffened. Although the agent's statement sounded harmless enough, Shane construed it as not merely a warning, but a subtle, deadly threat. "I will be careful."

Indeed he would, especially around Radnor. Shane turned and hurried upstairs to his bedchamber.

A few minutes later, Dobbins and two other footmen appeared with the copper tub and hot water he had ordered.

All three looked to be in a high state of indignation and pique over having been ordered to carry the water. Clearly they considered this service beneath them. They looked at Shane as though they longed to boil him in the contents of their pitchers.

After they left, Shane soaked for a long time in the tub. He felt his mouth curling into a pleased smile as he recalled Kathleen and their shared kisses.

How hard it was to put her from his mind. But

he had to deal with Radnor and his perfidy. The magnitude of the agent's crimes against Shane and his tenants was still beyond his comprehnsion.

The man was an evil little rat, but a sly and dangerous one.

How was Shane to repair the damage the agent's greed had inflicted upon Canamara? It would not be easy to set things right. If Shane restored the land to those few families who had leased it under his grandfather, he would be ousting all the others who lived there now, leaving them with nowhere to go.

How was he to find a solution to this coil that would be equitable to all his tenants?

No wonder Kathleen and the other Irish at Canamara hated him with such passion. Could he ever regain their trust and respect?

Especially Kathleen's, once she discovered he was Devil Sherbourne, the man she regarded as her husband's murderer?

God, what a bloody mess!

Shane's bathwater had cooled to lukewarm by the time he stepped from the tub. He dressed in clean breeches and shirt but did not bother with a cravat.

Shane looked at the muddy coat he'd worn that afternoon and rang for a maid.

Siobhan appeared at his door a minute later. She no longer manifested the nervousness she had when she'd come to his room the night he'd arrived. "You be wantin' somethin', Yer Honor?"

Shane held out his muddied coat to her. "I wonder whether someone could manage to make this presentable again."

"Sure, and we'll try." She took the garment from him.

"I know it will be difficult, but I will be grateful for whatever can be done to save it."

Siobhan hesitated, then burst out in unguarded candor, "So different ye be from the other Englishmen His Lordship sends us."

That startled Shane, for Robert Sutton had been the only visitor he had dispatched to Canamara. "Does His Lordship send you many such visitors?"

"Maybe a half-dozen a year. Some have returned more than once." She unconsciously wrinkled her nose in revulsion.

"I gather you have not liked them."

She hesitated, then said boldly, "Sure, and I don't mind tellin' ye none of them, 'ceptin' poor Mr. Sutton, who got himself killed, is the gentleman ye is."

"Tell me about these other visitors. What were they like?"

"Ben Tilton and his brother stayed here before His Lordship leased them the Malones' farm." She shuddered. "Much as we hated what was done to the Malones, thankful we maids were the Tiltons was gone from this house. Not a maid here was safe from them. Afeared we was they'd come back here to live after they was burned out but they haven't—at least not yet."

Nor are they likely to do so while I am here. Radnor could not chance Shane mentioning these scum he passed off as "friends of Sherbourne" to His Lordship. "When the Tiltons stayed here, did you complain to Radnor about their behavior?"

"And bring more trouble down on me head? Them bein' friends of His Lordship and all." Siobhan's mouth set in bitter lines. "Radnor don't care. Irish we be, and to his mind, deservin' of anything an Englishman be wantin' to do to us."

A repulsive suspicion flashed in Shane's mind. "Does Radnor also demand, er, improper services for himself from the maids?"

"No, but only 'cause we ain't grand 'nough for his taste. If ye ask me, it's under Mrs. McNamara's skirts he's wantin' to get." Siobhan clapped her hand over her mouth, and Shane saw the bright color rising in her cheeks above her fingers. "Sure, and I've shocked ye now—her bein' a teacher and all."

"I am not easily shocked." Shane recalled Radnor's lascivious leer as he had looked at Kathleen. Was that why he'd ordered her husband killed? Had the agent wanted her for himself?

After Siobhan carried his stained coat away, Shane picked up a candlestick holding a lighted taper. During Radnor's absence tonight, Shane intended to do some investigating.

He pressed the spring concealed by the Celtic cross and, candlestick in hand, went down the secret staircase to the gun room. There he unlocked the door that led into the hall and locked it again behind him. Relying on his mother's long ago description of the house, he made his way to what he believed was the estate office.

When he opened the door, he discovered he'd guessed right. A large oak desk dominated the room. He lifted his candlestick so its flickering taper illuminated a wall of bookshelves lined with ledgers. Examining these books, Shane saw that they dated back to when his grandfather had assumed control of the estate.

He opened the ledger for the previous year. To his disappointment, he discovered it simply mirrored the falsified records that he had been sent.

These were the show books, should anyone be sent from England to examine them.

Radnor was corrupt, but he was careful.

Somewhere, though, he must have hidden another set of ledgers that reflected the true accounts of Canamara—and all he had stolen from his employer.

Shane looked around for a place where the accurate ledgers might be hidden, but he found nothing.

He returned upstairs the same way he had come down. Back in his bedchamber, he considered what room Radnor would have taken for himself after Shane had ousted him from this apartment. Most likely he'd picked the house's best guest room.

Shane went there and discovered that again his guess had been accurate. A quick search of the room produced no ledgers, although Shane did find that Radnor possessed a wardrobe that would have filled many a peer he knew with envy.

As Shane considered the suffering of his starving tenants who had paid for the agent's finery, he itched to wrap his hands around the agent's neck and strangle him.

Shane remembered the locked cabinet in his own bedchamber. Perhaps what he sought was there. He changed the object of his search to a key that might open the cabinet.

After much looking, he found a large ring of keys hidden beneath a pile of silk smallclothes in the bottom drawer of a cupboard.

Hoping that one of the keys would open the locked cabinet, Shane hurried back to his apartment. One after another he tried each of the seventeen keys on the ring in the cabinet's lock.

None would open it.

Staring in frustration at the keys in his hand, Shane told himself he should not be surprised. If the cabinet contained what he suspected it did, Radnor most likely carried the key on his person at all times.

Unable to sleep, Kathleen lay in bed thinking of Shane Howard. She recalled the lightning swiftness with which he'd rescued little Timmy from the puddle. She could not help smiling as she recalled his gentleness as he comforted the child.

And his concern for Maurea had touched Kathleen too. He'd said he'd heard a cough like the girl's before, and he clearly knew how poor her chance of recovery was.

His appalled expression when he saw the tiny plots into which Devil Sherbourne had carved Canamara had been genuine. No one could have faked that.

But Kathleen had not fully appreciated how terribly disturbed he was about what he'd learned until she saw how it had robbed him of his appetite.

Yes, Shane was a kind and good man, even though he was English.

Only half-English! And half-Irish. That made her feel better.

Kathleen grew warm and aching with frustrated desire as she recalled Shane's kisses and caresses. They had awakened in her suppressed passions that she had not felt since before her husband was murdered.

A lusty lover Patrick had been, and she had enjoyed the pleasures of the marriage bed. She'd missed them after his death, but never with the gnawing hunger that she felt tonight.

She turned restlessly, her body crying out for the

comfort of a man's arms—no, for *one* man's arms alone—and for the sinuous dance of love between a husband and wife.

Her skin felt heated at the thought of lying with Shane Howard, of having his hands court her body and his sweet words woo her heart.

But, dear God in heaven, he was a friend of her husband's murderer. Kathleen would be betraying her Patrick and his memory.

She felt so ashamed. Yet even that did little to cool the fire that raged out of control within her.

Kathleen cursed her weakness. *You fool. The only greater sin you could commit against Patrick's memory would be to make love with his murderer, Sherbourne himself.*

Chapter 15

The next morning, Shane rose at dawn, dressed in worn, nondescript riding clothes, and set out to tour the outer reaches of his estate.

The half-starved occupants of the miserable sod hovels that dotted the land watched him with sullen expressions and hollow eyes as he rode past. Although he offered several people he met on the road a friendly greeting in Gaelic, their only response was startled suspicion in their eyes before they turned hastily away, as though he represented some kind of trap.

The bay gelding he rode betrayed him as a hated Englishman as surely as an *E* branded on his forehead. He felt conspicuous and alien, even though this was his land.

Kathleen had been right. All of Canamara that was not visible from the great house and the road leading to it had been divided into fragmented bits.

How clever Radnor must have thought himself. In the unlikely event his employer should visit Canamara, he would see only what the agent had so carefully manicured for his eyes.

The rage that boiled up as Shane considered the sins Radnor had committed washed away the aim-

189

lessness and grief, the lethargy and hopelessness that had gripped him since his son's death.

I swear to God that I will put things to right! I will see justice done!

Shane was filled with purpose and determination, stronger than anything he had felt before in his life.

Sitting at the writing table with its splendid view overlooking Canamara's park, Shane applied sealing wax to close the letters he had just written and imprinted them with his signet ring. He put the ring back in his pocket where he kept it.

Now he must find a way to post these missives that would prevent them from falling into Oliver Radnor's hands. Shane was certain that had been the fate of Robert Sutton's letters that he'd not received.

Shane decided the only way to assure his own letters reached their destination was to rise at dawn and ride all the way to Killarney on the morrow to post them there. He did not look forward to doing so, but better that than chance having them seized and destroyed.

In his letters, Shane had set in motion machinery that would eventually bring justice to Canamara. Unfortunately, thanks to the turbulent, unpredictable Irish Sea separating him from England, it could be weeks before his messages reached the recipients, and the answers to his requests, in turn, arrived in Ireland.

He ached to announce his true identity immediately and begin at once to right the wrongs on Canamara, but he must be patient. Shane knew no one in County Kerry or even in all of Ireland who could verify he was the Marquess of Sherbourne.

Beyond a doubt, that devious little snake Radnor would dispute his identity and very likely even try to have him killed.

Although he was convinced the agent had been behind Robert Sutton's and Patrick McNamara's deaths, Shane had no proof. And he must have that if he were to make certain the wily little bastard could not find a way to wiggle out of the charges.

The final reason for patience—and if Shane was honest with himself, perhaps his most important— was not practical, but emotional. Once Kathleen learned his real identity, he knew she would refuse to have anything to do with the man she considered her husband's murderer.

After school that afternoon, Kathleen walked wearily toward home. Overhead, ominous clouds darkened the sky, and she feared the downpour would begin well before she reached Rose Cottage.

She'd had precious little sleep the night before, torn as she was between the hunger that Shane Howard aroused in her and the guilt that stirring caused her.

All day she had resolutely tried to put him from her mind, but she had rarely succeeded. Now as she rounded the curve leading to the bridge where she had first met him, she felt her pulse quicken at the thought that he might be waiting for her, as he had been the previous afternoon.

And it's a fool you are! He won't be there.

But Shane stood in the middle of the narrow bridge, staring down into the rushing water. Kathleen's heart leaped, and she felt a delicious heat curl within her as she remembered his kisses.

Apparently he heard her footsteps, for he looked toward her. Her heart stumbled when she saw his somber expression, as dark and bleak as the sky above them. "What's wrong?"

"I rode about Canamara today. You were right, *alainn*. All the land that cannot be seen from the house has been chopped up into tiny parcels. It made me sick to see it."

He seemed so disgusted and distressed, as though somehow it were his fault. Wanting to comfort him, Kathleen smiled and reached up to touch his cheek lightly with her fingertips. "You are a good man, Shane Howard."

His expression defied her analysis. "May you always think so, *alainn*," he said hoarsely.

"I'm sure I shall." She had not intended to invite him to dinner, but now, anxious to offer him solace, she said, "Come, dine with us tonight."

His smile was like sunshine breaking through black storm clouds. "I should like nothing better."

Her breath caught. His smile was irresistible. Dear God in heaven, how could she deny this man anything?

Shane rode the next day to Killarney, where he paid for express delivery of his letters initiating Oliver Radnor's downfall.

How long before Radnor's reckoning depended on the fickle winds blowing across the Irish Sea. In the meantime, Shane would work in small ways to relieve some of the suffering at Canamara.

When he returned to his estate that evening, he rode toward Rose Cottage.

He found Brigid arcing through the air on a swing suspended from an oak tree on the edge of the meadow.

"S'ane, S'ane," she cried when she saw him. She

leaped from the swing as it still moved, landing on her hands and knees. Undaunted, she jumped up and ran toward him.

As she neared him, she cried, "Mama says you are coming to dinner."

"I am. Would you like to ride home with me on my horse?"

Her Irish blue eyes sparkled with delight. "Oh, please, may I?"

In answer, he reached down and swung her up in his arms, placing her sideways in front of him on the gelding.

"Oh, it's very high I am up here," Brigid exclaimed, her excitement tempered suddenly by nervousness.

"Do not worry, *sidhe*. I will not let you slip."

As they rode up to the cottage gate, flanked by rose bushes, Kathleen came down the path toward them.

"Mama, Mama, see me on the big horse!" Brigid cried.

"I see, darling." Kathleen smiled at her daughter, a mother's love and pride bringing a special glow to her eyes.

Shane wondered hungrily what it would be like to have her look at him with such love in her emerald eyes and such indulgence in her husky voice.

Both Shane and Kathleen started when the tall clock in the hall chimed midnight. Rather than leave when she had put Brigid to bed, he'd waited for Kathleen to come back down. They had been talking ever since on one of the settles in the kitchen.

"I had no idea it was so late," she said as the chimes died away.

"Nor I." Shane rose reluctantly, hating to leave. He had to force his feet toward the front door.

He could not remember ever having been so engrossed by anyone's conversation that hours flew by without notice as they did with Kathleen.

Tonight she'd told him about her childhood, so atypical of most Irish. As the daughter of a rich Dublin merchant, she had lacked for nothing from clothes and food to the finest of educations, culminating with study in France.

Clearly the academic standards of the schools she had attended were much higher than those in England that catered to the daughters of the aristocracy, for her range of knowledge was quite astonishing for a woman.

Nor did the fiery widow hesitate to argue when she disagreed with him. Only very rarely in England had anyone dared challenge him, a powerful marquess, as Kathleen did, and he loved it, especially since her arguments were well reasoned.

He liked her directness, too. She said what she thought without trying to soften her views with modifiers or euphemisms.

Her humor was equally sharp. Shane savored the way she laughed at witticisms that would have baffled his late wife.

Kathleen told him too how she had met her handsome, idealistic husband, another well-educated product of the wealthy Dublin merchant class. He had been fired with determination to right wrongs inflicted on his countrymen and had convinced his wife, then pregnant with Brigid, to come with him to County Kerry and Canamara.

Rose Cottage had been vacant—Radnor had been living in the great house even then—and he had rented it to them. Brigid had been born there.

Since Patrick's slaying, his father and hers sent Kathleen money to pay the rent, allowing her to live comfortably with her daughter.

When Shane reached the front door, he turned and, cupping Kathleen's face tenderly in his hands, kissed her with all the aching longing he felt for her. She returned his kiss fervently, but when he tried to kiss her a second time, she drew back.

"Goodnight," she said firmly.

"If you kiss me again like that, it will be an even better night," he teased.

She smiled. "You'll have to settle for good."

Rather than try to push her, Shane nodded and walked to his horse.

As he rode up the hill to the great house, he thought about the woman he had just left.

Shane saw in Kathleen's eyes the same consuming love for Brigid that he had felt for his son. She shared too the same determination he had felt to try to be both parents to her hurting child.

He had seen her concern for others and the respect in which she was held by them. She was a woman capable of enormous love and caring.

As for her daughter, that adorable little pixie delighted him. No one would ever replace Jeremy in that special nook in his heart that only his firstborn son could ever occupy, but the effervescent Brigid was carving out her own niche there.

She was so lively and full of fun that she absorbed Shane's attention and banished his loneliness.

So did her mother. Kathleen and her daughter had made his days at Canamara by far the happiest he had enjoyed in many months.

Or perhaps ever.

And he did not think he could bear to lose them,

but he would when Kathleen learned his real identity. Her implacable hatred of "His Devilship," even though terribly misdirected, would foreclose any possibility of a future for them together.

Chapter 16

As Shane escorted Kathleen through the gloaming to the Lughnasadh dance, he hoped he could remember all the Irish steps his mother had taught him years ago. He'd never had a chance to perform them except with her.

For a man faced with so much trouble ahead, he was oddly contented tonight.

And why should I not be? He had just had another excellent dinner at Rose Cottage with Kathleen, her daughter, and Maggie.

Shane tightened his grip on Kathleen's hand. She gave him a smile that turned his blood hot. But then just the sight of her did that to him.

As she guided him toward a circle of pine trees, Shane heard Irish pipes playing. Looking in the direction of the music, he saw a building through the trees and guessed that was where the dance would be held.

The twilight was fading rapidly into darkness. The trees, young Scotch pines with branches to the ground, had been planted in a circle around the structure, all but hiding it.

Not until they had passed between the pines did Shane realize that the building had been partially demolished. Only one end of it still had its roof and walls intact. It was from that section the music came.

"What happened here?" Shane asked.

"More of His Devilship's handiwork," Kathleen answered. "He ordered it destroyed, but Ollie Radnor secretly left one end of it standing."

The wily, lying bastard, pretending to be the tenants' friend when he was the real villain. "Did he now?"

Kathleen gave him a questioning look. Clearly she had not missed the irony in Shane's tone.

"What was it used for before?" he asked.

"It was always an assembly hall. It was also home to Lyon Fitzgerald's secret Irish school, and the Catholic priest said Sunday Mass here each week."

"Both illegal activities." Shane's love and respect for his grandfather soared even higher.

"Neither is held here now."

Disturbed by a sudden edge to Kathleen's voice, he placed his hand on her arm and turned her gently toward him. "I was merely making an observation. I would be happy if both school and Mass were still held here."

"Don't be letting Sherbourne hear you say that, or new employment you'll be seeking." She smiled approvingly at him. "You are a far better man than His Devilship is."

"Am I?"

"Still determined to defend your friend Sherbourne, are you? Don't be doing so to people at the dance."

"What would befall me if I did?"

"Tarred and feathered, you'd likely be."

Shane suspected she was right.

They reached the half-ruined structure. Kathleen

led him to the portion that still had walls and ceiling, which turned out to be one large room. Much of it was devoted to a dance floor where dozens of couples were performing an Irish reel.

Their clothes were shabby and mended, but neat and clean. Many of them were so painfully thin, Shane wondered how they had the energy to dance. Yet all of them seemed to have forgotten their troubles in the lively music.

Shane recognized among the dancers several of the people he had met in the Vale of Kincaid. He said wonderingly to Kathleen, "They look as though they had not a care in the world."

"The Irish know how to have fun, no matter how grim their lives," she replied proudly. "I sometimes think all that carries them through their daily misery is their love of music and dancing and their conviviality."

Shane noticed Mrs. McNulty among the onlookers watching the dancers. If ever anyone needed some respite from the bleakness of her life, that woman did.

People standing on the sidelines, men and women alike, greeted Kathleen with deference and respect. They eyed Shane speculatively.

The music ended, and the dancers streamed off the floor.

Shane heard a woman's voice say, "Sure, and it's Mr. Howard. Happy I am to be seein' ye lookin' so spruce."

Shane turned and saw Mrs. McNulty approaching him with a man who was as gaunt as she was.

"Tom, this be the man that hauled our Timmy from the mud. Never seen a man move so fast as when he went over the wall." She looked at Shane. "This is me husband, Tom McNulty."

Shane had heard the name before, but in what connection? Then it came to him. His grandfather had included McNulty on the list of tenants that he most prized.

Extending his hand to the man, Shane said, "I am happy to meet Timmy's da, Mr. McNulty." They shook hands. "I'm Shane Howard."

"It's Tom me friends call me."

"Did you not have a larger farm on Canamara at one time?" Shane asked.

Kathleen's head swiveled toward him in surprise. McNulty too looked startled. "Aye, a bonny piece of land I had when the ould Lion was alive. And how would you be knowin'—"

"A fine man the ould Lion was," a stocky man standing next to them interjected.

Shane slowly let out the breath he'd been holding. He was grateful to the stocky man for interrupting McNulty before he could finish a question that Shane would have trouble answering without revealing more than he wanted.

From the curious look Kathleen gave him, though, Shane feared she would ask him about it later.

"One of us, the ould Lion was," another man agreed. "Not like that damn English grandson o' his. Ain't that right, Conn."

The speaker appealed to a gray-haired man with a strong weathered face that reminded Shane of carved granite. A deep cleft split the man's wide chin. From the deferential attention accorded Conn, he was clearly a man who commanded great respect.

"Aye," he answered, nodding his head.

A drummer began to beat his *bodhran*, and the

pipers struck up an Irish jig that instantly captured everyone's attention.

The music fairly set Shane's toes to tapping. He had always loved the infectious energy and joy of Irish jigs. He did not think anyone—no matter how heavy the burden of his heart—would not feel his spirits rise when that music began.

Hearing it now did exactly that to Shane's. It also brought back to him memories of some of the happiest hours of his childhood spent learning from his mother the dances of her native island.

Shane took Kathleen's hand and led her to the dance floor. She tugged him to a stop. "Sure, and an Irish jig do you think you can dance?"

"Just watch me." He turned and faced her, his feet moving in perfect rhythm to the lively music. He wanted to laugh aloud at her amazed expression. Then she began to dance too. To his delight, she was as good as his mother had been.

After a while the others on the floor stopped and watched them. Finally, they were the only two left dancing.

But Shane scarcely noticed. He had eyes only for Kathleen. What a glorious creature she was.

When the music ended, he led her from the floor, and their audience applauded heartily.

Shane smiled at Kathleen, and his heart caught. Her beautiful face glowed. Her cheeks were rosy from exertion and her brilliant green eyes sparkled with pleasure. How he longed to take her in his arms and . . .

Would her eyes look like that after he made love to her? The thought had such an embarrassing effect on his body that he resolutely pushed it from his mind as they were quickly surrounded by people praising their dancing.

One of these was Conn, the gray-haired man with a face like carved granite. "Fine dancing, me boy. The likes o' it I've not seen since I was a wee lad, and the Lion was still young. Used to come down and dance with us, he did. A better dancin' man I never seen."

Shane's mother had said much the same thing about her father's talent.

"But nearly as good are ye." The man studied him with a perplexed expression. "Remind me of the ould Lion, ye do. *Nil*, not in the face, but in the grace with which ye move and in the way ye hold your body."

"A high compliment you've just paid me." Shane meant this sincerely. He extended his hand to the man. "I am Shane Howard. We have not met."

The man took Shane's hand and gripped it strongly. "Conn Malone be me name."

"Ah, the patriarch of the Malones. I am honored to meet you." Shane studied the man who had grown up with his mother in those happy days before a too handsome marquess had visited County Kerry. The English lord had wooed and married her, then carried her off to his country where they lived unhappily ever after.

Shane laid the blame for the failure of his parents' marriage on his rigid, pompous father, who quickly grew ashamed of his Irish wife and the half-Irish son she bore him fourteen months after he brought her to England.

Shane smiled at Conn. "I have heard you are a fine dancer yourself, Mr. Malone."

"In me youth, but me legs don't move like once they did. Hobbled me, the rheumatism has."

Remembering what Radnor had said about the Malones taking refuge with a married daughter,

Shane asked, "Did you come all the way from County Clare for the dance tonight?"

The question clearly perplexed Conn. "From County Clare?"

"I was told that after you were driven from your farm, you'd gone to stay with a married daughter in County Clare."

"No daughter have I, married or otherwise, but blessed with four strong sons I am."

Another one of Radnor's damn lies, designed to keep Shane from talking to Malone and finding out the truth.

The musicians struck up a country dance, and Shane led Kathleen out. She reminded him of a fairy sprite, so light was she on her feet. The touch of her hand sent electric waves coursing through him.

After two more dances with him, she begged off from a third. "I must have a few minutes to catch my breath. Ask Mrs. McNulty."

Shane frowned, displeased and irritated. "I want to dance only with you."

Their gazes met. Kathleen smiled; her emerald eyes glowing. She caressed his hand gently, making him feel as though the world had just tilted on its axis. "And I want to dance only with you, but a great act of kindness you'd be doing her. She loves to dance and her husband dislikes it."

That explained Mrs. McNulty's wistful expression as she watched the dancers. Shane made his way to her and led her out for a reel.

After that, he danced with Kathleen and then, at her urging, with a widow who had no partner. He returned to Kathleen, but she was already committed for the next dance, and he danced a second time with Mrs. McNulty.

When the music ended, the woman said with a smile that lighted her weary face, "Home I must be goin' now to me Maurea. Thankee kindly for the dances."

Shane returned her to her husband, who was standing beside Conn Malone.

As the McNultys disappeared through the door, Malone said to Shane, "Sure, and kind it was of ye to dance with her. A hard life she has. I fear her Maurea is not long for this world."

Malone's words reminded Shane of his own son's death, and he had to suppress a shudder. "If the child is to have any hope of surviving, she needs to be in a drier, warmer place."

"You've the right of it," Conn agreed.

"I noticed an unfinished, abandoned cottage on Kincaid Mountain behind the McNultys' land," Shane said. "If only that had a roof."

"I know the one ye mean. Talked we have of gettin' together and cleanin' it out and fixin' it up for them. God knows, plenty of sheaves for the roof we have."

"What an excellent idea!" Shane exclaimed, excited by the prospect. "Will you do it?"

Conn shrugged. "For naught, it'd be. No money have we to hire the *tuiodoir*."

Shane frowned. "The thatcher will not do it without pay?"

"Nay, a large family he has to feed. He says if one roof he thatches for free, everyone else will be wantin' him to do the same."

Kathleen had come up as the two men talked. Now she said, "Perhaps, Mr. Howard, you would be willing to contribute the sum my new skirt would cost you toward paying the *tuiodoir*."

"I will do more than that." Shane chose his

words with care. "I have a little money saved. I will gladly contribute it. Perhaps the sum will be enough to satisfy the thatcher."

Both Malone and Kathleen stared at him in surprise.

"Very generous of ye," Conn said approvingly. "I pray what ye have'll be enough."

Shane would make certain his contribution was sufficient, no matter what price the thatcher demanded.

Kathleen looked more skeptical. "And why'd you be doing that for people you hardly know?"

He remembered his dying son's agony, the terrible wrenching cough, the blood, the gasping for breath. Shane would do anything he could to spare another child that fate. "I want to do whatever I can to help that poor little girl live."

She smiled at him. "Very generous of you it is."

The way her eyes glowed at him, caressing him, made Shane's heart beat erratically.

The music started, and he led Kathleen out to dance another jig. After that, he refused to sit out a single dance.

When Kathleen begged off to catch her breath, he asked another of the women to dance with him.

Finally, late in the evening, as he danced again with Kathleen, he said breathlessly, "I cannot remember when I have had so much fun!"

Indeed, he could not. No stately English ball with its guests splendidly dressed in silks and satins had ever been half so enjoyable to him. He felt as though the joyous Irish music and dancing had released his soul from a gloomy prison where it had been captive too long.

Once again, he had the same sensation as he'd had that first day—that he had come home at last.

County Kerry was where he belonged.

With Kathleen McNamara at my side.

This unbidden thought filled him with intoxicating happiness, like drinking deeply of a fine, full bodied wine that left him feeling light-headed and exhilarated.

As the dance ended, Conn Malone came up to Shane and Kathleen. "Where—"

An angry voice boomed out. "What the hell is this English sonofabitch doin' here?"

Shane glanced toward the newcomer and saw the man who had challenged him among the ruins of the Boar's Head. The man he feared was Kathleen's lover. Seamus was pointing at Shane.

Everyone turned to stare, and absolute silence descended.

"Seamus," Conn began, "what kind o' welcome be that to a stranger?"

"Da, he be the damn Englishman staying at Canamara."

So Seamus was Conn's son. Shane could feel the silent rise in hostility against him, which the younger Malone's words generated among the dancers. Until that moment they had accepted Shane as one of them.

The elder Malone frowned. "But like a native, he speaks our tongue."

"So he does, but it's tutor to the divil's son he is."

Conn turned to Shane, his piercing eyes studying him with suspicion. "How is it, then, you speak Gaelic so well?"

"I am Irish as well as English. Both languages I learned as a child."

"So long as a drop of English blood flows in his

veins, no friend of Ireland is he," Seamus sneered. "Look at Sherbourne."

Conn shook his head sadly. "Sure, and I ne'er thought any son o' Maureen Fitzgerald or a grandson o' the ould Lion would be treatin' us as he does. Like me own sister she was."

The sad disillusionment in Conn's voice stabbed at Shane's heart. Before he could stop himself, he blurted, "Perhaps there is more to the story than you know."

"What more could there be?" Seamus demanded, looking at Shane as though he'd suddenly grown a second head.

"Stop it." Kathleen stepped between Shane and Seamus. "A friend of mine and my guest here he is, Seamus Malone, and I'll be thanking you to leave him alone."

Seamus looked as though Kathleen had stabbed him with a knife.

He is in love with her. Shane swiveled his head to see Kathleen's expression. If she was aware of Seamus's affection for her, she gave no indication of it.

"Right she is, Seamus," his father told him. "Because he has English blood does not mean he is an outcast among us. Judge a man on what he does, not on the blood in his veins. When a man bleeds, you cannot tell Irish blood from English."

Conn Malone turned to Shane. "Apologize I do for me son, but bitter he is over what's been done to us."

"And he has every right to be," Shane agreed. "I am sickened by it too, and I intend to do everything I can to see that justice comes to Canamara."

"Pretty words, English," Seamus scoffed, "but well you know a tutor like yerself can do nothing, even if it is the divil's own son you teach."

"And maybe 'tis a good thing he's tutoring the boy," Kathleen said. "Perhaps the son will grow up to be a better man than his father."

Her words, although they were meant to defend Shane, were like a blow to his gut. He was not a man to broadcast his personal losses, and no one in Ireland knew that his son would not grow up at all but already lay in his grave. That black pit of grief, which had imprisoned him before he arrived in Ireland, yawned before him again.

"At least Mr. Howard's heart is in the right place, Seamus Malone." Kathleen's championing of Shane pulled him a step back from the pit. "Give Shane credit for that much."

Seamus's lip curled in contempt. "Blinded you he has with his English charm."

"Nil, 'tis his Irish charm, for half-Irish he is."

Shane's spirts soared. No woman who loved a man would defend another man to him as Kathleen was doing. If Kathleen had a lover, handsome Seamus was not the lucky man. Shane felt almost giddy with relief.

"A fool you be, Kathleen McNamara!"

"It's you that's the fool, Seamus Malone," Kathleen shot back.

"Right she is," a woman said behind Shane. "Mr. Howard's not like most o' them that comes visitin' the big house."

Shane turned. Siobhan, the maid at Canamara, stood there, holding the hand of a redheaded young man whose earnest face was sprinkled with freckles.

After giving Siobhan a grateful smile for defending him, Shane introduced himself and offered his hand to her young man.

"James Sullivan's me name," he said as he shook the hand Shane had extended.

The pipers struck up another tune, and Seamus asked Kathleen to dance before Shane could do so.

A middle-aged woman came over to young Sullivan. "Jamie, it's a dance I'll be havin' with ye."

From the close facial resemblance, Shane guessed the woman was Sullivan's mother.

"Go ahead, Jamie," Siobhan urged. "Dance with yer mam."

He did, and Shane turned to her. "May I have the honor of this dance?"

"Wouldn't be fittin', ye bein' a guest at the big house and me only a maid."

"Why not let me be the judge of that?"

"Go with him, lass," Conn Malone said. "A fine dancer, he is."

Siobhan let Shane lead her out to the floor.

After the dance, as he returned her to her betrothed, she said, "Conn's right. A fine dancer ye be."

Shane left her with Jamie and moved away, looking for Kathleen. Finally, he saw her across the room and hurried to her side.

When he sought the next dance with her, she warned teasingly, "If you keep asking me, people will think you're sweet on me."

He answered with utmost seriousness, "People would be right."

Her smile vanished. "You don't mean that. You don't know me well enough."

"I know you better than you think, *alainn*." He led her out to the floor.

When the music ended, a man Shane did not know claimed Kathleen for the next dance. Reluctantly, Shane retired to the sidelines where he could watch her. Kathleen reminded him so much of his mother. She too had been a lively Irish colleen, full of energy and high spirits, with a love for music and dancing and people, especially children. And like Kathleen, his mother had had a strong sense of justice.

Conn Malone came up to Shane. "Talkin' to the men I've been, and if you have enough to pay the *tuiodoir* for the McNultys' roof, we'll start bringin' the reeds he needs tomorrow and cleanin' up the place."

"Wonderful!" Shane exclaimed. "The sooner the better for Maurea's sake. If you will give me the directions, I will ride to see the thatcher in the morning. If I can meet his price, I will ask him to start as quickly as he possibly can."

"A good man ye are, Shane Howard," Conn said as he turned away.

Will you still think so when you discover who I really am? Shane wondered sadly, watching Malone head toward a red-bearded man near the door.

When the music stopped, Shane looked around intent on reclaiming Kathleen, but before he could do so, a pretty colleen came up and boldly asked him to dance with her. Although he much preferred Kathleen as his partner, he agreed politely and returned to the floor with her.

From across the room, Kathleen observed Muire O'Rourke asking Shane to dance. The jealousy that spurted through Kathleen caught her by surprise. Why, she had not felt so much as a twinge of jealousy the once or twice Patrick had danced with another woman. So why should she feel it now—and for an Englishman?

No, a half-Irishman, she corrected herself, as though that made all the difference.

She thought of what he had said about being sweet on her. The wave of happiness that swept over her at his admission was so potent and unexpected that her heart beat like a *bodhran*.

Kathleen quickly reminded herself his being sweet on her did not mean his intentions were honorable. She dared not let herself believe they were. After all, she had a daughter to protect.

And her own heart.

Still, Kathleen could not remember when she'd had such a wonderful time at a dance. Not only had Patrick hated to dance, but he had not liked her to do so with other men. Patrick had made this clear to both her and them. They'd soon stopped asking. So she'd been forced to stand on the sidelines, yearning to be out on the floor.

That was why tonight she'd asked Shane to dance with Mrs. McNulty and the widow O'Connor. She understood how much these women enjoyed dancing.

Kathleen watched Shane as he moved through the intricate steps of the dance with a grace that thrilled her.

Siobhan came up beside her. "A fine dancer's Mr. Howard, and a real gentleman he seems too. Us maids at the big house all like him."

"Only *seems* a gentleman, Siobhan?" Kathleen asked teasingly.

The maid hesitated, her face troubled. She clearly wanted to tell Kathleen something and was having trouble with how to say it. Something about Shane distressed her.

Alarmed, Kathleen demanded, "What is it, Siobhan?"

The girl hesitated, then asked in a rush, "Do ye know who the handsome child be in the miniature Mr. Howard keeps by his bed?"

"What? How old a child?"

"Young—maybe three or four, with eyes and smile so like Mr. Howard's I'm wonderin' if it be his son."

Kathleen felt as though a sneak blow had just knocked the breath from her. Dear God, did Shane have a wife and son?

Chapter 17

Kathleen knew the maid meant the question as a kindly warning to her. "Thank you, Siobhan. Sure, and I'll be finding out."

The maid opened her mouth to say something more, but her soft voice could not be heard over an exchange of loud drunken shouts outside.

Siobhan grimaced. "It's Paddy Connaught and his drunken friends with a jug o' homemade whiskey."

Kathleen suppressed a groan. Under the best of circumstances Paddy hadn't the sense of a goose. Whiskey made him belligerent and combative, eager to start a fight or avenge some slight. She hoped he would not make trouble tonight.

She had not wanted Paddy in the Knights, but Conn Malone had convinced her the man would be more dangerous outside the organization than in it.

"To become a Knight he must take an oath of abstinence from drink and obedience to his captain when he's wearin' the Knights' shirt," Conn had argued. "Better to have him sober a little while and under control than off raisin' hell on his own."

After a minute, the clamor outside quieted down.

Kathleen and Siobhan exchanged looks of relief.

What the maid had told Kathleen dimmed her smile for Shane when he appeared at her side for the next dance. She was uncharacteristically silent and serious. All through the dance, she berated herself for not listening to her initial intuition that he must have children of his own.

As the music ended, Shane took her arm firmly in his hand and guided her from the floor and through the door into the night.

"What are you doing?" she demanded.

He turned to face her, wrapping his hands around hers, squeezing them reassuringly. She thrilled at the comfort and protection they seemed to offer, but after what Siobhan had told her, she wondered whether she dared trust him. She stiffened against his touch. Did he merely want her in his bed, or did he really care about her?

"Tell me what is troubling you, *alainn*."

How discerning he was. Patrick, never the most perceptive of men, would not have noticed anything amiss.

Kathleen was not a woman to hide behind coyness or euphemisms, and she asked bluntly, "Who is the child in the miniature that you keep beside your bed?"

His gaze met hers squarely, without evasion. "My son."

Even though this was the answer she feared, she flinched when she heard it. At least he did not try to lie to her.

"My *dead* son." Shane's voice sounded as though it came from the tomb where the boy lay. "My only child."

The agony she saw in his eyes brought a gasp to her lips. Her mother's heart went out to him. She understood his disconsolate grief. Were anything to happen to her precious Brigid she would feel the same way.

"He died five months ago. Until then he was my life."

"What of his mother?" The question popped out of Kathleen's mouth before she could stop it. She clamped her mouth shut, but her heart seemed to suspend beating as she awaited his answer.

"She died six years ago, giving birth to our son." For a moment, Shane seemed lost in his private hell, and Kathleen's heart wept for him. She knew what it was to have lost a spouse.

But then to lose one's only child besides.

It was unthinkable, beyond bearing. If Brigid were to die, Kathleen would want to curl up in the grave with her.

Now Kathleen understood the haunting sadness in Shane's eyes when he'd looked at Brigid that first day.

His gaze focused on Kathleen, and she saw disappointment in his eyes. He dropped her hands as though they suddenly burned him. "So you believe I am unfaithful to my wife and trifling with you. What a poor sort of man you think me, *alainn*."

"I didn't know what to think," she replied honestly. "So shocked I was when I heard about the miniature."

"Siobhan told you." It was not a question but a statement.

"Oh, please, don't be angry with her." This time it was Kathleen who seized his hands. "She meant it for the best. Perplexed more than anything, she was. She clearly likes you, and most rare that is. Canamara's maids usually despise His Devilship's guests."

From inside the hall came the announcement that the next dance would be the final one of the night.

As the musicians struck up, Kathleen asked, "If you do not mind my asking, how did your son die?"

"Consumption. You see why I want Maurea out of that damp cave. I could not save my son's life, but perhaps I can help save hers."

In the moonlight, Kathleen saw tears in Shane's eyes. He pulled his hands from hers and rubbed at his eyes, clearly embarrassed. "You must think me a fool, *alainn*."

She thought him the dearest man she had ever met.

This realization both stunned and intrigued her. "*Nil*, your tears show me that at heart you are a true Irishman." She smiled at him.

He returned the smile, his eyes glowing. "I think that may be the nicest compliment anyone ever paid me."

Inside, the musicians were playing the final bars of the night's last dance. Kathleen held out her hand to Shane again. "Come, will you walk me home?"

He held her gaze for a long moment, then took her hand.

She delighted in the gentle strength of his long fingers wrapped around hers. And the love and grief she'd seen in his eyes for his lost son spoke volumes about his character. She held that knowledge close to her heart like the winter memory of a perfect summer day.

From time to time puffy clouds drifted across the face of a bright moon, momentarily darkening the path they followed toward Rose Cottage.

By the time they reached a narrow bridge across

the stream, the clouds had moved on, and they stopped to admire the moonlit water plunging down a series of small cascades. The scent of roses and lavender drifted over the night. Somewhere in the distance, a nightingale trilled its sweet song.

"How lovely it is here," Kathleen murmured. She felt Shane's gaze upon her.

"Not nearly so lovely as you, *alainn*." Shane cupped his hand and placed it beneath her chin, turning her face toward his in the silver moonlight.

He watched her, his eyes glowing with appreciation and something else Kathleen could not define. "If I do not kiss you now, I will go mad."

Her heart pounded in anticipation as Shane lowered his head and his mouth moved ever so slowly to claim hers. It was as if he was giving her time to back away if she did not want this.

But she did want it.

She ached for it.

For him.

With a sudden wanton impatience that startled her, she turned toward him and raised her lips to meet his.

There was nothing tentative about this kiss. It was fierce and wild, hungry and passionate. On and on it went, a man and a woman exploring their feelings for each other and discovering unexpected depths and heights.

With a flash of insight, Kathleen realized it was the clinging of a man and a woman who had believed the light of love had been forever extinguished in their lives and were now discovering that perhaps they were wrong.

He moaned softly, and Kathleen wondered if his body felt as heated and excited as hers suddenly did.

He buried his fingers in her hair, and she could feel him removing the pins and combs that struggled to hold the untamed locks in place.

She felt her wild mane tumble down, covering her shoulders and back. He combed through the thick curtain with his fingers.

"So lovely, *alainn*, so lovely," he murmured.

His fingers massaged her head gently, sending contrary sensations of relaxation and excitement through her. "How good that feels," she murmured.

Clouds rolled across the moon again, blotting it out.

He turned her around so that her back was to him and massaged her neck and shoulders, banishing the tension there and feeding a desire for his touch in more intimate places.

"You have magic hands," she whispered dreamily.

He turned her to face him, and again he kissed her, this time with loving thoroughness and growing passion.

Raindrops began to fall on them. Still they clung to each other, reluctant to leave the moment. Finally though, as the drizzle grew heavier, they moved on again, hand in hand.

After a while the sprinkles and the clouds disappeared again. Shane looked at Kathleen and was proud and happy that this remarkable woman walked beside him in the moonlight. He could not help smiling as he remembered Kathleen's passionate defense of him to Seamus Malone.

From her response to his kisses, he suspected she would be even more passionate in other, most pleasurable ways.

Lucky, the man who won this woman's heart.

And he wanted to be that man, wanted to spend the rest of his life with Kathleen.

He no longer wanted her to share only his bed, but also his life.

He wanted her to be his wife, his marchioness.

And he wanted to be Brigid's da.

Between them, mother and daughter had dissolved the numbness that had gripped him since his son's death. They had helped him to heal.

Life was worth living again.

Happiness beckoned like a lighthouse in the darkness.

At least until Kathleen learned his real identity. After she discovered he was "Devil" Sherbourne, he would not stand a snowflake's chance in hell of winning her.

Even if he could convince her he had not ordered Patrick killed, had not even known of his murder, she would hate Shane for having deceived her about his identity, and he could not blame her.

But neither could he bear to lose her now. He loved her too much. Shane was caught in a trap that he himself had unwittingly constructed. What was he to do?

Kathleen was not a woman who would give herself lightly to a man. But once she did, she would be his for life.

He could think of only one possible path, one slight glimmer of hope. Frantic as he was to win her, his only tenuous hope of doing so lay in seducing her into loving him before she learned who he really was.

At the same time, it went against his grain as a man of integrity not to tell her the truth, but he could see no other route. He hated himself for continuing to deceive her, but he felt trapped, unwilling to do anything that might cost him this woman.

Shane had to bind Kathleen's heart to his own so tightly that nothing could break these ties. Even the revelation of his true identity, when it came, would not be able to fatally wound her feelings for him. And her love for him would help her accept that he was not guilty of the crimes of which he was accused, including her husband's murder.

He hoped he would have enough time to make her his before she learned the truth, but he could not push her too fast.

And to ease his conscience, he swore to himself he would tell Kathleen the truth before he asked her to marry him.

She had to know to whom she would be committing herself.

They were almost to Rose Cottage when Shane stopped. Surprised, Kathleen glanced at him questioningly.

"Please, sit here with me for a few minutes." He tugged her gently down beside him on the fallen trunk of a large oak.

She was happy to join him there, for she was reluctant to part from him tonight.

A shaft of moonlight illuminated him through the space the downed tree had left in the leafy canopy above them. The look in his eyes as he gently took her face between his hands set her heart to beating triple time.

He bathed her face with kisses, then her throat. His hands slid from her face to the buttons of her bodice. He lifted his head. "May I, *alainn*?"

She nodded, a little dazed by the strength of the sensations he had aroused in her.

His fingers nimbly unfastened the buttons. His mouth rained more kisses on her neck and breasts. Then his lips sucked one pink crest. Kathleen felt as though her body had been set afire.

All the need and passion that she had suppressed since her husband's death exploded within. She pulled his shirt from his waistband and pushed her hands beneath the much laundered material, testing the hair of his chest that felt like raw silk beneath her fingers.

They explored each other with questing hands and lips. After a while, he lifted her in his arms and placed her gently on the bed of fallen leaves beside the downed trunk. He joined her there, pulling her against the hardness of his body, caressing her with busy, talented hands.

Places in Kathleen's body that she thought had died with Patrick now came alive and begged for Shane's attention.

He gave it, his hand moving slowly up her thigh to her secret place, already crying its welcome to him. She saw his delighted smile as he discovered the moistness. His finger tormented the hidden folds with slow, sure movements.

Then a shout in the distance, too far away to make out the words, spoiled the silence, and Kathleen froze. To her, it was a cry recalling her to sanity—and to guilt.

"Dear God, what am I doing?" Her breast heaved with desire, yet she tried to scoot away. Even though her body yearned for him to continue, she was no loose woman who gave herself to a man like this. And him an Eng—no, a half-Irishman.

She saw the questions flicker across the masculine planes of Shane's face as she waged silent battle with herself, reason warring with passion.

"I can't let you make love to me. Can you understand?" she asked despairingly, not certain that she did herself.

"Yes, it is too soon for you." His expression was a peculiar mixture of sympathy and disappointment. "You are not a woman who gives herself easily to a man ... but still you need what I can give you."

She stared up at him. It was as though he had read her mind and given voice to her own thoughts, as though he could feel the burning ache that pulsed through her body.

He smiled at her, a sad, knowing smile. "So at least, *alainn*, let me give you what you want." His hand, still buried beneath her skirt, resumed its courtship of her womanhood.

Had he given her the chance, she would have felt embarrassed that he'd so accurately read her need. But desire spiraled again, so hot, so fast, all other thought vanished. All she could do was *feel*.

With clever, deft hands he brought her to the brink of madness, held her there. No man had ever ministered to her this way, so selflessly, so expertly.

She writhed in pleasure, and then she shattered in a glorious release. So powerful were the tremors that shook her she was caught between ecstasy and amazement.

Kathleen gasped for breath, feeling as though she were in heaven and drifting gently on the arms of a cloud.

But it was Shane's arms that held her, and now he smiled down at her in the moonlight. "I think, *alainn*, you enjoyed that."

The pleasure he'd just given her went far beyond

mere enjoyment, far beyond anything she'd experienced before. She could not find words to express what she felt.

But what of him? He had pleasured her, yet she had given him nothing in return. But she was not—

"Nil, *alainn*, for now that is all." Again he seemed to read her mind. "Only when you have no more reservations do I want you to give yourself to me."

Kathleen looked at his face in the moonlight. He called her *alainn*, but to her eye, he was the one who was beautiful with those glorious lashes, thick and black, sweeping over his eyelids, his elegantly sculpted nose, and his well-formed mouth.

Dear God, with all the responsibilities resting on her shoulders, this was the wrong time to fall in love.

And the wrong man.

But was it already too late?

Chapter 18

⟨~∽OᴼC~⟩

In the kitchen of Rose Cottage, Kathleen savored the taste of Shane's goodnight kiss on
her lips and wished that he were still with her.

When he left after bringing her home from the
dance, her emotions were still in too much turmoil
for her to go upstairs to bed, and she decided to
make a cup of tea first.

Now as she waited for it to steep, her body still
hummed with the pleasure he had given her.

Kathleen thought she heard a quick rap at the
cottage's back door. But the sound was so soft she
decided it must have been her imagination.

Then she heard it again. She hurried to the door
and whispered, "Who's there?"

"It's Danny Malone with a note fer you from me
da."

Kathleen's heart sank. Danny was Conn's youn-
gest son. And Conn, one of only three men who
knew she was Captain Starlight, could have a single reason for sending her a message at this ungodly hour.

Trouble.

With a worried sigh, she unbolted and opened

the upper half of the door. Danny handed her the note.

After thanking him, she shut the half-door, lighted a candle in the turf coals glowing in the fireplace, and read the note by the taper's weak light.

As Kathleen had feared might happen, Paddy Connaught in his cups had harangued a half-dozen other drunks. They had set out for Canamara's park looking for trouble.

Kathleen only hoped that Captain Starlight could reach them in time to head them off. She ran out to the shed where she hid her uniform and, shivering in the cold early morning air, donned it quickly.

As Shane emerged from the frigid water of the stream, he wondered if Kathleen could possibly guess what it had cost him not to let her reciprocate the pleasure he had given her tonight.

He had nothing with which to dry himself, save his shirt. As he used it for this purpose, he cut directly across the park toward the house. He was too bloody cold to stop and dry himself or to keep to the more roundabout path. The temperature must have dropped ten degrees while he'd been in the water. He could not stop shivering.

What a damn fool thing to have done, but he'd been desperate to stop the intensely painful need for Kathleen that racked his body.

By the time he finished using his shirt as a towel, it was too soaked for him to wear. He hung it on the branch of a bush while he pulled on his coat. Then he set off again, carrying the wet shirt in his hand.

As he hurried up the hill past a large clump of

wild rhododendron that stood taller than himself, he heard drunken curses from beyond the bushes.

He stopped in his tracks, wondering if he were the target of the voices. They fell silent, but a moment later he heard another voice, this one pitched too low for him to make out what was being said.

Shane crept closer to the rhododendron and nearly tripped over a large boulder in the darkness. He hoped his chattering teeth would not betray him.

As he searched the heavy foliage of the bushes for a peekhole through the leaves, he heard the low voice, clearly quite sober, again. It was berating someone called Paddy.

Finally Shane managed to find a space in the foliage through which he could see. The moonlight illuminated the profile of a man in a green uniform. A green hood covered his entire head and neck, making identification impossible.

Captain Starlight.

He was not as large a man as Shane would have expected, and, despite his broad shoulders, the rest of him was surprisingly slim.

Half a dozen burly men, who appeared to be in various stages of advanced drunkenness, faced the captain.

"Now go home and be quick about it, Paddy and the rest of ye," the captain ordered, "or ye'll be ousted from the Knights for breakin' yer solemn oath."

"Ne'er broke me oath in me life," Paddy protested in slurred tones.

"Not yet, but ye will if ye disobey me order to disperse and go home."

The smallest man of the group tugged at Paddy's sleeve. "He's right, Paddy. Took an oath before

God to obey the cap'n, we did. So ye be comin' along with me now."

Although Paddy grumbled loudly, he allowed himself to be led away, and the other men followed.

Captain Starlight headed in a different direction. Shane wanted to follow him, but he was so cold he had to get back to the house and warm himself or he could be in serious trouble.

Cursing his luck that prevented him from following the man, Shane started toward the house. At least now, though, he had some idea of the captain's height and build.

Early the following afternoon, Shane slowed his sorrel gelding to a walk as he approached the narrow bridge where he had first met Kathleen. He should have continued up the lane that led directly to the great house, but instead he followed the path to Rose Cottage. He had no reason to visit there except his yearning to see Kathleen. He loved her, and he wanted desperately to make her his own. But he feared he would fail.

And the possibility shriveled his heart.

When he reached the cottage, Brigid was playing in the yard. "S'ane, will you be stopping for tay?"

"Of course." He quickly dismounted.

As he stepped through the gate, flanked by fragrant rose bushes, Kathleen came down the path toward them. She fixed her attention on her daughter and did not look at Shane. He suspected she was embarrassed by her passionate response to him last night.

"It's to tay I've invited S'ane, and he's accepting."

Kathleen's gaze met Shane's for the first time.

She smiled at him almost shyly, a blush rising on her cheeks.

He winked at her and her color deepened. She looked so young and beautiful and flustered, it was all he could do to keep from kissing her.

As he followed Kathleen and Brigid into the kitchen, he was struck by the sensation he had felt before of having come home at last. How much more inviting he found this large, cheerful room than any at Canamara or even at Sherwood, his principal estate in England.

"So it's tay ye be wantin'," Maggie said from in front of the fireplace. "A few minutes, then, it'll be."

She bustled about pouring boiling water into a porcelain teapot from the kettle suspended over the peat coals in the fireplace. She covered the pot with a cozy while the tea brewed.

"I am in no hurry," Shane answered with a smile. Indeed he was not. He'd be happy to stay here for as long as they would let him.

Kathleen and Shane sat down at the trestle table, and Brigid ran over to tell Maggie about a strange bird she had seen and did not recognize.

As her daughter chattered, Kathleen asked Shane quietly, "Where have you been riding?" She seemed to have recovered from her earlier embarrassment.

"To see the *tuiodoir* about thatching the roof on the cottage for the McNultys."

"And?"

"He will do it."

"Wonderful! Waste no time, do you?" Amusement and some other emotion Shane could not read gleamed in her eye. Her tone turned teasing.

"And it's not even Monday. Perhaps you're not a true Irishman after all."

Puzzled, he inquired, "What do you mean by that?"

"Sure, and don't you know about Monday and Irishmen?"

Kathleen's smile was so infectious that Shane was swept by an overwhelming desire to take her in his arms.

"No important undertaking in Ireland can begin except on Monday morning," she explained. "Always it's 'On Monday morning, we'll do this,' and 'On Monday morning, we'll do that.' A true Irishman would've put off hiring the *tuiodoir* until Monday."

"And what about a true Irish woman?"

"Ah, then, she'd not be wasting her time till Monday comes. Far too much to do, she has, for that nonsense."

"You admit your countrymen are guilty of nonsense?" he teased, winking at her again. "But I promise it will be our secret forever."

"When will the *tuiodoir* begin work?"

"Tomorrow." Shane grinned. "Now I know why he is so eager to start then. It's Monday."

Brigid skipped back to the table. "Maggie says the tay's ready."

Kathleen removed the cozy from the pot and poured the tea.

"Can I have a biscuit, Mama?" Brigid asked.

"Don't be spoiling your dinner. Remember we're invited to the Farrells today."

Acute disappointment seized Shane. He had hoped to dine at Rose Cottage tonight. He remembered the truant he'd met in the Vale of Kincaid. "Are they Jimmy Farrell's parents?"

"His aunt and uncle," Kathleen said.

"Is Jimmy still skipping school?"

She smiled. "No. He's been there every day since we met him."

"You clearly put the fear of God into him," Shane observed.

"Or at least of his parents," Kathleen observed, her eyes bright with amusement.

"What of Mike Kelly?" Maggie asked. "Has he come back to school?"

The sparkle faded from Kathleen's eyes. "No, nor do I think he will while I am the teacher, more's the pity. Such a bright, delightful child. Too ashamed to face me, I'm fearing."

"Ashamed? Why?" Shane inquired.

"His father is Alban Kelly, the gamekeeper."

Shane's eyes widened. *And the man who fatally shot your husband.* Yet Shane was not surprised that she clearly felt no animosity toward Kelly's son. She was too wise and kind to blame an innocent boy for his father's sin.

"Talk to his mother," Maggie advised.

"I've tried, but she'll not answer the door to anyone, especially me."

So that was why Shane's knocks the several times he'd visited the gamekeeper's cottage had received no response.

After a while, Maggie lured Brigid outside with the promise of pushing her in her swing.

"Don't you want to come with us, S'ane?" the little girl asked as she followed Maggie.

"*Nil*, Brigid, he wants to talk to your mama," Maggie said quickly.

Bless you, Shane thought, giving Maggie a grateful smile.

When they were gone, he said, "Tell me about

Seamus Malone." He wanted to hear Kathleen's assessment of the man who loved her.

"A good man is Seamus . . ."

Shane's jealousy sprang to life again.

". . . but too impetuous and hotheaded." Kathleen sighed. "A pity it is, for otherwise he'd have made as good a leader as his father was, but he has not Conn's patience and farsightedness."

Shane let out a breath he'd not been conscious of holding, and his green-eyed monster retreated. "Then Seamus is not Captain Starlight." Not that Shane had thought he was. The man was too big.

"No." Her eyes narrowed suddenly and an odd flush crept into her cheeks. "And don't be asking me who he is for I'll not be telling you."

Her change of color puzzled Shane. "Which means you know him."

She shrugged. "*Nil*, I do not know him."

Something about the way she accented her answer fired a sudden unwelcome suspicion in Shane as to Captain Starlight's identity.

He prayed that he was wrong.

Chapter 19

Shane had been gone from Rose Cottage only two or three minutes when a knock sounded on the front door. Thinking he had returned, Kathleen's breath quickened. She turned away from the small mirror in the hall, still holding the bonnet she'd been about to don, and opened the door.

Oliver Radnor stood on the doorstep, his gray eyes narrowed in furious slits. "What was that damn Howard doing here?"

She had never seen little Ollie so angry, and she was as much taken aback by that as by his rude question. "No business of yours is it," she answered sharply.

"I pray you did not talk to him about those damn Irish hooligans driving the Tiltons from their farm and burning it."

Puzzled, she asked, "And why would it matter if I did?"

"I had hoped to keep what happened there from Sherbourne, but now I will not be able to do so. Howard will tell him."

"What if he does? Why would you want to keep the burning of the Malone farm from Sherbourne? I should think you'd be wanting him to know the hatred and hostility his policies are breeding."

"You think things are bad here now." Radnor snorted. "His Lordship warned me if anything like what happened to the Tiltons occurred on his property, he would send in troops to ferret out those responsible, and he will see them all hanged."

A shiver of fear shook Kathleen, and she only barely managed to suppress her involuntary urge to bring her hands to her vulnerable neck. But she refused to be cowed.

Stiffening her spine, she pointed out, "I can't see it matters whether Howard knows. The Tiltons, who are Sherbourne's friends, will surely tell him themselves, whether Mr. Howard does or not."

For a moment, Radnor seemed at a loss for words. Then he said sharply, "Be very careful what you tell Howard. He is Sherbourne's spy."

Kathleen's jaw dropped in surprise. Dear God in heaven, was that true? "How do you know that?"

"His Lordship's secretary is my friend, and he warned me."

"But why would His Devilship send a spy here?" Kathleen asked incredulously.

"To ferret out Captain Starlight and his followers and see them hanged. His Lordship apparently heard rumors about them. Not, however, from me."

Kathleen fought down a momentary panic and applied reason to the situation. "If Mr. Howard is a spy sent to do that, I should think, since he speaks excellent Gaelic, he would have come here disguised as an Irishman. He would not be openly living at Canamara as a guest of His Lordship."

Having said this aloud, Kathleen felt calmer.

"Ah, but you see, he said that was what people

would think, and they would be less apt to suspect him if he came as he has."

If Shane was what Radnor said, Kathleen had made a terrible mistake telling him all that she had.

And an even greater mistake in letting yourself care so much for him. Kathleen felt as though her heart were shattering like a porcelain plate dropped on granite rock.

"Howard is also spying on me," Radnor said.

"Why would he be doing that?"

"Because whenever I possibly could, I mitigated Sherbourne's cruel orders, and he now suspects that. Take your own situation. Exorbitant as your rent is, he wants to raise it even higher. Thus far, I have managed to dissuade him, but I can do so no longer."

She recalled what Shane had said. "You told Mr. Howard you let me have Rose Cottage rent free."

"I told him nothing of the sort!" Radnor answered indignantly. "He clearly chose to misunderstand what I said."

"And what was that?"

"I said *if I were His Lordship,* who after all ordered your husband murdered, I would at least allow you to live in the cottage rent free. As I have learned to my regret, however, His Lordship seems to have no conscience. But I have thought of a way to outwit him on his latest rent increase."

"What is it?"

He lowered his voice to a whisper. "It must be between the two of us. Perhaps we could go into the parlor where no one else will hear us."

Radnor's conspiratorial manner unsettled Kathleen. He had always acted with perfect propriety toward her, but his behavior now alarmed her.

"Oh, the parlor is all shut up and much too stuffy. Let us go outside instead."

She brushed past him and stepped into the yard.

He followed her, leaning so close to her that her nose twitched in revulsion at the heavy, musky scent he wore. How much she preferred the subtle, spicy fragrance that clung to Shane Howard. "And how is it you propose to outwit His Devilship?"

Radnor gave her an oily smile that set off an alarm in Kathleen's brain. "You must know how much I admire you."

"Do you indeed?" she asked warily, afraid she knew what was coming next. "I had no idea."

"I assure you I do. You will not have to pay the rent increase." He eyed her slyly. "Or any rent at all."

Kathleen pretended wide-eyed innocence. "But how can that be?"

"You can live in the great house."

He reached for her hand and would have taken it in his own, but she snatched it away and put it to her mouth as though his offer astonished her. The mere thought of his touch made her skin crawl. "I . . . I do not understand." Unfortunately, she understood all too well.

"Would you not love to live in such splendor?"

She shook her head. "No, a much greater fondness have I for my simple Rose Cottage."

"You cannot mean that," he protested incredulously. "Only think, you would eat in the grand dining room off fine silver and china and be wait—"

She interrupted him. "And me not knowing which fork and spoon to use"—which was a lie, for she knew very well. Radnor had no notion of her wealthy, privileged background. "Mortified, I should be."

"I will teach you," he said smugly. "I shall make you very happy."

She widened her eyes in feigned surprise. "Why, Mr. Radnor, are you proposing marriage?" she asked, knowing full well he was doing no such thing.

For an instant his eyes hardened, but then he was all smiles again. "I wish so much that I could, but Sherbourne would never permit it. He would turn us out in an instant because I am English, and he is rabidly opposed to intermarriage with the Irish."

"Is he now? A bit of a surprise that is, him being the product of such a union."

Radnor shifted from foot to foot for a minute. "Ah, well, ah, perhaps that is why he is so adamant on the subject. I am told he was ashamed of his mother because she was Irish."

Kathleen felt only disgust for any son who could feel that way about the woman who had given him birth.

"He hates anything and anyone Irish. He refuses even to set foot in this country."

"Sure, and sorry I am for him. He knows not what he is missing." Kathleen turned and strode toward the door of Rose Cottage as though their conversation were concluded.

Radnor came after her, grabbing her hand. "What of my offer?"

His fingers were thick and stubby, his palm clammy. Kathleen could scarcely keep from shuddering. She recalled last night. Shane's long, shapely hands had been lean and strong. And his fingers. Ah, those talented fingers!

She pulled her hand away from little Ollie's

grasp and faced him. "I'm shocked, Mr. Radnor. A respectable woman, I am—a widow and the mother of a little daughter for whom I must set a good example."

She turned away and, with head held proudly, started back into the house.

He seized her arm roughly with his hand and jerked her around to face him again. "You must tell no one, especially not Sherbourne's spy Howard, what I have suggested. I warn you that Howard will try to wheedle whatever information he can from you about me. He's handsome and he knows it. He has already seduced three of the poor stupid maids who bring him his bath."

Kathleen felt as though a bull had just gored her in the stomach. She gaped at Radnor, unable to hide her shock.

He looked triumphant. "Ah, I see word of such reprehensible behavior rightfully disturbs you."

Yes, it did. But surely Radnor must be lying.

Or was she merely lying to herself rather than facing the truth about Shane's character? Kathleen remembered how seductive—and persuasive— Shane had been the previous night with her. Dear God in heaven, was she just another easy conquest for him?

"Now you know how despicable Howard's real character is," Radnor said. With that, he turned and stalked down the walk. Kathleen shut the cottage door, her emotions roiling.

If what Radnor said about Shane being a spy was true, she should have nothing more to do with him.

Anger set in.

But Kathleen was not certain at whom it was directed.

At Radnor, if he were lying.

At Shane, if he were indeed a spy for her husband's murderer.

As Shane rode up the hill to Canamara, he looked out upon the pristine beauty, lush and verdant, of its park.

Three deer wandered among the greenery in the distance. Shane observed with disgust that these animals looked considerably better fed than most of the estate's Irish tenants.

Fury and impatience rose in equal measure in Shane, but for now he would have to content himself with catching fish and hunting game in the park to distribute among the tenants. Perhaps he would also raid Canamara's larder.

When Shane reached the house, the footman Dobbins opened the door to him, his eyes lingering on the frayed collar of his shirt. "Visitors await you in the drawing room."

Since no one Shane had met since he'd been at Canamara would be likely to call on him at the great house, he exclaimed in surprise, "Who are they?"

"Sir Tobias Smoot, his lady, and daughter." Dobbins sounded as though he thought the Smoots paid Shane a great honor by calling on him.

He frowned, for he recognized the name. His grandfather had written him that he had no use for his neighbor Smoot, whom he characterized as a weakling who drank too much and a gambler living far beyond his means, who held a vastly inflated opinion of himself. His grandfather had wanted nothing to do with the man and advised Shane to follow the same policy once he inherited Canamara.

Shane, who valued his grandfather's judgment,

sighed wearily. He had hoped to avoid local society in general and those the old Lion had so disliked in particular. "I suppose I must see them. You need not bother to announce me, Dobbins."

Shane strode into the drawing room to greet his visitors. They did not immediately notice him, giving him a moment to take their measure.

Short and rotund, Smoot had the unhealthy complexion of a man who spent much of his time in his cups. His gaze was fixed longingly on the decanter of brandy on a pier table between the windows.

His wife, thin and equally short, with the small, narrowed eyes and downturned mouth of a disapproving shrew, looked to be busily engaged in estimating the monetary value of the room's contents.

Their daughter was more attractive than Shane would have suspected, given her parentage. Or at least she would have been had it not been for her sullen expression that indicated louder than words she did not want to be there.

Her lovely pink silk gown trimmed with lace showed her complexion and figure to excellent advantage, but it was far too light for such a cool, damp evening. She appeared to be in her midtwenties, an age at which an unmarried woman was considered firmly on the shelf.

Shane knew immediately the reason for their visit. He had seen too many determined mamas seeking husbands for their aging daughters not to recognize Lady Smoot's intentions.

"Good evening, I am Shane Howard. You wished to see me?"

Two pairs of female eyes instantly fastened on him. Their disparate reactions amused Shane so much, he had difficulty keeping a straight face.

As Mama studied his worn, unfashionable clothes, her initial eagerness faded to dismay. His inelegant garments told her he was not prosperous enough for her daughter's hand.

Her daughter, on the other hand, after a sulky first glance at Shane, visibly brightened and gave him a longer, more appreciative perusal.

The male visitor reluctantly tore his gaze away from the brandy decanter. "Sir Tobias Smoot here. Heard a guest of Lord Sherbourne's was visiting. Since we are the marquess's nearest neighbors, my lady and I felt it our duty to come over to welcome you to County Kerry." Tobias sounded as though he had rehearsed this speech several times.

Shane suspected that if Smoot had not had an unmarried daughter on the shelf, he would not have been so anxious to welcome a visitor. "How very kind of you."

Smoot inclined his head toward his wife, who remained seated. "This is Lady Smoot."

With her disapproving gaze fixed on Shane's worn clothes, Her Ladyship acknowledged his welcome with an almost imperceptible nod of her head.

"And this is my daughter Alicia."

The younger woman curtsied to Shane, who, in turn, bowed politely in acknowledgment.

"I am sorry if you have been kept waiting," he said. "Indeed, I fear you caught me at a most awkward time. I only returned to the house to change my clothes before going out to dinner." Shane hoped the Smoots would take the hint and depart quickly.

Lady Smoot said coldly, "The footman failed to inform us you had plans for tonight."

"How very remiss of him!" Although Dobbins was innocent of this particular sin, he was guilty of so many others that Shane felt no compunction laying the blame on him.

"Where have you been?" Her Ladyship asked.

"Taking a solitary walk," he lied.

Smoot jerked his attention away from the brandy decanter, where it had again settled. "Hell's bells, man, surely you do not walk *alone*?" He looked aghast.

"Why should I not?" Shane inquired.

"It is not safe, man, you being English and, worse, a guest of Sherbourne."

"Why does being Sherbourne's guest make it worse?"

Lady Smoot answered for her husband. "The Irish hate Sherbourne because he treats them as they deserve to be treated, unlike that stupid grandfather of his who coddled them disgracefully and paid them ridiculously high wages in the bargain."

Shane's anger flared at hearing his grandfather called stupid for treating his people like human beings and paying them wages that permitted them to feed their families. He felt his face harden.

Her Ladyship, however, was too fixated on his clothes to notice. "Why, until old Fitzgerald died, it was nearly impossible to hire servants and laborers at an affordable wage. They had such an inflated view of what they were worth."

The ledgers Radnor sent to Shane in England indicated he still paid those "ridiculously high wages."

"Sherbourne is very lucky to have the younger Mr. Radnor as his agent. Such a fine young man he is, and always so fastidious too." Lady Smoot pointedly looked Shane up and down. "He was well educated in England and knows how a gentleman should dress. He always looks his best."

In his fine clothes paid for by stealing from me and enslaving my tenants.

"And he keeps a firm hand on the rabble," Smoot interjected. "We all envy Sherbourne having Mr. Radnor as his agent."

Smoot was welcome to Radnor. They deserved each other.

Clearly puzzled by Shane's worn clothes, Lady Smoot said slyly, "You must be a close friend of the marquess for him to let you use Canamara."

Her expression told him she was certain that could not be true. He decided to gratify her suspicious mind and put an end to any matchmaking efforts she might still contemplate. "No, but I have been ill, and His Lordship, knowing I yearned to visit Ireland, very kindly offered to let me stay here."

She looked shocked. "Why would he have done that?"

With great satisfaction, Shane repeated what he had told the men in Killoma. "I was his son's tutor."

From the look on Her Ladyship's face, he might as well have said he was a leper.

She rose so hastily that she nearly tripped on her skirts. "Well, then, a good evening to you, Mr. Howard. We would not dream of keeping you from your walk."

He bowed politely to her. "You are very kind, my lady."

Her daughter rose more slowly. Despite Shane's sudden demotion in status, she looked less happy about leaving. Her father, still staring thirstily at the brandy decanter, was the last to ease his bulk from his chair and stand.

His wife swept from the room without a backward glance.

Shane heard Radnor's voice in the hall. "Lady Smoot, are you leaving so soon?"

"Indeed, I am. You did not tell us, Oliver, that Howard is nothing more than the tutor of His Lordship's son."

"What! I did not know myself. His Lordship said nothing in his letter about that."

"I just heard it from the man's own lips," Lady Smoot said.

"I am shocked, truly shocked, my lady."

Shane suspected that for once Radnor was actually telling the truth.

"I had no idea," the agent continued indignantly. "Why, the lying impostor passed himself off as a close friend of His Lordship."

Shane walked over to one of the long windows and watched the Smoots get into their carriage.

"Mr. Howard, I must speak to you," Radnor said, advancing into the drawing room. Gone were his smile and his fawning manner. "Lady Smoot says you are the tutor for His Lordship's son."

"I acted in that capacity."

"Then why did you pass yourself off to me as a close friend of His Lordship?"

"I did not. If you got that impression, it was from Lord Sherbourne's letter introducing me. I suggest you reread it."

"I do not require advice from a damn lowly tutor," Radnor snapped.

"Not as lowly, however, as an estate agent," Shane shot back.

Radnor flushed angrily. "And why would the

marquess write that *you* are his friend?"

"He is not nearly so high in the instep as you are. He and I are very close. Is that what you wished to discuss with me?"

Shane's frigid tone clearly irritated Radnor, and he said sharply, "No. I have just come from Mrs. McNamara's. She complained to me that you are bothering her."

Shane thought of her response to him last night and could hardly suppress a smile. Yes, indeed, he'd bothered her, but not in the way Radnor alleged. What lies had the agent told her about him? Shane had no doubt they would amaze him. When it came to falsehoods, Radnor had the most fertile imagination Shane had ever had the misfortune of encountering.

"She does not want you to go near her or Rose Cottage again."

"If Mrs. McNamara tells me to leave her alone, I will. So far, she has not."

"She begged me to insist that you cease annoying her."

"Really?" Shane's voice dripped with scorn. "Why would she ask you, instead of telling me herself?"

Radnor smirked. "Because she is my mistress."

Not for an instant did Shane believe that. Radnor was lying about Kathleen, just as he lied about every other damn thing. The bastard! It was all Shane could do to keep from giving him the beating he deserved. "Do you intend to marry her?"

The question clearly shocked the agent. "Good God, no! She is Irish."

"What difference does that make?"

Radnor looked at Shane as though he were an idiot. "I am English, sir. I would not lower myself so drastically as to marry an *Irish woman*." His mouth curled in an ugly sneer.

"Then she is free to decide which of us she prefers. May the best man win, Mr. Radnor." Shane turned on his heel and went upstairs, his fingers itching to wrap themselves around the evil little agent's neck.

Chapter 20

D awn was not yet a glimmer on the eastern horizon the next morning when Shane rode out of Canamara's stableyard toward the Vale of Kincaid. His bulging saddlebags were stuffed with cheese, ham, cold beef, bread, and butter that he'd purloined from Canamara's larder.

When he reached the valley, he tied his horse to a gorse bush and distributed all but a small part of the food he'd taken from the larder, quietly leaving it at the entrances of the hovels. He was particularly generous to the McNultys.

As he left the vale, dawn was breaking. He was certain many of the food's recipients would be blessing the *daoine sidh*, the good fairies, for bringing them this windfall.

Shane turned his mount toward the game-keeper's cottage, urging the gelding to a gallop.

At the modest cottage, he tied his horse to the gate. As he strode up the path to the door, it flew open, and a woman emerged. Two ragged, bare-foot children, neither of whom reached to her hip, clung to her skirts.

"And what trouble, then, be ye bringin' me news of at this ungodly hour?" she demanded shrilly.

Shane frowned as he saw the fear on her plain face. Her wide, sagging body bespoke of having borne too many children in too short a time. He remembered Kathleen saying the gamekeeper had nine under the age of twelve. "No trouble," he assured her. "I have merely come to see Alban. Is this not his cottage?"

Relief flashed across her face before her eyes narrowed suspiciously. "Ye won't be findin' himself here. And what ye be wantin' with me Alban?"

Shane smiled at her in the hope of quieting her obvious alarm. "Merely to talk to him. Can you tell me where I would find him?"

She swept her hand toward the hills in the distance. "Most likely ye'll find him wanderin' the bog. But ye'll not be gettin' himself to talk. Mother of God, a miracle it'd be if ye did." She tapped her forehead. "Not quite right in the head is himself since that teacher died."

Shane thanked the woman and rode off. Hunger chewed at his stomach, reminding him that he had not taken time to eat breakfast.

He stopped beside a large rock beneath the spreading branches of a maple. Letting his horse's reins dangle on the ground, he pulled what was left of the food—a little bread and cheese—from his saddlebag. He settled himself against the boulder, using a smaller rock nearby as a makeshift table. He appreciated the maple's shade but his view—of a scraggly hedgerow—left something to be desired.

As he ate, the feeling he was being watched tingled along his nerve endings. He carefully studied the hedgerow. After a minute, he detected a slight movement.

Shane stood up casually and strode to his horse

as though he intended to get something from his saddlebag.

As he deliberately turned his back and bent over the bag, he saw from the corner of his eye a flash of movement through a gap in the hedgerow. He whirled and caught a young boy by a rope tied round his waist to hold up his ragged pants.

The child, as skinny as a young sapling, struggled desperately to escape, but Shane was far too strong for him. Nevertheless, the boy managed to get in a couple of hard kicks to Shane's shins with his bare feet.

Shane grabbed the boy around the arms and the legs to halt his wild flailing. "Stop fighting me or I will take that rope from round your waist and tie you to the tree with it."

The boy apparently did not realize the rope was too short to do that, and he went still in Shane's grip.

Shane set the boy's feet on the ground. Keeping a firm grasp on his shoulders, Shane turned him so they faced one another.

The urchin's blue eyes were huge and terrified in his gaunt face. From his size, Shane guessed his age to be about nine.

"Dia dhuit. Is mise Shane Howard." Shane gave the child the traditional Irish greeting of "God be with you" and told him his name in the hope of putting the child at ease.

"Dia is Muire dhuit." The boy returned the traditional response of "God and Mary be with you." But he did not volunteer his name. When Shane asked him what it was, he stared down at his feet and finally said, "Mike."

Shane remembered what Kathleen had said about Alban Kelly's eldest son. "Mike Kelly, is it?"

The boy's forehead creased in a frown, and he nodded reluctantly as though he expected Shane to turn away from him in disgust. Mike's hungry gaze skittered longingly toward the food Shane had left on the rock.

"Very pleased I would be, Mike, if you would share me breakfast with me." Shane deliberately spoke as the Irish did so that he would not alarm the boy any more than he already was.

The boy's head jerked up, and he stared at Shane with mingled incredulity, hope, and hunger. "Ye not be meanin' that."

"Sure now, and I don't waste words saying what I don't mean."

Shane sat down again by the rock, divided the bread and cheese, and handed half to Mike. The boy hesitated only a half-second before his hunger overcame his doubt. He took the offering and gobbled it up as though he feared Shane might change his mind before he could finish it.

Realizing Mike needed the food far more than he did, Shane gave the rest to the boy. "Eat this a little more slowly so you do not get a stomachache."

Mike did as he was admonished. Between bites, he said, "It's a handsome horse ye have."

Shane smiled. "Would you like to ride him with me?"

For a moment, Mike looked as though he'd just been offered a trip to paradise, then the glow faded from his eyes. "Sure, and ye won't be givin' no ride to the likes of me."

"I'd be honored to give you one," Shane said gravely.

Mike eyed him suspiciously. "Then what'd ye be wantin' to talk to me da fer?"

"I must be a slowtop, Mike, but I can't see how

giving you a ride has anything to do with wanting to talk to your da."

The boy hung his head. "People that know who me da is don't want no'hing to do with me."

"Well, I hate to disappoint you, but I want to take you for a ride. We will go as soon as you finish eating."

And they did. Shane rode through Canamara's park, holding Mike in front of him, keeping up a stream of questions and observations designed to put the boy at ease.

By the time he returned Mike to where he had found him, the boy was talking to Shane as though they were old friends.

But when Shane asked him if he would lead him to his father, the boy suddenly became silent. He did not, however, deny he knew where Alban was.

Much as Shane wanted to talk to the game-keeper, he decided it would be premature to press Mike further today. Instead he headed back to Canamara to explain to Siobhan about the miniature of Jeremy.

After school that afternoon, Kathleen walked along the path to Rose Cottage. Overhead, the rising wind drove dark rain clouds across the sky.

She had slept badly the previous night, thanks to Oliver Radnor. Strange, it was less his dishonorable proposition to her, which was infuriating enough, than his allegations against Shane that had ruined her sleep.

Bad enough that Shane might be the devil's spy, but had he seduced the maids at Canamara? Did he, like every other damn Englishman including little Ollie, think they'd the right to bed any Irish woman they wanted? Damn them all!

Kathleen rounded a bend and saw Shane coming toward her. Her heart skittered at the sight of him, and that made her angry at herself.

She stopped abruptly, noting with perverse pleasure that he looked almost as weary as she felt. "What are you doing here?" The sharpness of her voice startled her as it clearly did him.

He responded with a smile. "Hoping to run into you, *alainn*. Why else would I be here? Will you take me to your school one of these days? I would like to see it."

Remembering what Radnor had said about him, Kathleen's suspicion flared. "Why? Because you are Sherbourne's spy?"

His smile vanished. "Why would you think that?"

"Little Ollie says you are."

Shane's eyes glinted with anger. "He also claims you are his mistress."

Kathleen was so shocked she gasped. "You're hoaxing me."

His lips thinned to a grim line. "No, he told me you were, but I was certain he lied." Shane's eyes reproached her. "Just as he lied to you about me. I am disappointed and hurt that you did not doubt what he said of me."

Kathleen felt herself flushing at Shane's rebuke. "Oh, I did *doubt* it." She wanted to ask him about Radnor's other accusation that he'd seduced the maids, but she could not find the words to do so after Shane's chiding. She told herself this allegation must be as false as Ollie's other one had been. "And I thank you for not believing him about me. Counting chickens he is that'll not be hatching."

"Has he made you, er, an improper offer?"

Shane's expression told her his question

stemmed from concern, not prurient curiosity, and
she answered frankly, "He stopped at Rose Cottage
a few minutes after you left yesterday. Sherbourne
is raising my rent again. Radnor offered to let me
live with him in the great house so I wouldn't have
to pay rent—at least not with money."

"How generous of the bastard! What did you tell
him?"

"That I am not that kind of woman, and I have
a four-year-old daughter to be setting an example
for."

"Radnor is lying about Sherbourne raising your
rent. It is merely a ploy to get you into his bed."

Kathleen blinked. Was little Ollie *that* devious
and manipulative?

"Why do you seem so surprised?" Shane asked.
"You have only Radnor's word for your rent being
raised. And remember he told *me* you paid no rent
at all."

"He says you deliberately misunderstood him on
that point."

Shane laughed. "His ability to explain away his
evil actions never ceases to astonish me." His sensual mouth sobered. "Now listen to me, *alainn*.
Demand to see the written instructions from Sherbourne raising your rent. If Radnor agrees to
show you, take me with you to look at them, for
I know His Lordship's handwriting."

If Shane were right about this, little Ollie was
even more repugnant than Kathleen had begun to
think him.

She stared at Shane silently for a long minute, an
internal battle waging over whether she dared trust
him. What if he were the liar and not little Ollie?

What if Radnor's other accusation against him,
that he had been bedding the maids, was true?

That possibility hurt more than she wanted to admit.

Shane rested his hands gently on her arms, sending an involuntary tremor of excitement through her. "Do you not trust me, Kathleen?"

Dear God in heaven, so much depended on her not making a mistake. Her own life and that of the other Knights of Rosaleen would hang in the balance if she misjudged Shane.

She did not want to leave Brigid an orphan, nor the children of the men she led without fathers.

Kathleen felt as though the weight of the whole county was on her shoulders. She felt overburdened, overwrought, and terribly confused. She didn't know whom or what to believe anymore.

She recalled Shane's horror at the conditions he had seen in the Vale of Kincaid, his concern for little Maurea, his paying the thatcher to put a real roof over the child's head.

Yes, in her heart, Kathleen did trust him.

But was she being a fool, led by her emotions rather than logic?

"Trust me, *alainn*. You will not regret it."

Shane sounded so certain, determined, strong. Kathleen stared up at him. A breeze stirred, wafting stray locks of hair about her face.

He lightly brushed a strand away from her mouth. This gentle skimming of his fingers against her cheek sent an exciting current through her. God help her, she could not resist this man.

"Will you trust me?"

"Yes," she whispered.

He smiled at her, his eyes silently applauding her. Kathleen tingled to the tips of her toes. He made her feel as though she were the most beautiful creature alive.

His lips lowered toward hers, and her heart raced in anticipation.

Shane's mouth courted hers, by turns tender, coaxing, searching, demanding, infinitely exciting, firing her body's cry for more.

His hands joined his mouth in slowly pleasuring her, stroking her hair, skimming her body, cupping her breast.

He groaned and pulled her against him. Kathleen could feel the hard length of his arousal pressed against her, and she yearned to feel him within her, to assuage the hunger that gnawed at her body. She wanted him desperately . . .

"Mama, is that you?"

Kathleen and Shane sprang apart at Brigid's voice only a few yards away. Kathleen stifled a frustrated groan. Of all times for her daughter to appear. For the first time in her life, Kathleen was not entirely overjoyed to see her.

"Late you are, Mama," Brigid said reproachfully. Then she saw Shane, and her eyes lit up. "Oh, S'ane, you're here."

"Yes, *sidhe*, your mama and I were, er, talking."

"Coming to dinner tonight, are you?"

Shane smiled at the little girl. "If your mama invites me."

"She does, don't you, Mama?"

When Kathleen nodded, Shane said, "Let's get the fishing poles, Brigid, and we will see whether we can catch a fish to eat."

The last time he'd fished with Brigid, he'd left the gear at Rose Cottage, saying it was ridiculous to carry it up and down the hill all the time.

A few minutes after Shane and Brigid left with rods in hand, a knock sounded at the door. Fearful that it might be Radnor again, Kathleen answered it reluctantly. "Siobhan, what brings you here?"

"I'm wantin' to set something right about Mr. Howard. An injustice I done him. He told me this morning the little boy in the picture be his son. But the boy's dead and so's his mam."

"So Mr. Howard told me too."

The maid shook her head sorrowfully. "Poor man. No wonder he was lookin' so sad when he came here. What troubles he's had."

Kathleen thought of what Radnor had alleged of Shane. "Siobhan, who are the maids who bring Mr. Howard his bath?"

"None o' us do. Sure, and that's one o' the reasons we like him. He requires the English footmen to bring it to him. He says the water's too heavy for us maids to carry, and right he is. But what a temper he's put them footmen in. Cheerfully murder him in his sleep, they would."

That eased Kathleen's concern, but to eliminate any doubt, she asked, "Has he made any dishonorable advances to any of the maids?"

"*Nil*, a true gentleman he is, always polite and courteous, and ne'er tries to take any o' the liberties with us some o' the other guests have."

Kathleen's relief was so powerful she felt dizzy. She reached out for the door to steady herself.

What a liar Radnor was proving to be.

When Shane and Brigid returned, Kathleen said, "You were gone so long I was getting worried."

"But here we are, safe and sound," Shane answered, handing her the trout he had caught.

They were late because Brigid had shown Shane her secret "fairy" cave, a cavity in a hillside near the stream, only large enough, she assured him, for the "little people." Or, he'd thought with a smile, for a child no bigger than Brigid. But even she might have difficulty getting through the tangle of blackthorn and laurel that concealed the entrance.

Brigid had made Shane promise he would tell no one, not even her mother, who did not believe in fairies, about the cave. The little girl had been so insistent, he'd reluctantly agreed.

Now, rather than explain why they'd been gone so long, he asked Kathleen, "How was school today?"

"In high excitement were the students from the Vale of Kincaid, claiming the little people visited there during the night, leaving food at the doors."

"See, t'ere are fairies, Mama," Brigid piped up, her eyes wide.

Kathleen arched an eyebrow at Shane. "Are there?" she asked so softly only he could hear her.

He asked blandly, "Who do you think it could have been?"

She gave him a suspicious stare, but she did not press the subject.

The rest of the week was busy for Shane. He began each morning before dawn, distributing food from Canamara's larder to the hungry. Then he fished with Brigid and breakfasted at Rose Cottage.

He spent another two or three hours each day searching for Alban Kelly in the mushy bog with its sedges, bogbeans, and hummocks, where the gamekeeper was said to wander. Although Shane did find a sort of desolate beauty to the black bog rush and purple moor grass that grew in tussocks from the hummocks, he uncovered no sign of Alban.

All week the Irish tenants of Canamara carried sheaves of reed to the McNulty cottage and aided

the *tuiodoir* in thatching the roof. Shane helped
the tenants clear the accumulated debris from the
structure and seal the cracks in the walls. The
McNultys would be able to move into the cottage
the following Sunday.

Each night Shane dined at Rose Cottage and became an after-dinner fixture in that inviting
kitchen. He remained after Brigid and Maggie went
to bed to have a little time alone with Kathleen.
These were both the happiest and most frustrating
hours of the day for him.

He ached to make love to her, but where was he
to do it? The privacy required was not to be found
at Rose Cottage. Upstairs Brigid shared Kathleen's
bed. Downstairs Maggie slept in a room between
the kitchen and the never-used parlor.

Even if Kathleen had not been so obviously nervous about Maggie overhearing them, he was not
willing to make love to her on the hard stone floor
of the kitchen or the narrow cushions of the settles,
which were hardly wide enough for one person
and would never accommodate two lovers.

Conscious by now that his real rival for Kathleen's heart was the dead Patrick, Shane wanted
the first time they made love to be perfect for her.

But how was he to do that?

On Saturday, Shane gave up trying to find Alban
Kelly and went looking for his son instead.

Shane found Mike near the boulder where they
had first met.

"I am certain you know where to find your father," Shane told the boy bluntly, "and you must
take me to him."

Mike looked at Shane suspiciously with eyes

older than his years. "Why ye be wantin' ta see him?"

"I want him to tell me what really happened the day Mr. McNamara was killed and who actually killed him." Shane hoped he was guessing right. "I know your father didn't."

The hope that appeared on the boy's face was breathtaking. "How'd ye know me da didn't kill Mr. McNamara?"

"Because I'm convinced Oliver Radnor did."

Mike looked at Shane with such awe and astonishment, he knew his supposition was right. "Did your da tell you who killed Mr. McNamara?"

"Him says he did. Don't dare be sayin' otherwise, but I know the truth."

"How do you know?" Shane asked in surprise.

"Seen it all, I did. Followed me da that day."

"Am I right? Did Oliver Radnor kill Mr. McNamara?"

Mike nodded and broke into a smile. "Afeared I was no one'd believe me. How'd ye know?"

"I know Radnor—unfortunately. Now, tell me what happened."

"Mr. Radnor, he came after me da, sayin' he'd seen Mr. McNamara poachin' game in the beech wood, and me da had to stop him for once and all. If he didn't, me lord markess would be orderin' us from the estate and makin' certain me da never worked again. Me ma, she started cryin' we's all goin' to starve."

The boy paused. "But when me da got to Mr. McNamara, his hands were tied behind his back and his face was all bruised like he'd been in a fight, and a big ugly man were standin' guard over him."

"Did he have a scar down the side of his face?"

Mike nodded. "That be the one. Then Mr. Radnor, he hands me da a pistol and says for him to kill Mr. McNamara for poachin', but me da says he doesn't see no dead game. Mr. Radnor says if da don't do as he's told, the markess'll see me da never works another day in his life."

Mike paused, and Shane prodded, "What happened then?"

"Me da says he can't shoot a helpless man that's got his hands tied behind his back. Mr. Radnor, he keeps cussin' and yellin' at da to do it, but he won't. Finally Mr. Radnor grabs the gun from me da, shoves Mr. McNamara onto his knees, and shoots him in the back o' the head, then says to me da his family'll starve if he don't say he done it."

"Just as I thought," Shane said. "Now will you take me to your father?"

Mike looked frightened. "Gotta ask me da if I can first."

"Tell him you told me the truth and I believe you. I give you and your da my solemn oath that I will protect him if he'll tell what really happened."

"I'll try," Mike promised.

The boy had to succeed. Shane was determined that Radnor would pay for his murder of Kathleen's husband. "Tell your da, it is crucial I talk to him as quickly as possible."

When Kathleen came downstairs that night after tucking her daughter in bed, Shane had pulled one of the settles over near the hearth. He was staring somberly at the glowing coals of the turf fire, which turned the room to a soft, romantic pastel pink.

He had been quiet tonight, and she wondered

what was bothering him. She sat down beside him on the settle.

He smiled then and put his arm around her, drawing her tightly against him, as though by doing so he could banish his troubled thoughts. Kathleen settled there willingly, breathing deeply of his unique spicy scent.

Shane nuzzled her ear with his mouth, and his warm breath sent desire spiraling through her. She hungrily recalled the pleasure his hand had given her that night they'd walked home from the Lughnasadh dance.

Kathleen was shocked—and ashamed—by how much she wanted to make love with him.

After Patrick's death, she'd said she'd never marry again, but now ... if Shane were to ask her ...

But he won't ask you, you fool. When all's said and done, he's an Englishman, and you are Irish.

She must have tensed at this thought, for he pulled a little away and looked at her quizzically. "What is it, *alainn*?"

So perceptive he was. "We should not be doing this."

"Why not?" His breath warmed her cheek.

"You are English, and I am Irish. We are enemies."

He ran his fingertips lightly over her lips. "Only if you insist we are."

"You do not understand what it is like to be Irish," she cried passionately, "to be constantly looked down on and belittled simply because the blood of an old and proud people fills your veins."

"You think I do not know?" His tormented answer sounded as though it had been ripped from his soul.

She looked at him, and the bleakness of his eyes shocked her.

"You forget I am half-Irish. I am the son of an Englishman who fell in love with a wonderful Irish colleen, as passionate as she was beautiful, as intelligent as she was good. He wooed and won her in a whirlwind courtship."

"And then?"

"They married and he carried her away to England, where his friends treated her just as you describe." Shane's mouth hardened in anger and contempt. "But what is most unforgivable, so did my father."

Kathleen felt the angry tension in Shane's body.

"My father, who was as proud and vain a man as ever lived, soon grew ashamed of his Irish wife and the half-Irish son she bore him. He locked us away in the country so we could not embarrass him with his friends, while he spent much of his time in London. So you see, I do understand how it feels to be looked down on by the English."

"Your own father?" Kathleen's papa was such a loving man, delighting in his children, that she could not imagine a father like Shane's.

He nodded. "We were an embarrassment to him, my mother and I, not for anything we did, but for the blood that flowed in our veins. As a boy, I used to try so hard to please him, not knowing that was impossible." His voice seethed with painful emotions.

Kathleen's heart bled for the bewildered little boy Shane had been, desperately seeking approval from a man incapable of giving it. She took his hand in hers and squeezed it, trying to comfort him.

Shane's fingers tightened around hers, accepting the solace she silently offered.

A distressing insight shook Kathleen. Perhaps Brigid had had the same problem with Patrick. He'd had little time or patience for her, and she'd never seemed able to please him. Frequently, he'd acted jealous of her and of the attention, once his alone, that Kathleen gave their baby. "What a miserable childhood you must have had, Shane."

"No, actually, it was not. My mother more than made up for my father." The desolation in his eyes gave way to gleaming appreciation. "She was a remarkable woman. Her understanding was vastly superior to his. She was full of passion and love and enthusiasm, while he was a hollow shell of a man, caring only for outward appearances. How could he appreciate inner beauty and resources when he had none himself?"

Shane paused, staring thoughtfully down at the stone floor, the toe of his shoe idly tracing an abstract pattern there. Kathleen waited.

After a minute, he looked up at her. "You remind me very much of my mother."

Kathleen suspected that was the highest compliment Shane could pay her, and she was both honored and thrilled.

"My mother taught me so much—from fishing and hunting to the Irish language and dancing. She tried so hard to make up for my father's neglect and resentment of me."

"It sounds as though she succeeded," Kathleen said with a smile.

"She did. When I learned my wife was pregnant, I swore I would never be a father like my own was. By then, I hated him. I saw him for what he really was, a damn weakling who did not deserve a woman like my mother!"

Shane's mother might have been unlucky in her husband, Kathleen thought, but not in her son.

He continued, "When my wife died giving birth to our son, I could not imagine a child growing up without a mother. I swore I would do everything in my power to be both mother and father to him, to make up for her loss, as my mother had made up for my father."

"I am certain you succeeded too."

His smile was bittersweet. "Jeremy was a happy child." His voice faltered. "Unfortunately, though, he inherited his mama's delicate constitution . . . and he fell prey . . . to consumption." Shane's eyes were bright with unshed tears. *"Oh, God, I miss him."*

Shane's wrenching cry was filled with such enormous pain that Kathleen had to fight back her own tears. She let go of his hand and wrapped him in her arms, again offering him silent comfort.

He hugged her as a drowning man clung to flotsam.

After a minute, her thoughts turned from consolation to yearning. She pulled back a little.

Their gazes met, desire arcing between them. He lifted her onto his lap and hugged her to him.

They kissed deeply, passionately, fueling a hunger within Kathleen that cried out for the sustenance she instinctively knew only Shane could give her.

She yanked at the buttons of his shirt. When she popped them, she pushed her hand through the opening to stroke his muscular chest, loving the feel of his warm skin beneath her fingertips.

Shane showered her face and neck with kisses.

"Mama, isn't you coming to bed?" Brigid's voice called from the stairs. "It's so late."

Kathleen and Shane hastily straightened.

"I'll be coming in a few minutes, darling. Go back up to bed." Kathleen broke away from Shane, trying to ignore the aching need within her. "You had better go now."

The disappointment and frustrated desire she saw in his eyes mirrored her own, but he did not argue with her.

She should have been relieved, but as she shut the door behind him, she wished that he would have argued with her—and won.

Chapter 21

Shane used a large cart from Canamara to transport the three residents of Rose Cottage and several bowls and platters of food to the celebration of the McNultys moving into their newly roofed cottage.

He had taken much of the food from Canamara's larder and had supplemented it with two large salmon he'd caught that morning and given to Maggie to cook.

The cart also held a small bed with a feather mattress that Shane had found in a storage room at Canamara. He suspected it had been his mother's when she was little.

When they reached the cottage with its newly thatched roof, Shane carried the bed into the room that would be Maurea's and placed it beside a window so that she would be able to look out over the Vale of Kincaid.

Once he stepped outside again, he saw his companions had already unloaded the bowls and platters of food and put them on a rough trestle table. Noticing that most of the other dishes were potatoes in one form or another, Shane realized that many of the families had nothing else to contribute, but what they did have they shared generously.

As he looked around for Kathleen and Brigid, the *tuiodoir*, a hawk-faced man in his late forties, came up to him. "I'm needin' to talk to ye," he said under his breath.

Puzzled, Shane followed him to the back of the cottage, where they were alone.

"Visitors, we had yesterday," the *tuiodoir* said. "Went through the cottage as though they owned it. Something weren't right about 'em. Up to no good, I'm sure."

"What did they look like?"

"Big men. One had a scar from the corner of his eye to his chin. As ugly a man as ever I laid eyes on. And as rude and rough."

Ben Tilton. From the description Shane was certain of that, and he did not like it. "I appreciate the warning," he said, knowing the thatcher meant it as that.

A shout went up from the crowd gathered in front of the house. Shane and the *tuiodoir* hurried back there.

Maurea's da was carrying her out of the hovel and up the slope to her new home amid the cheers of those who had helped bring this moment about.

When McNulty carried the gaunt little girl inside the newly roofed and freshly redone cottage, the joy on her face brought a lump to Shane's throat.

From inside the house, he heard Maurea's excited cry, "Da, a bed o' me very own. Oh, and so comfortable it is. And a window too! And so much I can see from it. Oh, Da, I'm so happy."

From the corner of Shane's eye, he saw Kathleen brush away tears.

When she noticed him watching her, she gave him a smile that warmed him like a noon sun. "So happy I am for the McNultys, especially Maurea. And so grateful I am to you for paying the thatcher."

"I only pray that she will live long enough to enjoy the roof," Shane replied.

Once Maurea was installed in her new home, the celebration began in earnest. People moved around the table with plates in hand. Laughter rang out. A young man began playing a penny whistle. Then an Irish piper joined in.

Conn Malone came up to Shane, moving slowly, painfully. His rheumatism was clearly bothering him badly today. "A good deed ye've done, me lad. May heaven reward ye."

"The look on Maurea's face was reward enough. All I want in addition is for her to get better."

Conn regarded him with shrewd, penetrating eyes. "Do ye know, families in the vale here say the little people have taken to visitin' them in the wee hours, leavin' them food."

Shane schooled his face to give away nothing. "Then I hope the *daoine sidh* continue to do so. The people here deserve more than they have."

"To me way o' thinkin'," Conn said, "the *daoine sidhe* of Kincaid Vale is not so little, and he speaks with an English accent."

Shane smiled. "I am flattered, Conn, but do not make me out to be better than I am."

Conn's expression remained grave. "Be careful, me lad, that ye don't be bringin' more trouble down on yerself than ye can handle."

Kathleen returned to Shane's side. He reached for her hand and took it in his.

Two men joined them, and one of the newcomers, Mike Whaley, complained unhappily to Conn about having been ordered, along with every other male tenant in the Vale of Kincaid, to report early Tuesday morning for a workday that each was required by his lease to give Sherbourne.

"How very odd," Kathleen said with a frown. "Usually the only time all the men are required to work at the same time is during planting and harvest. I wonder why Tuesday? And what must be done that requires so many men?"

"Sure, and it's Divil Sherbourne doin' what he can to make our lives harder," Whaley said.

Two fiddlers struck up a reel, and the dancing began. Shane led Kathleen out. He managed to monopolize her for a half-dozen dances before Whaley claimed her for the next number.

As Shane stood on the sidelines watching Kathleen dancing, her eyes alight with gaiety, her cheeks flushed from exertion, he was once again struck by how much like his mother she was. Kathleen loved life as his mother had loved it before his father had sucked the joy from her with his sour, rigid, ceaseless fault-finding. The fifth marquess had been so certain of his enormous superiority, which had existed only in his own mind.

In truth, Shane's father had been so much his wife's inferior, lacking her energy, joy, enthusiasm, intelligence, and, most of all, her heart.

Shane had not thought to find the likes of her, but now he had in Kathleen. And he wanted her more than he'd ever wanted anything before.

Word of Shane's contribution to the McNultys' cottage had spread among those celebrating, and he was welcomed with friendly smiles and greetings, a rare circumstance for him.

Although the tenants of his English estates respected, even revered him, they treated him with the deference and distance that a marquess's position demanded.

But here, among people ignorant of his real identity, he was accepted as one of them. For the first time in his life, he did not feel like an outsider looking in, the unwanted Irish son of an English father, but as though he belonged.

He had Kathleen partly to thank for his acceptance. Her friendship and her championing of him counted for much with the people here.

But he also knew that no matter how much these people welcomed him now, once they learned his real identity, he would instantly become the lonely—and here the hated—outsider.

All that remained in doubt was whether he could convince Kathleen to remain at his side.

Two hours later, the musicians finally took a rest, and Shane was happy for it. He marveled at the capacity of these Irish to enjoy themselves. They had so little to celebrate, but they made the most of it.

Brigid rushed up to Kathleen. "Mama, Theresa wants me to stay the night at her house. Oh, please, Mama, I wants to so much. Please say yes!"

Kathleen was clearly reluctant to do so, but finally she agreed. Brigid jumped up and down in delight, and Shane was strongly tempted to do the same. *Perhaps tonight . . .*

Later, after he'd helped Kathleen and Maggie collect the now-empty dishes they had brought and stowed them in the cart, Maggie announced she would be spending the night with her dear friend, Bridie O'Reilly. Although Shane wasn't certain, he thought Maggie winked at him.

*   *   *

The ride to Rose Cottage had seemed to Kathleen both interminable and far too quick as she vacillated between hoping Shane would make love to her tonight and guilt that she ached so for this illicit pleasure.

Shane took Kathleen's hand to help her down from the cart, sending a shiver of desire through her.

After he helped her carry the empty bowls and platters from the cart to the kitchen, he turned to her. Cupping her face with his hands, he kissed her with a fervent hunger that matched her own. She wanted this man so much.

Still holding her face in his hands, he looked at her gravely, his face rosy from the glow of the turf coals. "Shall we go upstairs?"

Kathleen swore the man could read her mind. "Yes," she said so enthusiastically that she was embarrassed.

But her eager response seemed to delight him, and he bent to brush her mouth with his lips. Then he lifted the lamp from the trestle table, and she guided him up the stairs to her bedroom.

There Kathleen was suddenly shy and all too aware of the big bed. She took a nervous step backward from Shane.

"Afraid I will ravish you?" he asked dryly. "You need not worry. I was born a gentleman and I intend to remain one until I die . . ." His gaze moved slowly, appreciatively over her from the top of her head to her bare toes peeking from beneath the wrapper. "No matter how delicious the temptation."

His sensual perusal stoked into flames the embers of passion within Kathleen that had been smoldering since she met him. She ached to lie with him, to cure the throbbing within her. If the truth be known, she wanted to ravish *him*.

"I want to make love to you desperately, my darling Kathleen, but the decision is yours. I will not do anything you do not want."

She wondered whether he had any idea of all that she wanted. Since the night of the dance, her body had throbbed with desire at the thought of sharing a bed—and more—with him. She desperately wanted him to make love to her, to join their bodies, to feel him within her.

But he's English, a contrary voice within her whispered.

He's also half-Irish, and as good a man as ever I've known.

But he's a friend of His Devilship.

That was harder for Kathleen to dismiss. She'd been told once that the tenants of Sherbourne's English estates considered him the best landlord in Britain.

So perhaps Shane could be forgiven his blindness to Sherbourne's faults.

She reminded herself of all Shane had done to help the McNultys and, she suspected, others too. Although Shane refused to accept credit, she would wager all she owned that he was the *sidhe* of Kincaid Vale.

She thought of his dead wife and son. This was a man who understood suffering, for he had suffered himself.

"Is this what you want?" Shane asked gently, glancing toward the bed.

Too choked with emotion to trust her voice, Kathleen gave him a hesitant nod of assent, torn between happiness and nervousness.

She would remember until her dying moment

the look of joy and happiness on Shane's face.

He crushed her to him. His mouth came down on hers with hot, urgent need, firing her own, burning away any doubt that she might have still had about her decision.

When he finally broke the kiss, they were both breathless.

Slowly, almost reverently, he undressed her, first undoing the buttons of her gown.

When he pushed it off her shoulders, baring her breasts, his eyes turned hot and liquid with desire.

For a moment he continued to stare appreciatively, and she felt herself blushing. She was not used to a man looking at her like that. Patrick, the only man with whom she had lain, had always made love in the dark.

"How beautiful you are," Shane breathed.

He cupped her breasts gently, reverently, in his hands. Then with his thumb, he lightly stroked an already pebbled nipple, and passion burst into full flame.

With fingers made awkward by desire, Kathleen tore at the buttons of his shirt, then caressed his chest with her fingertips. The tantalizing hair curled around her fingers like black silk. When she reached his small, hard nipple, she heard his sharp intake of breath, followed by a groan of pleasure.

Shane finished undressing her, then pulled back the covers on the bed and settled her on it. Sitting beside her he quickly stripped off his boots and clothes, then returned to pleasuring her.

His thumb resumed its attention to her breast. He dipped his head and caught her other nipple in his mouth, licking and sucking in a way that made her womanly core clench and ache and cry for more. Now it was Kathleen's turn to groan with pleasure.

In a voice husky with desire, he murmured his appreciation of her in both English and Gaelic.

Never before had she heard such words while in a man's arms. Nor had she enjoyed such lingering, arousing preliminaries. Kathleen found Shane's husky whispers and his slow, loving exploration of her body sublimely exciting and erotic.

Then she forgot the past, forgot everything but the building pressure within her body that had her writhing and moaning with the need for release.

Finally she begged, "Please, Shane, come to me."

And he did, entering her slowly, carefully, as though she were a virgin trembling on the verge of her sexual awakening.

In his skillful hands, she almost felt as though she were. She had never experienced such an all-consuming fever of desire before. She had not known how intensely, how fiercely she could need and want a man.

This man!

Now her passion matched his. She undulated her hips as he thrust into her, and it was his turn to moan.

They danced to the age-old melody of love. Never had the song seemed so beautiful to Kathleen.

Together they soared to the music only they could hear until she reached beyond the hills and dales of County Kerry, beyond the mountain peaks, beyond all she had ever known. A second or two later, with a smothered cry, he joined her in that sublime place.

Her climax was so powerful, the spasms it unleashed so strong, her release so complete that she felt as though she had been consumed and reborn.

And perhaps she had.

For life suddenly seemed bright and beautiful again. She was young and lusty. And life, colored rose by the love she felt for Shane, was again something to be seized and enjoyed.

For a few moments, they lay intertwined in body and heart, too shaken and spent to move. Then he rolled on his side, bringing her with him, hugging her to him, as though he could not bear to separate from her.

"Oh, *alainn, alainn*," he murmured, his mouth at her ear. "What a rare and wonderful woman you are."

Never had she felt so cherished.

Later they made love twice more, and each time seemed better than the previous.

Kathleen felt utter contentment as the mists of sleep wafted about her.

She awakened as daylight crept into the room. Shane lay next to her, close enough that his spicy scent teased her nose. His face was relaxed and surprisingly boyish in repose.

Much as she had enjoyed the marriage bed with Patrick and thought herself a lucky wife, well pleasured by her husband, what she'd experienced last night with Shane soared far beyond mere pleasure into celestial realms that she had never imagined. It had been as near to heaven as she was likely to get on earth.

Shane was so generous and understanding, so skilled as a lover, so determined to give her pleasure. Patrick had never worshipped every inch of her body as Shane had done with such slow, careful attention.

Her late husband had rarely lingered on preliminaries, and she, a virgin when she married him, had known no different.

Until last night.

You don't miss what you've never known.

How different—and more exciting—Shane was from Patrick as a lover.

And that made her feel terribly guilty and unfaithful to the memory of Brigid's father.

Chapter 22

❦

Shane's temper rose as he stood at the corner windows of his bedchamber and watched the tenants from the Vale of Kincaid weed gardens that were weedless, prune trees that required no pruning, and whitewash fences that were already a gleaming white.

That these men had been pulled from their own land for such useless, wasted labor infuriated him. What the hell had possessed Radnor to order them here today? Merely to show his authority over them?

Shane went downstairs, where he found Radnor on the terrace, watching the tenants labor with smirking satisfaction. A hard west wind was blowing, and the sky was dark with clouds.

"Why are you having those men do totally useless tasks?" Shane demanded.

"His Lordship requires it."

Shane responded with a pungent obscenity that branded the agent a liar. It was all he could do to keep from identifying himself and putting a stop to this ridiculous waste of his tenants' time and labor.

Only the fear that he would lose Kathleen and

Brigid forever kept Shane from delivering a scathing indictment of Radnor and all his crimes against both the tenants and his employer.

Radnor turned to him, his cold gray eyes mere slits. "Were our mutual employer to hear your language, he would be your former employer. As for what he requires of these men, you clearly do not know His Lordship as well as you think you do, Mr. Howard."

"And you do not know him at all."

A flush darkened Radnor's already ruddy color. "I know him well enough to appreciate I must carry out his orders, and that is what I am doing."

Shane thought of demanding to see those orders, but he would be wasting his breath.

Shane remembered Kathleen's remarking at the McNulty celebration how odd it was that all the men had been summoned for this workday. Furthermore, Radnor's demeanor disturbed Shane. The suppressed air of excitement about the little snake warned he was up to something.

But what?

Hard as Kathleen tried to put Shane from her mind, she could think of nothing else.

He was as different from Patrick out of bed as in it, she mused. The respect Shane accorded her ideas and opinions surprised and flattered her. Nor did he mind when she challenged his views and argued with him. Instead he seemed to enjoy the give and take.

When she'd done that with Patrick, he'd been infuriated. He was not a man to have his ideas challenged, especially not by a woman.

Kathleen could no longer deny to herself that she loved Shane.

But did he return her love? Even when they'd lain together, he had said nothing of loving her, let alone of wanting to marry her. Now those omissions took on ominous overtones in her mind.

Tonight she intended to find out the truth.

The sound of the knocker on the front door startled her. She glanced at the bracket clock, confirming that it was a quarter-hour too early for Shane to be arriving for dinner. Fearing Oliver Radnor was calling, she walked reluctantly to the door.

Seamus Malone stood there. "Pa must see you in the green immediately."

Kathleen froze at this coded message that told her the assistance of the Knights of Rosaleen was needed. "What's happened?"

He looked beyond her to make certain no one else was within earshot, then whispered, "While all the men was away workin' at Canamara this afternoon, the Tiltons drove the McNultys out of their new home and moved in."

The burst of rage within Kathleen was so intense that the world before her eyes turned to a shimmering red haze, and she was incapable of speech. It took a minute for her vision to clear and her mind to function again. "I'll be there as soon as I can."

Shutting the door, Kathleen recalled the blissful look on little Maurea's face as her da carried her into her new home. Tears welled in Kathleen's eyes. That poor sick child thrown out into this cool, blustery weather. It was beyond cruel. It was criminal.

The Knights would move immediately, this very night, to thwart this wicked outrage.

Kathleen ran into the kitchen. Maggie looked up from the fireplace. "Who's at the door?"

"Seamus. I must leave at once. I'll not be here for dinner." Kathleen swallowed hard. She had been looking forward so much to tonight with Shane.

"And what am I to tell himself when he comes? And little Brigid too?"

"The usual excuse: I have been called to help the midwife with a difficult breech birth." Although Kathleen had once or twice rendered such a service, she had used this excuse several other times to hide from Brigid that she was going on Knights' errands.

A worried frown furrowed Maggie's forehead. "Sure, and it's goin' to be a long night, is it?"

Kathleen tried to affect a puzzled expression. "Why would you be thinking that?"

"If that be the excuse you're offerin', you're not expectin' to be back soon."

"I don't know," Kathleen answered honestly. She would argue for driving the Tiltons out this very night. She strongly doubted they'd be anticipating such a quick retaliation.

"I've no fancy to be lyin' to yer Mr. Howard," Maggie said nervously. "Them eyes of his, they see too much. I'm thinkin' ye could be trustin' him with the truth, Kathleen McNamara. Weren't he the one who paid fer the McNultys' roof?"

"I cannot take the chance, Maggie." Although Kathleen was certain Radnor had lied about Shane being Sherbourne's spy, she had to face the possibility that her emotions were blinding her intellect. "Too many lives depend on my not making a mistake."

When Shane knocked at Rose Cottage, he was still fuming at Oliver Radnor. Not until a few minutes ago had the damn agent dismissed the tenants from the ridiculous make-work tasks he'd had them doing all day. Perhaps Kathleen could help Shane figure out what Radnor was up to.

Shane's breath quickened at the prospect of seeing her. As befit a suitor, he had dressed with special care tonight, wearing the best coat and the one frilled shirt he had brought with him.

Once Kathleen admitted the love he was certain she felt for him, he would put an end to his damn charade, even if the aid he needed from England had not yet arrived.

He had no illusions doing this would be easy. Radnor would dispute his identity and perhaps try to have him killed. What Shane most needed was someone of undisputed repute who would identify him as Sherbourne, but he knew no one in Ireland who could do that.

Nor would telling Kathleen the truth be easy. He prayed she would have him, once she learned he was "Devil" Sherbourne.

Shane was about to knock again when the door opened. Instead of Kathleen, Brigid stood there. Much as he'd come to love the little girl, he was disappointed that she, rather than her mother, had answered. "Where is your mama, *sidhe*?"

"Helping a lady who's having a baby." Her face puckered a little. "Hours she may be gone."

Brigid took his hand and led him to the kitchen, where the enticing smell of cooking food reminded him that his stomach was ready for dinner.

Maggie stood at the fireplace, stirring the contents of a pot with such vigor that he smiled. Before he could speak, she said without raising her eyes from the pot, "Now ye and Brigid be sittin' yerself down, and I'll be dishin' dinner up in a minute."

Shane blinked in surprise. Whenever he came into the kitchen, Maggie always looked up from what she was doing and greeted him with a broad smile. But tonight she did not take her eyes from the pot. She looked as though her life depended on her stirring it just right.

Something was wrong.

He glanced down at the trestle table and saw that only two places had been set there. "Are you not eating with us tonight, Maggie?"

Still she kept her eyes fixed on the pot. "*Nil*, too many other chores I've to do."

Something was very wrong.

What the hell was going on? Maggie set the spoon down, picked up a bowl and ladle, and began to dish out the stew.

Shane said casually, "I did not know Kathleen was a midwife as well as a teacher."

The ladle dropped back in the pot with a splash. Maggie retrieved it, keeping her gaze fastened on it. "She's not, but it's a breech birth she's helpin' with."

As soon as Maggie finished serving the stew, she rushed out of the kitchen, mumbling that she must get to work.

Something was very, very wrong.

Brigid looked as puzzled as Shane felt. "Maggie does not seem herself tonight," he observed.

The little girl nodded. "She's nervous like this sometimes when Mama goes to help babies be born."

"But not all the time?" Suddenly Shane had no appetite for the stew that had smelled so delicious only moments before.

"*Nil*. Maggie says she worries cuz Mama don't get home till the wee hours of the morning."

"Does your mama go often to help babies be born?"

"No."

He idly poked with his spoon at the stew in his bowl. "When was the last time?"

Brigid looked puzzled and shrugged.

"Let me guess." Shane masked his concern with a teasing tone. "Could it have been the night before I first met you fishing?"

She thought for a moment, then broke into a smile. "It was! How did you know?"

He was so shaken he could hardly keep his voice steady. "I remember you asked her about the baby."

And he remembered how strangely flustered Kathleen had been by the question.

By now Shane was thoroughly alarmed. Oliver Radnor had been entirely too pleased with himself today and with his ridiculous requirement that the tenants report to Canamara for a workday. Some gut instinct told Shane that the agent's behavior and Kathleen's sudden need to help at a "birth" were connected.

Damn it, he had to get Maggie to tell him the truth.

"S'ane, you're not eating," Brigid observed.

"No, sweetheart, I suddenly am not feeling quite the thing. I am afraid I had better go home." He stood up, and the little girl put down her spoon, clearly intending to follow suit.

"No, Brigid, I insist you stay here and finish eating your dinner while it is still warm. Maggie will be truly insulted if you do not eat either. She will believe it is her cooking, and we don't want her to think anything so untrue as that, do we?"

Brigid shook her head and dutifully picked up her spoon again.

Shane dropped a kiss on the top of her head and hurried into the hall, shutting the kitchen door behind him. He found Maggie in her room, kneeling beside her bed, praying.

"What are you praying for, Maggie?" he asked quietly, afraid that he knew the answer.

She jumped and gasped, clutching her hands over her breasts. "Holy mother, scarin' me to death."

"Where is Kathleen?"

Her gaze flittered nervously away from his. "Told ye, I did. She's helpin' with a baby."

"We both know what she is helping is the Knights of Rosaleen."

Her gaze snapped to his. Her eyes were wide with shock.

"I have to find her, Maggie. Radnor is up to something, and I fear he has laid a trap for the Knights. I must warn her. Where is she?"

He could see in Maggie's honest blue eyes the conflict raging within her. Did she dare trust him with the truth?

"Maggie, I give you my oath that I would never betray Kathleen or the others. What happened that the Knights are marching tonight?"

"I don't know."

Her eyes told him this was the truth. "I believe you, but I have to find her. I swear to you that I only want to help her and the Knights."

Tears glistened in Maggie's eyes. "Sure, and I pray to God, ye be tellin' me the truth. If I was ye, I'd be tryin' Conn Malone. Stayin' with the Finnegans in Kerian Vale to the south of Kincaid Mountain, he is."

The vale was a considerable distance from Rose Cottage, and Shane feared he had no time to lose. He'd better take a horse from Canamara's stable.

Kathleen stopped to see Maurea on her way to meet with Conn. The McNultys had taken refuge in the miserable damp cave that had been their home before they moved into their new cottage.

Never had Kathleen seen Mrs. McNulty look so defeated and dejected as when she met her at the hovel's door.

Kathleen took the woman's work-hardened hands in her own and squeezed them comfortingly. "So sorry I am. How is dear little Maurea?"

"Poorly. Never seen nothin' like it. That divil Tilton picked her up and tossed her out the door like me darlin' were a piece o' trash. Deliberately threw her in the mud, he did, and then laughed."

Kathleen gasped. The image that flashed into her mind nauseated her. "How could any man do anything so cruel to such a sick child?"

Tears dripped slowly down Mrs. McNulty's cheeks. "And now, do you know, me Maurea's fever is risin'."

"May I see her?"

The woman nodded. Inside the damp cave, Maurea tossed restlessly on a bit of straw, her eyes that had been so bright on Saturday when she saw her new home were now dark and hollow.

Kathleen laid her hand on the girl's forehead, which was as hot as an ember to the touch.

"Dear God in heaven, what justification did Tilton give you for ousting you from your home?"

"Said his friend Sherbourne told him he could have any home on Canamara that he wanted. Since the Malone house was burned, he'd be takin' ours."

Kathleen swore silently to herself that she would do everything in her power to see that Maurea would be back in her new home that very night.

After Kathleen left the McNultys, she hurried toward the Finnegans' home, where Conn Malone and his family now lived.

She could not put Tilton's treatment of Maurea from her mind. Not only was it cruel, but it was senseless. It was as if he were deliberately trying to inflame the Irish against him. That thought raised a vague uneasiness in Kathleen.

Shane rode across the narrow bridge where he had first met Kathleen. As he rounded the curve that had hid her from him, he met three young men whom he had never seen before. How odd to meet strangers here in the heart of the estate.

Nor was that the only thing peculiar about them. Although the wind was raw and unpleasant, Shane thought the long capes in which they had wrapped themselves so only the toes of their boots showed beneath them were excessive. They were young men, perhaps not yet out of their teens, and they looked far too well fed to be Irish.

And then there was their posture, straight-backed and head high. It reminded him of . . .

. . . *Soldiers.*

What in bloody hell was going on? Alarmed, he reined in his horse and asked them, "Are you lost?"

" 'Tis no business of yours," one of the young men answered. "Be off with you, you damn Irishman."

Shane fixed the trio with a contemptuous stare. "Does this horse look like a five-pound animal?" he thundered in his most correct British accent, nodding at his brown thoroughbred, one of the finest horses Canamara's excellent stables had to offer. "Do I sound like an Irishman, you damn insolent young puppy?"

What Shane sounded like was an arrogant, affronted English aristocrat, and the "puppy's" rigid posture dissolved in fear. He began stammering.

Shane cut him off, "I am the Marquess of Sherbourne's closest friend and his guest here at Canamara, and you will address me with respect. Now what are you doing here?"

All three soldiers looked as though they wished the earth would open and swallow them. The puppy stammered, "We's part of the troops 'Is Lor'ship asked for to catch them Irish 'ooligans 'eaded by some man what calls 'imself Cap'n Starlight. We'll 'ave 'im in our trap this night."

"Surely you do not think these hooligans mean to attack the house itself."

"Nay, nay," one of the other soldiers assured Shane, "'tis some cottage in the Vale of Kincaid."

"Then what are you doing here instead of there? The Vale of Kincaid is on the opposite side of that mountain."

"Most o' the men will be moving in there soon as 'tis full dark," the soldier assured Shane. "We was ordered to guard some cottage near the big 'ouse to keep any o' the 'ooligans from 'iding there."

Rose Cottage. No doubt that was Radnor's idea, Shane thought, in the hope he might gain more leverage in his quest to make Kathleen his mistress. "Very well, I will not keep you any longer."

Shane held his horse to an easy pace until he was out of earshot of the soldiers, then he urged the thoroughbred to a gallop toward Kerian Vale. He prayed he could catch Kathleen before she and the Knights moved.

"It is agreed then," Kathleen said to Conn and Finn, the two men who, together with herself, made up the local governing council of the Knights. "The Knights will strike tonight."

Conn nodded morosely. "But I'm not likin' it."

"You know we must," Kathleen argued. "If we wait, we only give the Tiltons time to dig in and prepare defenses against us. We'll not be taking them by surprise, that's for sure, unless we move against them this very night."

"But the Tiltons be armed?"

"We'll be, too."

"Well, you know the punishment fer havin' a weapon," Finn said. "What if ye be caught?"

Kathleen thought of Brigid. *I can't be caught. I can't!*

When Shane reached Kerian Vale, he rode along until he saw Conn Malone sitting in a rocking chair next to the door of a large house.

Conn tried to rise on his arthritic limbs to greet his visitor, but Shane, seeing what pain it caused him, said hastily, "No, please, do not get up. I have come to talk to you, and we can do it here."

"So ye've heard about the McNultys, have ye?"

Foreboding seized Shane. "No, what about them?"

"Sure, and I thought ye'd know by now. While the men were working at Canamara today, the Tiltons ejected them from their new home and moved in themselves."

Shane swore under his breath. "I knew Radnor was up to no good. I should have guessed. Is that why the Knights of Rosaleen are meeting tonight?"

"Knights?" Conn looked perplexed. "Sure, and I don't know what yer talkin' about."

"Yes, you do, and we must stop them."

"And let those bloody Tilton bastards sleep beneath the roof you paid for?"

"Better that than to have many or most of the Knights captured or killed. That cottage is a damn trap. Soldiers are hiding all around it, waiting for the Knights to walk into their arms."

Conn turned pale. "How do ye know this?"

"I met some of the soldiers. That is why we have to stop the Knights. Tell me where they gather, so I can warn them."

Conn studied him suspiciously. "Why d'ye take our part like ye do? It can cause ye only trouble. Why d'ye care what happens here?"

"I want the wrongs done the tenants of Canamara righted. I believe in justice, and I will see it done here. I have another reason, too. I am in love with Captain Starlight."

Malone's sharp intake of breath was raspy. "Sure and she's not the one that told ye!"

"Of course not. I guessed. After the Lughnasadh dance, I had the advantage of observing the captain haranguing the drunken Paddy and his companions."

Interest and something else flickered in Malone's eyes. "A remarkably acute young man ye are— sharp as the ould Lion himself."

"Please, we have very little time. Where will I find Captain Starlight and her Knights?"

Conn drew a map in the dirt to help Shane understand the complex instructions.

After Conn finished and Shane was leaving, he heard the older man say softly, "I pray to God you will be in time."

So do I, Conn. So do I.

Chapter 23

Concealed behind the branches of a yew, Kathleen, in her green Captain Starlight uniform and hood, watched the Knights of Rosaleen arrive by twos and threes in the meadow.

Night had settled, black and stormy. Jagged streaks of lightning across the sky illuminated the scene for her. She was thankful for this nasty storm, thinking it provided a fitting backdrop for what was about to occur.

But Kathleen was worried too. Never had she heard the Knights as fractious as they were tonight. They were outraged at what had been done to the McNultys and especially to poor little Maurea.

As Kathleen had foreseen, Tilton's behavior toward the child had the Knights thirsting for revenge. The more Kathleen considered Tilton's intentionally provocative behavior, the more it puzzled and worried her.

She prayed that she could hold these angry men together tonight in the cohesive, disciplined group necessary to take effective action, but she was doubtful.

Some, like Paddy Connaught and a half-dozen of his cohorts, were drunk, even though that violated their membership oath. She wanted to order them home, but if she refused to let them accompany the Knights, they were certain to go off looking for trouble on their own.

A flash of lightning in the distance was followed a moment later by the low rumble of thunder. Time it was for her to leave her concealment and take her place on the tree stump Captain Starlight used to address the Knights.

As she stepped from behind the yew's concealing branches, she heard the sound of a horse racing toward them. She froze.

A bolt of lightning, much nearer this time, zigzagged down the sky, illuminating the scene as though a thousand candles had been lit for a few seconds and then extinguished again.

Before the light faded, she saw the horseman veer away from the meadow and direct his spirited mount toward where she stood. No horse costing less than five pounds was he riding.

Which meant he had to be an Englishman.

Deafening thunder drowned out the horse's hooves and seemed to rock the earth beneath Kathleen's feet.

Another streak of lightning revealed Shane's face as he jumped from his still-moving horse a few feet from her. He was yelling at her, but his words were lost in the thunder.

Unwilling to face him in her disguise, she turned to walk away, but as the thunder died, he grabbed her arm and pulled her back to face him. "Listen to me, Kathleen."

She froze in shock. How had he known who she was?

Affecting her deepest, gruffest voice and heaviest

brogue, she said, "Insultin' me ye are, stranger, callin' me by some colleen's name. Captain Starlight, I am."

He grinned. "If you say so, *alainn*." His smile vanished. "Now listen to me, Captain Starlight. The McNultys, the cottage—it is all a trap to catch you and the Knights. Soldiers are waiting there for you to come to oust the Tiltons."

"And how'd ye be knowing that?" she asked, still speaking in her deepest voice.

"I talked to some of the soldiers."

"And they'd be spillin' all their secrets to ye like that?" she scoffed.

"Living at Canamara as Sherbourne's guest has certain advantages," he said dryly.

Nor did Kathleen doubt what Shane told her. It confirmed her own uneasiness about Tilton's gratuitously provocative action.

"God, *alainn*, I was terrified I would not find you in time to warn you." Shane's voice was filled with such emotion that her heart did a somersault. "I would hug you except I would not want to start nasty rumors about Captain Starlight—or about myself."

"What the hell are you doing here, Howard?" Kathleen heard Seamus Malone's angry voice behind her.

Shane sighed. "Is that the only way you know how to greet me, Seamus?"

Clearly Shane had no more difficulty seeing through Seamus's disguise, a blackened face, than he had seeing through Kathleen's green mask. She longed to ask Shane how he had guessed she was the captain, but to do so would confirm to him that he was right.

Kathleen told Seamus, "He came to warn us that

the McNulty cottage is a trap. Soldiers are waiting there to capture us."

"And you believe that, Captain?" Malone demanded scornfully, his tone proclaiming that he did not. "How could soldiers have gotten here so quickly?"

"Because Radnor undoubtedly sent for them last week before the McNultys even moved in," Shane answered patiently. "Did you not wonder why he ordered all the men from Kincaid Vale to report to Canamara for a workday today even though there was little enough for them to do?"

Kathleen too had wondered about the timing, and she silently berated herself for not having made the connection.

"What does the workday have to do with the McNultys?"

"Radnor assured that no men would be around to interfere when the Tiltons ousted the McNultys. Nor would they be tending their fields where they might see soldiers moving into the area to wait for full dark to set the trap at the cottage."

"He couldn't be knowin' we'd move tonight," Seamus objected.

"True," Shane said, "but he could order Ben Tilton to toss poor Maurea into the mud as though she were a piece of trash to inflame you into trying to restore her and her family to their cottage as quickly as possible."

Shane was right, Kathleen thought. Now everything fit. She told Seamus, "I'll be sending the Knights home tonight."

"Because of what this *Englishman* claims?"

"I *claim* nothing," Shane retorted. "I speak the truth. If the Knights go to the cottage tonight, they may well be slaughtered. At the very least, they will be taken prisoner."

"I can't chance that," Kathleen said.

"What if the men won't listen to you?" Seamus asked.

She knew, as enraged as they were, that was a very real possibility.

A drunken shout rang out and was answered by another.

Kathleen said sharply to Seamus. "Get rid of Paddy Connaught and his drunken companions. Our rules are clear."

He nodded and headed toward the clearing.

"I suggest you warn your Knights, Captain Starlight, what will happen if they move tonight," Shane said. "Tell them too that they would be wise to go home as quickly as possible to make certain their wives and children stay inside."

"Why is that?"

"Untested young soldiers tend to be exceedingly nervous and often fire at shadows in the night or anything else that moves."

"Dear God in heaven, the women and children!" Kathleen's eyes pleaded with Shane. "Please, I beg of you, ride to the Vale of Kincaid at once and warn them to stay inside their homes. Likely as not, they'll be gathering near the cottage, not realizing the danger they're in."

To her relief, he nodded and mounted his horse.

She started toward the clearing, but he guided his horse into her path.

Bending down from the saddle, he said quietly, "Whatever you do, Kathleen—"

Driving her voice even deeper, she said, "No Kathleen am I. I—"

He cut off her denial. "Do not go back to Rose Cottage in that uniform, *alainn*."

Exasperating man. She might as well not have spoken.

"Soldiers are guarding your home." With that, he rode off, leaving her gaping after him.

Why were soldiers at Rose Cottage? Kathleen took a deep breath, girding herself for the challenge ahead of her, then hurried to the tree stump she used as her platform.

"I come to tell ye, me brave soldiers, a trap's been laid for us tonight. We cannot attack the Tiltons."

The air crackled with angry, rebellious objections.

"If we move against the Tiltons, the trap will snap shut upon us. By now, soldiers surround the cottage, and you will be killed or captured if you go there. Do you want to die a martyr tonight? Or do you want to live to fight another day?"

Slowly and with much grumbling, the men began to disperse, moving shadows in the night. Kathleen watched them leave, then jumped down from the stump, feeling utterly drained and exhausted.

She longed so much for Shane's strong arms around her, supporting her, comforting her, that she almost wished she had not sent him to warn the Kincaid women.

And what if the soldiers detected him? She might have sent him to his death. The thought turned her legs to putty, and she sank down on the rock.

She did not know how long she had been sitting there when a thin, bony figure hurried toward her. He wore an oversized white shirt over his clothes, had a blackened face, and carried a pitchfork.

As he reached her, she was surprised to see Seamus appear at her side. She thought he had left with the others.

"Cap'n, Cap'n, hopin' I'd find ye here." His voice told her he was a very young man. "Paddy Connaught and his friends, they ain't believin' soldiers be at the McNultys'. They say they'll be drivin' the Tiltons out themselves."

Kathleen jumped up from the rock. As their Captain Starlight, she must prevent them from carrying out their suicidal effort. Even though they were going against her orders, they were her men and her responsibility.

"We must stop them," she cried frantically to Seamus.

"Maybe we can head them off on the flank of Kincaid Mountain," Seamus said.

"Pray we succeed." Kathleen set off toward the mountain at a run. *How brave Paddy and his cohorts are when they're drunk.*

As they picked their way through the rocky countryside, Kathleen was thankful for the little patches of moonlight that lighted their way.

The youth with the pitchfork trailed behind them.

Determined to protect him from danger, Kathleen turned and ordered him in her gruffest, sternest voice, "Go home. I shall deal with Paddy and his friends."

With an expression that was part reluctance and part relief, the boy left them.

With only occasional flashes of lightning for illumination, Kathleen and Seamus picked their way in the darkness along the boulder-strewn flank of Kincaid Mountain. The accompanying thunder cracked sharply.

The feeling that she was being watched seized Kathleen, raising the hair on her nape. She told herself she was being a silly coward. The bone-jarring thunder must be unnerving her.

How desperately she wished that Shane, not Seamus, was with her. Shane's presence gave her a sense of security that she'd never felt with another man, not even Patrick.

A slurred yell from near the newly roofed cottage shattered the silence between rounds of thunder. "Come out o' there, ye damn Tiltons. It's yer brother, the divil, callin' ye to yer judgment."

Kathleen groaned as she recognized Paddy Connaught's voice.

"Damn!" Seamus exclaimed. "We're too late."

Suddenly the night came alive with shouts and shots, with the clump of running boots, and with shadowy figures that sprang up from behind boulders along the path Kathleen and her companion were on.

Dear God in heaven, the trap had been wider than she had suspected, and they had stumbled into it.

"Run!" Seamus cried, taking his own advice.

Kathleen followed him, then darted sideways to evade a soldier who jumped up from behind a large boulder.

She succeeded, but a pistol shot roared. A ball whizzed past her head and lodged in the side of the mountain, kicking out a shower of dirt and rock chips.

A dozen feet farther on, another burly figure materialized from the shadows, seized one of her arms, and jerked her to him, nearly knocking her off her feet with his roughness.

"So what's me got 'ere?" he asked, shoving his

face close to her mask. He reached up with his free hand, clearly intending to yank off the green silk hood that covered her head.

Before he could succeed, she brought her knee up as hard as she could against his groin. He let out a hideous shriek and released her as he doubled up in pain.

Free again, she sprinted away. The injured man's howling momentarily drew the other soldiers' attention from her.

"What 'appened?" one called.

"Irish bastard must of 'ad a knife," another cried.

Kathleen left the path and fled down the hillside toward a collection of alder and buckthorn.

"After 'im," a soldier yelled. "'E's getting away!"

She heard boots thumping after her.

Seamus must have eluded the soldiers, for she heard no sounds of them pursuing any quarry but herself.

Just as she reached the trees, another shot boomed. This time, however, the ball went wide of its target, sending out a spray of chips from an alder several feet from her.

When Kathleen emerged on the other side of the grove, she raced across a stretch of open land that offered no concealment, thankful that the soldiers were still trying to navigate the dense growth of buckthorn and alder into which she had led them.

No shots rang out before she reached the protective cover of a birch wood.

Panting for breath, Kathleen ran on, taking a zig-zagging course. But behind her, she again heard the soldiers that she could not seem to elude.

Then she remembered a thicket of blackthorn that Radnor had ordered be left to grow unchecked because he wanted the wood.

She fled toward it. Thank God, Kathleen had the advantage of knowing the countryside. But the soldiers had the weightier advantages of numbers and weapons.

The half-dozen soldiers, now spread out in a single line, gained on her, and her heaving chest felt as though it were on fire. She had to make the soldiers think she'd run directly into the blackthorn.

As she reached the thicket, a bolt of lightning illuminated her for a second.

"There 'e goes into them bushes, men. Follow 'im!"

As soon as the lightning gave way to blackness again, she threw herself on the muddy ground and began crawling as fast as she could around the edge of the blackthorn's dense core.

She had reached the other side, when she heard the men trampling into the thicket.

Almost immediately, loud curses rang out as they became entangled in the impenetrable blackthorn and its cruelly sharp thorns.

Kathleen sprang to her feet and ran along a path that led to Canamara's park. When she stopped to catch her breath, the sounds of running footsteps that had dogged her since Kincaid Mountain were finally silent.

She followed a roundabout course toward Rose Cottage, praying that the soldiers Shane had warned her about had left there by now.

When she reached the edge of the meadow around her home, she paused, wishing that Shane were waiting there for her. She wanted nothing more than to have him hold her in his arms, to comfort her and cheer her with his wonderful grin and dry wit.

She prayed that he had made it safely to the Vale

of Kincaid and back to Canamara. But what if he had been shot in the dark? Her shoulders slumped. She tried to push the unbearable thought from her mind.

Kathleen started to step into the meadow when she noticed the light in the parlor window of her cottage.

What on earth? They never used that room. She drew back hastily into the protection of the trees. Why would a light be there?

Only as a warning or a signal of some sort.

As she stood silently, trying to decide what to do, lightning flashed in the sky behind Rose Cottage, illuminating it and . . .

. . . the soldier standing guard at the front gate.

Dear God in heaven, they were still here.

But why? Did they suspect she was Captain Starlight?

Keeping to the cover of the trees, Kathleen moved carefully to a small rise that offered enough height for her to see in the lighted window.

She saw Brigid's and Maggie's profiles sitting side by side. Beyond them, in a chair facing the window, sat a man in the uniform of an English officer.

Fear gripped her, and her hands went involuntarily to her neck. She could almost feel the noose around it, and she gulped hard. What was she to do now?

How would she ever be able to explain her absence from the cottage all these hours?

Worse, how was she to change out of her distinctive uniform that convicted her as surely as a confession would?

The lightning flashes were coming more frequently now, and she was terrified one of them would betray her presence to the soldier at the gate.

Kathleen had never felt so alone and frightened in her life. What if, as at the Vale of Kincaid, sentries had been posted farther away from the cottage in the woods?

As she struggled to stifle her rising panic, a strong arm suddenly imprisoned her, pinioning her arms to her sides so that she could not fight. A hand closed over her mouth, sealing it against a scream.

Dear God in heaven, she had been captured in her Captain Starlight uniform.

And now she would be hanged.

Chapter 24

❦

For a moment, Kathleen was too shocked and terrified to move. Her heart was thudding so that were it not for the wailing of the wind through the trees and the rumble of thunder her captor surely would have heard it.

He brought his mouth so near to her ear that she could feel through the silk of her hood the stubble of his beard against her cheek.

"Do not make a sound, *alainn*."

The words were as faint as a breath on the wind, and for a second Kathleen wondered whether she only imagined them. Then she breathed in the spicy scent that was uniquely Shane's. She was certain it was he.

Keeping his hand across her mouth, he let go of her arms. Grabbing the back of her head with his suddenly free hand, he turned her to face him.

Another flash of lightning revealed his taut, anxious face.

Relief beyond anything Kathleen had ever experienced swept over her.

She felt that a great burden had suddenly been lifted from her shoulders. A confidence, irrational though it might be, sprang up in her that Shane would protect her from danger and keep her safe.

When the thunder roared two seconds after the lightning, he removed his hand from her mouth. He must have feared she would scream.

Instead she threw herself into his arms, hugging him as though their lives depended on it. He embraced her with equal fervor, then pulled off the green hood that covered her head. "And now, Captain Starlight, will you tell me you are not Kathleen?"

Before she could answer, his mouth claimed hers in a long, exquisite communication that obliterated the need for words.

When he released her, he put a finger to his lips, cautioning her to silence. Then he nodded to the left and the right, and soundlessly mouthed the word *soldiers*. He gestured for her to follow him, and she did.

They kept to the trees. Only Shane knew where they were going.

He made so many changes of direction that she was no longer certain where she was. Even when a long, crooked lightning flash illuminated the countryside, she was not certain of their location. The light was followed instantly by a clap of thunder so loud that it made her ears ache.

Shane appeared to know his whereabouts, for he moved purposefully. Odd that he who had been here so short a time seemed to know Canamara better than she, who had lived here for years.

Finally, they emerged from the trees, and she discovered they were on the back side of the hill that had as its crown Canamara's Palladian mansion. He took her hand in his, and they walked up the hill toward the house.

"You can't take me there," she protested in a whisper.

"It is the *only* place I can take you, *alainn*, where you will be safe. It is the one place where Radnor has not thought to look for you tonight."

"Look for me? Why would he be doing that?"

"When Radnor discovered you were not at Rose Cottage, he questioned the midwife, who knew nothing of any imminent birth. Naturally, he wondered why you lied about where you were going. The obvious answer is you did not want anyone to know where you would be."

"With the Knights, does he think?"

"Perhaps. Since he did not look for you in the great house, we can safely say you have been there all the time."

"But someone may see us going in," Kathleen objected.

"No, because I will take you in a secret entrance and up to my bedchamber."

"What if we are discovered there?"

He stopped and turned to her, brushing her face gently with the fingertips of his free hand. "I am afraid tonight you have to choose between your life and your reputation, *alainn*. Radnor is determined to see Captain Starlight hang."

Kathleen gulped.

"I hope you choose life for Brigid's sake, if for no other reason, but for mine too." Shane said somberly.

"You know I would do anything, give up anything for my daughter." *And for you.*

"I thought so." Shane brushed her cheek gently. "Which is why we must give Radnor a perfectly plausible explanation he is not expecting."

"That we have spent the night together?" The

mere thought made Kathleen hot and achy with need.

Shane nodded. "Yes, in my bed at Canamara."

He led her through a small opening in a circular hedge that was taller than he was. Kathleen saw they'd entered a small private garden, adjacent to the house. She looked about her while Shane approached the wall of the house.

When she looked back toward him, she could scarcely believe what she saw. A small section of what she had thought was a solid wall swung inward, and she saw a room beyond it.

Shane stood in the opening, silhouetted in a light behind him, and held out his hand to her. "Come, *alainn.*"

She took the hand he offered. As she stepped through the entrance into a small lamplit room, she noticed how the outside of the door had been cunningly faced with stone, perfectly fitted so it appeared to be part of a solid wall.

The secret door swung noiselessly shut behind them, becoming an indistinguishable part of the interior wall's oak paneling. The room was small and windowless, with only one obvious door, and that was bolted from inside.

Gun cases stood against three of the walls. On a small table, a candlestick with a lighted taper supplemented the lamp's illumination.

Kathleen looked at Shane, who'd moved across the room, and gaped in astonishment. He stood before another hidden opening in the wall paneling. Through this secret door, she saw a narrow staircase. She recalled his saying it led up to his bedchamber. The tempo of her heart quickened.

Shane picked up the candlestick from the table and held out his other hand to her. She took it, and his fingers curled reassuringly around hers.

He led her to the staircase and handed the taper to her. "Take this and go ahead of me. It will be easier for you if you carry the candle."

She released his hand reluctantly, took the candlestick, and started up the hidden passage. It reeked of damp and mildew.

At the top of the stairs, she swung the door inward and stepped into a large room.

Now she had no need for the candle she carried. Several tapers had been lighted about the room, which must surely be larger than any other bedchamber she'd been in.

A corner room, it contained an impressive collection of beautiful and expensive furnishings, including one of the biggest tester beds she had ever seen. In daylight, the windows along the two outside walls must offer a marvelous view of Canamara's park.

She glanced back toward Shane. His hair was disheveled, his face drawn and weary, his chin darkened by the faint stubble she had felt against her cheek. The front of his once white ruffled shirt was as mud-stained as her uniform from having hugged her.

He'd removed his neckcloth and unfastened the upper buttons of the shirt, revealing the curling black hair on his chest. Kathleen had to crush a powerful desire to slip her hands beneath his shirt and run her fingers through it.

"You must get out of that uniform as quickly as you can. You can use the dressing room." Shane gestured toward an open door. "You will find soap and water and a robe of mine you can use."

Kathleen went through the door and closed it behind her. Sitting on a chair, she yanked off her boots. Then she stood to strip off her muddy Captain Starlight uniform. With a sigh of relief, she removed the cloth that flattened her breasts painfully against her chest. She poured water into the basin to wash herself.

After she finished, she donned the robe, smiling as she detected his spicy scent clinging to it.

When she stepped back into the bedchamber, Shane hurried past her into the dressing room and quickly gathered up her discarded uniform, rolling it up around her boots. He carried the bundle over to the staircase they had used and left it on the steps.

Then he pushed the door to the stairs, and it swung closed, again becoming an undetectable part of the room's oak paneling.

Shane stripped off his muddy shirt, and suddenly Kathleen was all too aware that she wore only a thin robe.

He gathered her in his arms and held her tightly to him, murmuring, "Safe at last. I was terrified you would be killed or captured."

"So was I," she admitted, nestling against the warmth of his hard chest, feeling secure in the protection of his arms.

For the first time in months, Kathleen felt as though she no longer faced a dangerous world alone. Shane would be beside her. It was as though he had shouldered with her the burden of responsibilities that weighed so heavily upon her.

Not many men would have taken the chances he had tonight. "Why did you risk so much to help the Knights?"

"It was not to help the Knights but to save you. I did what I did for you."

She tipped her head back so she could see his face. "But why?"

"Surely you know why," he answered softly.

Perhaps she did, but she wanted to hear it from his lips. "Please tell me."

"Because I love you, *alainn*." His eyes glowed with it, silently confirming what his lips said.

It was the answer Kathleen had wanted but hardly dared to hope she would hear. She felt as though she might die of sheer joy.

And he said it with as much ease and assurance as he danced an Irish jig. Those three words had been as difficult for Patrick to say as the jig had been for him to dance.

Shane gently, lovingly smoothed her hair with his fingers, sending little shivers of pleasure through her. "And when a man loves a woman, he wants to protect her from all danger, from all unpleasantness. By bringing you here, I removed you from danger. But I fear much that is unpleasant still lies ahead of you, *alainn*."

He was right, of course. Kathleen would be the object of much gossip and censure, once it became known she had shared the bed of His Devilship's guest. But with Shane at her side, she felt as though she could deal with whatever happened. "No doubt, but now I want to think only of you and our love."

He looked as though she had just given him a priceless gift. "Do you love me, *alainn*? Perhaps I need to hear the words too."

She smiled. "I love you, Shane Howard."

He hugged her to him with such exuberant passion that she could scarcely breathe. "Now, let me show you how much I love you."

And he did, slowly, thoroughly, mouth and

hands exploring every inch of her, every erotic place. When at last he entered her, he brought her to the brink of fulfillment, then retreated over and over until she thought she would go mad with pleasure and need.

When at last he allowed her to climax, her body convulsed around him and, with a triumphant cry, he too found his release.

Afterward, as he had their first night together, he kept their sweat-slick bodies joined as he rolled on his side.

She drifted to sleep in his arms.

When she opened her eyes again, Shane still held her, watching her with a strange haunted expression, simultaneously happy and sad.

Perplexed, she asked, "What is it?"

The light of the candles that still burned cast a soft, shadowy light over his face. "I love you so much, *alainn*. I have never wanted a woman as I want you."

Joy so strong she trembled surged through her, and she smiled sleepily at him. "Then why does that make you look sad? Especially when I love you too."

He hugged her to him, his mouth so close to her ear that his breath tickled it as he whispered, "I hope that no matter what happens, you will always believe how much I love you. And I pray to God that your love will be strong enough to keep you with me always."

That so startled her, she broke the embrace and propped herself up on one elbow so that she could study his face on the pillow. Even with his jaw darkened by emerging beard, she had never seen a face she liked more. "I don't understand."

He sighed and reached up to brush her hair gently away from her face. "Life is not always as easy or simple as we would like, *alainn*."

Puzzled, she looked beyond him, and her gaze fell on the miniature of the small boy on the table beside his bed. She reached over Shane and touched the frame. "May I?"

"Of course."

She picked up the tiny portrait of his son. The boy had a charming smile upon his lips and a mischievous glow in his bright blue eyes so like his father's.

Other than the eyes and the smile, though, he did not resemble Shane very much. The boy's face was thinner, his features more delicate, and his hair blond.

"After my wife died, I devoted myself to him. He was the center of my life, the sun around which it revolved."

As Brigid had been Kathleen's.

"When he died, I wanted to die too," Shane confessed in a raw voice. "My life seemed without purpose or meaning."

"Seemed, past tense?"

"Yes, *alainn*. You and Brigid have restored my appreciation for life."

As he has mine! Kathleen looked down at his son's sweet, little face in the miniature. "What about purpose?"

"That too. I swear to you, *alainn*, I will right the wrongs that have been done to the tenants at Canamara."

As if His Devilship would stand for that! What terrible disillusionment Shane was courting both about his friend and about what he himself could accomplish. "And how—"

A loud pounding sounded on the door of the bedchamber and immediately the door flew open.

Radnor burst into the room, followed by an officer in an English major's uniform.

Chapter 25

Shane pulled Kathleen down on the bed and yanked the covers over her to hide both her face and her nakedness.

Pushing himself into a sitting position, he demanded in a voice that held all the authority of an angry and affronted lord of the realm. "What the hell do you mean, bursting into my bedchamber like this?"

The major stopped abruptly, clearly recognizing a man of superior power.

Radnor was not so perceptive. "We were told . . . I cannot believe it . . . We were told . . ." He was in such a fury, he could not seem to spit out a coherent sentence.

"Shut up," the major ordered him bluntly. "I will handle this. I must ask, sir, who is in the bed with you?"

"That, Major, is none of your damn business— nor anyone else's," Shane answered brusquely.

"Perhaps not under ordinary circumstances, sir," the major said politely. "But I fear tonight is not ordinary. We are searching for a missing woman, a Kathleen McNamara."

"That gives you no right to invade my bedchamber. Kindly explain why you have done so."

The major looked as though he preferred to depart at once. "We were told she was with you."

"By whom?" Shane demanded.

"I cannot divulge that, sir. Is she with you?"

Shane parried with a question of his own. "What earthly reason could you have to be searching for her?"

"She was not at home, and she lied about where she was going," the major said.

"I fail to see how that signifies," Shane retorted.

The major looked at Radnor, clearly exasperated with him. "When she was not at home, this man seemed to have some nonsensical idea that she was part of a band of Irish insurgents, perhaps even its leader."

"What absolute nonsense," Shane agreed indignantly. "As if any woman—and particularly a woman of Mrs. McNamara's gentle nature and sensibilities—would lead, or even be a part of, such a traitorous band."

Shane heard Kathleen's sharp intake of breath. No doubt she'd give him hell for that later.

"You seem to know the woman quite well," the major observed. "While I appreciate your chivalrous concern for her reputation, believe me, you will be doing her a great favor to tell me if she is the woman in your bed now."

The major gestured at Radnor. "If this man's suspicions are correct, she faces the hanging tree. Now, sir, is this Mrs. McNamara in your bed?"

"Yes, I am." Kathleen popped up beside Shane, clutching the covers about her neck.

"I can testify she was with me in my bed all night." Shane gave the major a smile that silently assured him what an exceptional time it had been.

"Why did you lie about where you were going, Mrs. McNamara?" the major asked.

"Of course she lied," Shane answered for her. "Do you think she would tell her little daughter and the rest of the world that she was coming to my bed?"

Until now Radnor had seemed transfixed by the sight of Kathleen. But now he started toward her, screaming, "You goddamn Irish slut!"

Shane, as naked as the day he was born, jumped out of bed to stop the agent. He was saved from having to do so by the major.

Several inches taller than the agent, the officer reached out, grabbed Radnor by the collars of his shirt and coat, and yanked him back. "You damn fool!"

"Take your hands off me," the agent screeched. "Your general will hear about this!"

"Indeed he will," the major snapped. "It appears you persuaded Lord Sherbourne that a large band of insurgent Irishmen was about to attack one of his tenants, who is his old friend, and that he must ask General Northrup to send troops."

As the major talked, Shane went to the wardrobe and pulled on a robe.

"So I and my men were dispatched on a fool's journey to capture this 'dangerous band' of a half-dozen drunken louts who posed more danger to themselves than anyone else."

Radnor cried, "The marquess will be in touch posthaste with General Northrup . . ."

Even sooner than that, little Ollie. Tilton was no old friend of the marquess, but General Northrup was. Shane had not known until now that Northrup had been sent to Ireland.

". . . to inform him, Major, of your ineptness and insubordination," Radnor concluded.

Shane said, "Major, if you would be so kind as to remove this obnoxious man and wait for me outside the door, I should like a word in private with you."

The major nodded, forcing Radnor toward the door.

As the door shut behind them, Shane snatched up his breeches from the floor and said to Kathleen, "This will only take a minute."

He sat down at the writing table in the corner and scrawled a quick message to Northrup, then fumbled in his breeches' pocket for his signet ring. Melting a bit of sealing wax in a candle's flame, he sealed the note shut with the signet.

Shane went to the door and stepped into the hall, where the officer waited. "Major, I will be happy to vouch to General Northrup for your handling of this situation. The general is a good friend of mine. I was unaware he had assumed a command in Ireland."

"He did so less than a fortnight ago, sir."

"Will you be so kind as to take an important message to him from me?"

The major nodded.

"When will you see him again?"

"I plan to leave at first light, and I should see him tomorrow night."

Shane handed the major his sealed note. "Tell the general this is an urgent message for him from Shane Howell."

"Howell?" The major frowned. "I thought that fool agent said your name was Howard."

"As you have already discovered, Major, much of what Radnor says has only a passing acquaintance with the truth. One other thing, Major, the *lady* in my bed is my future wife."

Shane prayed that he spoke the truth, that Kathleen would still marry him when she learned his true identity. "Naturally, under these circumstances, I would be outraged if the slightest breath of scandal attached to her name as a result of tonight."

"I am the soul of discretion, sir."

"Good. Who told you and Radnor that Mrs. McNamara was with me?"

"Maggie O'Brosnan, but not willingly."

"Bloody hell, what do you mean?"

"Radnor led Mrs. McNamara's little girl to think something had happened to her mother, reducing the child to terrified tears. He would not let the woman talk to the child except in his presence, and finally she had to tell the little girl to try to quiet her."

"Bastard," Shane muttered. "Did Maggie succeed in quieting Brigid?"

The major smiled. "The little girl seemed overjoyed that her mama was with you and promptly fell asleep."

When Shane went back into his bedchamber, Kathleen had donned the borrowed robe. "I must go home," she told him.

He hurried to her and took her hands in his own. "You have no clothes but that uniform," he reminded her. "I will borrow a gown from Siobhan in the morning."

"But Brigid will be worried about me."

"She already knows you are safe with me." He quickly related what the major had told him. "You might as well stay. The damage has already been done."

"I suppose it has," she agreed sadly.

He kissed one of her hands that he held and then the other. "Do not look so dejected, *alainn*."

She tried to smile, but she was not very successful.

He kissed her first on the tip of her nose, then on her lips, a sensual, coaxing kiss. Shane loved her taste, her passion, everything about her. He released her hands and untied the belt of her robe.

As he pushed the cloth aside, his mouth claimed the rosy tip of one breast while his thumb tantalized the other. She moaned with pleasure.

He brought his lips to her ear and sucked lightly on the lobe before whispering, "Come back to bed, *alainn*."

She let him lead her to the big tester bed.

As Kathleen settled on it, her gaze fell on the miniature of his dead son. She looked up at him. "Did you love your wife?"

"It is why I married her." Amiable, fragile Sarah had been Shane's first love. Timid and easily reduced to tears, she had inspired in his young heart, inexperienced and chivalrous, an eagerness to give her the world and to protect her from it.

Their marriage, like their love, had been quiet and sweet, lacking the fire and the passion that crackled between him and Kathleen.

Now, in retrospect, making love to Sarah had been like having a china doll in his bed. No matter what he tried, and desperation could indeed be the mother of invention, she had lain like a stone beneath him. Nothing he did elicited a response.

Her mama had instructed her with great firmness that no true lady could enjoy her husband in bed. And Sarah had been far too docile and obedient ever to question what her mother taught her.

Or to disagree with any opinion put forth by her husband.

When Sarah had died giving birth to their son, Shane had been filled with terrible guilt. God knew, and so did he, that she had gotten no pleasure out of the begetting of their child.

Now looking back, he saw he had been bored in his marriage. Shane had unconsciously yearned for a woman who would be his partner and companion in life, rather than a pliant, unquestioning wife, who was more child than adult.

He wanted a woman with whom he could share his passion and his problems, his joys and his dilemmas. Until he met Kathleen, he had not known what he was missing.

Not only was she the most exciting woman he had ever known, she was the loveliest. And it was not just her perfect oval face with its glowing emerald eyes, alabaster complexion, and sensual lips he ached to kiss. No, her beauty was not merely physical. It was soul-deep, a beauty of heart and spirit.

Shane made love to Kathleen again with the same thorough slowness that he had before, and once again they arced to a sensual paradise.

He collapsed against her, murmuring, "I love you so much, *alainn*."

Kathleen smiled at him. "And I love you."

She seemed to expect him to say more.

"What is it?" he asked, puzzled.

"I am wondering what your intentions toward me are."

Shane smiled. "Honorable, only honorable."

She waited for him to continue.

And Shane wanted to do so. He ached to ask her to marry him then and there, to bind her to him

before she learned who he really was. But that
would be wrong, cowardly.

No, he could not ask her until she knew to whom
she would be committing herself.

But would she accept him then? Kathleen must
be one of the very few women who, he expected,
would reject a marquess, his fortune, and all that
he could give her.

She continued to regard him with a perplexed
expression, still waiting.

Finally, he said, "I want to marry you, Kathleen,
but I cannot ask you, at least not yet."

"Why not?"

He hesitated. "I want you to be certain you want
to marry me."

Her eyes narrowed at that. "And you're thinkin'
I don't know my own mind? I don't understand."

"In time you will." He kissed her with passionate ardor. "No matter what happens, remember,
alainn, that I love you with all my heart and I always will."

Chapter 26

When Shane took Kathleen back to Rose Cottage the next morning, she was very quiet. He knew he had hurt her by not asking her to marry him. Perhaps he was a fool for not doing so, for not trying to bind her to him before she learned the truth.

As they reached the gate of Rose Cottage, Brigid ran out to meet them. "Mama, Mama, so worried I was about you till I heard you were with S'ane." She threw herself into Kathleen's arms and hugged her.

Mother and daughter clung together for a full minute. When Kathleen released Brigid, the little girl turned to Shane, her eyes shining.

"Maggie says Mama not coming home last night means you're going to be my da." She eagerly awaited his confirmation.

"It is what I want, Brigid, more than anything," he assured her quietly, "but I cannot do that quite yet."

Brigid's crestfallen expression nearly broke his heart. Her mother did not look much happier.

"Why not?" Brigid asked.

"Another matter must be dealt with first, *sidhe*."

The following morning, Kathleen was gathering together what she would take to school when one of the odious English footmen from Canamara, accompanied by two soldiers, arrived at Rose Cottage to summon her immediately to the great house.

"Why?" she asked as an alarmed Brigid clung to her skirt.

The footman said haughtily. "It is not for me to say."

"And more important things I've to do than go with you," she retorted. "Good day to you."

The footman looked meaningfully at the two soldiers, "You *will* come with us."

Kathleen thought of resisting, but she feared the soldiers might drag her from the cottage, and her daughter would be terrified.

When they reached the house, she was taken in through the servants' entrance, as though she were not good enough to enter by the front door, and led into the library.

She looked at the great number of books that lined the walls and wished she had only a fraction of them for her students.

In the center of the library, Oliver Radnor sat behind a large, imposing desk. Ben Tilton, a cruel smile on his scarred face, stood nearby. Two other men were in the room, one a young man in a lieutenant's uniform and the other, the sheriff.

A cold chill shook Kathleen. Had they found some proof that she was Captain Starlight? She fought down the panic that threatened to envelop her. How desperately she wished Shane were there beside her, but she was on her own.

She demanded with a hauteur she was far from feeling, "What do you want of me?"

Remaining seated in front of her as though he were a judge on the bench and she a convict awaiting sentence, Radnor glared at her with silent fury for a long moment. "You will see soon enough, you damn slut."

The door opened again, and Shane, dressed in black breeches and a white ruffled shirt, was escorted between two of the sheriff's men, who looked much discomfited by the duty they had been assigned.

Kathleen could see why. Shane had never looked more formidable. Gone was the tender, teasing man who had made such beautiful love to her. In his place stood a stranger, his face as hard as the granite of Kincaid Mountain. And he radiated an authority that had clearly cowed his escorts.

"What the bloody hell is the meaning of this outrage?" Shane thundered in a voice that promised terrible retribution.

The lieutenant looked unnerved, and the sheriff stared at Shane as though he were seeing a ghost.

Only Radnor, smirking behind the massive desk, seemed oblivious to the aura of power that Shane projected.

"I will deal with the woman first," Radnor said, looking at Kathleen. "The marquess has ordered you evicted immediately from Rose Cottage so his friend Ben Tilton may live there."

"No, the marquess has done no such thing," Shane snapped. "I demand you show us Lord Sherbourne's eviction order."

Ben Tilton stepped menacingly forward toward Shane. "Shut up. Me's 'Is Lordship's friend, and—"

"And," Shane growled, "anyone with a modicum of intelligence can see you corrupt, stinking scum out of a London gutter could not possibly be a friend of the marquess." The contempt in Shane's voice was mirrored in his eyes as they swept Tilton.

Shane seemed to cow even the big scarred man, who shut his mouth with a snap.

"Far from being a friend of the marquess, Tilton, you would not recognize him if he were standing before you, you damn impostor," Shane continued.

"You are the impostor," Radnor cried shrilly. "Sheriff, arrest this man. He came here posing as a friend of the marquess and has been stealing His Lordship blind while he has been here."

"No, Radnor, I have stolen nothing. You are the thief who, as you phrase it, has been stealing His Lordship blind."

Radnor looked on the verge of apoplexy. "This man has been stealing food, Sheriff! I can prove it. Arrest him immediately."

The sheriff, however, continued to stare at Shane as though he could not believe his eyes.

"I am no thief."

"You deny you removed food from the pantry?" the lieutenant asked.

"No, I do not deny it. I took food to feed the people that Radnor here, in his greed, has been starving."

Shane looked at Kathleen, and she saw in his eyes a deep sadness, contrition, and heartfelt apology to her.

But why to her? He had not stolen from her, and as far as she was concerned, he had not stolen at all, although she knew English law would not agree.

Continuing to look only at her with that strange pleading expression, Shane said, "But I stole nothing from the marquess. That would be impossible."

Kathleen blinked at this. Snatches of other things Shane had said flashed through her mind:

Sherbourne knew nothing of this.

He is not as bad as you think.

Far from being a friend of the marquess, Tilton, you would not recognize him if he were standing before you.

Shane's gaze met hers squarely and held it with an anguished plea for her to understand and forgive him.

Slowly in her mind, the unthinkable became the thinkable. Finally she grasped the truth. The realization hit her with the impact of a lightning bolt, stunning her, robbing her of breath, and incinerating her heart. "Oh, dear God in heaven, no," she cried.

She clasped her hand to her mouth, trying to choke down the nausea that welled up, and ran toward the door. The attention of the two soldiers was fixed on Shane, and she eluded their belated attempt to stop her.

Kathleen fled the room and the house, still clutching her mouth.

She had not slept with a friend of the devil, but with the devil himself!

With her husband's murderer!

Shane saw the horror on Kathleen's face as she ran from the room.

The soldiers started after her.

"Let her go," he ordered in a voice that froze them in their tracks.

Damn it, Shane had not wanted Kathleen to find out his true identity like this. One more sin Radnor would answer for. He longed to go after her, but first he would have to deal with the lieutenant and the sheriff.

The officer said nervously, "But you just admitted that you took the food. How can you say that is not theft?"

"I cannot steal from myself, Lieutenant."

Profound silence fell on the room as the others stared at Shane with varying degrees of comprehension, from the lieutenant's complete and dismayed understanding to Tilton's total lack of it. Radnor appeared dazed.

"What's 'im talking about?" Tilton asked.

Shane said scathingly, "As I said, this lying impostor here does not know the Marquess of Sherbourne when he is standing before him."

Tilton still looked baffled. "What—"

"Shut up, you damn fool," Radnor snapped. "I tell you he is not the marquess. Who would know that better than I, his agent? You will find no one here who will identify him as Lord Sherbourne."

"Can anyone *of repute* confirm you are the marquess?" the lieutenant asked.

"Your commanding general can," Shane said curtly, irritated that these questions were preventing him from going after Kathleen. "Northrup is an old friend of mine. I have sent for him, and he should be here tomorrow. And shortly after that I expect my solicitor, my man of business, and my secretary from London. Will that be *repute* enough?"

"Y-y-yes, my lord," the lieutenant stammered.

"Do not believe him!" Panic and desperation were thick in Radnor's voice. "The man is an impostor, seeking revenge on me."

"I have no doubt he is the marquess," the sheriff announced.

"Are you Sheriff McKenna?" Shane asked. "My grandfather wrote me of you."

"And you, my lord, have the manner and bearing of your grandfather," McKenna said. "When you came into the room, I thought I was seeing a ghost of the old Lion as a young man. I was only a child then, but I've never forgotten him."

"You have just paid me a fine compliment," Shane said with a smile. "Thank you. Please take these two scoundrels into custody." He gestured toward Radnor and Tilton.

"What am I to charge Mr. Radnor with, my lord?"

"All the crimes, ranging from murder to fraud and grand larceny, that he has committed during the past six years, many of them against me. He has stolen hundreds of thousands of pounds from me, and I can prove it."

A strangled cry escaped Radnor, and he darted for the door.

Shane grabbed him by the shirtfront and brought him up short. As he held the agent, he realized he had grabbed more than merely cloth. Two objects— long, thin, and hard, hung from a chain around Radnor's neck.

Still holding him with one hand, Shane slipped the other under the shirt and grabbed the objects, yanking both them and the chain that held them over Radnor's head.

The sheriff told his men to take Radnor into custody.

"Give me those keys," Radnor shrieked. "They are mine."

"No, I suspect they are mine." Shane looked down at the two brass keys in his hand. "One I will wager is the missing key to the cabinet in my bedchamber."

The sheriff's men each took one of Radnor's arms.

"You say he is guilty of murder?" the sheriff asked.

"Yes, the murder of Patrick McNamara and I suspect also of Robert Sutton, Lord Sutton's second son."

"Good God!" the young lieutenant exclaimed.

Shane stuffed the two keys into his pocket. He should go immediately to see if one unlocked the cabinet in his bedchamber, but nothing was as important to him as seeing Kathleen.

"Now I must beg you all to excuse me," he said, starting for the door. "I have a piece of urgent business that cannot wait."

The most important business of his life.

Still in the grip of shock, Kathleen stumbled toward Rose Cottage, hardly knowing where she was or what she was doing. By the time she reached it, she could scarcely see for the tears streaming from her eyes.

As she slammed the front door shut behind her, Brigid darted into the hall. "Mama, Mama, what's wrong?"

Kathleen did not hold out her arms to her daughter as she'd always done when Brigid sought her attention. "Leave me alone, please, darling. I am not feeling well."

She ran up the steps to her bedroom. For the first time in the years she had lived in Rose Cottage, she turned the key and locked herself in her chamber.

Kathleen threw herself across the bed and gave

way to great gulping sobs. Shane had made the world's greatest fool out of her.

And turned her into a scandalous traitor to Ireland too.

And to Patrick and his memory, for making love with the man responsible for his death.

Kathleen understood now why Shane had not asked her to marry him. The Marquess of Sherbourne would not, could not, lower himself to wed an Irish woman. He could never make her his wife and marchioness.

She told herself Shane was just one more rotten Englishman, lying to an Irish woman so he could have his way with her.

And she found that the most painful, unforgivable sin of all.

She was merely, as Radnor had said, Shane's Irish slut. She could never be anything else to the mighty marquess.

Her heart shattered into so many shards she knew it could never be made whole again. She had never felt so used and betrayed in her life.

And she hated the man who had done this to her.

Hated him for making her love him.

Hated him for robbing her of her self-respect.

Hated him for deceiving her so easily and cunningly.

In that instant, her love for him was consumed in the flames of her outrage and fury over the wrong he had done her. She would never forgive him.

Now she hated Shane as much as she had once loved him.

*   *   *

When Shane reached Rose Cottage, the front door was ajar, and he heard weeping inside. He pushed open the door without knocking. Maggie was on her knees beside it, trying to comfort a sobbing Brigid.

"Is she hurt?" Shane asked in alarm.

"No, it's scared she is about her mama. Mrs. McNamara's locked herself in her bedchamber and won't let anyone in. She's never locked the door to Brigid before."

Shane gathered the crying child up in his arms and hugged her. "Do not cry, *sidhe*."

"Something terrible's wrong with Mama."

"No, sweetheart. Your mama has just learned some shocking news that has upset her a great deal. But it has nothing to do with you. She still loves you very much, and so do I."

Her chubby little arms crept around his neck. "If you loves me so much, will you be my da?"

He squeezed her, and his own voice was choked. "I want to be your da more than anything in the world, *sidhe*, but that is up to your mama. Only she can make me your da."

Shane set Brigid down. "Now let me go upstairs to her and see if I can convince her to do that."

When he knocked on Kathleen's door, she cried, "Go away."

He tried the door, but it was still locked. "Let me in, *alainn*."

"*You!* Damn you, leave me alone."

"Please, unlock the door. We need to talk."

"What about—the enormous fool you made of me? I hate you!"

He felt as though a great boulder were crushing his heart. "Well, I *love* you, *alainn*. Now let me in so I can tell you how much I do."

"You mean so you can seduce me again into believing your lies. I will never again believe a word you say. Everything you've told me has been a lie, Your Devilship! And I will hate you until my dying day."

He winced at that. "Listen to me, Kathleen, I told you no lies except by omission."

"You told me you were your son's tutor and taught him Gaelic."

"I was, and I did. He had no tutor but me."

"You murdered my husband."

"Damn it, I did not!" Shane was tired of being unjustly accused of murder. "Oliver Radnor killed him, and I promise you I will see him hang for it."

"Radnor? But Alban . . ." Her voice trailed off.

"No, Radnor killed him."

"But you ordered him to do so."

"I did nothing of the sort. I am as much Radnor's victim as your husband was. I had no idea what was going on here until after I arrived. Had I, I would have put a stop to it long ago."

"As if I would believe anything you say now. Go away."

"Please, *alainn*, let me in."

"No!"

"I will break the door down."

Silence.

The door remained locked. In exasperation, Shane kicked the door hard, then threw himself against it. The door groaned but held fast. He tried again with no greater success.

Finally on his third try, he heard the wood splinter, and the door gave way.

Kathleen jumped up from her bed, her eyes sparking like green flints, her hair tumbling all about her in burgundy waves. She looked like an avenging angel.

What a magnificent creature she was. Shane could not help smiling.

"I will have you arrested!" she cried.

"For what," he asked tersely, "breaking into my own property?"

She stiffened in obvious outrage. "That's right! Everything here belongs to you, doesn't it, Your Devilship?"

He made a conscious effort to control his anger. "Damn it, do not call me that. You know by now what kind of man I am."

"Yes, I do." She spit the words at him. "A man who lies to a woman about who he is, so he can trick her into his bed."

It broke Shane's heart to see the disillusionment in her eyes. "I did not. What happened there was your decision. I gave you the choice."

"And you know what my choice would have been had I known who you really were."

"Yes, I do," he admitted. "Because had you known, you would never have given me a chance to show you what kind of man I am. You would never have seen beyond the false image of me that Oliver Radnor so carefully constructed and nurtured."

"And if you loved me as you claimed, you scoundrel, you would have told me the truth. You would have trusted me. Love requires trust."

"Yes, it does, but it was not my trust that worried me. It was yours. I was less certain of your trust—and your love—for me. Given the way you are acting now, my apprehension was justified."

She waited as though she expected him to say more, but he did not know what she wanted from him. He only knew what he wanted from her. He looked beyond her at the bed where he ached to lay his fiery colleen and prove his love for her. He would like to take a week doing that if he could.

She apparently grasped part of what he was thinking, for her eyes suddenly radiated fury. "And now, just like Radnor, you will demand my body again as payment for Rose Cottage. Well—"

He cut her off. "Do not insult us both, *alainn*! I beg of you, do not tarnish what we have together."

"You are the one who has tarnished it beyond repair with your lies. Now go away. I never want to set eyes on you again."

Shane sighed. Kathleen was far too overwrought for him to reason with her now. Perhaps later, when the shock of discovering who he was wore off and she calmed down, he could persuade her of his love.

"Very well, I will go. When you come to your senses and want to talk, send for me. I will be at the house." He stepped past the door that hung crazily on its hinges and into the hall.

When you come to your senses. To Kathleen's tormented, raw emotions, pulled between love and guilt, he meant that when she was ready to accept the honor of being the almighty marquess's mistress, she should come to him.

It was like touching a spark to an explosive. "I will never change my mind, Your Devilship!" she cried after him. "I never want to see your face again. I will never forgive you! I loathe the sight of you!"

Chapter 27

As Shane crossed the hall toward the drawing room after returning from his futile visit to see Kathleen, Siobhan appeared in the doorway of the dining room. She stopped abruptly when she saw him, looking frightened. Curtsying to him, she backed through the door and shut it quickly.

The other Irish servants were clearly afraid of him too, even though he had given them no reason to be while he had been at Canamara. It was as though he had suddenly been transformed into a monster.

His Devilship was now in residence, he thought bitterly.

Hurrying upstairs to his bedchamber, he tried one of the keys he had taken from Radnor in the lock of the mahogany cabinet.

It opened immediately.

Inside, as Shane had expected, he found Radnor's private ledgers that reflected the real finances of the estate and a large stack of leases to which the agent had forged a very poor imitation of Shane's signature. Studying the outrageous sums Radnor had collected for tiny plots of land, Shane was incensed.

Now he had to determine how best to right all the wrongs that had been done in his name and devise a way to be fair to all the tenants in a situation where justice for some meant injustice for others. Could he find a solution to that conundrum? Was it even possible?

And then there was Kathleen. The look of betrayal and anguish on her face as he'd left her was seared into his memory. Her parting words echoed over and over in his mind. *I will never forgive you! I loathe the sight of you!*

He had lost her and lost too the future that had seemed so bright and promising with her as his wife. He had counted on her love for him removing the blinders that distorted so cruelly her image of Sherbourne. He'd prayed her love would be strong enough to bind her and temper her disillusionment when she learned the truth.

But he had been deluding himself.

She had not loved him enough. She had not loved him as he had loved her with every fiber of his being. His heart felt as though it had been ground to dust. He should never have hoped . . . dreamed. The agony of his loss was wrenching. He felt as bereft as he had when Jeremy died. He should have known better than to open himself to that kind of pain again.

Yet much as he wanted to crawl into his lair and lick his wounds as he'd done after his son had died, he could not do that now. Too many wrongs must be righted; too many injustices must be eliminated.

Beneath a seething sky dumping intermittent rain, Shane set out from Canamara, his thoughts as dark as the sky above him.

He'd ridden partway down the hill from the house when he heard, "Mr. Howard!"

Shane looked to his left and saw Mike Kelly running toward him. The boy dashed up, panting for breath. "I'll . . . be takin' ye . . . to me da. But hurry we must . . . or I'm afeared . . . we won't be findin' him."

Shane hoisted the boy in front of him on the sorrel gelding. "Show me the direction."

"That way." Mike pointed toward the bog.

The boy guided Shane to a section of the bog he had not seen before where the peat had been cut away for fuel. It looked like a giant black staircase.

On one of the steps sat Alban Kelly, a thin nervous man whose hair had whitened before its time.

When Mike saw his father, he slid off the horse.

Shane nudged his mount close to the elder Kelly. His work-hardened fingers twisted the buttons of his shirt. He did not meet Shane's gaze but stared at his chest. "Me Mikie shouldn't have been tellin' ye what he did."

"Are you telling your son he should not speak the truth, Kelly?" Shane demanded, now every inch the marquess. "How can you, or any father, instruct his son to lie?"

Alban looked stricken, and he stammered about for a time before managing to say, "It were that, or let his brothers and sisters die o' hunger."

"You have Lord Sherbourne's promise that your position as gamekeeper at Canamara is secure so long as you stop lying about who killed Patrick McNamara and tell what really happened."

"Sure and who be lyin' now?" Alban demanded. "How can ye be speakin' fer Devil Sherbourne?"

"Because I am the Devil."

Alban's face was a study in confusion. "What ye sayin'?"

"I am saying I am Lord Sherbourne. I know you did not kill McNamara. Nor did I order him killed. I assure you that your employment with me is secure as long as you tell the sheriff the truth about what happened that day and who killed Patrick McNamara. Now, Mr. Kelly, get on this horse behind me."

Alban stared at him. "W-w-why?"

"I am taking you to Canamara so you can tell Sheriff McKenna, who is there, the truth."

Shane looked down at Mike, who was gaping at him. "I want you to come to Canamara too, so you also can talk to the sheriff. You will have to walk, but I promise you a fine dinner after you get there."

Later that day, Shane rode up alone to the McNultys' hovel and dismounted. Carrying a goose-down quilt in his arms, he went to the opening.

Through it he saw Mrs. McNulty slumped on a three-legged stool beside the bit of straw that served as Maurea's bed. Her profile was a study in dejection and despair. He understood her emotions so well, for he had felt the same when Jeremy was dying.

"How is Maurea?" he asked softly.

She jumped. "Holy Mother, ye scared me! What ye be doin' here, Mr. Howard?"

"I have come to take you and Maurea back to your cottage. The soldiers are clearing the Tiltons out of it now."

She gaped at him. Then yells and curses rang out

from the hillside above the cave, verifying what Shane had said.

The little girl, only semiconscious, was tossing feverishly, fretfully on the straw. He lifted her from it and wrapped her carefully in the quilt he had brought. "Come, I will carry her up now."

"Won't do no good," her mother said. "Them Tiltons'll only come back and drive us out again."

"They will never bother you again, Mrs. Mc-Nulty. You have my word on that."

"Beggin' yer pardon, I'm meanin' no offense, but it be His Devilship's word we need."

"You have that too."

The haggard woman stared at him as though he belonged in Bedlam, but she followed him outside.

Several woman and children from nearby hovels were standing on the path, gawking at the activity on the hillside.

Shane carried Maurea up the hill. By the time they reached the cottage, the soldiers had led Tilton's brother and the two women away.

Taking Maurea inside to her bedroom with the window that looked out on the Vale of Kincaid, Shane laid her on the little bed, making certain that the quilt covered her and that she was warm. He had ordered a turf fire lit in the room's fireplace. He noted with satisfaction that it was already taking the chill off the room and sweetening its air.

He said to her mother. "I had the soldiers leave food in the kitchen for you, and I have sent for the doctor for Maurea." He turned to leave.

"The doctor won't treat the likes o' us," the woman said bitterly.

Shane smiled, even though his own heart was as cold as a glacier. "Yes, he will."

* * *

As the clock struck one A.M., Kathleen still lay wide awake beside her sleeping daughter in their bed at Rose Cottage. Her heart felt as though it were an open wound from which her lifeblood was leaking away.

Was everything Shane told her a lie?

Probably, she told herself bitterly. He was an English aristocrat. He'd protested he loved her, but he had said nothing more about marrying her.

She longed to throw herself into his arms and sob out her hurt and pain and have him comfort her. How ridiculous, she berated herself, to want the cause of her pain to cure it.

Yet her treacherous body ached for his beside her, cried out for the ecstasy of his lovemaking.

Damn you, Shane Howard! Damn you to hell and back, Devil Sherbourne!

Chapter 28

❦

"**W**hat a tangled mess, my lord." Leland Carter, Shane's man of business, looked up from the ledgers he was comparing in Canamara's estate office.

"Amen," concurred Christopher Benton, Shane's secretary, who worked at a table adjacent to Lee's desk.

"It may be weeks before we know how much Radnor stole from you," Lee said. "The total will be enormous."

"Radnor could not have spent even half the money," Shane mused. "He must have hidden it. If only we could discover where." He suspected when they did, the second key on the chain he'd taken from Radnor's neck would open the lock.

Through the open window, Shane watched the tenants gathering on the lawn beyond the side terrace for the meeting to which he had summoned them.

Whatever they might be saying was lost in the noise of carriages approaching Canamara's front portico.

Since General Northrup had come three days ago to confirm that Shane was Sherbourne, word had spread rapidly among the gentry that the marquess was in residence.

Every afternoon since then, a parade of carriages had traveled to the front portico, carrying callers eager to make the acquaintance of the English lord. One and all were told he was not yet receiving visitors.

The only carriage Shane had wanted to come, the one that had brought Lee and Chris, along with Shane's solicitor and his valet, had finally arrived at Canamara from Dublin the previous night.

Chris had presented Shane with letters that Radnor had written to his employer in London. In them, the agent had accused Shane of committing a host of crimes, as nefarious as they were imaginary, against himself.

The bracket clock on the wall struck the hour five times, and Shane turned toward the door, dreading what lay ahead of him. "Time to go out and greet my tenants."

"My lord, I must again advise you as strongly as I can against doing so unless the soldiers are present," Lee warned him. "The hatred I have heard expressed for you is truly shocking."

"They have been given good reason to hate me. I will not convince them they are wrong about me if I meet them surrounded by soldiers."

He turned to his secretary. "Wait by the French windows to the terrace, Chris, until I summon you to come out."

From the look on his secretary's face, he was more than happy to remain inside.

Shane chose to go out through Canamara's front entrance, cross the portico, and walk around to the side rather than use one of the French windows that opened directly onto the terrace because he wanted an opportunity to move among the tenants.

He quickly discovered he might as well have used the terrace doors. As Shane approached the men, their lilting voices fell silent, and they parted to clear a wide path for him. He felt like Moses at the Red Sea.

Men with whom he had been friendly avoided meeting his eye, looking instead at one another or the ground.

An invisible wall had risen between him and the tenants. He was no longer Shane Howard, but the despised Marquess of Sherbourne. Considering all the evil that had been done in his name, he supposed he could not blame them.

After climbing the steps to the terrace, he turned and looked out over the faces gathered before him. He felt the hatred, the animosity, and the fear that radiated toward him. He could force them to listen to what he would say, but could he make them hear?

As he looked out over the group, disappointment gripped him. The one tenant he most wanted to see had not come.

Kathleen was missing.

So was the other tenant he had hoped would be here. He had counted on Conn Malone to help temper the anger and hostility against him. But Conn too was absent.

Every eye was fixed on Shane when he began speaking. "As many of you must know by now, I am Sherbourne. I called you here today to explain my plans for Canamara and to give you a chance to ask me questions."

Shane saw surprise register on some of the unfamiliar faces as he addressed them in Gaelic.

"First, I wish to announce I am reinstituting a

privilege you had when my grandfather was alive. Each tenant is free again to take two fish a week from the estate's streams."

A murmur of surprise rose from the assembled men.

"I should like it to be more," Shane continued, "but I cannot risk the stream becoming fished out. That will do none of us any good."

Despite this concession, the faces before Shane did, not soften.

"The agent I placed in charge here, Oliver Radnor, has been arrested on numerous charges including murder, larceny, embezzlement, and forgery. The last charge arises from his forging my name to the leases that you now hold."

An ominous rumble rose from the tenants, but Shane continued, "Without my knowledge or consent, Radnor took the land from the tenants who held it in my grandfather's time and divided Canamara into ever smaller plots."

"Ye be sayin' then our leases ain't legal now harvest's only days away?" a belligerent voice cried from the crowd. "Sure and that's yer excuse then, to be takin' all our harvest and not just half."

The tenants' discontent turned menacing. Suddenly a little figure in a blue dress darted up to Shane and grabbed his hand in her two little ones.

Silence settled on the startled crowd as Brigid turned to face them, still clinging to Shane's hand. "Why're you so angry at S'ane?" she cried. "He's the nicest man I know."

Bless her, she had inherited her mother's spirit and courage.

But how had she gotten here? Could Shane have somehow overlooked Kathleen? He eagerly scanned the crowd for her, but only Maggie was there.

Smiling at Brigid, he said, "Thank you, *sidhe*, that is a great compliment indeed."

Men toward the back strained to glimpse Shane's little advocate, and he hoisted her in his arms for everyone to see.

The diversion she caused defused some of the antagonism toward him. Taking advantage of this, he said, "You do not need to guess what I might do. I am here to tell you what I *will* do. Since harvest is almost upon us, the leases, although fraudulent, will remain in effect until the crops are in. And because you negotiated the leases in good faith, I will compensate you by taking *none* of your harvest this year."

That silenced the men, who well knew Shane should have part of their crop. They stared at him incredulously.

Finally a man far back in the crowd found his voice. "If the leases be illegal, what about the harvest workdays they says we owes Yer Honor?"

Shane knew it would be impossible to harvest the crops on the sections of the estate he still held outright without the tenants' labor. "I ask you to honor that provision, but you will also be paid for the days you work."

"How much?" a man in tattered clothing near the front demanded.

When Shane named what was a fair, even generous sum, he was greeted by suspicion and more incredulity on the men's faces.

"Sure, and what happens after the harvest? Will ye be drivin' us from our land?"

"I will drive no one from Canamara, but I am absolutely opposed to rack rents. I would like to restore the estate to what it was when my grandfather died."

A murmur of alarm arose among some of the men. "What about all o' us that done come after?"

"I have not yet devised a plan that will be fair to all of you, old-timers and newcomers alike, but I am working on it. I do have a proposition, however, that is open to everyone now. I am hiring workers for Canamara. If you would prefer to trade the uncertainties of farming for steady wages you can count on, I will hire you."

"And what, then, would ye be havin' us doin'?"

"Where would we be livin'?" another man demanded.

"After harvest is in, my first objective is to repair housing on the estate that has fallen into shameful disrepair. My workers will live in the restored houses at a modest rent. In time, I hope to build additional homes."

Shane turned and nodded to his secretary to come out on the terrace. Chris did so, seating himself at a table behind his employer.

"Those of you who wish to come to work for me, please give your name to this man." Shane prayed that a large number of the tenants would opt for this choice. It would make reapportioning the land into larger plots easier.

"Sure, and why ye bein' so generous?" Seamus Malone demanded skeptically. "Tell us that."

"Although I was totally unaware of what Oliver Radnor was doing here, Canamara is ultimately my responsibility. I should have come here years earlier to make certain all was as he told me it was."

Shane gestured toward a table loaded with food that had been set up at the side of the terrace. "I hope you will be my guests for dinner before you leave. Plenty of food there is for all of you. Please do not hesitate to take some home to your families."

Still holding Brigid in his arms, he stepped to the side of the terrace, and the tenants began ascending the steps toward Chris.

"Where is your mama, *sidhe*?"

Brigid's face darkened. "Home. She says she hates you cuz you lied to her. Did you?"

The little girl's expression told him she could not believe he would have done such a thing. He was deeply touched by her faith in him. If only her mama shared her trust and depth of feeling.

"I failed to tell her all of the truth, and I should have, *sidhe*. It was very wrong of me not to do so." Shane held her close for a moment before he set her down. "Would you like some food?"

The little girl grabbed his hand again and smiled up at him. "I want to be with you."

She was the only one who did.

As his tenants moved to the food, they respectfully pulled at their forelocks, but their gaze avoided his. Not a one of them came over to him, not even Tom McNulty.

The men's eyes widened as they saw all the food on the table, and he noted that many of them, rather than eating, were carrying off bread, beef, and ham for their families.

Those who did opt to eat on the spot carried their plates far away from Shane, as though, he thought unhappily, his nearness would contaminate the food.

He was gratified, however, by the length of the line that formed in front of his secretary, seeking wages instead of land.

Now, if only he could convince Kathleen of his good intentions toward her and all his tenants.

But Kathleen gave no indication that she would see him. Shane had much to do, and he threw himself into doing it in a desperate effort to divert his thoughts from her.

That proved to be impossible. But he hoped he could show her by his actions how sincere his intentions toward Canamara were, and that, in turn, would help her forgive him for not telling her his identity.

By the time the harvest was in three weeks later, and the men who had chosen to work for wages were repairing the buildings, his tenants' hatred toward him was abating.

But, if anything, the new respect they held for him only seemed to widen the gulf between him and them.

Word of what Shane was doing for his tenants spread like wildfire through the gentry. The carriages lining up at Canamara with occupants hoping to meet the marquess vanished. Instead he received furious letters from them, branding him a traitor to both his country and his class. Some even threatened him.

Now he was persona non grata with everyone, English ascendancy and Irish alike.

Well, *not* everyone. There was still Brigid.

He often sought solace with his fishing rod in the early morning, and she would join him at the stream. At least her mother did not stop her from doing that.

Brigid was the only brightness left in his life. He wanted so desperately for her to be his daughter, for her mother to be his wife.

But as the days passed without any word from Kathleen to indicate her feelings toward him had softened, Shane's bright dream of a new family seemed less and less likely to happen.

For a brief moment, he had known blissful happiness, but apparently that was all he would have. Was he forever destined to live his life alone and cut off from others?

A few times he saw Kathleen out walking, but as soon as she noticed him, she turned abruptly and hurried away in the opposite direction, ignoring his calls to her.

Clearly, she could not even stand to speak to him.

And he had no stomach to hear again this woman he loved so much tell him she loathed him.

Shane called his tenants in one by one to tell them the acreage they would be given under a new lease. He did what he could to preserve the boundaries of the land that Conn Malone and other old-timers had held during his grandfather's time.

The tenants who had come after the Lion's death were given parcels in parts of the estate that had not been leased before. But the one- and two-acre plots that had become the norm under Radnor were eliminated. The smallest piece of land Shane would lease was twenty-five acres.

When Conn Malone learned that he would be given his farm back, tears trickled down his grooved cheeks. "Thankee, me boy, thankee. Proud the ould Lion'd be of ye."

"Would he?" Shane asked skeptically. "I should have come long ago. I could have stopped Radnor before he did so much damage. And your house and barn would still be standing."

"But ye didn't know. And now ye do, ye've
righted it. Don't be so hard on yerself."

Kathleen held her head high and pretended dis-
interest in all that Shane was doing. But every time
she heard his name, which was constantly, her
wounded heart bled anew.

Nor did it help that whenever he was mentioned,
people would look at her curiously, clearly specu-
lating on what had happened between her and His
Lordship.

By now Kathleen knew full well it had not been
Devil Sherbourne who was responsible for her husband's murder and for the terrible plight of the tenants at Canamara, but Devil Radnor.

How thoroughly little Ollie had fooled everyone
including her into thinking he had the tenants' in-
terests at heart even as he was stealing from both
them and Sherbourne.

Not only had Radnor slain Kathleen's husband
with his own hand, but Ben Tilton confessed that
the agent had ordered him to kill Robert Sutton as
he returned to Dublin and make it look as though
he'd died at the hands of an Irish bandit.

Tilton also disclosed that Radnor had wanted
Shane murdered too. All that saved him was the
agent's being told Shane was merely a tutor. Upon
hearing that, Radnor decided he'd settle for sending Shane to prison for crimes against the marquess.

It was thought highly unlikely that either Radnor
or Tilton would escape the hanging tree. Little Ollie
would go to the gallows for Patrick's murder, and
Tilton for slaying Lord Sutton's son.

After Alban Kelly had been absolved of Patrick's
murder, his son Mike returned to school, singing

the praises of his new idol, Shane, to the other children.

And Mike was joined in this chorus by many of Canamara's tenants. Even Seamus Malone had come around to admitting Shane was a good man.

And so had Kathleen.

Shane's damning words still echoed in her mind. *Had you known, you would never have given me a chance to show you what kind of man I am.*

She'd acknowledged to herself the truth of this. She could no longer be angry at Shane for not revealing his real identity to her, especially not when she knew now how dangerous—and murderous— Radnor was.

I will right the wrongs that have been done to the tenants at Canamara.

All around her, she saw the fruits of Shane's good intentions turned into action.

The estate rang with the sounds of men busy building and repairing. Kathleen, deeply moved by all Shane was doing, was tormented by guilt and sorrow over how unkindly she had judged him. She remembered with pain and embarrassment the insults and protestations of hate with which she had driven Shane away after she'd learned he was Sherbourne.

The first structures Shane had ordered restored on Canamara were the assembly hall where the dances were held and the Boar's Head.

Christopher Benton, Shane's secretary, had called on Kathleen, inviting her to use the hall for her hedge school when it was finished.

If only Shane had come himself with this offer.

Yet glad she was that he hadn't. For she feared if she saw him again, she would not be able to resist him. She loved him so much that she would throw aside her self-respect and her reputation to be with him.

But more was at stake than that, and she must resist him.

For Brigid's sake, more than her own.

I want to marry you, Kathleen, but I cannot ask you, at least not yet.

And not ever. No matter how much Shane might want to marry her, English marquesses did not marry Irish women, especially when they had no aristocratic blood in their veins.

Life is not always as easy or simple as we would like, alainn.

Kathleen no longer doubted that he loved both her and Brigid, but she also knew that all he could offer was to make her his mistress, not his wife. Their love could have no honorable status.

She felt her cheeks burn with shame, because even knowing that could not kill her love for him, her aching to be with him.

But loving him did not mean she would give in to it and become his Irish slut, for she would be foreclosing her daughter's future as well as her own.

Brigid deserved better than to be stigmatized as the daughter of the marquess's whore.

But that was small comfort when Kathleen ached to be in Shane's arms and in his bed.

If the truth be known, she was afraid to see him again, so afraid that the few times she'd encountered him at a distance, she'd turned and hurried away in the opposite direction, ignoring his calls to her.

She was terrified that if she did talk to him, she would not have the strength to deny him whatever he wanted, terrified that her resolve against becoming his mistress would evaporate altogether, like a drop of water on a hot pan. Each night as she lay in bed she struggled against the sizzling heat of her need for him.

No matter what happens, remember, alainn, that I love you with all my heart and I always will.

Kathleen buried her head in her pillow and wept for their star-crossed, doomed love.

"Heard ye be goin' to Dublin on the morrow," Conn Malone said to Shane.

He nodded. "I intend to address the Irish Parliament on the stupidity of its policies toward most of the Irish people. The penal laws must be repealed."

"They'll not be listenin' to yer plea."

"No, probably not," Shane agreed. "But, damn it, I have to try."

"And after that, what'll ye be doin'? Comin' back to Canamara?"

Shane desperately wanted to do that, but only if Kathleen would marry him. Without that, it would be too painful here for him. He'd sent a note to her yesterday, asking her to call on him if she could bear the sight of him, but had received no answer. Now he answered sadly, "Probably go back to England."

If he had not heard from her by the time he left for Dublin, that was what he intended to do.

"And what of ye and the widow McNamara, me boy? Said ye loved her, ye did, but I don't see ye courtin' her."

"I would if she would let me, but she refuses to see me," Shane said, unable to keep the desolation from his voice. "She no longer returns my love. She cannot forgive me for not having told her from the beginning who I am."

"And if she does forgive ye, what'll ye do?"

Shane looked into Conn's faded blue eyes and said with total honesty, "Spend the rest of my life at Canamara with her."

Kathleen saw Conn Malone slowly making his way to Rose Cottage. She opened the door and welcomed him. She would have led him into the parlor, but he said, "The kitchen, if ye please."

She took him there. Maggie was upstairs changing the beds and Brigid was outside on her swing, so Kathleen was alone with her guest.

"A great new day has dawned at Canamara," Conn said. "Have ye heard about the new leases? His Lordship found a way to be fair."

Indeed Shane had.

"The ould Lion would be proud o' the lad." Conn paused, his faded blue eyes suddenly penetrating. "He says ye will not talk to him."

"I have nothing to say to him." *Nothing except how sorry I am for all the dreadful things I said. I don't loathe you. I never could.*

"Loves ye, he does, lass. Told me so himself."

Her heart beat like the wings of a frantic bird trying to escape its cage. "When?" she croaked.

"The night he saved you and the other Knights from the soldiers. I asked why he was doin' that, and he answered 'twas because he loved you."

I did what I did for you . . . Because I love you, alainn.

"Himself says ye no longer love him 'cause ye can't forgive him for keepin' his identity from ye."

Better to have Shane continue to think that. If he were to guess how much she did love him, he would use that to pressure her into becoming his mistress.

She clenched her jaw in determination. "He's right," she lied.

Conn shook his head sadly. "Sure and it's a fool ye be, me lass."

Brigid burst into Rose Cottage, tears streaming down her rosy cheeks.

"What's wrong?" Kathleen cried in alarm.

"Mama, S'ane left for Dublin and maybe England and says he doesn't know when or if he'll be back."

Kathleen's heart seemed to shrivel in her breast. Shane gone, and he might not be back. Dear God in heaven, she did not think she could bear never seeing him again, never feeling his arms around her, never experiencing the sublime joy of his lovemaking.

Was that why he had sent her that note asking her to call on him? Had he wanted to tell her goodbye? Or had he meant to offer her one more chance to be the Marquess of Sherbourne's whore?

That night Brigid refused to eat dinner and cried herself to sleep in the bed she shared with her mother.

And, much later that night, so did Kathleen.

Chapter 29

On a dark, blustery day with a raw north wind that promised an early winter, Shane stepped out of a post chaise in front of Canamara's portico.

He had been in Dublin for a week. At this very moment, he should have been crossing the Irish Sea to England. At the last minute, however, he had decided he could not leave Ireland without visiting Canamara once more.

And without seeing Kathleen and Brigid a final time.

He loved this Irish estate that had been his grandfather's. He would happily spend the rest of his life there, but only if he could persuade Kathleen to marry him. And he could no longer hope he might succeed in that endeavor.

So when the Irish footman who opened the door asked him how long he would be staying, he answered, "Only for a day, two at most."

After he changed out of his traveling clothes, he stopped in the office to see Chris. Shane had left his secretary at Canamara to oversee the carrying out of his instructions. Chris assured him that everything was being done precisely as Shane specified.

Even if it were not early afternoon and too late to go fishing, it was too cold to do so. Still Shane started down the hill toward the stream in the hope of seeing Brigid.

He had walked only a few yards when a little cyclone in a green coat rushed up the hill toward him, crying, "S'ane, S'ane, you're back."

When Brigid reached him she hurled herself into his arms. He picked her up and hugged her to him. "I had to see you again, *sidhe*." Tears burned at the back of his eyes. *One more time to last me a lifetime.*

"I loves you, S'ane." She leaned back in his arms. "Does you love me?"

"Very much, *sidhe*. Very, very much."

"Then won't you be my da?" Her pleading expression squeezed his heart. "I want you to be so much."

"No more than I want to be your da, *sidhe*, but we cannot always have the things we want."

"Awful sad Mama's been since you left," Brigid confided.

Did Shane dare hope? He hugged the little girl again, then put her on her feet. "Does your mama know where you are?" *Does she know I am here?*

"Mama's teaching, but I asked Maggie. She said I could come see you."

"But all by yourself?"

She nodded proudly. "Cuz I'm five now and growed up. Did you know my birthday was last week?"

"I did not know, and I missed it. Would you like to join me for cakes and milk in a belated celebration of it?"

Brigid clapped her hands. "Oh, yes!"

He took her into the withdrawing room off the great hall's entrance because it was smaller and less intimidating for a child her size than the other rooms.

When a servant brought in a tray, Brigid carefully picked out an assortment of little cakes and biscuits while Shane poured her a glass of milk.

She started to nibble on one of the cakes. Then she noticed Shane had not taken a plate or glass, and she reluctantly put it down.

"You must have some too," she told him. "It's not polite, me eating in front of you."

Although milk and cakes were not his favorite, he gamely partook of them so Brigid would enjoy hers.

The little girl chattered with him long after she'd finished her food. She was clearly in no hurry to leave.

Nor was he anxious to have her go.

Finally, however, the howling of the wind through the trees caught his attention. He glanced out the window at the turbulent sky, swirling with ominous clouds. A bad storm was clearly about to hit, and Brigid's green coat was not heavy enough to offer her much protection against the cold wind.

"I am afraid it is time for you to go home, *sidhe*. It is going to storm soon, and you are not warmly dressed."

He helped her into her green coat. With her hand in his, he escorted her out the front entrance, across the portico, and down the steps.

But as they moved down the hill toward Rose Cottage, she pulled her hand from his and told him, "You go back now."

"But I want to walk you home," he said, holding out his hand to her.

"No!" she cried so emphatically that his hand dropped and he stared at her in surprise. "I know the way home, and I am a big girl now. Growed-up girls don't need people to walk t'em home."

The proud tilt of her head as she said this reminded Shane so much of her mother that he could not help smiling. "All right, *sidhe*, but hurry home."

As she left, she turned back and reached up to him as though to whisper something in his ear. He obligingly bent down, and she grabbed him around the neck, giving him a great smacking kiss.

As she released him, she announced, "You *will* be my da."

Before he could recover his tongue, she scampered off down the hill.

Twice she looked around. Seeing him still watching her, she waved to him. He watched her until her little figure reached the low stone wall surrounding Rose Cottage, then he went slowly back into the house.

When Kathleen came into the kitchen, Maggie looked up from the potatoes she was scrubbing and gave Kathleen a sly look that puzzled her. "Home early today, are we?"

Kathleen nodded. "A terrible storm's brewing. I let the children go so they'd not be getting caught in it." She looked around the kitchen for her daughter. "Where's Brigid?"

"At the big house. Lord Sherbourne returned to Canamara today."

Kathleen's heart suddenly began thudding like a wild thing. "For how long?" She tried to sound cool and disinterested, but she failed miserably.

Her voice cracked, and she could feel the color rising in her cheeks.

"Only a day, two at most, before he sails for England."

"Did he send for Brigid?" Kathleen hoped that he had.

"No, she heard he'd come. Travels like the wind, such news does. She begged me to be lettin' her visit him, and I told her she could." Maggie gave Kathleen a defiant look, as though she expected her to protest.

All that protested was Kathleen's heart. She wanted so much to see Shane, to ask him to forgive her all the dreadful accusations she had hurled at him. "Has Brigid been there long?" *And is it too much to hope that he will bring her home?*

Maggie shrugged. "Near three hours. Should be back shortly."

But Brigid did not come. The wind grew more intense, the sky blacker. A worried Kathleen asked Maggie to go up to the great house to bring her daughter home.

Maggie planted her hands on her ample hips. "Sure, and cookin' dinner, I am. Why not be goin' after her yerself?"

Kathleen wanted to go, but what if she saw Shane again? She feared her broken heart would shatter into even smaller fragments. But most likely she would not see him. A footman would answer the door and fetch Brigid for her.

By the time Kathleen banged the knocker on Canamara's entrance door, she could scarcely breathe.

A new footman, an Irishman if she ever saw one, answered the door. She'd been told Shane had sent the English footmen packing across the sea and hired Irish instead.

"I believe my daughter, Brigid, is here with Lord Sherbourne. I have come to take her . . ." Her voice trailed off as the door nearest the entrance opened and Shane stepped into the hall.

He looked magnificent and every inch the marquess in his superbly tailored royal-blue coat, frilled shirt, and elegantly tied neckcloth.

But he did not appear at all pleased to see her. Instead he looked upset and alarmed.

Her heart and her foolish fantasies of him . . . of them together . . . sank into the murky darkness of her wounded soul.

So much for hoping Shane would want to see her.

"But Kathleen, Brigid went home more than an hour ago." Shane crossed to her, moving with that grace she so admired, and she remembered what it had been like to dance with him.

"I watched her until she reached the wall around the cottage," he said. "Are you saying she is not there?"

Kathleen was so unnerved by seeing Shane again that it was a second before the full import of his words sank into her consciousness.

Then every other thought fled her mind. She brought her hands to her mouth to smother the anguished cry rising in her throat. She did not entirely succeed, although it came out as a frightened, muted moan.

"Summon all the servants," Shane ordered the footman. "Tell them to come immediately, no matter what they are doing."

The footman exited the hall at a run.

"We will begin a search for her at once," Shane

said. "Damn it, I should have insisted on walking her to your door."

Kathleen prayed, mumbling aloud, "Oh God, please God, don't let anything happen to her." Then she began to cry.

Shane pulled Kathleen, dazed and shaking from shock, into his arms. She collapsed against his strong, hard body, thankful for the support he afforded her.

He bent his head and whispered against her ear. "We will find her, love, never fear."

His certainty that they would locate her daughter calmed Kathleen's terror a little. She marveled that, no matter how frightening the situation, she somehow always felt comforted and reassured in his arms. How she had missed them.

And him.

"Now you must pull yourself together and help us search." He held her tightly, as though he were trying to infuse her with some of his strength. "Have you any idea where she might have wandered?"

Kathleen shook her head. "She's been upset lately, moody," *since you left*. "But she's usually very good about staying near home except when she goes down to the stream." She gasped as a new fear seized her. "Perhaps she fell in and ... and ..." She could not finish the horrible thought.

"Brigid is a good swimmer, is she not?" Shane reminded Kathleen. "Even if she somehow fell in, she would be able to swim to safety."

Kathleen nodded at his words, her fear receding a little.

Servants came running from all directions. Kathleen listened, only half-comprehending as Shane crisply directed where each was to search so that all of Canamara would be covered.

When he and Kathleen were alone again, he took her hands in his. "Come, love, we will search too around Rose Cottage and along the stream."

For the next hour, Kathleen and Shane looked in vain for Brigid. The fierce wind ripped the yellow and scarlet leaves from the trees and drove the cold rain against them with such force the drops felt like pellets of ice.

Their cloaks were soaked, and Kathleen no longer knew whether she shivered from cold or from fear. Probably both.

Nothing mattered to her now except finding Brigid.

Her ears strained to hear a happy shout ring out from one of the other searchers, signaling that Brigid had been found. But none sounded.

Kathleen knew Shane tried to keep her hopes up, but he could not entirely hide from her that, as time passed and the weather grew worse, he was increasingly more worried.

The gloomy, gray light of the day began to fade, and Kathleen had to struggle against panic. The night would be colder by far, and Brigid's little green coat would not be warm enough, especially not after it had been soaked by the driving rain.

Once darkness settled, their chances of finding Brigid were minimal. If they did not find her before the light failed, she might not survive until morning.

Finally, Shane stopped abruptly among a pile of newly fallen leaves, his eyes troubled.

"What is it?" Kathleen asked.

"Brigid said something strange when she left me today. I wonder if she could have . . ." His voice trailed away as he puzzled over something.

"Have what?" Kathleen asked in alarm.

He did not even seem to hear her question. Instead he said musingly, "Brigid once showed me a cave by the stream where she thought the *daoine sidh* lived. I wonder . . ."

Shane turned abruptly and ran through the sodden leaves carpeting the ground.

Kathleen followed him, uncertain where he could be going. He followed the path of the stream until he came to a tangle of blackthorn and laurel growing along the side of an eroded hill.

He pulled frantically at the thicket, heedless of how its cruel thorns tore at his skin and clothes.

"What are you doing?" Kathleen cried.

Peering over his shoulder, she saw he had uncovered a small opening, apparently to a cave hidden by the foliage.

He dropped down on his knees and put his head inside.

"*Sidhe*," he cried, "are you all right?"

For Kathleen, the silence that followed seemed to last an eternity before she heard her daughter's sleepy voice say happily, "S'ane."

"What are you doing here, *sidhe*?" he asked gently.

"Waitin' for you to find me," Brigid replied, adding in a tone of utmost confidence, "I knowed you would."

"I'm glad *you* knew," Shane grumbled. "*I* was frightened to death."

Kathleen smiled, for Shane's gruff tone failed to conceal his relief that her daughter was safe.

He wrapped Brigid in his cloak to protect her from the thorns as he carried her from the cave.

When he emerged from the thicket with Brigid

in his arms, hidden beneath the folds of his cloak, his own face and hands were scratched and torn from the thorns. "Your mama's here, *sidhe*."

"I'm glad."

"Darling, what happened?" Kathleen asked, reaching for her daughter.

But Brigid snuggled against Shane. Her little voice was muffled beneath the wool cloth of his cloak. "I'm so sleepy, Mama. I want S'ane to carry me home."

"Certainly, *sidhe*." Shane turned to Kathleen. "Brigid was dry and reasonably warm in the cave, and I'll try to keep her that way in my cloak. I am convinced she is fine."

Tears of relief welled in Kathleen's eyes.

The rain mixed with the blood on Shane's face and hands from the damage the thorns had inflicted, leaving watery pink streaks. His wounds had to hurt, but he seemed oblivious to the pain in his enormous happiness that he had found Brigid safe.

Shane started toward Rose Cottage with such long strides that Kathleen was forced to half-run to keep up with him. "Thank God, after Brigid got lost, she managed to take shelter in that cave."

"She was not lost, she was hiding from us."

"*Hiding!* Why?"

Shane looked at Kathleen quizzically. "Surely you know why."

Kathleen didn't, and she was torn between anger and incredulity at the possibility her daughter could have been deliberately hiding.

They reached Rose Cottage, and Shane carried Brigid up the stairs to the bedchamber she shared with her mother.

"Would you wait outside while I put her to

bed?'' Kathleen asked Shane as he unwrapped Brigid from his cloak and laid her gently on the bed.

"I wants S'ane to stay with me," the little girl protested sleepily.

"It is better I leave you with your mama while she puts you to bed," Shane said.

"Then will you come and kiss me goodnight?" she pleaded.

"Certainly, *sidhe*, if you wish."

After he left the bedroom, Kathleen asked, "Brigid, did you run away and hide in that cave?"

The little girl nodded.

"Dear God in heaven, why?"

"So you would talk to S'ane. I want him for my da, and only you can make him that." The determination in Brigid's expression reminded Kathleen of Patrick at his most stubborn. "Will you, Mama, please? Promise me you will?"

Kathleen closed her eyes against a wave of pain. She could not expect her little daughter to understand that English marquesses did not *marry* Irish women. She fled into the hall.

Shane pushed himself away from the opposite wall. "Is Brigid ready for her goodnight kiss?"

"I am," the little girl called.

Shane went into the room, and Kathleen followed. His expression, so full of love, as he looked at her daughter nearly broke her heart. Once he had looked at Kathleen like that too. If only he would again.

He bent over the bed and kissed the little girl gently on the forehead. She reached up with her chubby arms and hugged him hard around the neck.

When she finally released him, he straightened and hurried from the room. As he passed Kathleen, she saw that his eyes were glistening with tears.

She followed him out of the room. "You love Brigid, don't you?"

"I could not love her more if she were my own flesh and blood. She is the daughter of my heart."

He looked at Kathleen with such a mixture of love, longing, and sorrow that she could not breathe.

"I want to be Brigid's da almost as much as I want to be your husband. Marry me, love. Please say you will marry me."

Kathleen stared at him in shock. "Marry you? Be your wife, not your mistress?"

He looked so outraged that she took an involuntary step backward. "I would never insult you or my love for you by dishonoring you that way. Nor Brigid either! Why do you look so surprised? I told you my intentions were honorable. I told you how much I loved you."

Surely Shane could not be saying what Kathleen thought he was. "But that first night we made love, you said you could not ask me to marry you."

"Not *yet*, I said. Not until after you learned who I was. I could not ask you to accept me as your husband before you knew I was Sherbourne. And once you discovered that, you refused to talk to me again. You said you loathed me." He paused, looking puzzled. "Why are you crying, *alainn*?"

"I lied," Kathleen admitted, swiping ineffectually at her tears. "I don't hate you. I tried so hard, but I couldn't hate you. You are too dear and good a man, and I love you so much. But you can't marry me."

"Why not?"

"You're an English marquess and I'm Irish. I am

the wrong woman, born in the wrong country. You know you can't marry me!"

"I know nothing of the sort." His mouth turned up in a wry smile. "Besides, I am half-Irish myself—the better half at that—so don't give me any more arguments on that score."

She tried again to bring him to his senses. "What will your peers think?"

"The hell with my peers. I don't give a damn what they think. And I don't want to be a marquess without you as my marchioness. Would you have me renounce my title?"

She gaped. "You would do that for *me*?"

"I will do anything I must to make you my wife. Now, will you marry me?"

If this was a dream, Kathleen prayed she would never wake up. "Yes, if that's what you truly want."

He looked at her with such a comical mixture of happiness, joy, and incredulity that she could not help smiling.

"Of course it's what I truly want. How could you doubt that for an instant, love?" He pulled her into his arms and kissed her with such thoroughness and tenderness that not a single doubt she harbored survived.

Still, when the kiss ended, she thought of the enormity of the decision she had just made and what would be required of her. Suddenly she was frightened. "Are you certain? Remember how your father loved your mother until they returned to England."

"My father was a fool. Once he married my mother, he tried to stifle in her the very things that made him love her. He never appreciated the woman he had. Instead he saw her through bigots' eyes, rather than his own. I will never make that mistake, love. I am not my father."

"I am afraid I made the mistake your father did," she said sadly. "I saw Sherbourne only as the evil devil that Radnor created. When I first learned who you were, I saw you as that fictional monster instead of as the man you really are, the man I had come to know and love. Oh, Shane, I am so sorry."

Again their lips met in a kiss, in a silent vow of forever more.

Afterward Shane asked, "No more reservations?"

"I admit I do not look forward to living in England."

"I have no intention of returning there. We will live here at Canamara. For the first time in my life, I have found a place where I feel I belong. It is home to me."

"But you are about to return to England," she reminded him.

"Only because I could not bear to be so close to you and not have you as my wife."

"I heard about your speech to Parliament. It was brilliant and very brave."

"So brilliant that I was roundly booed and jeered," Shane said dryly. He cupped her face tenderly in his hands. "I must warn you I intend to continue fighting to redress the wrongs done the Irish people."

"Good!"

"But as my wife, you may be subjected to unpleasant and hurtful moments."

"Shane, my darling, only those I love can hurt me. Only you or Brigid has that power."

He hugged her exuberantly to him. "And you, my love, rescued me from the wilderness of grief in which I was lost. I love you so much, *alainn*."

Epilogue

"Now I must ask my other love to dance," Shane told his bride during the celebration following their wedding. "What a difficult life, being in love with two beautiful colleens at once."

Kathleen's heart swelled as she watched her daughter's face light up when her new da asked her to dance. As he led Brigid out on the floor, happy tears dampened Kathleen's eyes at the love glowing between Brigid and Shane.

"A good man you've married, lass," Kathleen's father told her. "And a good da he'll be for your daughter."

How true, she thought as she looked around the room. The guests were enjoying a rollicking time. An enormous feast had been laid out for them. Champagne and ale, wine and whiskey flowed freely. The celebration promised to go on until dawn or later.

To Kathleen's relief, Shane had invited none of the gentry, who'd promptly added both that slight and his making of a common Irish woman his marchioness to their growing list of grievances against him.

Instead, he had invited all his tenants and her family and friends. Initially some of the Irish guests had been uncomfortable in the great house, but Shane's ebullient happiness proved to be contagious, sweeping away whatever stiffness they felt.

Conn Malone came up to Kathleen. "Just like the ould Lion, yer husband be." Tears welled in his faded eyes. "Proud his mam would be of him too."

"And proud his wife is," Kathleen said, smiling.

Conn looked toward Maurea McNulty sitting in an invalid's chair. "Sure, and kind it was of His Lordship to insist Maurea come. The medicine the doctor gave her must be helping."

"I think what's helping her most is being back in her room with the window that looks out on the vale. She loves it there."

Some hours later, when Shane actually sat out a dance, Brigid climbed up in his lap and, despite the music and noisy merrymaking, promptly fell asleep there.

"Time to put her to bed," Kathleen whispered.

He nodded. "Come with me, love. I'll take her up."

With Kathleen beside him, Shane carried Brigid upstairs to the bedchamber adjacent to the one that had been his grandfather's. Brigid's new room was intended for the lady of the house, but Shane would not hear of Kathleen being anywhere but in his bed.

Nor did she want to be anywhere else.

Shane had ordered the lady's chamber, which had been closed up and shrouded in dust covers since his grandmother's death, redone for a little girl.

After the dust covers had been removed from the furnishings, both Kathleen and Shane had been dismayed by the massive bed with an oak canopy and enormous carved footposts. They both wondered aloud at how incongruously masculine and out of place it was in an otherwise feminine room. Worse, the bed was so high, even an adult had to climb bedstairs to get in it.

Shane ordered it replaced with a frilly canopied bed that was Brigid's size.

When the workmen started to dismantle the old bed, they found concealed beneath the high mattress a locked, flat-topped trunk. One of the workmen volunteered that Oliver Radnor had ordered the bed installed in the lady's chamber after he'd become agent.

Certain the trunk must be where Radnor had secreted much of his ill-gotten gains, Shane tried the other key he'd taken from around the agent's neck in the lock. It opened immediately, revealing a rich treasure of gold inside. More gold was found in the enormous, hollowed-out footposts, and Shane now referred to it as the Midas bed.

Shane carried the sleeping Brigid into her new room, and Kathleen pulled back the covers of the frilly bed.

He laid the child beneath the ruffled canopy. When Kathleen unbuttoned Brigid's gown and slipped it off her, she did not even open her eyes.

Kathleen nodded at the little girl's undergarment. "She's so tired, I'm going to let her sleep in her shift." Kathleen pulled the covers over her daughter and kissed her.

Brigid's eyes fluttered open. "Da, kiss me goodnight too."

Shane bent and kissed her cheek tenderly. Her little arms came up to hug him fiercely. "I love you, Da."

She promptly fell asleep again.

Shane straightened and held out his hand to

Kathleen. She let him lead her through the connecting door to his—no, their—bedchamber, illuminated by a candelabra near the bed.

The moment the door closed behind them, he pulled her into his arms. As his mouth descended to claim hers, she teased, "At last, my turn to be kissed goodnight."

"Not yet." His face was so close to hers that she could feel his warm breath tickling her lip. "Eventually—although I fear it may be morning by then. I have other things in mind first."

His blue eyes gleamed in the pale candlelight, and his suddenly husky, sensual voice sent a shiver of anticipation through her. "Many other, most pleasurable things."

Then he kissed her as though he were dying of a thirst only her lips could slake. His mouth moved from her lips to nuzzle her ear, and he began to undo the buttons of her gown.

"What about our guests?"

Shane kissed her again. "They won't miss us." He chuckled. "And I refuse to wait another moment to begin my honeymoon. Have I told you how deliriously happy you have made me by becoming my wife?"

"As you have made Brigid. Now she has the da she herself picked out and wanted so desperately."

His smile faded. "But what of you, *alainn*?"

"Impossible though it seems, I'm even happier than my daughter. I love you so, Shane, that I ache with it." Smiling mischievously, Kathleen looked at the big tester bed. "Speaking of aches, my darling . . ."

A long time later, as they lay in each other arms, sated and satisfied from their lovemaking, Kathleen yawned deeply as sleep stole over her. "Now that you've taken care of all my aches so beautifully, will you kiss me goodnight?"

As Shane's mouth moved to hers, he whispered, "Yes, my love—tonight and every night for the rest of our lives."

Dear Reader,

Heat up your summer with some sizzling June romance reading from Avon Books, beginning with Judith Ivory's Avon Romantic Treasure SLEEPING BEAUTY. This unique twist on the popular fairy tale is lushly sensuous. And the romance between Sir James Stoker and the delectable Coco Wild is unforgettable!

If you love Regency-set romance, don't miss ONLY IN MY DREAMS by Eve Byron. Eve's love stories are filled with passion, humor and a touch of intrigue. Here, Lorelei Wildewood had been forced into a marriage of convenience with Adrian Winters—a man she barely knew. Adrian promptly went off to sea, but now he's back, and his fiery kisses make Lorelei think that marriage might not be so bad after all...

Western settings are a favorite of mine, and Kit Dee's ARIZONA RENEGADE has everything western fans could ask for—a wild, beautiful setting, a sexy U.S. Secret Service agent...and an innocent temptress. Strong romantic tension, complex characters and a memorable love story all combine to make ARIZONA RENEGADE a book for your keeper shelf!

Fans of Contemporary romance won't want to miss Eboni Snoe's TELL ME I'M DREAMIN'. Nadine Clayton has had it with being a workaholic! So she sheds her business suits and takes off for the sunny Caribbean...where she meets a mysterious man she simply can't resist. This is the perfect love story to take to the beach!

Happy Reading!

Lucia Macro

Lucia Macro
Senior Editor

Avon Romances—
the best in exceptional authors and unforgettable novels!

Avon Romantic Treasures

*Unforgettable, enthralling love stories,
sparkling with passion and adventure
from Romance's bestselling authors*

❋❋❋❋❋❋❋❋❋❋❋❋❋❋❋❋❋❋❋❋❋❋❋❋❋❋❋❋❋❋